EVE

Sheriff Jim Horse waited for Thora Gunn to get bundled against the cold, standing in the doorway to the jail cells, watching her without looking like he was.

Thora was nervous and excited about going to the party, but, if the truth were known, most of the nervous part came from being alone with the sheriff. There was something about him that made her feel like the first time she'd seen a bald eagle. Awed, overwhelmed.

He unlocked the cell and swung the door open. "Ready?"

She stepped out of the cell. "Aren't you going to tie my hands together?"

He looked at her. "That's not needed, is it?" He got the direct gaze of her eyes. "Or is it?"

"I can't promise anything. Maybe I'll run for it."

"Then maybe I'll shoot you."

He held the door open for her.

Until she paused under the bower of his arm, Thora didn't realize where she had placed herself which was . . . under the bower of his arm. She looked up at his hard face, intending to answer sharply, but her voice came out as soft as a sigh. "Please let me go."

"No." He was looking off somewhere, and then he looked down at her and during the long moment that followed her anger left and something else took over. Her eyes fell to his lips—which were mere inches from hers—and of their own will, her lips parted and her hand half lifted.

Then it struck her how moony she must look and the anger returned, this time against herself.

They walked to the party in heavy silence, Thora chewing on her anger and Jim wondering about the strange girl beside him. A girl who fascinated him, a girl he would like nothing better than to drag into the woods and screw blue.

"Wynema McGowan is a name destined to be on every romance reader's lips. Truly a master of her craft, McGowan draws you in, makes you fall in love with her characters, and keeps you turning the pages. Her voice is unusual, with a wonderful blend of gritty reality, down-home earthiness, and a touch of magic."

—Catherine Anderson on *Catching Fire*

Books by Wynema McGowan

BEYOND THE RIVER

WHILE THE RIVERS RUN

CATCHING RAINBOWS

THE IRISHMAN

CATCHING FIRE

Wynema McGowan

Pinnacle Books
Kensington Publishing Corp.
http://www.pinnaclebooks.com

PINNACLE BOOKS are published by

Kensington Publishing Corp.
850 Third Avenue
New York, NY 10022

First Printing: December, 1997
10 9 8 7 6 5 4 3 2 1

Printed in the United States of America

To Tony & Dianne Mills

Chapter 1

There was a timber wolf inside the jail. Not in back where the two cells were but in front where the sheriff's and deputy's desks sat. Outside on the street stood the sheriff, staring at the slammed jailhouse door. It was snowing. "My butt!" Jim Horse squinted up, which was sort of like sticking his head into a feather pillow. "This's a blasted blizzard!" It was the first storm to hit town this season and it was going to be a corker. "Town," by the way, was Two Sisters, Minnesota, a fledgling community with a reputation to improve.

Located square between the Ontario border and Duluth, Two Sisters had recently successfully survived a regional, rather precipitous decline of the lumber industry. Now, what had once been little more than a tent town had become a bustling hamlet that continued to draw new settlers every month. Some of this growth was due to its location—it was only a day's rail travel from the Twin Cities of Minneapolis and St. Paul—but most of it was due to its hardy population which was primarily made up of German, Swedish and Norwegian immigrants . . . all of whom wrote regular letters home.

It was indeed a place of incredible beauty . . . when you could see it. Six months out of the year, that was more easily said than done. Since it rimmed the body of water that the natives called Kechi-gami (the whites called the same water Superior) its weather was greatly influenced by trade-like winds which could change in a heartbeat, especially in the spring and fall. Consequently, a snowstorm like the one Two Sisters was experiencing that night was quite a common occurrence, even in November.

A lot of people liked it (Really!) and were quick to point out that the lake was not the town's only lure. (Here they'd poke the newcomer in the side and point at the water. "Lew-er. Get it? Hah! Hah!") Belting the town from behind was virgin wilderness, a towering mountain forest of spruce, jack-pine, birch, alder, aspen and oak about which the residents were equally vocal. They were apt to drag a newcomer outside—in a raging blizzard if necessary—in order to point proudly and say that within that forest "right dere" flourished scores of birds and flowers and most of the wild game known to the northern hemisphere! Mistaking a frostbitten grimace for disbelief, they'd cry, "Yah! Iss trew!"

Naturally that wild game to which they alluded included the species *canis lupus*, more commonly known as the timber wolf.

The sheriff removed his hat to knock the snow off it, rocked it back into place and then stuck out a hand to stop his deputy who arrived breathless and skidding in the hand-tooled leather-soled boots that he insisted upon wearing year around. The deputy was slow to learn. He'd cracked his tailbone the winter before and had had to stand till spring.

"Thanks." Deputy William Peavy "Bull" Durham gathered his feet under him and looked about. A minute earlier the deputy had heard two shots, but right off his trained lawman eyes noted that Jim Horse had neither his gun nor knife drawn. Matter of fact, his fleece-lined jacket was hiked up in back and his hands were stuck in his hip pockets. Strange. "You signal me?"

"Yeah."

Bull looked around again. "So, uh, what's up?"

"I just didn't want you hellin' into the jail without a warnin'."

"The jail?" He looked toward the snow smeared building, its single window an orange daub in a world gone white. "How come?"

" 'Cause there's a wolf in there."

Deputy Durham looked at his boss. "A what?"

"A wolf."

"Yer kiddin'!"

Jim called to mind the animal that had bowled him over earlier. Short-eared and yellowy-eyed. Long snout and thick ruff. Silvery grey and measuring right around seven foot from nose to tail. "No. I'm not kiddin'."

"I'll be damned!" Durham looked at the jail then back at his boss and squared his shoulders. "What do you want me t'do?"

"I'm not sure yet."

There was a pause, then, "I could circle 'round in back an' on yer signal, I could open the back door exactly as you open the front door an' then . . ."

"An' then?"

"We both open fire."

"An' riddle each other with bullets?"

Bull looked insulted. "I was gonna aim at the wolf."

When Jim didn't answer, Bull pondered some more but he didn't come up with a better plan. "There ain't no earthly reason for a wolf to come around all these people unless . . . Hey! Mebbe it's got that disease, that you know."

For obvious reasons Bill Durham's nickname was "Bull" but, as far as his appearance went it would've been more apt if his last name had been Crane and his nickname "Icky." He was the sort who ate six times a day and still had his gut stuck to his backbone. He was a tall, long-boned man with a narrow expressive face and small pale eyes. Late twenties or, at the outside, early thirties. When he had first arrived in Two Sisters he'd said he was from some place west of Dallas. He had never said precisely where and nobody'd ever asked. Not why he'd left either. Two Sisters was not that civilized yet.

Bull studied the toe of his boot and then the rim of his hat. "Aw hell! You know the disease I mean."

Jim Horse looked back at his deputy. He liked the man, but if he had any annoying habit, it was that he always smoked his twirlies down to the lipline. At the moment a butt was hanging off his lower lip like a grub. "Hydrophobia?"

"Naw, hell. That's what you got when you can't pee." He looked off and thought some more.

Bull had not been hired because of his pumpkin-sized brain, but because he was keen-eyed, honest and skillful with all manner of firearms. Oh, yeah, there'd been one other thing in his favor (at least as far as the town council was concerned); he was a bachelor, same as his boss. Like a lot of other boom town lawmen, the ones in Two Sisters used to be kinda short-lived.

"Well, however we go about it, we're gonna have t'shoot it afore it bites somebody." Bull removed his gun from the holster and spun the cylinder to check the load.

"What about the girl?"

Bull's head snapped up and the butt fell off his lip. "What girl?"

Jim was about to explain when out of the white whirling clouds came the sound of jingling bit chains, creaking wood and tinkling bells.

"Somebody's comin'!" Bull went buzzard-necked and squinted in that direction. Pretty soon there appeared a black horse trailing a plume of frosty breath and a sleigh. In it were Joe Willie Everett and his wife Sissy.

"Damn!" said Jim softly.

"It's the Everetts," said Bull unnecessarily. "I thought you said they was havin' a party tonight. I thought that's how come you wanted me to work. 'Cause you was gonna go to it."

"I was goin' to go, Bull."

"Oh, yeah. Then t'wolf . . ."

"Uh-huh. Then the wolf."

Joe Willie climbed out of the sleigh and went around to help his wife alight. Since she was several months gone, she did not exactly bound around like a bareback rider.

Bull chuckled, but not unkindly. "Looks like somebody could play catch with her." He paused then frowned. "Well, not one person by hisself, 'course but two people . . ."

Warningly. "Bull . . ."

"Yeah, yeah. Jus' funnin'."

Sissy Heck Everett had been Two Sisters' schoolteacher for the last four years but she was planning to retire come January first because of the impending arrival of the Everetts' second child. The party they were supposed to be hosting that evening was in honor of that event and in order to introduce the new teacher, a painfully shy young man named Nils Duuos. Duuos spoke fluent Norwegian which with all the Scandinavians in the area was no doubt the primary reason why he'd gotten the job. (According to those who'd been present, it certainly wasn't how he'd impressed the council members during his interview. Two out of five had dozed off.)

Jim Horse muttered, "I can't believe how word travels in this town."

The Everetts approached, Joe Willie holding Sissy's arm and hunched in order to take most of the wind. Bull imagined it must be like having a barn door roll alongside her.

"Hey, Jim, Bull."

"Hey, Joe Willie. Howdy, Mrs. Everett."

"Sissy, Bull. Remember?"

"Yes, ma'am."

Beneath snow-encrusted brows Joe Willie Everett laid a hard eye first on Jim Horse and then on Bull Durham. "Heard there was trouble."

Bull answered. "Aw. Hell."

"Anybody hurt here?"

"Naw. Hell."

Joe Willie was Two Sisters' most popular attorney, but before he took up lawyering he and Jim Horse had worked together as the town's sheriff and deputy. It was on Joe Willie's recommendation—and of course years of proven ability—that Jim had been offered the sheriff's job when Joe Willie quit.

So what, a person might wonder, had drawn Joe Willie out on a night such as this? Sleigh chasing? Was he the old weary hound who couldn't quit baying at the moon? Actually, neither. It was because of a sense of duty toward his old partner.

Joe Willie and Jim Horse were about as close as two men who were not kin could be. Had been almost from the moment they'd laid eyes on one another.

They had made a memorable pair back then, a duo any foraging owlhoots did not soon forget. Joe Willie had the sort of grim, scarred face that made him look more like a street fighter than a lawman. It fit. They used to say he was "greased hell on wheels with his fists!" He always preferred besting a man—or two—with his fists, and would resort to gunplay only if pushed.

By the way, that was the first thing a newcomer used to find out: that Joe Willie Everett did not push.

Now, Jim Horse, on the other hand, looked exactly like a wild Indian. Which fit. He was. Hard to believe, most would say, an Indian sheriff back in those times, but nobody had trouble believing it once they saw him. He had hair that was straight and shiny as an oil slick and blunt features like a kid's stick drawing in the dirt. He looked mean and liked it.

By the way, there was a second thing that newcomer found out: Jim Horse pushed even less than Joe Willie Everett.

Bull touched his hat to Sissy Everett. "I thought y'all was havin' a party, ah, Sissy." Tomorrow it would be Mrs. Everett again.

"We were," replied Sissy. "But in light of the storm we thought we better put it off until another night. Especially when Buddy told us that Jim couldn't come. We couldn't have the party without Jim."

Joe Willie said, "Buddy tore in about ten minutes back. Said there was some trouble at the jail. I tried to leave Sissy home. Might as well get a cat to bark." His wife smiled good naturedly but not Joe Willie. He nodded toward the jail. "What've you got here, Jim?

"Yes," said Sissy. A rabbit-fur hood rimmed her concerned face like a cowl. "Buddy said Thor's sister just got into town. Can that be true?"

"I guess it can. At least that's who she claimed to be before she keeled over."

"Oh, God!"

She looked from Jim to Bull but Bull looked at her ear. He'd learned his lesson. A man who looked into those chocolaty eyes was jus' askin' t'get his brain clabbered. Sissy Everett was a damn pretty girl, even if she was shaped like a tomato.

"What did you tell her, Jim?"

"The truth. I had to. It was the first question she asked. 'I've come to find my brother Halldor,' she says. 'Do you know him?' I said that he had been hung for a crime he did not commit and that's when she went down." To himself he added, "Like head-shot animal."

Sissy covered her mouth with a mittened hand. "Oh, the poor thing!"

Bull had a conspiratorial look when he elbowed Jim. "What about that um, other thing, Jim." He jerked his chin toward the jail. "You know."

All four people leaned with a cold gust of wind then righted themselves. With a hint of sarcasm in his voice Joe Willie suggested that "maybe we could chat more comfortably inside."

"I wouldn't recommend it," said Jim.

"Why?" asked Joe Willie. "The girl won't bite, will she?"

"No, but her wolf might."

"Wolf!"

"What wolf?"

Voices spoke in unison until Joe Willie lifted one gloved hand. "Hold on. Jus' hold on now. Jim, you better back up to the beginning." Jim set his jaw, something Joe Willie had seen him do many times before. More than anyone, Joe Willie knew how much Jim hated idle talk, or for that matter, talk of any sort.

"I was tryin' to fill out the papers on the Coffman arrest 'cause the deadline on the hundred-dollar-bounty ended tonight." Joe Willie nodded—he knew all about that kinda stuff.

Bull chuckled. "Looks like you can kiss that hunnerd good-bye."

"Fifty," Jim said with an evil smile. "I was gonna split with you, Bull, seein' as how you spotted him first."

Bull's gleeful look went south. "Damn!" he said and kicked at a clump of snow. "I probably coulda gone my whole life without knowin' that!"

"Then what?" Sissy prompted.

"Buddy stopped by about seven wantin' to know if I wanted to ride with her over to your place. I told her no. That I'd be along in a few minutes. Not a minute after she left the door opens again an' in comes this . . . girl."

He pictured her as he had first seen her, wearing fur-trimmed leather leggins and a coat that had been made from a prime timber wolf pelt. Staring at her he recalled thinking that he knew he'd never seen her before yet there was something strangely familiar about her.

"That's when she said that she was Thora Gunnlauger and that she'd come to find her brother, Halldor."

"Halldor!" Sissy exclaimed. "Why did everyone call him Thor? Oh, wait!" She put a mittened hand on her husband's arm. "I remember now. Buddy said that the last time the boy spoke was the day they found him abandoned in that old farm. She said he kept calling 'Thor! Thor!' so everyone just assumed that it was his name but if her name is Thora . . . Oh, Joe Willie!" She went into her husband's arms. "He must've been crying for his sister."

"Pathetic!" Joe Willie muttered. "That whole thing was just pathetic. Well, go on, Jim."

"That's when I told her that her brother had been hung . . ."

Sissy lifted her head from Joe Willie's chest. "Surely not like that, Jim!"

"Well . . . yeah."

"Oh, God!"

His wife was mortified but Joe Willie wasn't. Was Jim a damn good lawman? Yes. A crazy man in a fight? You bet! A silver-tongued devil? Nuh uh.

"I was about to lift her up off the floor when the door blew open and this damn wolf flew in! Since they seemed to know each other I took off."

"A wolf!" exclaimed Joe Willie.

"Yeah, imagine that," said Bull incredulously. "A durn wolf!"

"Oh, Jim!" cried Sissy. "Surely you didn't leave her like that!"

"Hell, I didn't have any choice . . ." He showed his rippled jacket sleeve. "It was either kill the animal or hightail it outa there."

Sissy looked at the rectangle of light that was the jailhouse window and then at her husband. "Joe Willie, I must go talk to her!"

"Sissy, we're havin' a durn blizzard . . ."

"I'll hurry."

"But what about the wolf?"

"From what you said it must be hers. I doubt if she'll sic it on an expectant mother."

"Well . . ."

"Thank you, darling!"

Dear! Darlin'! Bull Durham snorted. Everybody in Two Sisters agreed on two things: one, that little Sissy Everett had a hold of her husband by somethin', an' two, that it was not his nose.

Sissy closed the door and leaned back on it. The girl sat slump-shouldered at Bull's desk. The animal lay at her feet looking up at her with a quizzical wrinkle to his brow. Neither the girl nor the wolf—oh, yes, it most definitely *was* a wolf—paid her the least attention.

Sissy removed her coat and pulled up one of the ladder backed chairs and sat down and unwound her scarf. Without thinking, indeed without even looking, she removed one mitten and scratched the wolf behind his ear. The girl looked up at her then. Her hazel eyes were curiously dry. Her skin, however, was the color of cold lard. And oh, how she looked like Thor! Same color eyes. Same strong bones. Her hair was a shade lighter maybe, but the resemblance was striking.

"Who are you?" Thora's voice sounded strange to her own ears. Pinched and dry.

"My name is Sissy Everett. I couldn't bear to know that you were in here alone. I simply had to come in and tell you that I . . . I knew and loved your brother as if he were mine."

"A man said . . . he said that my brother was dead. Do you know if it's true?" Thora had been praying she was mistaken, but the young woman was nodding. She covered her face with her hands.

"I'm so sorry." Sissy longed to put her arm around her but dared not. "I'm sure you hoped he misspoke but I'm afraid he didn't. Actually the sheriff more than anyone . . ."

The girl looked up. "That's the sheriff?"

"Yes. Jim Horse," Sissy said and automatically Jim's face came to mind. "Oh, I hope he didn't frighten you. He looks a bit . . . rough but you have no reason to be afraid of him."

Rough? The hard face that had loomed over her was like

something from a bad dream! But it was the recollection of that single inky eye that gave her an involuntary shudder. It had been like looking into the bore of a rifle.

She only now recalled his hair, how very long it had been, and how very black—blacker maybe than anything she had ever seen before. A strip of red flannel cloth had held it . . .

The sheriff of Two Sisters was an Indian! And not a very civilized-looking one either. God, she was lucky to be alive! She'd pulled her knife on him only nothing had come of it. He'd just grinned at her and took it away. That was when Cocoman came boiling into the room and that was the last thing she remembered.

Thora looked at her visitor. She was awfully pretty with russet colored hair and big brown eyes. She was also perched on the edge of her chair and very anxious acting. "Who did you say you were?"

"Who am I?" The other girl clasped her hands. "Well, my name is Sissy. I'm presently the schoolteacher but I'm retiring in a few weeks. I'm married to the former Sheriff, Joe Willie Everett who is now an attorney here in town. We have one child, a son eighteen months old and . . ." She leaned closer and lowered her voice confidentially. ". . . I am expecting another child in early March." A soft whine and Sissy looked at the wold. The animal had not taken its eyes from the girl. "Think he ah you know . . . needs to go outside?"

"No. He's hungry."

"Hungry! Good heavens!" She jumped up. "Of course he's hungry! My stars! You too probably! I don't know what I was thinking!"

"Miss? Ah, Mrs. Everett."

"Sissy."

"Do you suppose the sheriff would let me stay here tonight?"

"Here?" Sissy looked around at the walls, bare except for an elkhorn rifle rack, a wavy mirror and a thousand flyspecked wanted dodgers. "Why, I don't see why not." She'd spoken before she thought and added, "Of course, I'll need to ask first, but I'm pretty sure it will be all right." She turned away then she turned back. "You know, you might be sorry tomorrow. The sheriff's day starts pretty early . . ."

"I'll be gone by the time he gets here, but right now I'm as tired as I've ever been."

Sissy nodded. Shock sometimes did that. She had a sudden thought. "You don't intend to leave town, do you?"

Thora shrugged. She wasn't sure what she'd do. She hadn't really thought much beyond tonight.

"Surely not! Well, look, we'll talk about that tomorrow. First we'll get you set for tonight. Let's see, I better check the wood supply." She lifted the lid on the woodbox. "Plenty! That's good! Now for some food."

Mindful of escaping heat, she opened the door only a crack. The three men were spotlit by the hurricane lantern hanging on a pole on the sleigh. Otherwise she'd have never seen them. She crooked her finger at Joe Willie, but he was already approaching.

"Sissy, we are freezin' our . . ."

"I know. I promise I'll only be another minute. Joe Willie, do you think you can you get your hands on some raw meat?"

"Mebbe I could. Then again mebbe I'd just as soon not."

"But we need some for her er . . . wolf."

"Ah. Well, I guess."

"And some good hearty soup or stew?"

"I suppose." Testily. "Anythin' else?" His cavalry-style mustache had frozen to his skin and it smarted when he talked.

Sissy looked over her shoulder and asked, "Would you take some tea or coffee?" After a second she turned back and shrugged. "Guess it doesn't matter. Just bring anything you can find that's hot to drink." She reached out and snagged her husband's sleeve and smiled winningly. "Thank you, dear."

The girl looked up when Sissy Everett resettled herself across from her. "The sheriff said my brother was hung for a crime he did not commit."

"Don't you think you'd rather talk about it tomorrow? Everything will be so much easier after a good night's rest."

"Please."

Sighing, "Yes, that much is true. It was an awful, awful mistake."

"How could it have happened? My brother was the kindest human being in the world."

"I know. I know." Two huge tears rolled down the girl's

grief-swollen face and Sissy put a hand to her throat and closed her eyes lest she start crying herself. "I know exactly how painful this is for you because I . . . I too loved your brother. Very much."

"When did it happen?"

"In 1881. In the fall."

"A year after we left."

The girl buried her face in her hands and sobbed. Sissy petted her shoulder and wondered if she dare draw her close. A guttural noise answered that for her.

More to think than because the room needed it, Sissy got up and added a piece of wood to the claw-footed heater. "Your brother had grown into a most handsome young man, but in his mind he always remained a child. I'm sure you knew that."

The girl lifted her head slightly. "Halldor was never like the other kids . . ." Her tone turned hard. ". . . which is why my father left him behind. Because he could not earn his keep."

Sissy couldn't quell her anger. "I can't believe that a man could do that to his own flesh and blood!"

She shrugged. "My father could. That and more."

Sissy digested that unpalatable statement. "Where is your family?"

"In Alaska. At least they are if he has anything to say about it."

"Alaska! My stars!"

"It's where he was determined to go when we left. He said he would get to Alaska or die trying." She looked far off. "My sisters and my little brother didn't want to leave Two Sisters either. We all liked it here. But that didn't matter to him. He told them they'd go and shut up about it." She looked at Sissy square on. "The only way they won't end up there is if he dies before they get there, or if he gets rid of some more of them along the way."

Sissy was shocked into silence. What else besides the forced abandonment of her brother had this poor girl endured? Finally she asked, "When did you last see your family?"

"Almost four years ago. We were on a ship bound for Alaska when I jumped off."

"My stars! You jumped off a ship?"

"Yes."

"Where?"

"Near a place called Puget Sound."

Sissy had to check a map but if Puget Sound was where she thought it was . . .

Then the girl asked, "Is this 1885?"

"Yes."

"That's what I figured."

"Glory be to heaven! You came back here by yourself? All that way? All that time?"

"I wasn't traveling all the time. I once spent a few weeks with some Indians right after I first left the ship and one winter the weather was so bad I had to stay in an abandoned cabin up in the mountains." She was quiet a minute, remembering how it had snowed that winter. Day after day. "It must've snowed for four months straight."

"Lucky you had your pet to keep you company."

"But I didn't. I've only had him for this past year." She touched Sissy's hand and her eyes were filled with entreaty and tears. "Please tell me what happened to my brother."

"Don't ask me to do that. Please. Not tonight. It is such a painful story. I don't think I have the strength for it myself. Besides, I must get home to my son before the storm really hits. And you . . . why, you're out on your feet. Please let's talk tomorrow."

Reluctantly Thora nodded. She told herself that one more day would not matter. Not after all this time. Still it was hard not to insist.

Sissy leaned close. "Listen to me. Not only will I tell you everything tomorrow but I will also gather several others who knew your brother before I came to town and they will tell you what they know about him as well. You must stay at least that long. Agreed?"

Thora nodded. "Agreed."

There came a smart rap on the door. "There's Joe Willie with your food." Sissy went to the door and opened it just enough to take in the tray. "Thank you! This looks wonderful." There came a warning growl—and it was not the wolf's. "Sissy, we're standin' out here . . ."

"I know. I know. I'll be right out." With his face in the

gap, trying to see inside, Joe Willie's misshapen nose was almost reshaped again.

One hunk of raw meat disappeared before it hit the floor, so Sissy dumped the newspaper's contents and purposefully did not watch the disposition of the rest. She could not, however, shut out the sound of massive jaws snapping and grinding. She poured steaming chicken-wild-rice soup in a bowl, and coffee into a cup and set both beside the girl. There came a tap on the glass then and both girls looked at the window.

"There's my husband again!" More rapping. "Ah . . . just a minute." Sissy opened the door slightly and poked her head out. "Yes?"

"Yes? Yes? Damnit, Sissy!" Joe Willie was a native Texan and although he'd spent eight years in Minnesota he had never learned to endure the winters with ease.

"Just one more minute."

Unlike many of his colleagues in the legal profession, Joe Willie could be a man of few words. "No! Now!"

"Joe Willie!"

"Goodgawdamighty girl! I can pound a nail with my cojones!"

"Hush, Joe Willie!" Sissy stepped outside and pulled the door to behind her. "She wants to know if she can stay the night in the jail."

Joe Willie's impatience was gone in an instant. "Poor thing's got no money, eh? Well, I don't see why not." He turned to Jim Horse who'd slogged up beside him. "All right with you, Jim?"

Jim shrugged. "Bull could put a sign on the door and stay the night at the North Star." The hotel was next door to the jail.

Joe Willie looked at the deputy. "What about you, Bull? Will that work for you?"

"Heck, yeah. The Star's beds're a hunnerd times better'n that l'il ol' pancake of a mattress in the jail." He swept a hand through the falling snow. " 'Sides, far as I'm concerned, any larcenous-minded fella that'll brave this, deserves whatever he wants."

Bull had a room in Ma Crosby's boarding house and Jim

Horse had his lodging above Buddy's Cafe but on the nights when either of them were "on call" they slept at the jail.

Sissy watched Jim. It was up to him. He removed his hat and knocked the snow off against his leg. The bowl of hair under the hat looked all the blacker in contrast to the snow-covered bottom half.

"Tell her all right."

"Great!" Sissy grinned big and then looked concerned. "Joe Willie, maybe you better bring me that blanket out of the sleigh."

"What're we gonna use on the way home?"

"Why our buffalo lap robe, of course!" She smiled. "It's ever so much warmer than that ol' Hudson Bay blanket."

What could Joe Willie say about that without pissing off Jim Horse? It had been Jim who had given them the buffalo robe as a wedding present four years earlier. Grumbling, he waded through drifted snow two feet deep and lifted the blanket off the sleigh. As he handed it to his wife, he used a proven ploy for lighting a fire under her. "Don't forget about little Joey's feeding."

"You're right! We really must go." She turned away. Turned back. "You know what, Joe Willie? I think that girl has walked all the way here from the West Coast."

"Goodgawdamighty!"

"You mean she walked to Minnesota?"

"On foot?" asked Bull.

"Yes, that's what it sounds like. Isn't that amazing?"

"Pretty close to unbelievable. Even for a full-grown man . . ."

There were more incredulous comments from the others but not from Jim Horse although he was just as impressed. Maybe more. Four years meant four winters. Not only could a person get turned around in blizzards just like the one they were experiencing, but the wilderness—even that which surrounded Two Sisters—was infested with all sorts of dangerous creatures. Four-legged and two-legged. A couple of years back a land survey crew had left town around the first of November and was never seen alive again. Hell, their remains weren't even discovered until the following August.

What she had done showed either great courage and an

excellent knowledge of the woods, or a run of harebrained luck the likes of which he'd never known before.

"You say somethin', Jim?"

"No."

"Four years walkin' only to get back here an' find her brother is dead." Bull swung his head. "Mm. Mm. Wonder what she's gonna do now. Whadda ya figure, Joe Willie?"

"I'm too damn froze to figure."

Sissy came back outside in only a moment. "Joe Willie, I've promised to come back first thing in the morning."

"All right. I'll get you here somehow." After assisting her into the sleigh, Joe Willie climbed in and turned the horse. "So long, boys."

"I'd stay on the road if I was you."

"Stay on the road. That's damn good advice, Bull."

Chapter 2

Jim Horse watched Bull tack a sign on the jailhouse door and then each man went his own way; a grinning Bull to a luxurious loll in a hotel bed, Jim to his quarters above Buddy's Cafe. He paused on the landing and looked across the road. It seemed he could just make out the jailhouse window. Then again, maybe not. He went inside.

He lived in a former attic, one large room with a dormer ceiling and exposed beams, a home to bats and cobwebs until Buddy Tangen decided—after twenty years of occupancy—that she suddenly no longer felt safe on the premises.

Ola Tangen, affectionately known as "Buddy" was as Norwegian as Oslo and about as subtle as a bull moose in season. Ever since she found out that Jim's grandmother was her dearly departed husband's long lost kin she was determined to adopt him. He was a bit big to fit under a wing but she would not be denied. Aside from her brother-in-law, Goody Tangen, she claimed that Jim was her "only kin left in America." So she'd had stairs built up the side of the building that housed her cafe and installed a coal heater and windows, and then waged a calculated battle specifically designed to get him moved up there. Rather than argue, he had given in. Surprisingly enough it had turned out fine. Not only was it closer to the jail and more private than the boarding house, but there was one big attraction that Buddy had neglected to mention: the sweet smell of home cooking that snaked up through the cracks in the wood floor. And the fact that all he had to do to partake of it was to tumble down the stairs.

There was something else beyond the advance indication of the bill of fare, something he'd only realized at this moment. Sometimes when he opened the door and the smell of home cooking struck him, he would briefly pretend that someone waited within. A woman with dinner on the stove and a relieved look on her face. A harmless fleeting fantasy. Unfortunately, that's all it was. Fantasy. Turns out that Buddy Tangen was his "only kin left in America" too.

His room had two windows, one that faced the street and one that faced the alley behind the cafe. On a clear day the back window gave him a bird's eye view of the outhouse and the chicken coop. Beyond that, however, were the woods, home to his people since time immemorial and as necessary to him as air. Some days it helped him just to know that the woods were there; other days being able to get into them for a couple of hours was about all that kept his head on straight. To an Ojibwe, not much equalled the north woods for restoring a sense of well being.

He had no cook stove but that was not a hardship. He ate all his meals out anyway and, on nights like this he could always scoop snow off the roof and make coffee on the coal heater. He decided that sounded good.

Sometimes—generally it was on just such a night like this—he'd recall exactly what a cup of coffee tasted like when it was laced with whiskey, but no matter how appealing the thought, he never poured himself one. He had not touched whiskey since his good friend Rope Thrower needlessly died because of it. It had been once too often that he had seen whiskey's adverse effects on his people and he wanted none of it. For some that was easier said than done but he hadn't found it a hardship. He had given up a lot of things more important to him than whiskey. Things such as most of the traditions he had brought with him to Two Sisters.

After stoking the heater, he whipped off his black hat with

its sodden eagle feather and hung it on a whittled peg on the wall.

When he first took the job as deputy to Joe Willie Everett he removed the sacred eagle feathers from the barrel of his rifle. A few weeks later, as a concession to some jittery townspeople, he had ceased openly carrying a spiked tomahawk. But he'd drawn the line at the feather in his hat.

The room was beginning to warm up. He hung his jacket on the back of a chair and removed his patch and dropped it on the bureau where it slithered to the edge and fell onto the floor. He retrieved it and looked at it. A frayed bit of cotton.

He was far from vain but he had taken to wearing it ever since the day a little girl ran from the sight of him. Locking one knee and laying his elbows on the bureau, he warily examined himself in the cracked mirror propped against the wall. Looked at with an impartial eye, (Hell, he only had the one!) he allowed that he would probably run from the sight of him too. He saw straight black hair and one slightly slanted eye the color of wet oak shavings. Opposite, where his other eye was supposed to be, was a dog-leg scar that ran from his temple to his cheek bone.

He shrugged then his face changed and he grinned. Sometimes the way he looked was an advantage. Turns out that some women . . . hell no, most *all* women . . . were drawn to a man who looked like a brute. Yeah. Like deer to a baited trap. He grinned again and yawned and stretched and looked at his bed with anticipation. He always slept particularly well when a storm raged outside. Which was understandable when one knew something about his tribe.

The principal Ojibwe clans were Crane, Catfish, Bear, Marten, Wolf and Loon, and it was believed that often (but not always) a person who belonged to a certain clan was most likely to have the characteristics of its totem. Those of the Loon Clan could be swift swimmers. The Wolf Clan people were often unequaled trackers. Stuff like that.

Jim's people were of the Bear Clan. Slow to anger. Ferocious once incited. Protective of their own. And, as one might imagine, very deep sleepers on cold winter nights.

Among the other tribes, the Ojibwe—or Chippewa as some prefer—used to have the reputation of being a generally pleasant people, fond of a joke and a good laugh. Not warlike to speak of. But that all changed when the ownership of their land was challenged. Then they became the most fierce fighters in the northern hemisphere.

About the time of the American Revolution, the Ojibwe and the Sioux were involved in a terrific battle of their own. It lasted years and exacted a terrible toll on both tribes but when it finally ended the Ojibwe had soundly whipped the more numerous, supposedly mighty Sioux and forced them south once and for all.

The Ojibwe were known perfectionists, but were also remarkably practical. If a man could not do something exceptionally well, he refrained from doing it at all. One man might tell another, I do not make a very good canoe. The other man would nod in understanding and say, I do not make a very good fish trap. How about if I make a fish trap for you and you make a canoe for me?

This was done all the time and neither man had reason to feel inferior. The tribe had no trials to prove a man's masculinity or a woman's worth. Certainly a manhood rite would not be how well a man made a canoe! But neither was a man judged by what labor he might undertake. Ojibwe men were very self-assured and, unlike the men of many other tribes, they did not think that doing heavier tasks for their women made them less manly at all.

Bear Clan or not, that night Jim lay sleepless. There was an odd sadness in his heart. As he stared up at the dark beams above his head, he found himself thinking of times gone by—of places he never expected to see again, of people he had loved and lost. Pretty soon his mind retreated to that long-ago time.

His grandmother was his grandfather's third wife (married after Blue Crow's first wives had both died young) a white captive who fell in love with her husband and bore him two sons and a daughter. Only her daughter lived to maturity and Jim was her only son. When his mother died, three-year-old Jim's rearing was taken over by his grandmother.

He was a handful for her. Not mean or cruel but like many

young, constantly testing any restrictions placed upon him. As he matured his grandmother worried about his direction. She was afraid he would swing too wide and end up joining some renegade band of drinkers and malcontents. Such boys were always getting into trouble and were not generally very long-lived.

When Jim was a boy, one of Blue Crow's daughters by his first wife was working at the home of a wealthy merchant in the Twin Cities when she fell in love with a Cherokee who owned a trading post in Tahlequah, a town in the recently formed Indian Nations. Jim's grandmother seized on an opportunity to get him out of the area. When Blue Crow's daughter married her Cherokee and they left for their new home, nine-year-old Jim Horse went with them. He stayed over ten years and might have stayed forever if not for the death of his friend Rope Thrower.

Rope Thrower's father was a Cherokee Indian and a policeman, as were all lawmen and judges in the Nations. He was a good lawman and the first fair non-tribal person of authority with whom Jim had had any dealings. It was he who taught Jim how to handle a gun . . . but it was many hours of practice on his own that made him so fast and deadly accurate.

The two boys were inseparable. What Rope Thrower learned, so did Jim. Not all was edifying but much was. One such thing was skill in riding, and the management and care of a horse.

Jim was no horseman when he arrived in Oklahoma. Far from it. The Ojibwe were fleet-footed warriors of the forest, and since traveling in drifted snow through trees a foot apart was easier done on foot, most Ojibwe didn't care for horses at all. Jim was destined to be different.

There in the Nations, among the plains tribes such as the Cherokee, Comanche and the Chickasaw, he was to become a horse wrangler of some repute. So much so that in riding contests even the Comanche men nodded their approval when he rode by. (Jim was pleased that the reaction of some of the Comanche girls was considerably more . . . robust.)

Not many men name themselves but by the time he left the Nations he was called Jim Horse. By the men and by the girls . . . who if they were white might have had their tongue-in-check.

Jim spent so much time at Rope Thrower's family farm he was looked at as one of their own, and as such, was subject to their rules of conduct. Sometimes this caused problems. Particularly when the two boys discovered whores. By the time they'd reached eighteen they were rarely not in rut and were considered—mostly by themselves—to be great studs. Since everyone knew them in Tahlequah, they often rode over to Paw-Paw or Briartown where they could whore in anonymity.

The accident took place on a sultry summer night. As often happened, they had spent most of their money on whiskey and had had to share a woman. (Ah, yes, and what better woman to share than Miss Beauty Simpson? A cross-eyed Choctaw with three gold teeth and a feminine form that would stop a sundial!) They were enjoying themselves so much they didn't leave until the early hours of the morning. Of course, they had both had way too much to drink but so had they many times before. Riding back, Rope Thrower's horse started giving him trouble.

Jim could still see that dun gelding, a small-eared, big-boned horse with wild glarey eyes that hinted of some evil thing hidden deep within.

They had worked that horse together, using skills handed down from generations of horsemen but it had still been very difficult to break the gelding to saddle and bridle. Jim told Rope Thrower that maybe some horses are not meant to be tamed. "Maybe some are just plain too mean to break." No, Rope Thrower replied. This is a born war horse!

That night that horse declared war on Rope Thrower and it won.

They were tearing across a field when the dun abruptly stopped and threw Rope Thrower over his head and snapped his neck like a twig. At first Jim didn't know what had happened. A cannon couldn't have unseated Rope Thrower if he hadn't been drinking. He leapt off his horse. After the dun's hoofbeats faded, there came a dead silence in which Jim stood frozen. It was his first close encounter with sudden death. One minute his friend had been hoo-haaing and carrying on; the next minute he was dead.

Jim was stunned sober that night and stayed that way. When the opportunity presented itself, he left there and returned to

Minnesota. It was not a joyful homecoming. That his grandmother's health was failing was bad enough, but he would soon find that there was more wrong than that.

It was as if he'd returned to a place he'd never been before! Most of his clansmen had scattered like seeds on the water. Those men who remained were drunk most of the time, many of the women too. The people even looked different. No longer forceful and vital but stark and haunted-looking. Jim wanted to ask: What happened to you? Why have you changed like this? Naturally he didn't. It wasn't something a person did.

A few days after he got home a clansman he knew by sight killed himself by cutting his own throat and Jim was astounded. Suicide was unheard of among the Ojibwe. Such a dishonorable, cowardly thing had never happened in his lifetime and yet, in subsequent days, he learned that there had been two other suicides in the six months previous. Something was terribly wrong. When he said as much to his grandmother, she replied that most of the people could no longer see the sun.

His grandmother rallied due, she claimed, to his return—but he could tell her time was close. He stayed near and it wasn't long before he had fallen back into the routine of his former life. Within a few months he had met a girl named Little Rain and decided to marry her despite what he sensed was disappointment on his grandmother's part. When asked, she said she had nothing against the girl who was quiet, amiable and hard working. On the contrary, she had said, "I like her."

Jim knew that the real reason she was not pleased was because marrying Little Rain meant that he would always live as a red man.

Poor Little Rain! Only fifteen years old and married and buried less than a year after they met. To Jim the nights were black and starless after she died, almost as if he were the dead one with a buckskin covering his face and, from that day forward, he vowed to limit his lovemaking to whore houses and keep his feelings to himself.

But when his grandmother died as well, he discovered that not all vows are so easily kept.

It was only when he looked at his grandmother's face, always pale and even more so now in death, that he realized how much he owed her. It was she who had given him what care and love and guidance he had received in life. It was she who had shaped him and encouraged him.

It was also she who had always insisted that he find a life with the whites.

In the beginning he'd thought that there was a perfectly good reason for her favoring the white man's world. She was, after all, white herself. Though he could not see the mark of her race on his face, his grandmother was full-blood Norwegian—one of two young girls after which the settlement of Two Sisters had been named. Abducted within a few weeks of her arrival, Hedy Tangen had been only sixteen when it happened, a small blond girl with a wry sense of humor and a slight overbite. But she was practical and free from prejudice and in time she grew to love her Ojibwe husband, Blue Crow. Ultimately she had a very happy life with him. Unfortunately she lived long enough to see all but her grandson Jim precede her in death.

Hedy Tangen had been smart enough to see beyond the misguided visionaries and the rifle shaking agitators to the end of the red man. After centuries of happy habitation, the Ojibwe way of life was over. She worried that it might be over for her grandson as well.

When she sent him to live in the Nations she hoped that it would broaden his horizon—literally—and simultaneously curb the wild streak she saw widening in him. She had hoped that spending time with a more advanced tribe like the Cherokees would make him want to adapt himself to the white's way of life. It didn't work. If anything he was wilder when he returned than he'd been when he left. Then Little Rain died.

The death of his friend Rope Thrower and then his young wife had embittered her grandson. He was angry and disillusioned and she knew she needed her best powers of persuasion to save him from himself. Though near death, she refused to pass over. She was determined to see him on the right path before she went.

"In the old days you would have been a head warrior, maybe the best warrior our people have ever known, but our war is over now and the white man has won. We are irrevocably defeated.

"Now, Grandson, I remind you how well I know you . . .

better I think, than you know yourself . . . well enough to know that you will not live long as a conquered man.''

She kept pointing out things he knew only too well: that the clan was disbanding and that the people were wandering away.

''You go too but not into the woods to rot like a broken stick. Go instead into the white man's world. Live there and prosper and in that way . . . win!''

It took weeks but by blatantly using her imminent demise, she finally coaxed him into complying. ''Two years,'' she had urged. ''If you will try it for two years I believe you will stay. You were born to be a leader of men. Not a drunk who does not have the sense to come in out of the cold.'' (She was referring to another death earlier that week, a man who had been found just so, laying dead in the snow with a bottle frozen to his hand.)

Half angry and half teasing, Jim recalled that he had asked her if what she wanted was a white man in a red skin and she had nodded. By God, looking at himself now, it was about what he had become.

She made him promise to contact her family in Two Sisters—Ola and Albin Tangen, who she'd heard were owners of a cafe there. In the unlikely event that they had moved or both had died he should talk to Gudmund Tangen who was the owner of the general store. ''Either of those people will help you simply because you are my kin.'' She removed a rawhide necklace. ''Take this to prove you are who you say you are.'' He'd opened the tarnished locket that contained the images of two girls, both blond and obviously related and recognized that one of them was his grandmother.

''The picture was taken the day we arrived in New York.''

''Who is the other girl?''

''My sister, Trina but I heard that she died long ago.'' He offered her water. She sipped it weakly then waved it away.

He studied the locket then said, ''They'll probably think I've stolen it.''

''Then tell them about what happened on the way to Minnesota. Tell them about the calf that broke its leg in a gopher hole and how my father was going to shoot it, but I carried on so that he bound the calf's leg and fashioned a sling for it under the wagon and that it rode there until it could walk again."

After she died he seriously considered not honoring his promise—it would have been the easier course but in the end he could not. So he went. He could not, however, bring himself to approach those Tangens who were respected and landed pillars of the community. Instead, when circumstances offered him the opportunity, he took the job as deputy sheriff. It was only after Al Tangen's death that he told Al's widow and his brother who he was. He didn't know what reaction he expected but it certainly wasn't the open hearted welcome he got. Now five years later, he was an accepted if not respected member of the community himself.

In the beginning there was no doubt in his mind that his acceptance was due to the Tangens being one of Two Sisters' "founding families." Now he was just as certain that it was because—Indian or not—he was the best man to do the job. He was proud of that fact. He realized that originally he may have come to Two Sisters only because he had promised he would, but he had stayed for another reason entirely: ambition, though where it had come from was still a puzzlement to him. He used to question himself about it all the time. Was it his grandmother's upbringing? Or maybe his years in the Nations? Or some old instinct that rose up and took charge? Maybe it was simply the stubborn belief that he would be at least one red man that the white man would never conquer!

For whatever reason, he had aspirations that many of his people did not. First among them was a passionate need to succeed on the white man's terms.

But now, on this strange snowy night he was feeling a vague dissatisfaction with his life. Why? He did his work fairly and well. He had a roof over his head, food for his belly and a woman two or three times a week. (More often if he wanted.) So what was wrong? What had brought all this on?

He would've liked to sleep on the question but by three o'clock he realized that it wasn't going to happen. He got up, added more fuel to the heater and made more coffee. Then, with one shoulder to the wall, he stood at the window to drink it. The storm's fury had died with the wind. Now moisture-laden, acorn-sized flakes fell straight to the ground.

Staring toward the treeline, he was thinking that maybe the best way to spend this night was with the new whore at the Inside Straight when some snowflakes gathered and started to form a faint image. He watched with interest. As a kid he often saw things in the falling snow, a foraging deer, a swimming moose, the face of a coyote. But this time something was different. This image looked like it might be a human being. Yes, it was. He watched the picture come together, a pale oval of a face, wavy and indistinct and yet unmistakable because of the honeyed hair.

Captured by the phenomenon, he had no idea how long he stood there; time had become meaningless. Coming closer then retreating, it once appeared so real that without realizing it, he reached out to it. The image wavered and a curtain fell across his eyes, and when it lifted, the image was gone.

For a long time he waited for it to reappear but it did not.

Instead of going to the Inside Straight, he went back to bed. With his ankles crossed and one arm crooked behind his head, he resumed his contemplation of the rafters.

The spirit of one who had gone before was trying to contact him. He had no doubt about that. It could have been his grandmother or Rope Thrower or Little Rain. Maybe even someone who had lived hundreds of years ago. Who knew? The only thing he knew for sure was that the spirit was using that girl in the jail to send its message. Interesting.

Chapter 3

Thora went into the cell and looked at the thin feather tick on the cot and the slop bucket that had been set in the corner. The cell smelled of tobacco, urine and harsh lye soap. It smelled of man. Coco-man closed his jaws on a soft howl and hummed unhappily. "All right. Come on. We'll sleep in the other room."

She positioned her coat in front of the stove and sat on it with the Hudson Bay blanket drawn squaw-like around her. Idly she picked up the bowl of soup and ate some. With the spoon halfway to her lips she suddenly started to cry, great wrenching sobs that hurt her chest and slopped soup onto the floor. It was some time before the onslaught passed and it left her body aching and her throat raw. She never would understand why some people swore by having a good cry. She sure didn't feel any better and it didn't seem possible that she ever would. Not if she cried from now to kingdom come.

She still couldn't believe that anyone would think that her poor addle-brained brother was capable of murder! Halldor would never hurt a bird, much less a human being. Yet if the truth were told, deep down she had been afraid that something like this would happen. He had always been too trusting of others.

Her plan from the beginning had been to get back to Two

Sisters, find her brother, find work and find a place for them to live. Naturally she'd worried herself sick about him the whole time. Stuck in mountain blizzards for weeks at a time, she would drive herself crazy, imagining him hungry and alone, or duped out of his shoes by some mean man, or harnessed like an animal and made to work for gruel. None of her nightmares were unrealistic; her brother was as helpless as a baby.

The only way she could stop the torment was to try to remember him happy. How he had looked the time a puppy piddled in his lap, or the time he stared up at the northern lights with his arms wide spread and his face shining with wonder. There hadn't been many of those happy times but she liked to think she'd had a hand in most of them.

Unfortunately those happy images would never stay with her for long. Another would keep intruding, one that had remained with her intact and undisturbed for over four years now . . . the way her brother had looked on the day their father decided to leave him in Two Sisters. Twisting his bound arms and legs. Tied by the neck to a ridge pole that supported the center of the house. His boy-man face awash in tears.

She'd been sent to look for the cow and hadn't known what was happening. She remembered running toward him and then something slammed against the side of her head. She woke in the flat bed of the wagon as it rumbled down some deeply rutted road. She looked around but at first she could only move her eyes. Her ankles were drawn up and tied to her hands, much as her brother's had been and her head—which rested in her sister Hekla's lap—felt like it was cracked.

Out the canvas opening she saw that the cow and her calf tagged along behind the wagon. In front her mother sat beside her father but her back was rigid and cold. The other five kids as well as all their belongings—such as they were—were in the wagon. They stared at her big-eyed and scared to death. Bebe, she noted, had gone back to sucking her thumb. Then she looked up but Hekla shook her shoulder and laid her finger across her lips in warning.

So they were moving on again. Only this time they were leaving more than debts behind. They were leaving one of their own! She had to get free! If the sun that shone into the back of the wagon was any indication, it was late morning. Her brother would have cried himself sick!

She struggled to get to her knees but she got so dizzy she sort of fainted again. When she woke her sister hissed, "You better be still, Thora!" She wiped her ear and then showed her the red on the rag. "See! You've started it bleeding again."

She couldn't just do nothing. Using her eyes she begged her sister to untie her, but Hekla was too afraid to go against their father. She had always been. Finding her voice, she beseeched her mother. "Please! Mother, please!" It was no surprise when her mother didn't even look around. If her mother had ever had any spirit it had been broken by her husband's wrath long, long ago. But she couldn't give up. She was Halldor's only hope. "Papa, please don't leave him. Please please don't. Let's go back and get him. He won't be any trouble. I'll take care of him . . . I'll do everything . . ."

He turned and pointed at her. "You keep it up and I'll give you a beatin' like you've never had before."

Words dried in her mouth. It was not what he had said but the look he'd thrown her. Like he'd kill her if she troubled him even a little bit. She settled back and made her face meek. She would be of no help to Halldor dead.

As the miles went by, she summoned a sort of blind hope from some place deep within her. And she planned. It was the only way she could keep from going crazy with worry.

Someone would find Halldor and he'd be all right until she got back. He knew she would not willingly leave him. He knew she'd come back and she would! She vowed it then. Somehow, someday she would be back.

Every minute of every hour she watched for an opportunity to escape but days became weeks and the weeks turned into months, and it seemed that her father was never going to let her out of his sight. On and on she walked beside the wagon counting every step that took her further away, knowing they were all steps she would have to retrace! And oh, how she had wanted to get at it!

Finally she did it! And then what followed was four long years of living like a wild animal. Dirty. Hungry. Scared and tired, always tired. Sometimes she was so miserably cold she could not draw a deep breath without terrible pain, sometimes she was so layered with sweat that her buckskins felt like fish skin. All that and she was too late!

Stop it! Stop! She shook her head to clear it. She hated when she got like this. Driving herself half crazy over something she could do nothing about. There'd been nights on the trail when she had not slept at all thinking . . . what if this happened . . . or this . . . or that . . . And in the morning nothing was different. The only thing she had accomplished was to exhaust herself. Which was exactly what she was doing now. She could no longer hold up her head. And tomorrow she must go on. Where or how she could not answer now.

Careful not to cover her deaf ear, she laid down. Coco-man curled up with his back to hers but in spite of his heat and that thrown by the stove she was trembling like a person with the palsy. Her last thought as she fell into an exhausted sleep was: God had to help her now. No one else could.

Unlike her older brother, Thora Gunnlauger had been born with a wealth of inherent ability and while it's true that she lacked a formal education, she was clever and very cunning. Early on she'd been forced to think on her feet, a skill that had saved her life more than once over the last four years. She also instinctively knew how to respond to new situations and never forgot something once she learned it.

There was, however, a certain lack of depth to her ability to reason. She did not know how to analyze ideas and then draw conclusions. As a consequence, it had never entered her mind to consider one certain, salient fact: just as she and her father shared the same nose and the same shade of hair, they also shared certain inherent traits. And single-mindedness was one of them.

The tenacity that got her from Puget Sound to Minnesota was the same determination that her father had demonstrated in his obsession about reaching Alaska.

That she had never come to this conclusion was probably just as well. She would have been stunned to learn that she was so much like the one person she hated most in the world. She probably wouldn't have been able to bear it and in the end she would have hated herself too. Fair or not, she was already beginning to blame herself for her brother's death.

That night she dreamt that she was wandering around town trying to find help. She circled every house and public building but none appeared to have any doors or windows! How did the people gain entry?

It was cold and dark. She was close to exhaustion when finally she saw a yellow rectangle cast onto the snow from a window on the second level of a building. A man was backlit by the light within. She called to him to raise the window and let her inside.

She woke before the dream came to a natural resolution. It had unsettled her and added to her feeling of isolation. She did not spend time trying to figure it out but in spite of her exhaustion, it was a long time before she slept again.

Chapter 4

The next day dawned clear but long-time residents knew it probably wouldn't last. Low hanging snow-swollen clouds sat a mile off shore and waited for the wind to carry them over the town. At six o'clock Jim Horse showed up for the morning shift, same as usual, except this time he knocked on the door first and entered only when he got permission. He stepped inside and shut the door behind him.

The girl was standing with one hand on the wolf's head. The animal wasn't making any noise but its gums were scrolled back to exhibit an impressive set of yellowy tusklike teeth. Damnit, he did not want to have to shoot that wolf!

To her the sheriff of Two Sisters looked no less formidable by daylight. Just the opposite. He was even taller and more solidly built than she'd thought. Understandable, she supposed. Last night he had been on one knee beside her and all she had seen was a deathly flat eye and a face that was without a flicker of emotion.

Today he wore a low-crowned wide-brimmed black hat with one feather slanted backward along its band. Beneath its brim were grim lips, a square jaw and the tail end of an angry scar. His eye was still deathly flat, his face still without a bit of expression.

"What's the wolf called?"

"Coco-man."

"Snowsnake?"

"Yes."

He hung his hat on a peg on the wall. As he took a seat on the closest chair he said, "Hu'ah," which she took as "Huh!"

Jim Horse leaned back and folded his arms and studied her from tip to toe. She had a strong face with wide eyes, a long nose, a chin that was almost squared.

And she had ties to his people. That was unmistakable. Her hair, a curly blond tangle, was poorly restrained by a beaded and quilled headband. Her deerskin moccasins were trimmed in the traditional leaf design of the Ojibwe and her pet had an Ojibwe name. Unmistakable ties.

All these things he had seen last night and his thought then had been that she was some buck's woman, but now he wasn't so sure. She faced him without fear, even with an air of defiance, yet there was a certain innocence about her.

A silence had fallen. She was probably waiting for him to speak, but he didn't. He had never been a chatterbox but he'd been a lot more talkative before the deaths of everyone close to him. Those losses—all coming within the same year as they had—had stunned his soul and sent him into a dark silence that had become a habit after a while.

On the other hand, the only way to find out what he wanted to know was to ask. "How'd you come by an Ojibwe name for your pet?"

She looked at the wolf. "He's not a pet."

"Should I keep a gun on him then?"

"That's not necessary."

Graceful as a doe she bent to say something to the wolf. Her hair fell forward like a veil of spun silver in the sunlight and worn buckskin breeches molded her rear like the peel on a potato. When she turned back she squared her shoulders which traced her breasts against her shirt. Jim decided that he definitely should have visited that new whore at the Inside Straight.

Whatever she said made the wolf unfurl its lips, but it still acted edgy. So did Jim, and the wolf was the least of it. "How did you come by your . . . friend?"

"For a time I stayed with a woman who thought that wolves

were better people than most people. She used to go all over springing any wolf traps that she found. Most of the time the trap had already done its job and the animal was either dead or too far gone to save.'' Half to herself she added, ''She was a crazy old coot.'' She shook her head. ''Anyway, when the old woman was sick I used to take over for her.''

''That how you got your coat?''

''Yes. A big male, biggest I'd ever seen. He was already dead when I found him.''

''Why'd that old woman make them her business?''

She shrugged. ''She liked wolves and she hated trappers, especially those who did not run their traps often. It drove her crazy to think that animals were starving to death or being attacked by other predators while they were held helpless by a trap.'' She nodded at the wolf. ''This one's mother had already starved to death when I found her. Two of her pups too. Coco was almost dead as well but I brought him to the old woman and she saved him. I named him Snowsnake because for a long time he was so scared he crawled on his belly every place he went.''

Before she remembered not to, she gave him a quick smile. She had even teeth. Wide and almost too white, like new snow in the bright sunlight. ''Looks like he got over that,'' he said gruffly.

''Yeah. Maybe I'll have to change his name to Fearless or Braveheart. He's not afraid of anything now.''

Jim merely grunted. He couldn't argue with that.

Once again silence swelled between them. She waited for him to go on but he didn't. Just pinned her with that fever-bright eye of his. ''Mrs. Everett told me to wait here for her.'' He nodded. She thought she heard someone at the window but it was only a passing wagon that rattled the ice rimmed glass. She looked out. ''There's about ten kids out in front. Fooling around in the snow . . .'' She looked back at him. Still looking at her.

A log thunked against the stove and from the street came the high-pitched squeal of a girl's laughter and still he stared. She imagined that she could hear her skin pebble and her arm hairs twang.

Suddenly the door flew open and a woman stuck her head

in. Once she got her heart swallowed, Thora was never so glad to see another human being in her life.

She was a pleasantly plump woman with apple cheeks, a button nose and white-blond hair. When she saw Thora she covered her mouth with both hands. Thora looked at the sheriff as if to ask: what's wrong with her? He looked from the woman to her and his normally firmly fixed mouth moved in a barely perceptible twitch.

Pressing in behind the first woman were a man and another woman who had the same stunned expressions. The man, though pale, was at least capable of speech. ''Please forgive us for staring, Miss Gunnlauger.'' With a kindly smile, the woman added, ''It is just such a shock!''

The sheriff introduced them. The man was the Mayor Rudy Fagerhaug. The matronly woman with the pouter-pigeon body and the no-nonsense air was his wife, Dorothy. The apple-cheeked woman was Buddy Tangen, owner of Buddy's Cafe. She made a little foot. ''Pleased to meet you, Miss Gunnlauger.''

''Thora, please. And I call myself Gunn now.''

''Why?'' asked Buddy. She was from the old guard who hung onto their old ideas. And names.

Thora shrugged. ''Sounds more American, I guess.'' She frowned. ''What was such a shock?''

''How much you resemble your brother, Thor.'' the Mayor replied.

''Thor?''

''That's what we called your brother.''

Buddy Tangen added. ''Yah, Thor. Iss true. Yew lewk yust like him.'' The woman looked familiar to Thora. Her face, maybe the way she wore her hair in coiled braids around her ears. Something.

''You sure knocked me for a roll.''

''Loop, dear.'' said the mayor's wife. ''Oh, but it's true.'' The mayor put one arm around his wife whose eyes had suddenly filled.

Hearing Dottie sniff and seeing Rudy grope for his handkerchief, Buddy Tangen realized she was coming perilously close to losing the stoic Norwegian rein she kept on her emotions.

This is not good, she thought. Not good at all. "Come to the cafe with me and I will fix you some breakfast."

Jim rolled his eye. His "aunt's" surefire cure for everything. Food. And lots of it.

"Thank you," Thora replied. "But I can't. I'm supposed to wait here for Mrs. Everett."

"Yah! Yah!" Buddy motioned. "Sissy told us that last night when they got home. We stayed with the baby while they came to the jail to see you. We . . ." She pointed at the mayor's wife and at herself. ". . . are the ones supposed to tell you all about your brother. Come."

Buddy had barely finished speaking when the door was pushed further open and a freckle-nosed boy skidded in. He was perhaps fifteen or sixteen and in a powerful hurry. Snatching off his cap made straw-colored hair rise from his head like a geyser.

"They said you were Thor's sister . . ." Pant-pant ". . . I had to see for myself."

Jim saw a hint of a smile on the girl's lips.

"Well? Am I?"

"Yeah, you're her all right."

"And you're . . . ?"

The boy hiked his pants which were six inches too short as it was. "Davey Cox, Thor's best friend. I been waitin' on you all this time. Sure took you long enough," he grumbled. Thora had to drown out exclamations of reproach to ask why.

"Why?" He acted shocked. "So's we can get to the bottom of this thing an' bring Thor's murderers to justice."

"I'd like nothing better."

Watching her closely Jim noted that her eyes had become calculating and thought: It was exactly as he'd suspected. There's a lot more to this girl than a well-shaped rear end.

"Good," Davey said. "After school I work at the paper right over yonder." He hitched a thumb over his shoulder. "Where it says The Daily Clarion. If you want we can get started soon as I get off work."

"All right . . ."

"Now hold on there, young man. Don't you dare start all that up again."

"All what?" Apparently no one heard her.

''Opening old wounds, Davey. That's about all you'd accomplish.''

''That's right. You know the investigation Joe Willie and Jim conducted four years ago led absolutely no where.''

The mayor agreed with his wife. ''Besides, what could you expect to find now, Davey? With a trail that cold.''

''Well, I figured we might . . .''

Buddy stepped forward. ''We better go to the cafe now. Sissy may be already there.'' When she took the girl's arm there came a sound not unlike distant drums, but the girl patted the wolf's head and it ceased. ''I have some raw beef over there for your . . . your guardian,'' said Buddy. ''And food for you too.'' It sounded like she said: Fewd fer yew tew.

Davey Cox pulled on his worsted cap. ''Well, I got to get back to work anyway. We can talk later.''

''I'd like to.''

''We will! An' don't worry about findin' me. I'll find you.''

My, he's dramatic! She smiled to herself, remembering when she was his age. About a hundred years ago. ''All right.''

When Sissy Everett arrived at the jail a few minutes later she found it empty except for Jim Horse who was lounging at the window with one palm braced on the window frame.

''Where is she?''

''There.'' He used his chin. ''Goin' into Buddy's.''

''Oh, good. I'll go right over.'' She got as far as the door and turned back. ''You all right, Jim?''

''Yeah, sure.'' He moved away from window. ''Why?''

''I don't know. I thought maybe something . . .'' He smiled at her then and she smiled back and went on out. Same old Jim.

Not exactly. Jim was still Indian enough to be bothered by that vision the night before. He sat at his desk and rolled a twirly. He ran his tongue along the paper, then ran a match under the desk and thought about it.

Sometimes people who had passed on into the next life would try to contact those left behind through one still living. Last night he'd been thinking about Rope Thrower, Little Rain and his grandmother immediately before the girl appeared to him in the vision. She did not look anything like Rope Thrower or Little Rain but she might look something like his grandmother had when she was young. He grimaced. If that was grandmother, he was in a lot of trouble. Last night he distinctly remembered thinking that it was too bad he wasn't a savage any more because what he would really like to do is cart that girl off and screw her blue.

Grandmother would not have approved at all. Especially if she knew that the idea held even greater appeal today.

Thinking of the end of his people's way of life made him sigh sadly. It was too bad. Taking captives had been one of the real advantages to living back in the old days. A man could take the good ones as wives—as his grandfather had done. The bad ones a man could be a little careless with their bonds and let nature take its course. He remembered one man who'd followed a captive for days in order to make sure she made it to her people and did not—under any circumstances—wander back to his village.

He pulled his chair to the window and propped his foot against the wall. The more he thought about the girl and the woods, the more "savage" his thoughts only he could readily foresee two major drawbacks to turning his thoughts into action: he would lose his job and he would have to shoot the wolf. He doubted that having her would be worth his job and he knew it wouldn't be worth the killing of that . . . he muttered aloud without realizing it . . . "beautiful animal!"

"Well, thanks, Jim. I didn't think you'd noticed."

Jim focused and saw Bull Durham standing in the doorway, grinning like an idiot. The two elevated legs of Jim's chair met wood with a resounding smack. Wordless, he unracked his rifle and stuck on his hat and went to the door. Then he turned. "Don't let it go to your head."

Chapter 5

No doubt the entire town would have found its way over to Buddy's Cafe if she hadn't finally put the "closed" sign in the window and bolted the door.

The mayor expressed his sympathy to Thora again, offered his services in any way and then he left the five silent women alone, sitting at a table of half-full coffee cups and smeared pie plates.

Thora looked at each in turn. Sissy Everett, the schoolteacher; Buddy Tangen, the owner of the cafe; and Dottie Fagerhaug, the mayor's wife.

Directly to her left was the last to arrive, a young woman named Meline Beckstrom. She, like Buddy, possessed the sort of skin that always looked freshly scrubbed. Blond Meline and russet-haired Sissy were of a similar age while Dottie Fagerhaug and Buddy Tangen appeared to be in their fifties or sixties but she wasn't very good at judging stuff like that. "I'm anxious to hear about my brother."

The four women looked at each other with expressions that said: Where to begin? Finally Sissy Everett took a deep breath and plunged in. "We called your brother Thor because the only time he ever spoke was the day he was discovered." She paused to swallow hard and Buddy leapt in.

"We didn't know until you arrived last night that he had been crying your name."

Dottie Fagerhaug spoke. "A man heard him as he was passing by your farm. It was no later than midday and near as we could tell he had probably been there only since early that morning."

"Thank goodness," said Meline.

"Yes! Think how horrible that would have been."

"Why, he might've been there for days!"

"First time I saw him I knew who he was."

"Everyone did."

"Yah," said Buddy. "I used to see you and him all the time, walking around town. One so big and the other so slight. I told my Al—She looks like a terrier leading a bull."

Now Thora placed Buddy Tangen. "Your husband used to give us fresh-baked bread with butter and sugar on it."

"Yah, that was my Al." She sat for a minute with her eyes downcast and her throat working. Finally she couldn't help herself and used her apron to swab her eyes.

"Your brother liked Buddy's bread better than a slice of pie," Sissy said, petting Buddy on the back.

"It's true."

Sissy added, "After your family left, many of the townspeople watched out for him. Buddy fed him. Meline patched his clothes. Dottie and Rudy gave him a place to stay."

"And Sissy read stories to him," Dottie exclaimed.

Thora looked at all the women then at the table. "I'll never be able to thank you for doing those things."

Dottie pooh-poohed her part. "It was just a little room off the back of our barn. In the beginning we tried everything we could to get him into the house but he insisted on staying by himself. Once he stopped wandering off, we let him be. It wasn't till later that we were able to figure out why he preferred that room to the house."

"Why?"

"Why, because of the unobstructed view of the road. As soon as the weather turned in the spring that's where he'd be every night."

"He'd bring a chair outside and just sit there like he was in church. Rocking a little and staring off to the west."

"I'd have to go get him inside if it started to rain." Dottie brought her handkerchief to her eyes. "Poor thing."

"He must've seen you go off in that direction."

"Funny how he could remember something like that and forget to wear his socks."

Sissy stepped in, trying to avoid a deluge of tears. "Can you tell us what happened after you left Two Sisters?"

Thora shook her head. "Not yet." To herself she added: Maybe never. "Why was my brother suspected of murder?"

Sissy sighed. Might as well get it over with. Obviously there would be no denying her.

The trouble began, Sissy said, not long after she arrived in Two Sisters, which was April 28, 1881. She said she had been fleeing a "bad situation" in New York and had chosen the place because it was the end of the line. With a smile at Buddy she told about getting a job waiting tables at the cafe and that it was there that she met Thora's brother.

"I'll never forget that day." She looked off. "He'd come by to pick up his lunch. Remember, Buddy? It was pouring cats and dogs but there he was, standing outside in the rain, patiently waiting for somebody to notice him. Oh, Thora, he was such a handsome man! That face! That form! Just like a Greek statue. And so strong!" She touched Thora's arm. "He saved my life once."

She told about three voyageurs who attacked her on her way home from work one night. How they had tossed a sack over her head and were about to carry her into the woods when Thor came out of nowhere and beat them off.

"If it hadn't been for your brother, I don't know what would have happened to me." Actually, after being married to Joe Willie for four years she now knew exactly what would have happened to her. The thought of those three . . . Lordy, it was enough to make her ill!

"Almost the same thing happened to me," Meline said and spoke about how Thor saved her from a man who had already murdered two women. She said she knew that neither she nor her daughter would be alive today if it weren't for him. "The man almost killed me!"

Buddy jumped in again. "Meline still can't lift her arm above her shoulder. Show them, Meline!"

She did but then she said she didn't care about her arm. "I was more than six months along and I might have lost my little Marne. Oh, when I think about it . . ."

The depth of her feelings were evident on her face but Thora had to listen carefully to her words. Like Buddy, her accent was as thick as overcooked oatmeal.

"And the night he died?"

The women exchanged looks then Dottie put her hand on hers which were clasped in her lap. "Are you sure you want to . . ."

"I'm sure."

"But it will be so painful . . ."

"I'm sure."

Dottie sighed and gave in. "Well, about four years ago there were three women who were killed, all murdered in the same way. Meline was the last person attacked and, like she said, she survived solely because of Thor."

"But unfortunately there was a lot of circumstantial evidence that pointed to your brother."

"The first girl who was killed was discovered in the well on your family's old place."

"And a necklace belonging to Meline was found in his room."

"Planted by the killer, of course."

Head bent and holding onto her self control with difficulty, Thora listened to the different women's voices in turn.

"As if fate had not dealt poor Thor enough low blows, Meline . . ."

". . . who could have cleared him."

". . . lapsed into unconsciousness and did not wake until months later when she went into labor."

"Of course, as soon as she regained her senses she told Doc O'Malley that your brother was not her attacker; rather that he had actually risked his own life to save hers. But by then it was too late. Some foolish people were convinced he did the murders."

"The very night it happened Joe Willie had considered all the evidence against your brother and told Jim to take him into protective custody."

"Jim Horse and Thor were walking from the Everett place

to the jail when Jim was shot in the back and your brother was . . . hung."

Sissy touched Thora's arm. She could not believe the girl's control. Though clearly close to tears she was able to hold them at bay somehow. "I'm sure it will be some comfort to know that Dr. O'Malley said your brother was probably rendered unconscious immediately."

"Why does he think that?"

"Because both Jim and your brother were very strong and would otherwise have put up a very fierce fight. It appeared that there was none. With Jim down and your brother helpless, it was easy for the five men to do the deed."

The girl looked up then. "Five men?"

"Yes, when Jim came to for a minute he saw that there were five men in all. Cowards with grain sacks on their heads."

"Hurt as he was, he recognized Mose Starr and Junior Buel by their outfits."

"What about the other men?"

"Jim could not tell who they were. To this day no one knows the identity of the other three men."

There was a long minute before Sissy continued. "Junior tried to beat Jim to death with his pistol. That was how he lost his eye."

"And he almost died from the wound in his back."

"It was touch and go for three days. Finally he gained consciousness and told Joe Willie about Mose Starr and Junior Buel. Only they'd already left town."

Sissy said, "Joe Willie went after them right away. He was gone for months and I was worried sick."

"He found Mose Starr in a saloon in Oklahoma. Nobody knows the particulars. Only that Starr was killed. He brought Junior Buel back to stand trial. I hardly recognized him when Joe Willie escorted him off the train . . .

The girl looked up again. "Was he dead?"

"I think he wished he were after Joe Willie got a hold of him. But no, he stood trial for manslaughter."

"His father was influential and very wealthy man and he hired two big-shot lawyers out of the Cities to defend him."

"His sentence was only four years. It was a terrible travesty."

"Four years!" Thora looked at each of the women in turn. "When does he get out?"

"Well . . ." Sissy thought. "Now that you mention it, I believe it maybe sometime fairly soon."

Buddy broke the silence that followed. "Meanwhile the real woman-killer shot hisself."

"Who was the real murderer?"

Dottie answered. "A man who had lived amongst us for eleven years. His name was Leon Cheever."

Sissy added, "He took something that caused his sanity to leave him for long stretches of time. Apparently he spent half his time in fifteenth-century Rome and the other half in Two Sisters."

Dottie tapped her head. "Crazy as a coot."

"And we all thought he was benign old man."

"But he was completely insane."

Thora was on an emotional edge. She needed to get her bearings and think it all out. For her own sake she allowed Sissy to steer the conversation back to earlier happier times.

They spent the next hours recounting things about her brother. One remembrance was the stimulus for another, like the time he won the weight-lifting contest at a fourth of July picnic and the caring way he'd nursed a litter of kittens when the Fagerhaugs' barn cat died. Not knowing his birth date, they had declared his to be the first of February. On that day they always had a party and every one brought some bright little thing they thought he'd like. Buddy always made a cake.

Thora was touched and very grateful. "I can never repay you for your kindness to him."

"Pah!" said Buddy. "Our payment was the pleasure of knowing him."

"Well said!" exclaimed Dottie. "That's exactly how I've always felt. Rudy and I talked about it many times, how having him stay with us helped ease the loss of our son, Harold. He was an infantryman with the First Minnesota and died in '62." Here she cleared her throat and for a few minutes nobody said anything.

'62! Thora thought. My brother was needed to ease a twenty-year-old loss?

Dottie then picked up something from the floor by her feet. "By the way, I've brought you some of Thor's things."

Thora had been fairly sure she wasn't going to embarrass herself until she produced that cigar box that contained the sum of her brother's "valuables." It was touch and go then.

First she just moved her fingers over it, knowing that Halldor had done the same. Then she opened it and laid each item on the table. Four dollars in coin. Three marbles. A broken jackknife. A gray feather similar to the one she'd seen stuck in the sheriff's hat. She could not keep tears from gathering. From Buddy's "Poor ting! Poor ting!" and the sight of Meline and Sissy's tear-streaked faces, seeing his things had gotten to the others too.

"Oh, look! Meline cried. "There is his first-place ribbon for weight-lifting." She smoothed a crink in the ribbon. "He was so pleased."

The box's last item was a small petit point sewing case which Thora recognized as having belonged to her mother, given to her by the wealthy girl she had been a companion to before she married. It must have been overlooked in the rush to leave.

So many times she had seen her mother take it out of her pocket to make some small repair. Those had not been particularly happy times but they had mostly occurred in the evening when the arguing and switchings were done for the day. It took everything she had not to bawl then. She put the things back and then handed the box to Dottie. "Will you keep this for me for awhile?"

"As long as you like. I'll put it right back on our mantel."

Meline dried her face and stood. "I must go." To Thora she said, "Our place is nothing fancy but we . . . Ketil and me . . . would be honored to have you stay with us."

"No, Meline. I have lots more room," said Sissy. She touched Thora's hand. "Please stay with us."

Buddy stood and drew herself up. "She will stay with me! I am all alone now that my Albin is gone and I have the most room!" The pleading look she gave Thora was quite different from her no argument tone. Thora looked around. Buddy added "Please?" and Thora nodded.

"Gut!"

"Only until I decide what I am going to do."

"You are welcome for as long as you like. Well, let's go now, why don't we?"

"I need a minute first to ah . . ." She looked around.

"Yah, yah-shure. The privy is right out back. What about your things?"

"My t'ings?' Oh, you mean my rucksack? I can pick it up later. If I can remember where I buried it."

"Bet your ah . . . dog can find it if you can't."

"You're probably right. Well, I'll be back in a minute."

Once outside she leaned back against the door, breathless and flushed, as if she'd been running. Her heart was pounding and her mind reeled. She pressed her palms against the rough wooden door and took deep breaths and finally the tumult ended.

She slid down the wall and hunkered there. So. It was true. Her brother was dead. The intense feelings had gone and left her dull and confused. What would she do now? Strange, but that was a question she had never had to ask before. One thought had possessed her for years: getting back to Two Sisters. Without that objective, she felt rudderless. Her brother had been her purpose, not just during the past four years but for as long as she had memory. "Watch your brother, Thora," her mother would say. "Don't forget to take your brother along!" The extra chore was one with which she willingly complied. She liked being with Halldor. Everything was soothing about him. He never screamed and he never cried and he was always the same. She gladly included him in everything, even in her dreams.

She would marry a wonderful man who was kind and soft-spoken. He would build them a big cabin on his land. It would have a separate sleeping room for their children, one for herself, one of her husband and one for her brother. Because her husband was so patient and understanding, Halldor's mind would grow and he would become more capable and would help her husband around the farm. He would be happy and never be hungry or cold. They would live there forever.

That was the most important part; that they would never, ever move away.

Finally she dried her eyes and sat staring at the great gap

that stretched before her. God, it was her life! Empty of meaning. Just . . . empty. She didn't know which way to turn.

Her eyes swept the yard. The town was strangely silent. The air had turned cold and the setting sun had left a pink tattered sky. She shook her head to clear it and some sounds came to her then. Chickens softly clucking, a dog barking in the distance. Ordinary sounds. Soothing sounds. She sat very still and allowed her thoughts to roam but they kept coming back to the same thing: Five men had a hand in hanging her brother but only two had been punished—one with little more than a slap on his wrist. Four years! Surely a man's life—even the life of a flawed man—was worth more than four years!

One question led to another and all went unanswered. There was only one thing she knew for sure: that kid Davey Cox was right. The three other men should be punished. No matter how much time had passed. And if the law could not or would not do it, well, then she should!

With that thought, that strange rudderless feeling left her. She would avenge her brother. She would see that justice was done. Even if she got killed for it.

But how? She supposed she could start by making that man Buel reveal the names of the unknown men and once she had their names she could . . . what? Kill them? Bring them to the law?

She brushed that aside. Better face that problem later. One step at a time. One day at a time. That was how she had walked for four years.

"I'll avenge you, Halldor," she said softly then closed her eyes and whispered, "So help me God. I will."

She whistled once, which brought Coco-man around the side of the building. She knelt and buried her fingers in his heavy ruff. He was her family. The only one she had now.

Chapter 6

Buddy had been so busy cleaning she apparently hadn't noticed how long she'd been gone. When Thora hooked the back door and wiped her feet on a rag rug there, Buddy looked up, surprised then smiled and went back to sweeping a minuscule pile of dust into the center of the room. "Can I help you do something?" Thora glanced around. Everything looked spotless.

"No. I am just finished."

Thora watched her return the broom to a narrow closet and pull the curtains across the front window and add wood to the heater and adjust the damper.

"Well, all right," she said and looked around. "We go." From her coat pocket she withdrew a huge skeleton key strung on a circlet of rawhide. "You must be very tired from trying to sleep on the floor all night, but I should stop at Goody's for a minute. Can you last?"

"Sure. I'm fine."

From the front step she pointed to the general store across the street. "My brother-in-law's place is there. Goody's we call it. His name is Gudmund Tangen, but everybody calls him Goody. Poor ting! He's a widow man all these years but he never found someone else after his Anha died. Such a good man too! Hardworking and clean. Much too old for you." She'd slogged half way across the road before she realized that Thora had held back. She turned and motioned. "Come. Yah. You come too."

As they mounted the cupped wood stairs a fat square-faced yellow dog lifted his head and thumped his tail on the boardwalk. Buddy stepped over him and into the shop. Thora bent and rubbed between his eyes before she followed.

The store was one long room with a wood-burning stove center square. Counters were piled high and ascending every wall were well stocked shelves with tins she recognized as Lytona Baking Powder and Arbuckle's Coffee and Bull Durham tobacco. Kegs of nails, barrels of crackers and sacks of flour made negotiating the aisles a tight squeeze. Hanging from spikes on the posts that held up the roof were harnesses, ropes, horseshoes, traps and axes.

Halfway up a ladder, was a small bald man wielding a feather duster like a flag. He squinted around the lantern that hung on a nearby post. "Halloo, Buddy. Hvat ar yew dewing here dis time of day?"

"I'm closed up, Goody, on account of Thor's sister being here." She pointed at Thora who nodded and gave a little wave. She hated being the center of attention every place she went.

"I heard about that," Goody said as he descended. "Pleased to meet you," he said with a little bow. He had a round florid face and wore his spectacles pushed up on his broad shiny forehead.

"Thank you."

"Sorry about all that bad that happened. Terrible. So sorry."

"Me, too." To discourage further conversation along those lines, Thora drifted toward a long counter where an impressive array of yard goods were displayed. She ran a finger down some checked material. A dainty card was pinned to each bolt of fabric and she traced each letter, wishing she could somehow divine their meaning. She had never owned any piece of clothing that was her own first. Everything had been worn by someone else before and was destined to be worn by someone else afterward.

"So, Goody," Buddy was saying. "Seeing as how the cafe is closed, do you want to come eat with Thora and me?"

"No, no. I still got some of that ham you gave me. Besides, I got four boxes to put up yet tonight."

Thora drifted by the men's section. Mallory and Stetson hats, work shirts, boots and belts, ready-made socks. From somewhere the thought occurred to her that the sheriff probably bought his clothes here. The sheepskin jacket. That flannel shirt that despite the weather had been open at the neck. The buckskin trousers tucked into knee-high moccasins. Why was she so keenly conscious of the way he looked? His smooth brown skin and the sheen of his hair. The strength of his gaze—so potent that when he looked at her it was as if he touched her. Maybe because he only had one eye. Made sense. They'd once had a baby chick who'd had a near-fatal run-in with a weasel and lost most of one leg. Somehow it survived and learned to get by with one leg and a nub. It was awkward and lopsided and had to fight all the other chickens for its food but it grew. So did its single leg. Much more than it should've. Matter of fact, it ended up being about three times bigger than an ordinary chicken leg. "Tough too!" her father said when he ate it. Oh, how Halldor had cried when their father wrung that chicken's neck and then chased him all around the yard with it, laughing and squawking, "Pock! Pock Pock!"

"All right," Buddy was retying her woolen scarf. "But you can come over if you want."

"Better not. A man's got to make wheat while the sun shines."

Thora bit back "hay" and waited for either to realize their mistake.

"Yah, is true. Maybe it is just as well." Buddy moved toward the door. "We would stay up and talk and this girl here is worn to death."

"It's shure no surprise tew hear dat!" He seemed to be looking for worn places on Thora. "A pleasure to meet you, miss. And I shure am sorry about your brother."

"Thank you. Bye."

"Bye."

They set off. In spite of the snow there were plenty of people on the street. A woman wearing a knitted hat and matching scarf waved to them and Buddy called, "Hvordan star det til?"

''Bare bra, takk,'' the woman replied in passing. ''Og med deg?''

''Bra, takk.''

A few feet further Thora commented on it, ''I'd forgotten how many people in this town are Norwegian.''

''Not so many now but just about everybody was in the beginning. The first settlers were even from the same village. Nine families, there were.'' Buddy looked at her. ''You remember how Two Sisters got its name, don't you?''

''I think so . . . There were ah . . . two sisters, right?''

''Yah!'' Buddy said and then told the story anyway.

The two sisters named Hedy and Trina were part of the original nine families. The first week the immigrants arrived Hedy was carried off by Indians and in spite of a tireless search by practically the entire town, was never seen again.

''We all thought she'd been killed and worse, but we found out some years back that she lived to be very old and had a happy life. Jim Horse, the sheriff, is her grandson.''

It was hard not to quit walking at that. ''He is?''

''Yah, Hedy sent him here before she died. It was five years last July. I remember 'cause he came the year before my Albin died.''

Thora was silent, picturing the sheriff once again and trying to see something Norwegian in that face. She failed.

Coco-man trotted alongside them, oblivious to the two lowly growling dogs who dared to challenge him—but only from beneath the safety of a porch across the street.

Now Buddy was pointing out things of interest. ''Over there is the Wind Fall Saloon. Doc O'Malley's office is right up those stairs. He is from Ireland. Hard working and real nice. The doc is a widow man too. A much younger widow man.'' She gave Thora a shrewd look, as if she was waiting for her to say something so she asked, ''What's that little place?''

''The newspaper.''

''Ah.'' Where her brother's ''best friend'' worked.

''Next door is the Inside Straight.''

They were walking in the road from which the snow had not so much been cleared as it had been packed down. Ahead she could see a burly man standing on a huge log which was attached by chains to two hairy horses. By directing the log first to one side then the other he was cutting a wide swathe down the center of the road.

"That house there belongs to the oldest person in town. Mrs. Willman. Ninety-eight, I think, on her next birthday."

Next they passed a field where in the distance she saw some white faced cows bunched beneath a clump of red oaks. Red and white trees. White and red cows. It looked like they had been fixed up to match.

Further on, Buddy said, "Here is Dottie and Rudy's place." They stopped while Thora looked at the Fagerhaug's stately house. Someone had shoveled the snow off a walk made from sunken nail keg lids. Hoarfrost rimmed the metal edges and glittered in the waning light.

"Rudy farms a little on the edge."

"On the side," Thora said without thinking.

"Yah," Buddy said and then, as if it explained most everything about them, she added, "They come here from Iowa, you know."

Theirs was a two-story house with steps leading up to a covered veranda that ran across the front and around one side. The front door was banked by two fancy windows with little panes. She was about to ask about them when Buddy said, "In the back there you can see the little place that was Thor's."

With those words Buddy effectively removed all but thoughts of her brother from her mind. What with all she had heard since she arrived, she'd forgotten that he had lived with the Fagerhaugs!

She stood there and pictured him, unlatching the iron gate, following the rutted path. Coco-man pushed his nose into her palm but she was staring at the peeled bark barn that was weathered to a dull silvery gray. *This is where he lived. That barn is the first thing he saw every morning.* Buddy touched her arm. "Come," she said softly. "There's no good in that."

In sad silence they went on. The wind had come up and a light sleet was falling that stung her face and, she hoped, veiled the wetness on her cheeks.

Only a short way out of town, and pines and spruce crowded their path and sent out a damp clean smell. "Not much further now," Buddy said. They came around a bend in the road and

Buddy said they were there. "My castle in the woods," she exclaimed.

Nestled in an expanse of white, her squat brown home looked more like a toad in a sugar bowl. It had a thick steep roof and a stone chimney from which there rose a narrow spiral of smoke. The place had a look of permanence, though, and having moved at least twenty times in her short life, that was the aspect that appealed to Thora. They followed a tiny footpath that led from the road to the house. "How long have you lived here?"

"Since the second month we came to Minnesota. A long time now." She clumped up the stairs. "Every one worked together to build all the cabins in the beginning. We drew straws. Longest straw got their cabins built first. Albin and me were straw number seven." She stomped her feet and then used a rusted piece of a scythe that served as a boot scraper.

"Now we get nice and warm. Come then and, Velkommin."

Inside she quickly rekindled the banked fire with a few pieces of birch that instantly caught and crackled and lent light to the cabin.

The living area was neat but cluttered with keepsakes. Rugged peeled logs ran across the ceiling throughout. A huge hearth was bracketed by two cushioned chairs and round tables with tatted covers. In one corner was an old spool rocker flanked by a little table. On it was a faded Bible that sprouted several pieces of paper. "Very nice," Thora said and meant it. "Homey."

"All the inside finishing we did ourselves, Albin and me. He was a good worker, my Albin."

There were two rooms off either end that were separated from the living area by bunched curtains hanging on wooden rods. Buddy pulled back one to reveal a four-poster bed with a colorful quilt and two plump pillows. "Goose down," she said and squeezed a pillow.

"Comfortable, I'll bet."

"Comfortable? Ho! You wait. Is like sleeping on a cloud. Ah! You are looking at that little chest."

"It's beautiful! Who painted it all up like that?"

"Anha. Goody's wife. Nobody did rosemaling better than Anha."

Buddy showed her all around pointing out this and that and

then she proudly escorted her into the kitchen and showed her the stenciled cabinets and blue eyelet curtains. ‘‘My good things,’’ she said and pointed to a shelf a foot beneath the ceiling where she had her fancy crockery and hand-painted dishes displayed. ‘‘Over there is the pantry.’’

‘‘Ah.’’

When Buddy opened yet another narrow door, Thora expected to see a broom and mop and bucket, but what she saw was a hand pump and a well cover. ‘‘A well? Right inside the cabin?’’

‘‘Yah.’’ Proudly. ‘‘At night after we were finished working on the others’ cabins, my Albin dug this well. Then when all the workers came, they built our cabin around it. Lots of people have had well trouble in the winter but not us.’’ She tapped her forehead. ‘‘Very smart, my Albin. You bet!’’

Chapter 7

Buddy had been right about the goose down; the next morning Thora woke later than she ever had before and she couldn't recall when she had slept so well. Upon rising she found that Buddy had already gone to work, but waiting on the stove was an agateware pot of hot coffee and a loaf of bread kept warm in a sacking towel. After she ate, she spread up the bed and washed and whistled up Coco and headed for town herself.

The snow shimmered with blinding brightness and a cold wind cut her face. The storm was over but to the north the sky was the sort of murky gray that said it could go either way. She pulled in her neck and stepped lively.

She was only a short way from town when she heard a child's carefree laugh. Walking backward and shading her eyes with her hand she searched for its source. There! On a small hill behind a cabin. A girl who appeared a few years older than her companion was pulling a boy on a wooden toboggan. She stopped to watch them.

The boy wore a rabbitskin cap with ear flaps. Every time they started downhill he'd snatch it off and flail the sled with it. Every time they got to the bottom the girl would patiently tug it on again and tie the legs under his chin.

She wished she could learn something about them but on

second thought, maybe it was better that she couldn't. This way she could think they were often happy like that, that they had a nice mother and a kind father and three brothers and sisters all perfect and healthy. And that they had a nice home and plenty to eat.

When she went on she turned onto a little used rocky footpath that followed the lake's shoreline. It took longer to reach town this way, but it was the path her brother had always wanted to take.

He never tired of the lake. If she had let him he would have stood there looking at it for hours. Sometimes she would see what he saw. How it could look like a hand mirror, or how the sun could make a rainbow in the water.

God forbid that they should see something really interesting! She thought she would never get him going again after the day they saw an Indian canoe crossing the mouth of the bay. Sleek and narrow, it had slipped through the water like an otter and then disappeared. Halldor wanted to wait for it to return. Till kingdom come if necessary.

With sudden clarity she remembered the last day they'd been here. As usual, they were just standing staring out at the water only there hadn't been much to see that day. A fog hung to the water like a curtain of smoke.

Suddenly three young men came boiling down the hill behind them. Tumbling, half falling, like puppies at play. They scarcely spared Thora and Halldor a glance but brushed by them to an old wood boat overturned on the bank. Two of the men righted the boat then waded in dragging it behind them. The last man handed their things over. Poles and a bait can, a woven reed hamper and finally . . . carefully . . . a gallon keg already bung-holed. Eventually the last man rolled up his pants legs and then dove into the boat belly first and they were off, soon to be swallowed up by the fog. "Well, let's go," she said and started off. She retraced her steps and shook his arm. "Let's go!" C'mon now, we gotta go!" But right then the sound of manly laughter drifted back to them. Her brother made a noise in the back of his throat and took a hesitant step toward the water. "Halldor! Halldor!" It was like she wasn't even there!

She had to hang onto his shirttail to get him stopped but he still wouldn't budge. She tried distracting him with a school of minnows. He looked down at them for a few seconds but he was soon riveted on the spot where the boat had disappeared. She thought she would never get him away that day!

It was times like those that she could swear her brother understood much more than she gave him credit for. That day she could've sworn that he knew he would never be like those young men and that it had hurt him terribly.

She sat on her heels and wrapped her arms around her legs. She had told him once that where the water met the sky was the edge of the world and he believed her. She'd told him that some little winged people lived above the clouds and he believed her then too. He had always believed her. Especially when she told him that they would be together forever.

Walking into town later she told herself that it was good that she'd gotten that out of her system because now she would never have to do it again. She had a job to do and had no time for this constant bawling.

Her first stop was the Western Union office where the clerk introduced himself as Dill Wyatt and said he knew everything about her. *A scary thought.* Finished with her business she went outside and found herself turned around. She wanted to talk to the doctor next but Buddy had pointed out so many places yesterday she couldn't remember which was his office. She opened the door and stuck her head in and Mr. Wyatt jerked and slammed the desk drawer, as if he'd been doing something he shouldn't.

"Forget somethin'?"

"No. Just wondered if you could tell me where the doctor's office is?"

"O'Malley?"

"Is there more than one?"

He ignored that. "Right over yonder."

Now that he pointed it out she recognized the small hand-painted sign that was nailed to the side of a building. "Thank you!" she said and pulled the door to again. She waited for a horse-drawn sleigh to pass and then crossed the street. Down the way Goody Tangen stopped sweeping snow off his walk in order to wave at her.

Such a friendly town. It was hard to believe that three of these people had participated in a murder.

Narrow stairs with a wood railing led up to the landing. She knocked and a man opened the door almost immediately. "Dr. O'Malley?"

"Yes."

In spite of Buddy's comment that the doctor was "not so old" he turned out to be even younger than she had expected, a bit over thirty maybe. His hair and complexion were both ruddy and soft cocker-spaniel eyes made a striking contrast to strong and rather uneven features. All in all, he was not unattractive in a manly sort of way.

Belatedly she noticed that he wore a coat. Was he coming or going? "I am Thora Gunn. Could I speak to you for a moment?"

"Of course. I should have realized who you were right away." He gave her a kindly smile and moved aside. "Please come in. If you'll give me a moment, I'll offer you some tea." He motioned her toward a cracked leather chair.

"No, thank you."

"Do you mind if I have some?"

She shook her head.

"I've just returned from a house call. A poor child with rickets."

While he busied himself elsewhere she looked around. The office was plainly furnished with a desk, three worn leather chairs and a glass cabinet with a bowed front. Other than that, the clutter was mostly books—a lot of books! Open and crosswise in a corner, on a table, on one of the chairs. The place smelled strongly of witch hazel and rubbing alcohol.

Through an open door she watched him put the kettle on, moving efficiently in what was obviously a very cramped space. Apparently he lodged here as well.

When finished he sat opposite her and began to prepare a pipe. He made it the old-fashioned way by breaking off a chunk of tobacco and mashing it in his palm with his thumb then filling his bowl from there. He had large square hands and surprisingly thick fingers.

He looked up at her. "You know that the entire town is

talking about your arrival'' She nodded. ''Everyone's very concerned about you.''

''I know.''

''Collective shame. I think that's what some of us feel. I know I did. That was the day when I was ashamed to be a part of the human race. Well, allow me to add my condolences, Miss Gunn. What a shock that must have been for you.'' He shook his head. ''It was for us as well. We were all stunned.'' He paused and looked at her.

''They said you could tell me about his death especially if he . . . if . . .''

''You want to know if he suffered or died instantly.'' He lifted his eyebrows. ''Right?''

''Yes.''

''He died instantly.''

''What makes you think that?''

She had the feeling he was thinking about holding back—sparing her feelings maybe—but then if he was judging her he must have come to a decision because he said, ''Because your brother did not die of strangulation. Aside from the fact that his neck was broken and aside from a knot on his head, there were no other marks on his body. Which is why I believe it is highly probable that he was rendered unconscious first. If he had strangled to death there would have been abrasions on his hands and feet where he had struggled against the bindings. There also would have been certain unmistakable changes in his facial expression . . .'' He met her gaze and softened his voice. ''I'm quite sure that he didn't suffer at all.''

More to herself than to him she said, ''So things did happen the way they said.''

''They?''

''Sissy Everett and Buddy and Dottie.''

''Yes, of course. Look, I can understand your suspicion but those women would have no reason not to tell the truth, would they?''

''No . . .'' *Unless they were protecting someone close to them.*

He took several drags on his pipe and looked at her cannily. ''I expect another concern of yours is whether everything possible was done to protect him.'' She nodded, grateful for his perception. It was a difficult question and one she would have been hesitant to ask.

"The answer is yes. Jim Horse was the deputy sheriff then and was with your brother the night he was killed. I spent the next three days trying to save Jim's life . . . darn thing!"

He'd lost his fire and spent some time fiddling with his pipe, striking a lucifer on the sole of his shoe, cupping it over the bowl and then puffing vigorously. After he got it going, his tone turned professional again.

"Jim Horse was shot in the back from a distance of fifty feet or less. The bullet would've taken down a moose and it took down Jim. After a six-hour operation I truly did not know if he would live or die but hoping against hope I turned my attention to his other injuries, the most serious of which was his eye. While unconscious he had been beaten unmercifully which irreparably damaged the small bones that support the globe. Since the chances were nonexistent that he would even be able to detect light and dark from that eye again, I decided I'd better enucleate . . . remove . . . it rather than take the risk of developing sympathetic ophthalmia."

"What's that?"

"Sympathetic ophthalmia? No one really knows, but often a person who has sustained an injury in one eye will begin to experience the same symptoms in the other eye even though that healthy eye is completely injury-free." He shrugged. "There are several theories regarding the phenomenon. Perhaps something to do with the nerves. All I know is that when the injured eye is removed the good eye stops exhibiting unhealthy symptoms. I believed at the time—and still do now—that Jim could have ended up completely blind. It simply wasn't worth the risk." She said nothing so he continued. "I've known Jim as long as I've lived in Minnesota and I've observed him to be diligent in his duties and completely unbiased but I don't think anyone knows him like Joe Willie Everett. If you desire further, more detailed information about that night then Joe Willie is your man. He went over everything, absolutely everything, trying to get a lead on the killers." He stopped, then: "By the way, how long have you been having trouble hearing?"

She just looked at him so surprised she didn't answer for a minute. "How did you know?"

He smiled slightly. "A trick of the trade, my dear, but the dead give-away is your habit of cocking your head when someone speaks to you. It's your left ear, isn't it?"

"Yes."

"Would you like me to look at it." She shook her head. "No charge." Another negative. She stood and moved toward the door. He followed. With her hand on the latch, she turned.

"Can you tell me where my brother is buried?"

He stepped out onto the landing and pointed to the crest of a hill to the north of town. "The cemetery's right up there."

"Thank you."

He called to her halfway down the stairs. "The grave's on the south side. Beneath two aspens."

"Thank you."

"No'atall." He watched her hop over a ledge of banked snow and then set off for the cemetery. To himself he added, "An' God's good luck t'you, lass."

The road out of town was a sea of muck but it was passable compared to traveling off it. In some spots she sunk into drifted snow to her moccasin tops.

She climbed over a low rail fence, more decorative than protective, and followed a narrow path between the wooden markers. The going was easier up here. Swept by strong winds off the lake, sections of the cemetery had almost no snow on the ground at all.

Right off she spotted the two aspens with leafless branches that formed a stark silhouette against the sky but she held back, unwilling to go on now that she was here.

From this height she could see beyond the protected bay to the breakers on either side and hear the waves crashing onto the rocks. Clinging gamely to the cliffs were bent and twisted pines, scraggly from being constantly buffeted by the wind. On the other side, Two Sisters lay in its protective bowl. Blue smoke from its many chimneys rose and hovered over it like a parasol. She stood there until she felt the cold and then she approached.

The wooden cross was hung with faded black ribbons that fluttered in the wind. Clumps of snow crusted flowers now dried and brittle lay at its base. A short epitaph had been burned into the wood with a poker. Her fingers traced that which she could not read. THOR—A gentle man 8*30*1881.

Despite her hour-old vow, her eyes blurred with tears. Then her legs went wobbly and she folded like a fan.

Chapter 8

No sooner had Conor O'Malley shut the door than there came another timid knock. He flung open the door and there stood a bundled figure. Boy or girl, he wondered and then she spoke.

"Dr. O'Malley?"

"Yes?"

"How do you do."

"Fine. May I help you?"

"Perhaps. I was wondering how . . . how much you charge for an appointment?"

"That depends." He observed her threadbare coat and tattered scarf and mumbled, "Often next to nothing." He opened the door wider still. "Come in and we'll discuss it out of the weather." The girl hesitated a minute and then stepped inside. "Well . . ." he said, watching her out of the corner of his eye. "May I hang up your things?" He indicated a row of wooden pegs on the wall.

"No, thank you."

Oh, God! he thought. This one will even have to be coaxed out of her coat! "Please take a seat." She did and he sat at his desk. "Now, then . . ."

"How much did you say it would be?"

"Normally one dollar . . ." She paled. "But often considerably less. Please don't worry about that now. Just tell me how I can help you. Miss . . . ?" She shut her eyes briefly and then just looked at him as if mutely pleading that he read her mind. It didn't work. He tried another tack.

"Well . . . you're interested in an examination, right miss?" She nodded. "All right then. I'll need just a bit of information for my file. Let's see, where is . . . yes. Here we go." He took a piece of paper and unstoppered a jar of ink and dipped his pen. "Your name?"

"Emily."

"Emily!" He looked up, frowning slightly.

"Yes." And then somewhat defensively, "Why?"

He shook his head and looked at the paper. "Nothing only my . . . my wife's name was Emily."

"Was?"

"Yes." He looked at her—she was an intent little thing—then looked away. "She died six years ago. On the ship to America."

"Did you blame yourself?"

"Blame myself?"

"Because with all your skills as a doctor you could not save her?"

Imaginative too. "My wife suffered from no illness. It was a shipboard accident. A sudden squall. She was up on deck and was swept overboard. A sailor just caught sight of her as it happened. Everything was done, of course, but her body was never recovered."

Time fell away and he was back in that cramped little cabin. They had argued earlier that evening. Not unusual of itself, but that particular argument had been worse than all the others. He had discovered she'd been stealing laudanum from his medical bag again. He might not have found out about it until they docked but earlier that afternoon he had been asked to treat a sailor for a nasty, quite painful cut on his foot. The wound had required suturing and he administered laudanum in order to relieve the man who was already in considerable pain. When the first doses had no effect, he gave him more. In the end he had given him enough to knock him out for hours and still no effect! One sniff of the bottle told him why: it was practically all water! Of course, Emily had denied it. Which was putting it mildly. When he confronted her, she had spat at him like a wet cat.

It wasn't the first time they'd had this row. He had caught her stealing the drug soon after they were married. She had denied it in the beginning, but he persevered and she finally admitted that she had been taking it in her evening tea for years. Originally it had been prescribed for the pains she experienced during her monthly moon time; over the years she had bamboozled a weak and forgetful family physician into prescribing more and more until finally she was hooked.

Patiently he had explained about the terrible addictive properties of opium and suggested that if she started reducing the amount she took every day, over time she could wean herself of it.

A dozen times they'd had that conversation; a dozen times she had promised she would comply, but obviously she could not.

There'd been no talking to her that night. She had soon worked herself into such a lather she was screaming all manner of demeaning imprecations at him. Then she slammed out of the cabin and to his everlasting regret, he had let her go. At that moment he didn't care if he ever saw her again.

Amazing what changes a year of marriage had wrought. Not so long ago he had been quite taken with Emily Van Clief. He had thought her sweet tempered and amusing. He discovered she was also quite an accomplished actress, for in reality she had the tongue of an adder and the wit of a rock. How had he been so blind? A fool could have seen that no two people were ever more unsuited to each other. Unfortunately the ability for him to see that had required hindsight.

They had met in Dublin at the home of one of his professors who was an uncle of Emily's by marriage, and after a whirlwind courtship, they married. Conor's parents had had a happy marriage, so his expectations were understandably high. He was destined to be disappointed. Emily was never happy. His coarse physical appetite disgusted her. So did his absentmindedness, his lack of ambition, his evening cigar and most particularly his interest in "those repulsive little urchins" at the free clinic.

She wanted to be wealthy and influential in society. She needed the first to realize the latter.

She was not above using any tactic to "bring him into line." Withholding her favors (such as they were) or not speaking to him for weeks on end. He tried placating her then he tried ignoring her. Finally, hard-headed Irishman that he was, he dug in his heels and war was declared.

When he decided to immigrate, it was a last-ditch effort to save the marriage . . . America and a fresh start and all. And then she was gone. Swept out of his life, but not out of his conscience. He still blamed himself. As a trained physician, he should have been able to help her. He should have done something to save her from herself.

Thanks to a legion of family retainers, very little of the Van Clief money came to him after Emily's death. One or two monumental investment mistakes and a few years of carefree living and Conor O'Malley was broke again. On a lark he traveled to Chicago where a school chum had set up his practice. While enjoying his friend's hospitality—and a few bawdy houses as well—he read an advertisement for medical men in Northern Minnesota. And now . . . here he was. Trying to coax sweet young things out of their outerwear.

He glanced at the girl and set pen to paper again. "And your last name, Emily?"

"Jones."

"Emily Jones?"

"Yes."

He set down the pen and looked at her. She was quite young—no more than twenty—and quite fetching with a wealth of brown naturally wavy hair and large, wide-set eyes the color of wet earth. She had a fine-boned face with a narrow freckled nose that reminded him of a doe. That chin, however, reminded him of the particularly stubborn offspring of a donkey and a horse. A brave girl and unless he missed his guess, inordinately mature for her years. He rested his own chin on his fist, oblivious to the fact that he was staring.

She looked away. Looked back. "What?"

"I was wonderin' if you were a Catholic, Miss . . . Mrs. Jones?"

"Land o' Goshen! Do you need to know that too?" There

was a hint of humor in her voice then she dropped her eyes and picked at something on her coat. After she'd worked it over good, she grudgingly said, "I guess I don't see that it is any of your business . . . but I am."

"You're right. 'Tis none of my business." He leaned back. "But knowing that you're Catholic saves me from explaining the doctrine of penance, now doesn't it?" She nodded but she looked very wary now. Like she might bolt. "What I'm trying to get at is this: a doctor is just like a priest in one respect. A patient can tell his—or her—doctor anything because, like a priest in the confessional, a doctor is sworn to eternal secrecy."

She nodded. "I knew that."

"You did? Well, then you know there's no difference between telling me something and telling your priest . . ."

"Oh, yes there is. When I go to see the priest I can't see him . . ." She pointed at him and touched her chest. ". . . like I can see you."

With a start he realized he was enjoying himself. "That could be worked out if we try. Here, let's pretend that you can't see me now and will never see me again. Turn your head. There. Now." He shaded his eyes and stared at the paper and made his voice holy. "Tell me, my child. Why have you sought my assistance."

He heard a little giggle.

"I didn't seek your assistance. I sought the assistance of the only medical man in town."

"No need to get snippy now is there. By the way, what brought you to Two Sisters?"

"I suddenly realized I was about to run out of money."

"Where were you going?"

"Canada, but the train fare was more than I thought it would be. I got off before I was tossed off."

"I doubt they'd do that."

He sensed she was looking at him, compelling him to look at her. Or maybe he just wanted to very badly.

"I only have three dollars to my name but I simply must know if . . ." She looked back at that place on her coat. "If I'm going to have a baby."

She was married. He felt a twinge of something suspiciously

like regret. ''Would that be so bad? A wee babe is a joyous event.''

''Not always.''

Another twinge. Hope? ''Are you unmarried, Mrs. Jones?''

''Yes.''

''And the baby's father is . . .'' He paused. Waited. Nothing. ''Well, no matter. Let's make sure first.'' He asked about her symptoms. Yes, she'd had some dizziness. Yes, she'd been sick in the morning.

''And your last monthly?''

''Three months ago.''

''You have the classic symptoms of a mother-to-be. Nausea, vomiting, inordinate appetite, lack of menses. Are your breasts painful and larger?'' He waited, looking at the paper, not looking up.

''Yes,'' she whispered.

''That's all the questions, Emily . . .'' He heard a sigh of relief. ''But I'll need to examine you to see if our suspicions are true.'' He pointed to an open doorway. ''Step right in there. It will only take a minute.''

He deliberately knocked out his pipe and straightened his papers—everything commonplace but out of the corner of his eye he watched her stand and pause then turn and walk toward the examining room as if she were approaching the guillotine.

The examining room had a cot, a head-high screen, two tables with various instruments arranged on a starkly white cloth and one window with a yellowy roll-up shade set at half mast. He pulled the shade down and turned the room to dusk. For the first time in his career he was aware of being in a room alone with a female patient. Strange.

''Please disrobe to your undergarments and recline on the cot and cover yourself with the sheet. I'll . . . I'll wait in the other room until you're ready.''

She stepped behind the screen and he exited the room. He listened. Heard rustling and then scurrying then the creak of the cot. ''Ready?''

''Yes.'' Strangled.

He stepped into the room and saw that she held the sheet under her chin with white knuckled hands. ''Well, now . . .'' He approached and was almost scared witless when she cried,

"Wait!" She held up one hand. "Please wait one minute. Please."

"Why? What is it?"

"You won't have to . . . you won't have to pull my teeth, will you?"

"Faith n' begorra! Why on earth would I have to do a thing like that?"

"One of the doctors back home had one solution to everything from broken bones to boils. Pulling all the patient's teeth."

He threw back his head and laughed. A booming laugh that carried through the thin wooden walls and into one of the upstairs rooms at the Wind Fall. The whore and her customer stopped writhing and stared at the wall.

"What t'hell was that?"

"A moose?"

"This close to town?"

"Lord, I don't know!"

"Good Grief!" Conor wiped his eyes and held up one hand. "I swear to you: I have never pulled a tooth in my life."

She smiled. "All right then."

"Now . . . I will slip my hands under the sheet but I will avert my eyes. All right?"

"All right."

"There's something you might do to take your mind off what I am doing."

"What?" She sounded disbelieving.

"Sing."

"Sing?"

"Yes. Do you know Oh Susannah?"

"Yes."

"Good. Sing it with me. 'Tis a fine rousing tune. Oh Susannah, oh don't you cry for me . . ."

Again the doctor's big booming baritone breached the walls that separated Hattie Mueller's brothel from his examining room.

"Christ! A singin' moose!" complained the man. *"I can't concentrate."*

The whore was practical and didn't want to be late for lunch. "Try thinkin' with your other head, sugar."

Tentative at first, Emily Jones lifted her voice. "Good!" he said as he lifted the sheet. "A little louder now."

A verse later he had palpated the abdomen and felt a slight distension. And a flattened navel. And skin as soft as a baby chick. Between verses he used his stethoscope to hear a faint fetal heart tone.

"Oh, Susannah oh don . . .

"You can stop singing and get dressed now."

"All right." She sounded a bit disappointed.

He turned away while she slipped behind the screen. "You were right." He poured water from a pitcher into a bowl and made a production of washing and drying his hands. "You are about four months pregnant. If all goes well—and I see no reason why it should not—you will have your baby two hundred and eighty days from the date of . . . er inception." He raised the window shade and they both jumped when it got away from him with a loud flapping. In the void that followed Conor heard a soft tapping against the wall, the familiar sound of an iron bedstead meeting wood.

At least a hundred times he had asked Hattie to pull the beds out from the wall! She swore she did but claimed they "walked."

Since the Wind Fall was the best brothel in Two Sisters and since Hattie had her girls checked for venereal disease once a month, he was one of Hattie's best customers and vice versa. This, however, was ridiculous. The girl was looking at him and he imagined that his face had turned the color of raw meat. He cleared his throat and, in what he hoped was a professional manner, asked, "Emily . . . Miss Jones. Is the father married?"

"Yes," came the whispered answer.

"You're running away?"

"Yes."

"I see." Briskly. "Well, it is a misfortune but not the end of the world. This is, after all, 1881. Such a . . . happening is quite common." None of his blather was true, of course but he had an uncontrollable urge to soothe her. "We'll say your husband passed on. No one need know."

He'd been pacing. She'd been standing with her hands clasped at her waist. He faced her.

"I'm sure the father will want to help you in any way he can." She shook her head. "But he must!"

"He doesn't know."

"Then you must tell him so he can help you financially. At least until you can support yourself." She was shaking her head. "Why not?"

"He was drunk. He doesn't even remember that it happened."

"You were raped!"

"Yes."

He felt his temper rising. "By whom? Really you must tell me because I can . . . I can . . ." She shook her head and he saw that he had been right about her chin.

"No, Doctor. I have no intention of telling you or anyone anything."

He held up one hand. "All right. All right. I won't press you on that." He walked one way. He walked the other. "All right. Let's see now. Can you work?"

"Yes, of course. I am a real good worker."

He thought a minute. "The mayor mentioned that there's a need for someone to clean the courthouse and my office and the jail. It is hard work . . ."

"Oh, I don't care. Whatever I am put to do I will do."

"Well, it would give you some money until . . ." He did not say *until I can get that bastard's name out of you and then choke the money out of him!*

"Thank you, Doctor! Thank you very much."

She was digging in a pouch purse dangling from her arm. "Put your money away. I'll not take it now." *Or ever.*

"But . . ."

He pointed at her. "No arguing. You can give me something later. When you get a bit ahead."

"But . . ."

He put his hands on his hips. "I suppose you're the sort who's going to tell me how much I should be chargin' for a visit?"

"No."

"All right then. Now. Come with me and we'll see to a place for you to live."

"Oh!" She cried. "Is there a place for me here in town?

Something I can afford?'' She had covered her mouth with her hands and her eyes were filling.

''Here now!'' His voice was gruff. ''None of that now. None of that.''

''I don't know what to say.''

''Say nothing and allow me to help you with your coat. Good. I'll get mine on and . . . we're off.''

They set out briskly although Conor tried to pace his steps to hers.

''Are we going to see about the job first or the place to live?''

''Both. A young lady named Meline Beckstrom may be able to help us with both.''

''Meline. What a pretty name.''

''She is a pretty person as well. Inside and out.''

Meline, who used to clean the jail and his office, also sold baked goods on the side. That business was doing so well she had recently informed the town council she would have to give up cleaning. At least that's what Rudy Fagerhaug had told him over lunch the day before.

Coincidentally, the only lodging that wouldn't cost Emily anything was an abandoned cabin near where Ketil and Meline Beckstrom lived. Conor then had a sudden, disturbing thought: Over the years several squatters had used it. Good grief! There might be someone living there right now. He hadn't considered that. He looked down at the top of the girl's head. She had her skirt lifted a demure inch and was watching her step. Poor thing! Broke and no roof over her head to say nothing of not knowing if there was a child on the way. She must have been worried to death. Was she still? Hopefully merely by verifying her pregnancy he'd at least relieved her mind about an illness. He knew these naïve little things. He once had a recently married pregnant girl with a strict, religious background tell him that at night her husband was bouncing her around on the bed so much that it was making her sick in the morning. He had responded that, in a manner of speaking, she was correct.

''Miss Jones . . .'' She looked up. Her lashes were wet but her eyes were dry. ''Everything'll be just fine.''

''I know.'' She gave him a brave smile. ''I . . . we will be fine.''

''There's the ticket!''

He took her arm crossing the tracks and left it there, ever so lightly, as they followed a narrow path to a large log cabin that sat some yards beyond. Screened by a stand of aspen was another much smaller cabin, just visible through the trees. It didn't look like much with a sagging roof and jagged windows. ''Hard to believe both of these places looked the same at one time. Ketil's done so much to fix his up.'' They were standing in front of the Beckstrom place, but she was staring off in the direction of the smaller cabin. He couldn't gauge her reaction. ''If the stove is working and roof doesn't leak too bad, it can be fixed up.''

''It's more than I expected.''

Conor knew exactly who to contact about linens and second-hand furniture. Dottie Fagerhaug and her Lutheran Ladies League could furnish a five-room house in an hour. He had seen it done before. The Moore place last year for example. Their cabin had been gutted by fire leaving the family of seven with nothing but a roof over their heads. Never fear! Someone alerted the Lutheran Ladies League and by sundown Dottie Fagerhaug and her troops had delivered everything from furniture to flatware.

So, he thought. That's settled. He'd just stop by the Fagerhaug place on his way back to town and set things in motion. Intuitively he knew Miss Emily Jones would not accept charity. Dottie would have to make it clear that she could pay for the things ''down the road.'' They ascended the stairs. At the door he smiled at her. ''Ready?''

''Yes.''

''Their name is Beckstrom. Meline and Ketil. Nice people. Salt of the earth.'' He knocked. The door opened and the smell of fresh-baked bread was like a slap upside the head. Ketil was thumbing on his suspenders and chewing. ''Good timing, doc!'' said he with a big grin. ''Meline just put the stew pot on the table.''

''Let's come back,'' said the girl for Conor's ears only but Ketil was already pulling them inside.

''Too late,'' Conor said gleefully. ''We can never get away without eating something now.''

Chapter 9

Thora's next stop was Joe Willie Everett's office which was supposedly next door to Buddy's place. She had no trouble finding it but she was careful to approach from the opposite direction so she wouldn't have to walk by the cafe's front window. Put simply, she had a feeling that Buddy Tangen had been born nosey and had been honing her skills ever since.

Just to be sure that she had the right place she waited outside until a man came by. ''Excuse me.''

''Yes?'' he said and glanced around as if he had only now noticed where he was.

''Could you tell me what this sign says?'' She tapped it.

''Of course.'' He looked at her again but just briefly. ''It says: Joe Willie Everett.'' Smiling he held up one mittened finger. ''Not Joseph William Everett, mind you. And then this next line says: Counselor at Law.''

He was a heavy-set, rather pale-faced man who wore a wool plaid scarf knotted under his chin like a kid. He must've seen the direction of her gaze because he blushed like a girl. ''I, um, forgot my hat.''

Though she wore none she said, ''Not a good idea in this weather.''

''No.'' He waited. ''Well . . .'' He looked at the girl. Looked at the lawyer's door. "Was there any thing else I can help you with?"

"No. I'm just working up my nerve."

"To talk to Joe Willie?" She nodded. He leaned closer. "You needn't bother. Joe Willie's a real pussycat."

"Is he?" He had a kid's mischievous eyes.

"You betcha!"

"Thanks!"

"Not at all." As he reached up to tip his hat, he remembered he wore none and reddened again. "Good day, miss."

"And to you, sir."

No one heard the bell above the door due to three men who were bunched in the center of the room arguing loudly. All had their back to her. She made herself small and hoped an end to the discussion was near. Between wood and tobacco smoke the air was thick as pea soup. She coughed quietly and stood shifting her weight from foot to foot until she caught the eye of the man lounging at the desk. Through the churning arms and swirling hands he smiled and held up one finger that said: Give me a minute. She nodded and settled back to wait. The argument apparently had to do with "the state of the nation."

"It's this damn wild inflation!" yelled one man.

"Caused, mind you, by the excess burden of debt." Which the second man claimed could be laid right at the bankers' feet for "urging men to borrow more than they need."

Replied another, "The day'll come when everyone will want to sell at once an' there'll be no buyers."

"But it's already happened," cried the third. "In Western Kansas and Nebraska."

"I heard that over a hundred thousand settlers have chucked everything an' gone back East."

"Can you blame them? Why stay when their farms're mortgaged past redemption?"

That last speaker turned a little and she recognized the mayor, Rudy Fagerhaug.

"Their dreams're dust."

"Poor devils."

Joe Willie jumped into the dramatic lull that followed. "You'll have to excuse me, gents. I see my next customer's here." All turned, saw her and doffed an assortment of headwear.

"Sorry, miss."

"Yeah, we didn't know you was here." The man's smile showed that he was missing several important teeth.

"Hope you haven't been waitin' long!"

"Only a minute."

"Gentlemen, this is Miss Thora Gunn. I believe you've already met our mayor."

"Yes, I have. Hello."

"This . . ." Joe Willie indicated the man with the missing teeth. ". . . is Curly Frye, undertaker and owner of Curly's Tonsorial." He put his hand on the third man's shoulder. "And this fella with the large-lookin' brain is Guy Corliss, owner of *The Clarion.*"

"It's *The Daily Clarion* now, don't forget," said Mr. Corliss proudly.

Though she had never seen one before, he fit her idea of what a newspaper man should look like. Scattered. Studious. Bespeckled and pale as paste. With his gray scarf wrapped several times around his neck he resembled an inchworm in a high-necked sweater. He told her, "Joe Willie's wife, Sissy, writes a column for the paper, you know."

"For which she is not only shamelessly encouraged but paid to boot!" exclaimed Joe Willie.

The men laughed. "He's fishin' for compliments again," said Rudy. "He knows Sissy's column is the first thing everybody reads. You'll soon see why."

Sure I will, she thought. I'll just pick up that paper and read it like a book.

Looking serious now, Mr. Corliss said, "Allow me to express my condolences about your brother, miss."

"Yeah," said the barber. "I thought he was real nice."

"Indeed he was. Such a gentle soul," Ben Coliss said. "Everyone liked him."

She turned to face Mr. Corliss. What they'd said had touched her and that made her mad. "You know, you're about the tenth person who's said that to me. If everyone liked him so much how come five men had a hand in hanging him?'' He stared at her plainly taken aback. Somebody mumbled something about Junior Buel and it spurred her on. ''I know all about Junior Buel and his partner Mose Starr. What I want to know is who were the other three?''

''I don't know what to say. Of course we all wondered the same thing at the time.''

''And . . . ?''

''We didn't know what to think. Who would take part in such a thing?''

''Everyone pretty much agrees in their opinion that Starr and Buel were the instigators of it.''

''Then why didn't the other three men stop it? Just tell me that, Mr. Corliss. Why didn't they stop it?''

''I don't know. Truly I don't. And unless one of them decides to tell us, we will never know.''

The other men nodded. ''That's it in a nutshell, miss.''

There was a long moment when no one had anything else to say and the uncomfortable silence grew.

''Well, I've got shearin' t'do.''

''And I've got a paper to put to bed.''

With that, Frye and Corliss gathered their things, said polite good-byes and left.

She could see them from the window. They stood talking a minute. Both glanced over their shoulders at least once before they peeled off in opposite directions. The barber was soon out of view but the newspaper man crossed the road to a shop almost directly across from Joe Willie's office.

Had he been one of them? That round-shouldered little figure? She didn't think so but she was not scratching anyone off the list yet.

Rudy Fagerhaug had hung back. She looked at him and waited. Obviously he had something to say, but he seemed to have trouble getting started. When he did, the words came rushing.

''I just want to say that I know it's hard for you to believe now, but what you're feeling will pass on one day. I know because we had a similar loss and the pain passed for us. Not fast, not easy, but it passed.''

His voice turned soft then, not at all the robust political voice she had heard earlier.

"It's an awful hard thing . . . losing someone you love. Dottie like to never get over it. In a way it's similar to what you're facing because we never did find out what happened to Harold. When the war ended, he just didn't come home with the other boys."

She studied her shoe, sorry now that she had spoken at all. "She said something about your son yesterday."

"There was a time when she wouldn't have. Back when she was so despondent. Why, one time she sank into such a deep melancholia she started acting downright . . ." Here he twirled his finger around his temple. ". . . dotty.

"I'll tell you, it scared me half to death. She'd say things like, 'I believe he's been grazed by a minie ball and has lost his memory.' And I'd say: 'But why hasn't somebody let us know?' 'Because,' she'd say, 'somebody bumped into him and tore off his sign.'

"She'd heard that the boys would write their name on a piece of paper and pin it on their shirt." He shook his head. "That's where she'd pinned her hopes. On a piece of paper. 'We'll just have to wait until someone finds it.' 'Good Lord!' I'd say. 'Finds the paper?' This is three years later, you understand. 'Well, either that or wait until it comes to him.' Until what comes to him? I'd ask. 'Why, where he belongs, of course.'"

He looked at Thora with shiny eyes. "She knew she was close to losing her reason but she couldn't seem to pull herself together. It went on for a long time. Or maybe it didn't and it just seemed that way to me."

"If it helps you any, she was all right the other day. Sorta sad, but not too much so."

"I don't know what caused her to finally let it go. She had several sessions with our minister and threw herself into her charity work even more than ever. I guess either one could've done it. Then again," he mused, "maybe it was divine intervention."

"Maybe that's what will have to happen to me. Divine intervention."

"Then I hope for your sake it happens soon." To himself

he added: before you drive yourself and everyone you meet crazy!

He picked up his hat. "Well, good day, miss and good luck. Joe Willie, I'll see you at the poker game tonight."

"I'll be there. Bring plenty of cash."

"Ha! I might say the same to you!" He nodded to her again and went out.

Joe Willie looked at her and she thought she detected pity in his gaze. That alone made her draw herself up and paste a smile on her face.

"C'mon in and sit down."

A wooden railing of the sort one saw around a tidy porch separated the waiting area from the office. He swung a gate open for her and motioned her toward one of two chairs that sat beside his desk. Like the room, the chair wasn't fancy, just bullhide stretched on a wooden frame but it was surprisingly comfortable.

"Looks like I interrupted a pretty heated argument."

"What? That?" Joe Willie settled himself and laid one boot on his knee. "Heated's rollin' around on the floor."

She looked down. "Sorry about saying that stuff. It's just that I'm getting sick of hearing how much everyone loved my brother. Somebody's lying. Three *somebodies* to be exact."

He waved her off. "Don't blame you a bit. You've got a right to be angry."

This was her first good look at Sissy Everett's husband; the night of the storm he had been only a dark silhouette in the doorway, a sheepskin coat and a western style hat. She'd imagined someone refined and was surprised to see that his appearance was anything but. He looked more like a street fighter than an attorney. How on earth had he gotten himself such a delicate young wife?

When he smiled at her, she realized that she was staring and turned her attention to some odd looking items that hung on the wall. "What are those things?"

"Those?" He pointed. "Well, that one there's a hackamore. That's a crupper and over there's a martingale."

"And that?" She indicated a wedge-shaped tool with a backwards handle.

"A froe."

"A froe?"

"Gesundheit! Haw-haw."

Having never heard that foreign word before, she gave him a contemplative eye before she returned her gaze to the thing. "What's it used for?"

"I haven't a clue," he said soberly and then grinned when she did.

"See, I inherited these things. This place used to be a leather repair shop that was owned by Buddy's husband Al. When Al died, Arne Stinson rented it from Buddy. He kept up the repair side of the business an' started makin' skiis an' snowshoes. Pretty soon ol' Arne'd branched out into furniture an' just about everything else known to man that's made outa wood. Finally got so busy he had to build his own shop. He moved out. I moved in. He left Al's stuff on the wall. Which was fine by me. I like old-timey things."

"I do too."

"Too bad you couldn't've met Buddy's husband. He was sure a fine fella." He held up a pouch of tobacco. "Mind if I smoke?"

"No," she said. It was the first time anybody had ever asked her permission for something and it pleased her. Made her feel womanly and well brought-up. Which was why she decided not to say that all he had to do was breathe in. He tapped tobacco into the paper cradle he held then closed the sack with his teeth.

"Now." He licked the twirly into shape. "What can I do for you?"

"Well," she said and paused.

He ran a match under the desk. "Go on and ask. Whatever it is there's no sense beatin' around the bush."

"All right. The night my brother was hung he was in protective custody."

"That's right."

"Well, it seems to me that it wasn't very good protection."

He gave her a piercing look. "Where're you headin' with that?"

"I'd like to know if the sheriff did everything he could to protect him."

"I was the sheriff the night your brother was hung."

"I meant Jim Horse. He was escorting my brother to jail, wasn't he?"

"Yes." He smoked a minute before he went on. "Listen here. I can understand where you're comin' from. There wasn't one amongst us who didn't ask ourselves: what if I'd been there instead of here or what if I'd done this instead of that. None of which, by the way, did anybody a lick of good, least of all poor Thor.

"I know Jim Horse asked himself plenty of questions too, but the thing is, his job was to protect your brother's life with his own, and that's exactly what he did. That's what he's always done. His job."

"Yes, but . . ."

"I know." He leaned forward. "You're probably judgin' Jim by what you see, a roughshod uncultured-looking man. Which is exactly what he is, but he is also a damn good lawman." He leaned back and squinted at the froe. "Let me tell you about our beginning."

She thought: do I have a choice?

"Ol' Jim and I arrived in town about the same time. Him from the north. Me from the south. I didn't find out till much later what had brought him to town. Myself, I was hunting bounty. Unfortunately the fella must've made it over the border 'cause I have never heard any more about him. Well, I hadn't been in town a week when I was offered the job as sheriff." He held up a finger . "I bet I know what you're thinking: why in the sam hill would anyone offer a gamey-lookin' stranger like myself the job of keepin' the peace."

She thought: I'll bet he's going to tell me. Sure enough . . .

"The council was at the end of their rope. There was nothing left for 'em but to try the ol' trick called it-takes-one-to-know-one." He chuckled. "You wouldn't have believed this town back then. It was about as rough as they come. We had 'em all. Hard-partying lumberjacks. Half-crazed trappers who hadn't seen a white . . . human being for years. Gamblers. Bank robbers. Scarcely a night went by that there wasn't two or three shootings and at least one stabbin'."

He moved like he was working a crink out of his neck and unknowingly called attention to the size of his shoulders. She was beginning to understand why a refined schoolmarm like Sissy might have found this man interesting.

"At the time I arrived there was a coupla no-goods who had the whole town buffaloed. The, ah, let's see . . . Give me a minute an' it'll come to me." He looked at the ceiling. "Yeah, they were the Hatcher boys. Coyle and Doyle. Not only brothers but twins. Meaner'n two wolverines in a sack.

"Well, one night—for no other reason than I was the lawful authority hereabouts—one of 'em braced me in the Wind Fall Saloon. Told me he collected badges and stars. Had over a dozen of 'em, he said. We did find two badges in his pockets. Which we pinned over the holes in his chest before we buried him.

"The other one, Coyle or Doyle—I never could keep 'em straight—was upstairs ah . . . restin' when his brother died. Several had later heard him vow revenge, but when nothing happened and he dropped out of sight, I figured he'd left for a less unhealthy climate. Well, I'd figured wrong. Two days later he tried to throw down on me in that alley right yonder. The durn wind must've been wrong for I had my back to him an' never heard him call out before he fired."

"What happened?"

"Turned out the area was unhealthy for him too. He succumbed that very night to a terrible lung draft." He tapped his chest and shook his head in mock sympathy.

She admired his way with words. "The night air?" she asked and he nodded sadly. "Huh!"

He rested his arms on his knees. "Now mind you what I'd done was something many others could've done faster an' smoother, but you'd've thought I hung the moon. The town practically threw a party and the next day Rudy Fagerhaug offered me the job permanently." He blew a ringlet of smoke. "I decided I would take it. Don't ask why 'cause I can't recall. Maybe I figured I'd just as soon die of a bullet as freeze to death.

"Well, I had my hands full, I'll tell you. I knew I'd have to have help but no one quite measured up for the job. An' then I ran into Jim." He dropped his smoke into a spittoon beside the desk where it sizzled like frying bacon. "First time I saw him he was squared off against four men in the same damned alley where I'd dealt with that Hatcher fella. I was about to step in and even up the odds but turned out that the odds were already even.'' He gave her a grin which she didn't return. He obviously thought very highly of the sheriff and that, unaccountably, annoyed her no end. Besides, all this wasn't what she came for. She wanted to know if Jim Horse had slacked off on his duties, not hear how admirable he was.

''But you hired him anyway . . .''

''Ultimately but to say that the council wasn't too keen on it was putting it mildly. It appeared that they'd had a lot of Indian trouble in years past and there I was tellin' 'em I wanted to hire one. 'Can't trust 'em,' they said. 'They can't leave the firewater alone.'

''Turned out that they were dead wrong about ol' Jim. Why, I have never known the man to take a drink. I don't believe he's sworn off it or anything. Just doesn't like what it does to him. Now, I'm not sayin' he doesn't have his faults. Who doesn't? Why, I was a big hell-roarer myself at one time. Back before I met Sissy.''

She acted disbelieving. ''No! Really?''

He ignored that. ''Took me a while to get used to his perplexin' nature and to how silent he is. But I came to appreciate his words when they came. And they did come once he'd learned to trust me. He's a complicated man living a complicated life. Born an Indian. Raised down in the Nations. Living now in a white man's world. I don't know if he's sure where he fits in yet. Sometimes I believe he'll make his life here. Other times I think he could . . .''

She moved again and he looked at her with a keen eye. ''None of this is what you wanted to know.''

''Well . . .''

''I know, I know. But I thought that once you understood what kind of man he is, you'd know that he would've died before he'd've let harm come to your brother. Not because he has any lofty ideals or anything. Simply because it was his job to get your brother to the jail safely and not much is more important to Jim Horse than his job. You understand what I'm sayin'?''

''Yeah, I guess.''

"Good." He leaned back. "Then I believe there's only one more thing to say."

"Yes?"

"If you want to really know what happened that night, why don't you ask Jim about it himself. He'll tell you flat out. I've never known him to tell a lie."

"I guess I don't need to. I just wanted to know if there was any chance he'd sided with those men."

"Sided with 'em? A compadre does not pistol-whip a man so bad that he loses an eye."

"I know but maybe they had a falling out at the end or maybe . . ."

"You are just lookin' for somebody to blame. It's human nature. You want to point the finger at somebody."

"I suppose you're right. I don't know what I was thinking."

"And now?"

She believed him; how could she not? She nodded again. "I'm sure he tried his best."

"Good."

"Mr. Everett . . ."

"Joe Willie."

She nodded again. "Do you have any idea who those other three men were?"

"No. If I did, I'd've killed 'em myself at the time."

She believed him then too. "Did you suspect anyone?"

"You mean have I got any hunches?" She nodded hopefully but he shook his head. "The answer's the same now as it was then. I don't have a clue."

Chapter 10

Jim Horse sat in the jail with his feet on the windowsill, watching the townspeople come and go. Though he knew everybody in town there were many he didn't recognize because of how bundled up they were. He recognized Thora Gunn easily enough, striding around with no hat and her coat flapping open. As if the weather didn't concern her a bit.

He saw her trudge to the Western Union office and then to Conor O'Malley's office then past the jail and up the hill to the cemetery. When she came back down the hill and went past again her face was pinched and red.

She was an independent little cuss. About as far from a shrinking violet as you could get. Not his sort at all. He liked his women a bit clinging and needful. Joe Willie and he used to talk about it sometimes. It was one of the several topics in which they had a common interest. 'Course that was back when Joe Willie was a bachelor too. Women. Guns. Knives. Women. Indians. Shootists. Women. The cavalry. Gamblers. Women. Keeping abreast—so to speak—of the new working girls in town meant that they never ran out of material.

One of the things Joe Willie had always claimed was that he just couldn't abide those women who couldn't take care of themselves. Give me a rough an' tumble whore, he used to say. The sort of woman who'll get into a fistfight or a wrasslin' match and bite and scratch like a cat. Said it excited the hell outa him.

And just look at who he'd married: a little prim miss about as tough as butter in August.

Now as for himself, he liked the clingers. Helpless, dependent, entwine-y little things. As he'd always told Joe Willie, if there was one advantage white girls had over Indian girls, it was their ability to make a man feel like he was in command in the hay. A lot of Indian girls—Cherokees are the worst—will tell a man when to get on, when to get off and exactly what to do in between. Jim's feet hit the floor and he pressed his cheek to the glass. There she goes again!

Later that day Dill Wyatt, postmaster and Western Union agent, hung a sign on the knob of the telegraph office door that said "Back in Five Minutes!" Limping slightly from a blister on his heel (This is the last time he'd let Herta talk him into ordering from a catalog!) he hurried across the street to the jailhouse. Bull Durham and Jim Horse both looked up as he came in. "Hey, Dill!" said Bull. "Got a wire for us?"

"No. But I sent a wire and got a response that I think you'll want to know about."

"Whose wire?" asked Jim.

"You know that girl . . . Thor's sister?"

"Yeah. What about her?"

"She came in earlier today an' said she wanted to send a wire to Stillwater Prison. To the prison warden hisself."

Jim Horse sat back and waited. He couldn't say he was surprised.

"An' she waited right there until the answer came in."

"What answer, Dill?" Telling him what was in the telegram was illegal. Dill knew it. Jim knew it. Both ignored it.

"The exact date and time that Junior Buel is due to be released from prison."

"An' when's that?"

"Saturday."

Jim Horse stood up and collected his hat which prompted Dill to say, "That ain't all."

"What then?"

"She asked how much the train fare was to Stillwater an' after I told her what it was, she whipped out this real purty beaded thing. Looked sorta like a coin purse."

A charm bag, thought Jim.

"Anyhow, she asked me if I wanted to buy it for my wife."

"Yeah?" Jim was thinking that train fare to Stillwater was pretty cheap. Especially if a person took the night train.

"Well, you all know how Herta likes doodads."

"Damn it, Dill."

"What?" He stuck out his chin. "Hell, I guess I can buy my wife a gift if I want to."

At the door Jim told Bull, "I'll be over at Joe Willie's." And then he was gone.

Jim didn't find Joe Willie in his office but rather at Buddy's Cafe, having an early dinner with Sissy. He wasted no time in telling them: it was better than an even bet that Thora Gunn planned to go to Stillwater and confront Junior Buel. To what end, he couldn't say, but that's what he figured.

"We must talk her out of that," said Sissy. "She doesn't know what a bad character Junior is."

"If she's set on goin', I doubt there's much we can do to stop her."

All three fell silent then Sissy said, "Too bad you couldn't hold her in protective custody. Just temporarily, of course."

She had no sooner finished speaking when the baby gave her a hard kick and instantly removed all other thought from her mind. She looked at the two men and then at her hands in her lap—or rather what used to be her lap—and she smiled to herself. It was a boy. She just knew it was another boy. She had told Joe Willie as much the night before, "My stars can he kick!"

"He?"

"Yes, he! No girl could be this rambunctious." He had thought she was exaggerating until she had held his hand on her stomach.

"Goodgawdamighty!" he'd said. "The kid kicks like a mule."

She had hoped for a girl this time but of course, she would be pleased with a healthy baby of either gender.

Joe Willie looked at his wife and then at Jim Horse. "You know, Sissy may have somethin' there." Sissy beamed. (This was nothing unusual as far as Joe Willie was concerned. He said she was always beaming.)

But now she was frowning. She had apparently lost the thread of the conversation. "I may have something where, Joe Willie?" Her husband was talking to Jim and didn't hear.

"Maybe you could keep her in jail until Junior Buel has left for where ever he plans on headin' when he gets out."

"Think so?" Jim said.

"I don't see how else you can keep an eye on her otherwise."

"Hu'ah." It was that part about keeping an eye on her that caused his non-committal comment. It struck him that he was already doing that about every chance he got.

Joe Willie didn't let on that he had recognized the carnal gleam in Jim's eye. Obviously Jim found the girl appealing but that wasn't what had hit Joe Willie. Any man under eighty would find her exciting. No, what had impressed him was the fact that Jim had allowed his feelings to show. It just wasn't like him to do that.

Sissy was looking at him with a perplexed expression but he could not explain what he'd just seen to his wife. In spite of her having the most vigorous love life Joe Willie could provide—and still hold down a job—Sissy was surprisingly naïve about things like that in other men. Of course, she had picked up on the gleam in his eye right off the bat. Which was due to all practice he had given her in spottin' it.

"Joe Willie? Are you listening?"

"Yeah. I was wonderin' what charge you can hold her on."

Another interesting notion thought Jim. Holding Thora Gunn. "I don't know that there is one."

"Hmm. You got that new list on you?" Jim nodded. "Well, haul it on out here and let's take a look."

Jim dug in his hip pocket and came up with a little book with a black pebbled cover. "Where do you want me to start?"

"At the beginnin', I suppose."

Jim started reading. "Fine of fifty cents for letting livestock run free within the city limits plus impoundment of said cow, pig, mule, sheep . . .''

''On second thought, skip to the stuff that warrants jail time.''

Jim licked his thumb and pushed several pages over. ''Here we go. Unlawful to hunt in town limits. Fine is one dollar plus one day in jail and impoundment of . . .''

''Hell, that won't work. Didn't you say Buel gets out on Saturday?''

''Yeah.''

''Then you're gonna have to hold her longer'n a day.''

Jim rolled another page over.

''What's all this, anyway?'' Sissy asked her husband.

''New laws enacted by the council last week. It won't be like the ol' days any more.''

''Good. A man used to be able to get away with murder around here.''

''Many did,'' said Jim dryly.

''But not any more.'' She smiled at Joe Willie and then at Jim. ''And the town can thank you two for that!''

Both men shrugged off her comment but neither said it wasn't true, because it was.

The year before Joe Willie and Jim Horse became the law there had been twelve murders, two missing persons (probable abductions), four forcings, eighteen maimings and one hundred fifty-two drunken rows. (And only those consisting of six or more people were counted; bare-fisted fights involving six people or less were written off as hoo-haa.)

People used to claim Two Sisters didn't have enough laws. Now there were those who said the council had gone too far! Infringing on a person's private affairs and all. In Joe Willie's opinion they had something there. Hell, there was even a law against peeing up a wall!

''Firing a pistol into the ceiling of any public establishment,'' read Jim. ''Four days.''

That last ordinance and its harsh sentence had had strong backing by the saloon owners. Though scarcely a year old the Inside Straight's tin ceiling was so puckered by bullets it looked like a milk strainer.

Jim droned on, ''Vagrants, artistic gamblers, extortioners and restless belligerents are strongly frowned upon . . .'' (Translation: when he worked someone over he didn't have to ask if they were Democrat or Republican first.) ". . . and are subject to arrest."

Sissy frowned. "There isn't anything about protective custody for someone who might harm themselves?"

Jim looked at the book a final time. "Appears not."

"Well, give it here then."

Jim complied and Joe Willie licked the end of his pencil and began to write.

Sissy was shocked. "Joe Willie!"

He looked up. "What?"

"You can't do that."

He dotted something with a flourish. "I already have." He returned the book to Jim who read, "Sheriff may temporarily restrain a person who appears to be willfully bent on self-destruction. Length of time shall be at the sheriff's dis . . . dis . . ."

"Discretion. Means you call it, Jim." He patted Sissy's hand. "You're right, honey. I can't do that, but by the time somebody gets around to lookin' into it, Junior Buel will—we hope—have left the state."

"There's no reason for him to stay here any more. Not since his old man died."

"I imagine he might head back to that saloon he bought down in Durango?"

Joe Willie nodded. "When I found him down there he looked like he'd settled in pretty good."

Sissy listened and remembered. With Jim literally at death's door, Joe Willie had left Two Sisters swearing that he'd bring Buel back to Minnesota to stand trial. He succeeded but he'd been gone for months. Besides being worried sick she had missed him something awful. They had only been married a short time when he left. Not that his leaving would be any easier now. Lord, she was so glad he was an attorney now instead of a lawman!

She looked from her husband to Jim Horse and told herself she was being silly. They both might have bent the rules a bit in the past but certainly neither would sanction the out and out invention of a law! Well, Joe Willie maybe but surely Jim wasn't going along with it!

Jim adjusted his eye patch and rocked his hat into position. "Guess I'll go arrest her."

He was!

Sissy sputtered, "But Joe Willie, Jim can't . . ." Jim stood and her eyes followed him up. "Can he?" She looked from one man to the other. In some respects Jim was a lot like her husband. Both were tall and muscular, though Jim might be a bit heavier through the shoulders, and while neither was handsome in the conventional sense, each possessed something that compelled a female's interest.

Joe Willie tipped his chair back until it was balanced on two legs and nodded. "Good!" Jim had reached the door when Joe Willie added, "Say, Jim?"

"Yeah?"

"We best keep this amongst us three."

"I don't think we can do that."

"Why not?"

"Well, what about Buddy, for example? The girl stayed there last night and I'm sure Buddy expects her to stay there again tonight."

Joe Willie considered that. "We could tell Buddy she just prefers the jail over her place."

"Oh, Joe Willie!" Disgusted. "You can't tell Buddy Tangen that."

"Why not?"

Jim came partway back. "Sissy's right. We'll have to let her in on it."

"Aw hell! You know what that means. Tellbuddy. Telegraph. Same difference."

"You have no choice." This from Sissy. "Telling her the other would hurt her feelings terribly."

"All right. You tell her, Jim."

"Why me?"

"You're her kin. That's why."

Jim mumbled. "I'll tell her the girl prefers the jail."

"Don't you dare!" But then Sissy sat back. Jim Horse was already gone.

Chapter 11

First thing Jim saw when he stepped outside was the wolf, sitting on the boardwalk in front of the jail. He had a feeling the girl would not be far away so he went over to Buddy's to pick up some raw liver and to tell her why they were going to hold the girl for a few days.

"Protective custody?"

"Yeah, that's right."

"What's that mean?"

"Somebody's got to help her 'cause she can't help herself."

"What's wrong with her?"

"She's a toe-biter."

"A what?"

"She sees a bare toe, she'll bite it every time. Can't help herself. You don't see much of it up here but it's common down south where most people don't wear shoes." He shook his head. "We might be able to break her of it."

He left Buddy with her upper lip curled and her mouth hanging open.

Having made a sort of friend of the wolf when he tossed the liver into a cell, the wolf followed it on in. He had just locked the door when he heard the street door open. "Coco?" The wolf yipped and she came on in, like Jim had figured she would. He picked her up and deposited her in the other cell and locked that door too. The wolf started throwing himself against the bars that separated him from the girl. The girl, however, hadn't even had time to get worked up.

"What's going on?

"Protective custody."

"What?"

"We're lockin' you up to protect you from yourself."

Understanding dawned and she grasped the bars with white knuckles. "You can't do that!"

"I guess we can. Soon as Junior Buel leaves the state, you'll be free to go."

"But . . ."

He pointed at the wolf. "You better get your animal under control before he hurts himself."

"Stop! Coco! Stop!" The wolf quieted and trotted to where her hand was inserted between the bars. "Let him come in here with me."

"No."

"Why not?"

" 'Cause I'm gonna have to open these cell doors once in a while an' I can't trust you not to sic him on me."

"You can't do this."

"I already have."

She walked to the window. The wolf sat on his haunches and looked back and forth between them. Jim didn't know who looked more forlorn.

She turned. "Look, all I want to do is ask Buel who the other men were."

"And you think he'll tell you? Just like that? Junior would take you and use you hard and then he'd slit your throat and go eat a hearty breakfast."

She showed him the willful set to her lips. "That's my worry, mister. Not yours."

He shrugged then he lied. "It's out of my hands." He softened his tone. "This way's best. Really."

And before she could say more, he pulled the door closed.

* * *

Glittering snow glazed the town like a gingerbread village in a confectioner's window, but Thora's thoughts were on her predicament. Surely sane people in this town would not allow her to stay a prisoner! She would holler to some passerby and ask them to get a message to the Everetts or Buddy Tangen. Yes, that's what she'd do.

She hung at the window and watched. There was a narrow alley between the jail and the North Star Hotel next door, but in two hours' time she saw only a young man, a boy really. He emerged from the hotel with a box of refuse. After he disposed of it, he carried in an armload of stove wood. He ignored her so completely she decided he'd been born deaf.

Meanwhile in the other room she heard Bull Durham come on duty and she heard Jim Horse leave. The deputy must've made a bed on the floor because less than ten minutes later she heard him snoring. She spent an awful night.

At sunup the sheriff returned carrying a tray which was covered with a red checkered napkin. He wasn't alone. Toting a mop and a pail was an owl-eyed person that he introduced as Emily Jones.

"Hello, miss. I've been hired to tidy up the jail. I won't be but a minute."

Thora said nothing in response. She wasn't going to cause any trouble but she wasn't going to make it easy on anyone either. She was allowed to stand outside the cell while Emily Jones cleaned. The sheriff set down the tray and lifted the napkin to reveal more food than Thora had seen in months. Flannel cakes swimming in butter and maple syrup. Crisp bacon cut thick. Sourdough biscuits and stirred eggs. Coffee. Intuitively she knew where the food had been cooked and amended her escape plan. She kept the coffee and pushed the tray into Coco's cell.

Before the sheriff left she called him back. "I want to let Coco-man go."

"Go where?"

"To his home."

"Can you do that?"

"I can." Smugly.

"It wouldn't do for him to be hanging around town. Somebody'd . . ."

"I said I can send him home."

When the wolf was just a pup she had trained him to return to the cabin by giving him a whiff of Wolf Woman's tobacco pouch. He had learned quickly. When he was big enough she would often send him back to the cabin with the sled full of wood or maybe some game she had shot while she went on working or hunting.

"Can I have your word that you won't tell him to attack?"

"Yes. Can I have your word that you won't shoot him?"

"Yes."

"Is your word any good?"

"Good as yours." He unlocked the wolf's cell then hers. "Go on then. I'll be watching from the door."

She went around the side of the building, still in sight but private. She knelt beside the wolf. "You're going back home, Coco. Now, I want you to be extra careful. Stay out of towns and away from people of all colors. Travel at night. Keep moving." She put her arms around him. "I'll be up that way as soon as I'm done here." She reached in her pocket for the pouch of Wolf Woman's tobacco and let him smell it. He gave a soft yip that ended in a whine. "Yes, I know but it can't be helped. Go on! Go now. Go!"

He might've hesitated a little but not for long. Standing she watched him trot down the road that headed north. "Hey!" She called him back. Doubling his speed he returned and staggered her by putting his paws on her shoulders. "No, now, you can't stay. I only want to remind you not to take food from anyone—even if you're starving—and if someone tries to coax you close, veer off. All right. That's all. Now go. Go on." A half mile away she saw him peel off the road and disappear into the woods. She felt like bawling like a baby but when she turned around her face was as much a mask as the sheriff's.

When they returned to the jail that girl, Emily was in Thora's cell pushing soapy water toward a convenient drain along the back wall. Thora sat on an overturned bucket and leaned back against the bars. She should've eaten that food. She was famished and could not be expected to be smart as a fox if she was starved. It had been a childish thing to do. She wouldn't make that mistake again.

While she watched the cleaning girl she reviewed her overall situation. She had been faced with obstacles before and early on she had learned that it did no earthly good to blame or complain. A person could spend a lot of time on that which would never get the person out of the fix they were in. No, what she had to do was concentrate her efforts on making a plan. Belatedly she realized the other girl had spoken. "What?"

"I said, I'm sure sorry."

"Sorry about what?"

"That this is the only place they had for you to stay."

"What?"

"The sheriff said you were staying here until you could find a place to stay. I suppose I got the last available spot in town."

Thora thought: what made her think I would choose to stay in a locked jail cell when I could make a shelter outside. At the least, the girl was light between the ears; at the worst, she might be dangerous. I better humor her.

Emily Jones stood looking at her a minute before she returned to work. "See, I just moved here too." She slid her a look. "And I don't know hardly anyone yet. Just the doctor and my neighbors next door. And now you, of course!"

Thora didn't know what to say so she said nothing.

"Have you met him yet?"

"Him who?"

"Conor O'Malley."

The girl had finished in the cell and came out. Thora traded places with her and pulled the barred door closed until it latched. "Yes. I've met him."

"He's been so nice to me." She blushed, something it appeared she did often. "He's the one who found me a place to live. I'll ask him if he knows of anything for you, shall I?"

"Uh, sure."

She collected her things. "Maybe you'd like to come over to my place sometime. When you're, er . . . out."

"Maybe."

A last look around. "I better get over to the doctor's." She pinked again. "I think I've been getting there a little too early. I thought I'd come here first instead. Are you an early riser?"

"Yes. Very early."

"Good. Well then I'll see you first thing tomorrow." With a clatter she tossed her scrub brush in the pail and picked up the broom. "Bye!"

The one person she could've given a message to had bats in her belfry! She slapped her palm against the bars and said something she'd heard a stevedore say once. She had no idea what it meant but it for sure wasn't "Pshaw!"

Conor O'Malley sat at his tiny dining table completely dressed, which was a far cry from the condition he had been in on the previous morning.

He had been sitting having his first cup of coffee. Fortunately he'd had on his pants and his carpet slippers but little else. What possessed him to holler "Come in!" instead of getting up and answering the door, he'd never know. He recalled that he briefly thought his early morning visitor was Ben Corliss who often stopped by for a minute on his way to his shop. That was before he saw Emily Jones standing there and all thought left him.

Now this morning here he sat, shaved, polished and pomaded. And waiting. He'd been checking his pocket watch every five minutes for an hour.

"Good morning!" she said.

"Good morning," he managed and half rose.

"I knocked. When no one answered I thought you might have gone about your day."

"No, not quite yet." She looked enchanting with her braided hair in a no-nonsense coronet, her small face scrubbed and shiny with health. When she removed her coat he saw that she had the same dress on as the day before and had made an apron by tieing a thin piece of sacking cloth around her waist.

"I came a bit later today." She hid her blush by moving toward the kitchen.

She would never forget the sight of him yesterday! All she got was a glimpse, but that wide hairy chest and those muscular arms were now apparently indelibly etched upon her brain because the image had reappeared in her mind's eye at least a hundred times since then. She turned and smiled at him. Today he looked like he was on his way to church, but since she now knew what he looked like underneath his clothes, that's what she saw. She firmed up a smile gone wobbly. "This isn't still too early, is it?"

"No. No. Fine. How did last night go?"

"Oh, fine."

"Not afraid?"

"No. I'm used to being alone. Besides Mrs. Fagerhaug and her two friends were there until quite late, cleaning and putting things away."

"Just as I told you. No project is too big for the Lutheran Ladies League. How was the roof?"

"Fine. Well, there was a little water near the stove but I set a bucket there and even before I left this morning a man named Terrance Byers had arrived to patch it."

Terrance Byers, Conor thought. Ah, yes. Unmarried. Youngish. Good-looking in a loutish sort of way. He stopped himself and thought: Great Scott! Am I jealous? He sat back down, shocked stupid.

He spent the next hour supposedly catching up on his paperwork but actually staring fixedly at his desk while Emily bustled here and there, back and forth. By God, he was jealous!

Chapter 12

Sissy and little Joey headed into town bright and early the next morning. Her motto being: The Sooner An Unpleasant Task Is Addressed, The Better. She was on her way to talk to Thora Gunn. But first she had to drop Joey at Meline Beckstrom's.

Meline and Ketil still lived in the cabin that they had moved into on the day they got married, although a person would scarcely recognize it as the same place. It used to be little more than a one-room lean-to until Ketil added a large bedroom and a well-equipped kitchen with a pantry full of shelves. The next spring he re-sided the outside with rough-sawed timber—rejects from the mill for one reason or another—and replaced the tar-paper roof with one made of cedar shingles. To accommodate their growing family—they had two children now—he had recently added another bedroom and yet another fireplace.

As the mill supervisor Ketil was doing well enough for Meline to stay home and not work at all, but she argued that most of her work was done at home anyway. So, for the time being, she continued to augment their income by baking for the North Star Hotel and Buddy's Cafe and by watching little Joey Everett for Sissy and Joe Willie. Initially Sissy had had to threaten all manner of things to get Meline to accept payment for her services—Meline's argument being that Sissy was her best friend and that she could not take money from a friend—but Sissy was resolute and once that hurdle had been overcome, it was an arrangement that had worked well for them both.

Meline baked in the morning and delivered to her customers in the late afternoon. When school was in session, that often meant that she had to wait to make her rounds until after four o'clock, which was when Sissy came to pick up Joey. Fine with her because they could walk the delivery route together. Meline and her two tots, and Sissy and little Joey. It had become an outing, a time that they both looked forward to with pleasure.

When Sissy arrived on the morning after Thora had been placed in protective custody, four-year-old Marne and two-year-old Lars were sitting on the kitchen floor playing with their blocks . . . on which various farm animals had been carved and on which many tiny teeth marks had been engraved.

Lars greeted Joey with a shriek of glee and a slobbery kiss and Marne immediately offered him his choice of the wooden toys that Ketil had made. After due deliberation—for he was a serious, thoughtful little boy—he opted for his favorite: a wooden dog with jointed limbs that moved when pulled by a string. With it in tow, his mother's imminent departure was of little interest.

Sissy smiled at Meline. "I won't be long."

"No hurry." Meline used her forearm to brush back her hair. "Hungry?"

"No! Gosh, Meline, if I don't quit eating I'll be big as a house!"

"You? Hah!"

"Not that I can't be tempted." Ruefully. "What smells so good anyway?"

"Apple strudel. Mrs. Willman gave me her recipe. You could have just a little slice."

Sissy buried her head in the crook of her arm and cried. "Get thee behind me, Satan!" She lifted her head. "Well, maybe just a little one!"

Sissy found Jim Horse sitting at his desk, tapping his pencil first on one end then the other. He didn't look particularly comfortable. Actually he looked like she felt. "Jim, I've been thinking . . ."

"I know."

"I mean, it's bad enough to keep Thora in jail but that wolf . . ."

"She just sent it on its way somewhere."

"Oh, good." She waited a minute. "Well?"

"Well, what?"

"How's she taking it?"

He shrugged. "She doesn't say much."

"Well, what's your opinion?" For an answer he shrugged again.

My stars! Sissy thought as she approached the other room. Can you imagine the two of them trying to talk?

The prisoner was standing staring out the cell window. This is wrong, Sissy thought. No matter what anyone says, it's wrong. She closed the door behind her and waited for Thora to turn. As she might've expected, she confronted her with it right away.

"So you're in on this too!"

"Thora, Jim and Joe Willie are trying to save your life, to prevent you from doing something very foolish."

"My life is not your concern. What I do is nobody's business but mine."

Sissy set down a needlepoint bag that held her knitting, a jug of heated spicy apple cider and a piece of Meline's strudel. "They . . . we don't want you to do something you may be sorry for."

"Like what?"

"Like go to Stillwater and confront Junior Buel." Thora turned back to the window. "It's only for a couple of days, Thora, just until a cooler head prevails."

"What's that mean?"

"You've just received the devastating word that your beloved brother was wrongfully killed. It's human nature to be hurt and angry and to look around for someone to take that anger out on." Sissy could not see the other girl's face but she moved her shoulders impatiently. "Believe me, Thora, you don't want anything to do with Junior Buel. He is a coarse, terribly cruel man, a bully who enjoys hurting others so much that he seeks out people weaker than he.'' She might have gone on and told Thora how Junior used to torment her brother every chance he got but she knew that to do so would only inflame her more.

''I trusted you. I thought you were my friends.''

''We are. Thora, we are trying to protect you. Please please be reasonable.'' To that she received not one word in response. *My stars, she's stubborn. Well, I am not leaving.*

Sissy sat on a three-legged stool and almost went ass over teakettle. Rocking a bit she found that one leg had been broken off and was an inch shorter than the others! It was probably safe enough if she remembered to offset her stomach by leaning back a bit.

Looking around, she thought: the odds and ends in this place are abominable! The town simply must allocate the funds to buy better furnishings! Did it merit a column? Yes. Maybe so.

Sighing, she removed from her bag a half-finished baby's cap that was only the size of a teacup. She smoothed it lovingly and thinking about of the benefits of motherhood, grimly set to work. The silence stretched.

After a bit, Thora heard the sound of quiet counting and looked at Sissy who was—as they say—tending to her knitting. She acted perfectly content to be spending her morning with a sullen prisoner but Thora knew she wasn't. Sissy Everett's face was the sort on which all her inner emotions played. The sight of it, tight and white, made Thora feel terrible too. She wanted to hate her but she was so engaging. ''I thought you said you were a schoolteacher.''

Sissy lifted her head, grateful. ''I am. At least until the first of the year. The night you arrived we were going to have a party for the young man who's taking my place but what with the blizzard and all, we put it off.''

Thora sat on the cot. Though separated by the bars they were now mere inches apart. ''Then why aren't you at school now?''

''Because it's Saturday.''

''Don't kids go to school on Saturday?''

''No. Nor Sunday either.''

''Huh!'' A moment passed. ''Did you decide to quit on your own?'' Thora couldn't imagine anyone leaving school voluntarily.

''Yes. Why?''

"Well, I thought maybe your husband . . ."

"Oh, my, no. Joe Willie lets me do anything I want. Well, he doesn't like me to stay up too late reading but that's because . . ." She glanced at Thora and finished lamely. ". . . of getting too tired."

"Won't you miss it?"

"I already do. Oh, you mean the teaching? Oh, yes. Very much." She skewed her mouth. "From a purely practical side, I will miss the twenty dollars a month plus the three dollars lodging allowance. Not that we need it. Joe Willie is a wonderful provider, but I like having my own money." She leaned closer. "Makes it easier for me to buy things for him without him finding out ahead of time. He's very, very difficult to surprise."

Thora imagined what a secret would look like on Sissy's face and knew exactly where her husband got his clues.

"But, of course, what I'll miss the most is the children. Very very much."

"How many children are there?"

"Fifteen. The youngest is six and the oldest is sixteen, and they are as different in age as they are in personality." She went on to tell about "Poor Karl" whose his parents were killed in a wagon accident the year previous and how overnight he'd gone from a carefree kid to a responsible young man. "There is only his grossmutter left now and he has to do everything around the farm that his father did. So sad! I don't think he'll be in school much longer."

And a boy named Floyd Dobber whose name was the least of his problems. "If he doesn't change direction he'll end up just like Junior Buel. Only the Dobbers are not wealthy and Floyd will end up on the gallows!"

Realizing she was on shaky ground, she hurried on and told about Clara, a beautiful little girl who had been tragically scarred by small pox. "She comes in every day with an inch of flour pasted on her face. I've cautioned the other children against saying anything and pray that she'll outgrow it but she hasn't so far."

And she talked about Davey Cox. "What's there to say about Davey? Having met him, you know what a character he is! He is also as smart as any child I've ever taught. I'm hoping he'll be a writer or a journalist like Guy Corliss. He has such a vivid imagination and a knack with words.''

Then there was sixteen-year-old Nils who lived with his father on a wannigan. Which, she explained, was a house built on a flat-bottom boat. ''I think he comes to school this time of year just to get warm!''

She looked up then. ''By the way, are you warm enough in here?'' Thora nodded. ''That's good. Let me know if you're not. We used to freeze at the school until our new Waterbury was installed. I got so I was hesitant to send the children outside to play for fear they couldn't get warm again.''

''Play? Do kids play at school?''

''Play . . . exercise . . . whatever you care to call it. There are days when it's essential. Particularly right after lunch when the little ones start to droop.''

''What do they play?''

''What? Well, let's see, that depends on the time of year. Sometimes I just have them put on their coats and snow shoes and run around the building for a while, but on a nice winter day they might go sledding or ice skating on the little pond in back. In the summer they play almost anything. Ante ante I over. Black sheep run. Tug of war. Hopscotch or London Bridge. Again, it depends on the weather. Some days if it is raining or snowing so hard that I simply *have* to keep them indoors then we play what color is my bird or hide the thimble or dominos or drop the handkerchief.''

With a leaden heart Thora listened to her prattle on. She was trying to hold onto her sulk, but she couldn't help asking questions about school. Besides, Sissy actually seemed to like talking to her! It was a kindness she had experienced only rarely before.

For the time being, an inner voice cautioned. *Watch her opinion of you drop when she finds out you are as ignorant as they come.*

She had always wanted to go to school but her father used to say that even if he had the dollar it cost to send her he wouldn't spend it on a ''useless thing like school.''

Neither girl spoke for a time then Thora heard herself ask, ''What do you teach?'' Damn! She ought to bite her tongue!

''Oh, a lot. School's not all play, you know.''

No. I don't know.

"Well, let's see. There's arithmetic and grammar and geography and spelling. Penmanship. The golden rule." She looked sort of sad. "I hope that along with their numbers and letters I've also taught my pupils how to get along with others and how to be thankful for what they have. I've tried to teach a love of God and country by beginning each day with the "Star-Spangled Banner" and ending it with a prayer."

Sissy refocused and saw that the other girl was sadly staring at a place between her feet. An awful thought struck her. "Thora! Didn't you get to go to school?"

Almost musingly she replied, "Go? I have never even seen the inside of one."

"But you speak so well!"

"That's because my mother was a ladies' maid and sat beside her mistress when the girl was being tutored. She even learned how to read a little."

Sissy looked at top of the other girl's head then a smile broke on her face and she snapped her fingers. "Thora, the first school you will see will be ours!"

"What?"

"Yes. The Two Sisters' school. I'm going to ask Jim to bring you to my surprise going-away party."

"A surprise going-away party?"

"Yes. I'm not supposed to know about it but I do. Oh, what fun it will be!" The stool rattled as she jumped up and made for the door. "I'll go talk to Jim right now!"

"Mrs. Everett?"

"Sissy!"

"Sissy. When everything is over . . . Well, what I mean is this, if I stay in Two Sisters . . ." Thora's throat worked and her hands clenched and finally she blurted, "Would you ever consider teaching me to read?"

"No."

"No?" she repeated. She hadn't expected that answer.

"No. Not when everything is done or when you get out of here but now! Right now. We'll begin today."

Thora's heart pounded and her palms got clammy and she croaked, "Today?"

"Absolutely! I'll ask Jim for some paper and a pencil and we'll begin immediately!"

That's how they passed at least three or four hours that day and the next as well. Sissy finished the baby cap and started on a bootee. She insisted that Thora eat the strudel Meline sent—it didn't take much, while she showed Thora her printed cards of words. The way she did it—laughing and talking and knitting—it didn't seem like such a big thing when Thora made a mistake. But then, she was trying very hard to make none.

As far as her vow to confront Junior Buel went, learning to read was the worst thing that could've happened. That first night she fell onto the cot feeling like she'd stuck her head inside a beehive. She was so caught up in all those words she didn't even think of Buel again until in the morning. And then what she thought next was that Sissy had said she would be back at nine o'clock that day. She hated herself, but there it was. Apparently she would rather learn to read than just about anything. Including avenge her brother.

Thora was, as Sissy told Joe Willie later, one of the smartest pupils she had ever taught. "Every bit as quick as Davey Cox. Why, she had a head start on reading and didn't realize it." She told him that Thora's mother used to read to her from an old Bible. It had been written in Icelandic, of course, but she had taught Thora to sound out some of the words. It wasn't much harder to do the same in English.

The next morning the sheriff came in before Sissy did. For a minute he stood there. What did he want? Bull Durham had already escorted her out back to tend to her business.

"Nice day today."

"What?"

"I said, Nice . . ."

"I heard what you said."

He looked mildly perplexed. "Then why'd you say 'what'?"

"Because I didn't believe my ears."

"Why?"

"Because that's such a . . . dumb thing to say."

"It is?" he said, playing along. What did she think? That he was right off the turnip wagon.

"Yes."

There was a long moment when each stared at the other's face. She thought his held a hint of humor; he thought hers held a lot of suspicion. She narrowed her eyes. "Exactly what are you up to?" He steepled his fingers on his chest. "Yeah. You. You're thinking about doing something."

He looked away. He looked back. Should he say what he had in mind: *I was thinking about dragging you into the woods and screwing you blue.* "I just thought maybe you'd like to talk."

He loomed large there in the doorway and she told herself that it was fear that caught her breath in her throat. "Talk to you? Why on earth would I want to do that?" She must've seen something on his face because she knew she got him then.

"Guess I was wrong," he said before he left.

"I guess you were!" she called through the slammed door. *What was all that about?*

Jim retrieved his still-twanging knife from a "wanted" dodger and threw himself into his chair. So much for light-hearted conversation . . . breaking the ice . . . and whatever else he had heard it called. He often did not know the words to use to express his thoughts, in English or Ojibwe, but he had never thought of it as a shortcoming before. At this moment, however, it seemed that it was. A big shortcoming.

Damnit! Jim Horse was who he was and Jim Horse would not change for anyone! He threw his knife again . . .

Unfortunately at that exact instant Buddy opened the door with a tray full of food. She did not see Jim, half cocked off his chair and looking twenty times paler than normal. What she saw was the knife stuck in the wall about an inch from her nose. She stared cross-eyed at it until it quit quivering then she let out a hair-raising scream and blindly threw the tray. Hiking her skirts, she took off down the middle of the street, throwing her arms around and screaming "INDIYUNS."

Bull raced into the jail. He spun, slipped and slid on the syrup and brained himself on his desk. Emily Jones and Conor O'Malley appeared in the doorway in time to hear the thunk of skull meeting desk. Emily's eyes, however, were drawn elsewhere. They were not happy eyes. "Crimany!" she cried. "There's egg on the ceiling."

"What the hell's going on, Jim?" asked Conor as he tiptoed through the syrup to a now groaning Bull.

With as much dignity as he could muster with a piece of bacon riding on his brim, Jim silently retrieved his knife, sheathed it and left.

Chapter 13

On that Saturday night Jim was waiting for Thora to get bundled against the cold, standing in the doorway to the jail cells, watching her without looking like he was. She rolled up her moccasins and tied them in place with strips of rawhide and then faced him.

Thora was nervous and excited about seeing the school but, if the truth were known, most of the nervous part came from being alone with the sheriff.

There was something about him that made her feel like the first time she saw a bald eagle. Awed, overwhelmed. She had walked right off a little ledge and about jarred all her teeth out.

Yeah, she better watch where she was going all right! He unlocked the cell and swung the door open. "I guess this is pretty unusual, isn't it?"

"What?"

"Taking a prisoner to a surprise party."

"The whole thing's unusual." He was seating his hat. "Ready?"

She stepped out of the cell. "Aren't you going to tie my hands together?"

He looked at her. "That's not needed, is it?" He got the direct gaze of her eyes. "Or is it?"

"I can't promise anything. Maybe I'll run for it.

"Then maybe I'll shoot you."

Smirking, she looked at his rifle, at the decorative designs carved on stock and then up at him. "And here I thought I was in protective custody. Then again, maybe this is the same sort of 'protective custody' you gave my brother." Soon as she said it she wished she hadn't. He held open the door.

Until she paused under the bower of his arm, she didn't realize where she had placed herself which was . . . under the bower of his arm. She looked up at his rock-hard face. She intended to be sharp, which would let him know she didn't regret her words. Instead her voice was soft as a sigh. "Please let me go."

"No." He was looking off somewhere. "This time tomorrow night maybe."

"That'll be too late."

"That'll be too bad."

And then he looked at her and during the long moment that followed her anger left and something else took over. Her eyes fell to his lips—which were mere inches from hers—and of their own will, her lips parted and her hand half lifted.

It was then that it struck her how moony she must look and anger rose again—this time at herself!

She stomped through the main room and flung open the door and plowed right into two women who were passing arm and arm. Scrambling like a frog in a skillet and slapping away his helping hands, she eventually righted herself, but when she looked at the women, her words of apology died in her throat for she was face to face with a couple of "fancy ladies." The same sort her mother had shunned on the wharf in Seattle. "Don't even look their way," she'd said. Only, like that day four years earlier Thora was hard-pressed not to look at them. It wasn't their clothes—which were too bright and too tight. Or their hats—which were too big and too feathery. It was their hair. Nobody's hair went like that.

"Hellooo, Jim," said one, simpering. She had corn yellow hair and a loose painted mouth.

"Ladies." He touched his hat then Thora's arm.

"Comin' by later?" asked Brasshead. Her mouth might be

soft but when she turned her eyes on Thora they were hard and cold as flint.

"Mebbe."

Brasshead was giving her a look that started at the end of her nose and she was trying to give Brasshead a look right back, but the sheriff had a strong hand on her elbow and was steering her off the wooden walk. A few steps and she pulled free.

"Friend of yours?"

"Not exactly."

"I see." And she did too. She had seen what male animals liked to do to female animals. Figuring what humans did when they mated had been a simple progression for her—even without an Indian and his wife who had coupled in her presence. (She'd pretended to be asleep but later realized she needn't've. They were too lost in their activities to give a hoot about her.)

They walked to the school in a heavy silence, Thora chewing on her anger, Jim wondering about the strange girl beside him.

He had to admit that she fascinated him, not unlike the first snapping turtle he ever saw. There was a quality about her—as with that turtle—that he'd never seen in any other creature. Maybe he should tell her that. Maybe she would appreciate his honesty. He looked over at her.

Then again, maybe not.

Women, he discovered early on, thought differently from men about all manner of things, but especially about conversation of an informal nature. After considerable personal observation and firsthand experience he made a decision: Don't talk to them.

Woman had no judgment concerning what was important and what was not. It was not their fault; either they were born that way or the ability was removed from them within the first year or two of life. The failing was never more obvious than it was when a man tried to talk to a woman. He had only to recall what happened earlier that day to reinforce his conviction.

Here's how he saw it: a man talked about ordinary things to another man. The other man responded. Their words swirled around them like sage-sweetened smoke. When finished, both men would probably agree that they'd had a fine discussion but since it had not been an important talk, chances are neither man would mention it again.

Not so with a woman. The same words spoken to a woman could pierce her and stick in her liver. Four days later she would be picking them out and looking at them. Or worse, reciting them back to the man. Why did you say that? Or what did you mean by that?

It was, he had discovered, about the only way a man got into trouble with a female: by talking to her. Which was why he was happy he was known as a man who did not speak a lot. Women who had heard that about him expected no conversation. He could then conserve his energy for other, much more important forms of communication.

He snuck another look at her—tromping along beside him, swinging her arms and stomping her feet—and he shook his head slightly. It was as if they'd had a lovers' quarrel! Then he had a sudden thought. Maybe he had not selected a subject that interested her. Suppose—for the sake of proving his point—he were to try again with a more absorbing topic. He gave that some thought. She had evidenced curiosity about the yellow-haired woman. If she were a man and had shown the same curiosity, he would have told what happened the first time he was with the woman. He remembered it like it was yesterday. Because it was.

As soon as he walked into the Wind Fall, he found that the new woman was one of those who are drawn to a man who looks like a brute. She was on him like a blanket. Five minutes more and he'd learned that her name was Serena and that she was from St. Louis. Those preliminaries dealt with, they went upstairs to get better acquainted.

She cried out so when she reached her pleasure that Hattie, the whorehouse owner, had come and knocked on their door and inquired if the woman was all right. No, Serena had yelled back. I am dying! Which was when the owner opened the door and came in and stood beside the bed and looked at them. He did not pause; he had, after all, paid for an hour. Hattie Mueller had smacked him on his bare butt and said, 'Don't go ruinin' her for the others now!'

Now, he had not told Joe Willie that story but he could've.

Joe Willie would've listened carefully and might've advised him to prop a chair under the doorknob next time.

But would this girl like to hear that tale? He shot her another look. No. As with the turtle; something told him that she would not.

After a further search he decided that about the only story she might like—well, hell, anyone would!—was the one about the time he shot two turkeys with one bullet. Far and away, that was the best story he knew!

Smiling a little, he opened his mouth only to shut it again. Hu'ah! Too bad! Ahead was the school.

Thora had seen it too. The kerosene lanterns hanging on the trees that lined the path drew attention to the building from a long way away. She started walking a little faster.

It appeared crowded already. Several horse-drawn sleighs were tied up in front as was a large wagon with bales on hay piled on both sides of the flatbed. With excitement bubbling inside her, she walked up two wooden steps and into a mass of bodies.

Once inside she was mildly disappointed. She'd expected to see a sea of little happy faces sitting at their desks but the desks were pushed to one side and piled on top of each other.

Other things, however, met her expectations. In one corner was an American flag and center square the teacher's desk. Behind the desk was a blackboard, with a pointing stick hanging by a string from a nail. Tacked to the wall, below the big and little letters of the alphabet, were kids' drawings, mostly of animals and mostly unrecognizable. A few were of buildings that looked like a cat could blow them down. Some flowers and suns. She drew a deep breath and smelled books and pencil shavings. *A school! This is a school!*

"Want to put your coat in there?" Jim asked.

"Where?"

"The cloakroom."

"Oh!" *I better see that.*

The cloakroom contained mounds of coats, overshoes, mittens and scarfs and smelled strongly of wet wool. It was also dark and close and, except for herself and the sheriff, empty. She added her coat to a pile and half fell over a boot in her hurry to get out.

Safely back in the main room she was greeted by Sissy and her husband. Buddy was there. Rudy and Dottie Fagerhaug. Meline and Ketil Beckstrom. She saw many others she knew as well. And just arriving was the one person she had hoped to see the most: Davey Cox, self-professed best friend of her brother.

She had brief conversations with several townspeople, some of whom acted so sheepish she knew they must've been apprised of her situation. She showed no mercy and acted miserable. She was particularly gratified to see the unhappy faces of those traitors, Buddy, Dottie and Meline. Little by little she worked her way over to the opposite side of the room. "Hello, Davey." He'd been in the process of drinking some cider. He gulped hard and ran his sleeve across his mouth before he turned.

"Hey! I just heard about your bein' thrown in jail."

"I wasn't 'thrown' and I won't be in for long."

"What're you gonna do?"

"I'm not sure yet." She looked across at Jim Horse with speculation. "But I'm going to do something."

Quite suddenly a howl emerged from the cloakroom and brought a mother scurrying passed them. A few squeals and harshly whispered words and a moment later the mother exited holding two youngsters each by an ear.

The fletching-like hair on one of the boys reminded her of the time when she'd looked the same. Her brothers and sisters too. They all had a raging infestation of lice. Their father'd said, "Oh, leave 'em be. Those lice'll die off come winter." But their mother quietly took money from someplace and bought carbolic acid and green soap. The next day, after their father had left, their heads got shaved and treated with acid and everything they owned got boiled in green soap. That was one thing about her mother. Their clothes might've been patched but they were clean.

She felt someone watching her. She looked at Jim Horse first and saw that he was talking to Joe Willie. Yes. Talking. Joe Willie chuckled and threw a furtive glance at his wife before he responded then he made a motion with his hands like he was jamming something under something.

Her eyes moved on and locked with a scabby-faced boy with

a mile-wide smirk. He looked right at her and extended the middle finger of his right hand.

That puzzled her. A club signal of some sort? An Indian sign?

"Who's that boy over there?"

"Which boy?"

"The one glaring at us." Davey took another swig of cider and this time turned his head and wiped his mouth on his shoulder. *He must have to wring out his shirt at night.*

"That's ol' Floyd Dobber."

"Looks like there's no love lost between you two."

"I hate his guts."

Probably because he knew he was being observed, Floyd walked up behind Marne Beckstrom and yanked on one of her braids. "Hey!" Davey yelled and pushed off from the wall. Before Dobber sauntered off he threw Davey a look that said, This will be continued when there aren't so many people around.

"What a . . . !" He swallowed that last word. "He's always doin' stuff to the little kids . . ."

She was listening—sort of. Mostly she was watching Jim Horse and Joe Willie move toward the door. Probably going outside for a smoke. Unfortunately she had already checked and saw that there was only one door.

Suddenly the sheriff turned and looked right at her. Caught staring at him she felt her face heat but jutted her jaw as if she didn't care. When he smiled slowly and secretly, she dropped her gaze to the fingers of her left hand and looked at them as if she'd just noticed they were there.

"Hello, Davey. Miss Gunn."

She was grateful when Conor O'Malley's large body arrived and blocked her from the sheriff's scrutiny. "Hello, Doctor. Emily."

"Hey, Doc."

Conor O'Malley turned to his companion. "Miss Gunn, you've met Emily Jones."

"Yes," said Thora and smiled. She'd been wrong about Emily Jones. Turns out she wasn't crazy as a coot after all. They'd visited every day, as much as Emily's work allowed.

She was not one to waste much time or motion, and Thora liked that about her.

"Miss Jones, this is Davey Cox."

Davey croaked, cleared his throat and turned the color of blood. Everyone studiously ignored his discomfort and he finally managed "Hullo." in an almost normal tone of voice.

The doctor considerately pointed at the refreshment table laden with decorated cookies and a keg of hot cider. "Shall we have some cookies?"

"Yes. Let's," said Emily.

"Davey, Miss Gunn? Can we bring you anything?"

"Not for me."

"Me neither. I already et . . . ate twelve."

"Twelve!" exclaimed Emily Jones.

The doctor laughed. "You may have need of a purgative powder, Davey.

He stood straighter. "Not me. I can eat rocks."

"An interesting boast. Well, in any case, you know where my office is."

Watching them move away, Thora reflected again on the ways that she and Emily were alike. Things like being alone and being poor, for there was no doubt that Emily Jones was both. She always looked neat and clean but Thora had never seen her in any other dress than the one she had on. It was of the plainest material and patched at the elbows yet she wore it with a quiet dignity and Thora was willing to bet that such things as clothes just weren't important to Emily Jones. She admired her for not giving a fig what anyone thought. It used to bother her a lot to have patches on her clothes.

Jim Horse and Joe Willie Everett came back in with reddened cheeks and wind bright eyes and she sensed that Jim immediately searched for her. She looked away before meeting his gaze and said, "Well, Davey."

"Yeah?"

"I'm thinking you'd be the person to help me out with something."

"Yeah?" Davey peered up at her, his eyebrows in a quizzical scrunch. "What?"

She looked around, real casual-like. *Yes, still watching.* "I want you to tell me exactly what Buel looks like."

"Junior Buel?"

"Mm."

Davey paused but not for long. "Dirty-colored hair and not much of it. A thick body with long arms and a big butt for a man. Lizard-lids an' eyes like ice. A scar acrost the bridge of his nose that he got from Joe Willie Everett in a fight at the Wind Fall Saloon. He's about um . . . twenty-eight or thirty years old."

By the time he finished she was looking at him with new respect in her eyes. "You are going to make a great newspaper man, Davey."

"I thought that's what I was gonna be but now I'm pretty sure I'll be startin' up my own detective agency. You know, like Pinkerton's."

"Ah."

"Cox Criminal Catchin'."

"Ah, good name."

He looked across the room and lowered his voice. "I haven't told Mr. Corliss yet." Ben Corliss stood beside his cousin, Toussaint Boullard whom she'd met when she first came in.

"He's got his heart set on me takin' over *The Clarion* one day."

"Mm. Tough situation."

"Yeah."

"Well, I'm sure you'll work it out." She checked Jim Horse. Still talking to Joe Willie, still watching her. Matter of fact, now they both were. "Listen, Davey . . ."

"Yeah?"

"Tell me what you know about the other three men."

"You mean the ones who were with Junior and Mose Starr." It was a statement.

"Yes. Do you have any idea who they were?"

He shook his head. "I thought on it and thought on it. Till I thought my brain was gonna go on me. I finally had to say all right, somebody'll slip up sometime and when they do, I'll be there to point the finger at 'em." He shook his head again. "But it just hasn't happened. Not in all this time. There hasn't been a thing."

Someone rapped a fork on a glass and everyone looked.

Sissy stood, holding the wooden plaque into which each kid's name had been burned. Her face looked happy and sad at once.

"I can't thank you enough for this beautiful keepsake. I will treasure it always. Thank you!" Her eyes roamed the room. "You know, this is a great joy for me! Every day I am reminded how fortunate I am to be here in Two Sisters, and to have you all as friends. Why, when I think that I came here quite by chance . . ." She looked at her husband who held their son who had an ear-to-ear cookie smear. "Frankly I just can't imagine . . ."

Under his breath Davey said, "She'll be bawling like a baby any minute."

". . . and I am so grateful for all the blessings that I have received, not the least of which are you . . . my . . . my dear, dear friends."

Davey had been right. Shoulders heaving, she now had her face buried in her husband's chest. Half laughing, half crying himself, Joe Willie was patting her back and dropping a kiss or two on her curls.

"Davey, can you get me a pistol?"

He looked at her sharply. "A pistol?"

She nodded and waited. "Well . . . can you or not?"

"I guess I can. Yeah." He was thinking of the guns in a glass cabinet over at Ben Corliss's house. Though Mr. Corliss said the guns belonged to his cousin, he knew all about them and had shown them to Davey one by one. They'd been all sizes and styles; one with a nine-inch barrel, one kept in a felt box that was about as big as a bird. "Careful," Mr. Corliss told him when he bobbled that one. "Don't let that gun's size fool you. It's a vicious little pistol."

"If I'm going to be there when Junior Buel gets out of prison, I've got to get out of jail tonight. And if he's anything like they say he is, then I'll need to carry a weapon." Seeing the look of awe on Davey's face, she laid it on a bit thick. "I may have to kill him, you know." She couldn't help this tendency to exaggerate. It had come on her at birth. She took a sip of cider. "Where can you leave it?"

Davey thought then said. "There's a rain barrel in back of Goody's store. If you stand up on it, you can reach a ledge above it. It'll be there."

"Good."

When she smiled at him he noticed that her eyes were the color of tarnished copper. She set her cup on the edge of a tiny desk. "Thanks."

"Say?" He'd had a wild and crazy thought.

"Yes?"

"How old are you?"

"Seventeen. How old are you?"

"Fifteen." Two years! Davey thought. There was only two years difference in their ages! She was looking at him very intently and something turned over in his chest.

"Davey?"

"Yeah?" Hopeful. Yearning. Ready to drop to his knees and propose.

"I just wanted to say that my brother would've appreciated the help you're giving me now."

Davey toed a place on the floor but inside he swelled with so much pride he thought he'd bust.

Another part of him swelled as well, an embarrassing reaction that befell him every time a female under fifty spoke to him. But this time, his emotional reaction coupled with the other made the sensation a hundred times more powerful than ever before.

When Thora Gunn walked off, Davey Cox's young heart went with her.

Chapter 14

With each of them intent on their own thoughts, it was a silent walk back to the jail. Had they had a mind reader's skills, Jim would have been surprised at just how far Thora was willing to go to secure her freedom. Thora, on the other hand, would have been surprised at just how close Jim was to handing it to her. But since neither possessed more than a thimblefull of perceptive ability (much less precognitive skill) each thought the other an utter mystery.

Jim recalled what Joe Willie said earlier. "I think she'll go after Buel where ever he is."

"I think you're right."

"Well, if we let her go now at least now she'll only have to travel as far as Stillwater. In a week or two seeing Buel'll probably mean a trip clear down to Durango."

In the end, they had agreed that she should be released right off. What Jim did not tell Joe Willie was that he had already decided that, on his own, even before he and the girl left the jail. He would've told her, if it hadn't been for that smart-mouth comment she made about "protective custody."

Jim's reason for letting her go was simple. Maybe she just wanted to talk to Buel. Maybe not. But what mattered was: the boy who died was her brother and Jim was an Indian and as such believed that if anyone had the right to revenge, she did. Of course, she didn't comprehend the danger she was placing herself in but he knew enough about her now to know that even if she knew, it wasn't going to stop her.

There'd been a stink at the party. Several people had heard she was being held. "The idea!" Dottie Fagerhaug said with a squinched mouth. "Holding her in that filthy old place!" She was so irate that she threatened to go to Judge Rice if Thora wasn't released that very night. Joe Willie got his dander up and told her that sometimes a person can carry their do-good meddling too far. Which had put Dottie in a snit and Joe Willie in the doghouse with Sissy. Since Jim had kept his mouth shut, he wasn't in hot water with anyone. Except Thora Gunn.

So he was faced with a dilemma: He wanted to let her go because it was the honorable thing to do. But he didn't want to let her go because he had a feeling he would never seen her again. And he did want to see her again. He now accepted that fact in the way that one does not question the change of seasons. That was simply the way it was.

There was something else that had a bearing on things. Once free to do as she pleased, she would probably leave Two Sisters forever. He would if he were her. But for the sake of the argument going on in his head, suppose she didn't. The only place he would ever see her was in passing and it stood to reason that if he couldn't speak to her tonight . . . alone and witnessed only by the stars . . . he sure would not be able to speak to her on the street. Then what?

The last two days had made one thing painfully clear. He had declined to speak to women for so long, he had lost the ability to do so.

He looked at her side-eyed. She acted as if she hated him and she did not even know him. It bothered him that now she never would. He would have liked to tell her things about him. Like where he was born. How he grew up. The mistakes he had made and the fights he had won. What hopes he'd had and what sorrows he had suffered. Everything.

They had reached the door and she was waiting for him to unlock it. This was his only chance. He had five minutes to become a talking fool or she would be gone forever, yet there he stood. Like wood outside. Miserable inside. She brushed by him and on into the back.

Thora stood in the cell, waiting for him to lock her in but he was just standing in the opening, staring at her. So she said it all again one last time. She explained about her vow and how the failure to keep it—whether it was her fault or not—would haunt her forever. It was like talking to a log. Granted, a very keen log, but a log. "Buel is the man who caused you to lose your eye."

"I seem to remember that."

She ignored his sarcasm. "Then why do you care what happens to him?"

"I don't." *But I care what happens to you.*

While Jim was politely hearing her out before he stepped aside, she believed he was unmoved. She canted her head toward him—unaware that he found the habit very provocative.

Somewhere along the line some instinct had emerged from a heretofore unheard from place and told her that he liked her the way a man likes a girl. On the basis of that wee inkling, she threw caution to the wind. It was a last resort, but she didn't know what else to do. "Suppose I was to offer you something in return for letting me go."

"Like what?" This had possibilities. Maybe he would angle for a kiss.

"Like me."

If he was ever going to go slack-jawed in his life, it was at that moment. Fortunately, by calling on all the skills he had learned from birth, he managed to control his face. But not his body. A familiar heat rose in him.

Thora watched him carefully but his hat shaded his face. *Well, say something! Even if it's only no thanks!*

From the street came the sound of some drunks singing so poorly it was impossible to tell the tune. Inside however there was only the sound of a branch scraping against the roof.

Finally, he said, "Just like that?"

"Just like that."

"You know what you're askin' for?"

She nodded. She knew exactly what she was asking for: pain. For years she had heard her mother through thin wooden slats, or through a blanket laid over a rope, or through the worn planks of a wagon flatbed. Pleading before. Crying after. If that wasn't enough, she'd had her own firsthand experiences, once with a trapper and once with a crazed woodsman.

After dark she and Halldor used to sneak down to the dock to watch the trappers load the flat-bottom boats by lantern-light. One night one of the men took her arm and walked her behind a pile of pelts. Her brother followed them. When he saw that the man was trying to wrestle her to the ground, he held the man off the ground by his neck until the man turned purple and his friends came and chased them off. That trapper had said he wanted to show her some kittens. She was very wary after that, but the woodsman had used no deception at all. While he was trying to tie her he told her everything he was going to do, how many times he was going to do it and in what places. She'd been so shocked at some of the crazy things he said she almost forgot to fight!

He'd caught her sleeping in the woods an hour or two before dawn. She lay well hidden—she thought—in a little dip between two stands of cedar. He must've been quiet as a snow-flake for he took her completely by surprise. The first indication she had that she was in trouble was when he jumped on her and knocked the air out of her. "I gotcha! I gotcha now!" The low light from her fire's embers allowed her only a glimpse of his face, but it was enough to see that he looked half human with broken-off teeth and face hair that started at his eyes.

He pinned her legs with his and tore off the rope holding up her pants. Using his knife—and not very gently—he had her skinned out of the rest of her clothes in seconds. It was only because she got a thumb in his eye and somehow managed to roll him into the fire that he didn't succeed in getting his male part into her. A handy rock either knocked him out or killed him; she didn't stop long enough to find out which. After hurriedly gathering the tattered remains of her clothes and her few precious things she backtracked until she found where the man had left his horse. And then she rode for three days straight.

Looking at Jim Horse, she stuck out her chin and hoped he didn't notice the wobble. Their eyes met and held. "I know what I'm doing."

Jim was having difficulty doing a midstream change of opinion about her. This little gal was as hard as a whore on a busy Saturday night.

She was getting worried. It seemed he was taking an unusually long time to think about it. She no sooner had that thought than he spoke.

"Let's see what you've got."

She told herself she had to expect this but for a private person—and she was one—it was awfully hard to bare her body. The only person who had ever seen her buck naked was her mother and that was back when she was still wearing three-cornered pants.

She disrobed and then stood partly in the shadows. Not trusting his voice he lifted one hand and motioned her into the moonlight. She took two halting steps and he said. "That's good." The sight of her hit him with a physical force. Good? That is like saying snow is cold and fire is hot. In spite of her slenderness, hers was a woman's body with fist-sized breasts, rounded hips and skin like a water lily. She was beautiful. Long-legged and sleek as a yearling colt. Soft and strong-looking at once.

His eye gleamed like a rain-wet coal as it moved over her. Digging her fingernails into her palms she willed herself to stand still and prayed that he wanted her.

He turned away—in rejection she thought—until his gunbelt slipped and he dropped it on a chair. Shuddering with relief—or was it fear?—she went to the cot and lay down and pulled the thin blanket up to her shoulders. He had his shirt off now and was unbuttoning his pants. From somewhere he removed a knife and a short-handled ax—neither of which she had seen before—and laid them on the chair as well.

Unwillingly her eyes were drawn to his legs and back and then when he turned to the muscles defined in his dark-skinned chest. A star-shaped scar duplicated itself on his back and chest. A round scar puckered the skin at his waist and yet another zigzagged down his thigh.

Other than those scars the only thing he wore was a bear claw necklace.

He stood there with his feet slightly apart, his muscular torso as straight and strong as a lodgepole pine. He was compact and well proportioned except for one part of him which appeared to be . . . not right for a man of any size. She closed her eyes. She had been mistaken. She hadn't known what she was asking for.

Then he was beside her. He didn't waste any time in feeling every fold and curve of her, touching her as if he were a blind man who did not know what he had a hold of. Not surprisingly he didn't speak but made low soft sounds of satisfaction. Then his hands were no longer exploring but urgent and insistent and while they moved, he kissed her mouth, her eyes, her cheeks, her neck. Mostly her mouth. Long, long kisses that drew the strength from her, and then also apparently her ability to think for she started to kiss him back. Gently he pulled the blanket off her and kissed his way up one side and down the other. By the time he reached her breasts again she was digging her heels into the cot and pushing herself at him.

What Jim could not say with words, he tried to say with his hands. That her hair smelled like a field of spring wild flowers. That her mouth tasted like a cool mountain brook. That her skin heated his hands and seared his soul. But soon nothing mattered to him except having her . . . now.

He went into her too quick and could not stop when he discovered that he was her first. The thought shocked then pleased him but it wouldn't have mattered. By then he was beyond the point of no return. He thought only of his possession of her. It was like nothing else he had ever known. Powerful, yet pure and sweet. Indescribable. His heart pounded with a drumlike rhythm and sweat beaded on his skin and when she caught her breath once the sound gripped his insides like a fever. His mind ceased to function; his body ceased to be of this earth.

Finally the fury ended and his body went slack. A minute, then two, and he lifted his face from the pillow and yawned contentedly. God, he felt good! Not only had it been better than any other woman he'd ever had, it had been a thousand times better than when he shot two turkeys with one bullet! He turned to her and the gleam in his eye was now one of pride. Yes, and ownership. She was his. Mine first, he exalted. Mine always! "Thora!" he said gruffly. It was a moment for whispered words and peaceful companionship but he was met with only a terrible silence. He brushed her hair back but she turned her face away. Moonlight gleamed dully on her cheek and on her breasts, pale white and dusty rose. He lowered his head but she drew up the sheet so he traced it with his finger. "I'm sorry," he said. "I didn't know."

"You didn't know what?"

"That I was your first."

"Would it have mattered?"

"No. Not once I saw you."

"Will you keep your bargain?"

"Yes."

"That's all I need to know then."

She rose and dressed in the corner and again the words to stop her would not come to him. How had their lovemaking meant so little to her and so much to him?

She was at the door when she turned and faced him. She looked at him for a brief moment. "It wasn't that bad. Really."

He half rose but she was gone.

She found the gun right where Davey Cox had said it would be and had to swallow a cry of disappointment when she saw how small it was. Telling herself to be grateful for what she had, she slipped it into her pocket and climbed off the barrel. She guessed the gun would kill if it was fired from close quarters. She'd just have to make sure she got close enough for it to be effective.

She followed the alley until it emptied into the street. Smoke from the tar-barrel flares on all the corners gave the town a ghostly appearance but there were no ghosts—or humans—about.

Which was why she was so startled when twenty men roared out of a saloon she'd just passed. She slipped into a narrow doorway and hoped no one noticed her.

In the center of the storm were two men who were going at it hammer and tongs. All the others had apparently come outside just to lend moral support. No one paid her any mind; all eyes were on the battling men.

In mere moments, Deputy Bull Durham had arrived and waded through the ring of spectators to use the butt of his pistol on first one man and then the other. While everyone's attention was on the felled men she flew down the street and away from the flares. She set off at a fast trot for the Fagerhaugs', thinking: *I sure hope they don't have a dog.*

So far so good she thought as she crept up the Fagerhaugs' porch stairs undetected. The door opened readily and noiselessly.

There was enough moon for her to see that the old farmhouse's rooms were all off a center hall. She went into an eating room first and had to backtrack. But in the room opposite she found the fireplace. Above it was a mantel and on the mantel, next to a picture of a big-eared boy with Rudy's unruly hair and Dottie's gray eyes, was her brother's cigar box. She turned the boy's likeness toward the window. Harold, the son who never returned from the war, was wearing a uniform and a somber expression and did not look a day older than herself. After carefully removing Halldor's four coins she realigned the box just so and tiptoed out.

She briefly considered going back to the stunted scarecrow-shaped tamarack beneath which was buried her rucksack of necessaries and her oilskin-wrapped rifle, but she decided there wasn't time. She had the boot gun. It would have to do.

On the road again her heart pounded in unison with her feet as she raced toward the depot. She purposefully kept her mind blank, not thinking of Jim Horse, nor about the sticky soreness between her legs. She had vowed to avenge her brother. Her first step was to confront Junior Buel. The cost was immaterial.

Though she told herself these things, she was awash with feelings she had never experienced before. She had no name for the powerful sense of loss she felt as she ran away from Two Sisters, and Sheriff Jim Horse. The only thing she knew was that deep inside something hurt something awful.

Jim made his rounds later with her parting words stuck in *his* liver. Damnit, there are too many women around to pick a hard one to please. *It wasn't that bad. Really.* Half angry, half insulted, he told himself she was out of his mind and out of his life and good riddance! But then it seemed that the stirred syrup scent of her remained on his skin so he stopped and scrubbed his face and hands with snow before he went on.

He paused in front of the mercantile. Inside he saw Goody Tangen locking up for the night . . . only it wasn't Goody's round smiling face that he saw reflected in the glass. That's about enough! Straightening, he looked up toward where the spirits lived and shook his fist. "Damnit, don't start this shit with me."

"You say somethin' t'me, Sheriff?"

The voice was muffled, as was the boy who stood in the middle of the street holding a rope that was attached to a homemade sled. On it were newspapers peeking from beneath a protective cover.

"Naw, son. Somebody else."

It was young John's job to pick up the unsold newspapers Guy Corliss gave away, first come first served. The Dobbers were using newspaper to insulate their drafty attic. John wished his father would send Floyd because John was secretly scared of the dark. Sometimes he imagined things like . . . voices. Without moving his head, young John looked one way and then looked the other. No one. Just him and the sheriff. Young John's neck hairs twanged and suddenly he needed to pee . . . bad.

Next thing Jim knew the kid was dashing down the street so fast a person could've balanced a glass of water on his coattail!

Well, hell! He kicked at a clump of snow. Why shouldn't he talk to spirits if he wanted to? There sure as hell wasn't anybody else!

During the rest of his rounds, he rattled twenty doorknobs and peered into twenty windows. But he saw only one face and it was not his own.

While she waited for the train she hid behind a shed several yards from the station. It was cold. Her breath curled out of her mouth and ice crunched whenever she moved. She put her hands inside her coat and pulled in her neck and told herself she didn't feel it. She also told herself she wasn't afraid.

Fear was not new to her. She had experienced it plenty of times before and with practice she got pretty good at fooling herself into shunting it aside. Not this time. This time her sense of impending trouble was too persistent and too relentless to shake. Nothing would work this time.

There were two cabins beyond the tracks; one large and well lit, the other quite small with no visible signs of life. Suddenly the door of the larger cabin opened, startling her by tossing a knife of light on the snow. The scent of pine smoke floated out, then a thin piping voice raised in query, then a manly grumble, then spontaneous laughter.

A little girl came out. She was backlit by the lantern within as she paused to pull on her mittens. Straight blond hair stuck out from under her hat and muffler, and she had a man's buckled galoshes on her feet. A voice called from within the cabin, the words indistinct but the tone plaintive. The little girl went back and shut the door and then she clumped across the porch and down a path, headed, it appeared, for the privy. A minute later she came trotting back with a funny little fat-legged run. When the girl opened the door, Thora heard a familiar voice. "Bed now, Marne Beckstrom. No more doodling!"

So that's where Meline and her family lived. Ketil the husband. Marne the little girl and a son named Lars who was almost two. A family.

Suddenly hot tears of wanting crystallized on her cheeks. That was the only thing she had ever asked God for. A family who cared so much about each other they would do anything to stay together. Apparently God had answered her and apparently His answer was no.

Now that she thought about it, it seemed pretty mean-spirited of God, considering that it was all she had ever asked for.

A coyote howled somewhere in the nearby hills and set every dog in town to barking in response and she almost didn't hear the far-off whistle of the train.

Chapter 15

No one bothered her on the train. Probably because there were only three other travelers, a salesman reading a feed catalog and sneaking looks at her when he thought she wasn't looking and two veiled women dressed all in black who leaned into each other and slept most of the time.

She had not thought about how she would do it but she did now. Given what she'd heard about Junior Buel she didn't think she could trick him into telling her who the other men were. She also didn't think there was anything she could offer. (Funny isn't it: how she knew Jim Horse's word was good and how she knew Junior Buel's wasn't.)

Now that she thought about it, she realized she actually knew quite a lot about Junior Buel. For example, she knew that he had tormented her brother unmercifully and that he liked to hurt people and animals and she knew he probably wasn't going to be intimidated by a woman—even one with a gun.

So. Knowing these things about him, it was clear to her what she ought to do. Ask him once and for all for the names of the three other men and if he would not tell her, she should kill him.

How, though? She imagined herself walking up to him on the street. She'd ask him, "Are you Junior Buel?" and when he said ''Yeah? What's it to you?'' she'd say, ''Tell me the names of the men who helped you hang Halldor Gunnlauger.'' And he'd say, ''Go eat rat turds.'' And right then's when she'd fire.

No. Every time she got to that part she backed off. It was too fast, too hard.

Damn, of course it's hard! she argued. Death is damn hard.

She imagined herself in a cafe, sitting at a table next to his. She would lean over. ''Are you . . . ?''

All the while she was thinking about Junior Buel and Stillwater, snippets of thoughts about Jim Horse and Two Sisters intruded. How he'd looked when she'd seen him last, one arm crooked behind his head, his black hair turning the gray pillowcase white.

Damn it, Thora!

All right, all right!

She imagined that she climbed into a boarding house window and saw him asleep on a four poster bed. ''Junior Buel!'' she'd cry. ''Wake up and meet your Maker!''

Her mind had decided it had a mind of its own because she could not keep it on the business at hand. With relentless regularity, images of Jim Horse came again and again. If she were honest, one memory more than others. Because she allowed it. No, because she summoned it.

It was the moment when she had looked up at him and saw his face, tight and strained and his eye fever-bright on hers. Their gazes had locked and held as he strove for whatever it was that he had to have. God, the intensity! The passion!

Then as now, her body responded with a strange, new sensation. She closed her eyes and clasped her hands between her legs and rocked slightly . . .

She came to. She wiped her mouth—which was slack and rubbery-feeling—and looked around and saw that the feed salesman was staring at her with speculation in his gaze. Flushing she turned to stare out the window.

All right. All right!

She came up behind Junior Buel and said, ''Don't look around. Just head for that alley up ahead . . .''

* * *

"You can't miss the prison." The man she had stopped was delivering hay by horse-drawn wagon. He pointed over his shoulder. "Yonder's the top of it. Biggest building on the river."

At a few minutes before nine in the morning she was standing in the shadows of an open doorway across from the red brick jail. The dismal daybreak had done little to lighten an overcast sky or her spirits.

What on earth was wrong with her? She should be proud of herself. She had broken herself out of jail—without getting herself killed or killing anybody, and she'd gotten here to Stillwater—without a hitch and with time to spare. Now all she had to do was . . . face down Junior Buel.

She had been thinking about it all night and she honestly didn't know if she wanted Buel's life to last longer because she was afraid to end it or because the deed had more import for her—and for her brother—if it did. Either way she could not see herself shooting him on the street.

But she imagined that she could see herself hanging him. Yes. Now that would be justice. That would be right.

Thus did she reach a decision: If Junior Buel would not tell her the names of the other culprits, she would take him back to Two Sisters and she would hang him as he had hung her brother.

About an hour later the gates clanged and creaked open and two men emerged. One was a seedy-looking young man with unruly hair and ravaged skin. The other was Junior Buel. They looked around. Buel clapped the other man on the back and the younger man did a little jig. In general they both looked as pleased as Punch.

From across the way came a woman—a girl really—who was leading a towhead boy. The younger man moved forward to meet her and they stood together talking. Buel shouted something and the younger man flashed him a look but then he hung his head and stayed put. Buel called out again and though his words were lost in the wind, his tone was clearly jeering. He stood watching the reunion for a minute and then he turned and looked directly across the street toward where Thora stood. His face was cruel and sneering. When he walked off in the opposite direction, she followed. Within two blocks he turned into a place called the Midas Touch.

The saloon had two doors. The front one was guarded by a black man in a stovepipe hat that had been made for a much smaller head. The back door had no watchman and opened into an alley. Since she couldn't be certain which one her quarry would leave by, she positioned herself across the street where she could see both doors.

Three hours later a door slammed and there was a commotion in the alley. Casually she moved in that direction and saw Junior Buel being escorted outside by the black man—without his hat but with a long-barrelled pistol. The black man propped Buel against the brick wall where he hung like a clot of blood. The black man threw some angry words at him and went back inside.

Buel had a cut on his lip, a bruise on his chin and a ripped jacket sleeve. A bottle dangled from one hand like a short club. Putting as much sashay into her step as possible she started toward him.

No one who knew him before would've believed that grim, silent Jim Horse could become such a dreamer. Hell, he couldn't hardly believe it himself. But it was a fact. And now that it had come on him—this dreaming thing—damned if he knew how to get it to quit!

Of course, he used to dream when he was a kid—back before he knew better. Naturally, like kids do, he had dreamt big. The one he'd especially enjoyed was about when he led his people in a bloody but highly successful war against the white man. Through his personal cunning and heretofore unseen feats in hand-to-hand combat, the white armies fell in battle after battle. As victor, he demanded that an Ojibwe nation be formed. Afraid to chance his anger, the white men deeded the best hunting and fishing areas over to his people, and swore to leave them in peace forever.

Naturally his people insisted that he be their chief and he was awarded the biggest lodge, the best weapons, the first choice of any game killed. And the girls! God, the girls were shameless, sneaking into his wigwam during the night and insisting that he share his buffalo robe with them.

Stuff like that.

On a more serious level, there had been an occasion years back when, as part of the ritual of becoming a man, he'd experienced his personal spirit dream. Unfortunately the time the elders deemed right for him to seek his personal spirit was ona'binigi'zis. The snow-crusted month to the Ojibwe. February to the whites. Damn, but it had been cold that year!

After four days of sitting up on that wind- and snow-swept rocky ledge (during which he'd abstained from food, water, sleep and a fire) all sorts of strange visions appeared to him. Which was understandable. He was half-starved and lightheaded from lack of sustenance. Since he was also almost buck naked, he was near froze to death to boot.

That previous experience did not compare to the state of his body or the state of his mind on the night after Thora Gunn left Two Sisters. That night he'd had two helpings of fried chicken, several glasses of liquid and a woman who had offered to hang him out to dry. Apparently he was half dead because instead of taking her up on the offer, he'd gone home and gone to bed. And dreamt. With thousands of people and hundreds of animals. But in the end, in the early hours of the morning, it was her face that formed in his mind.

It amazed him how well his mind worked. Without conscious effort he could recall every detail about her. He could see the wisps of hair that gathered at her temples and the broad, full shape of her mouth. He could still feel the soft beating of her heart against his chest, like a moth's wings against a lampshade.

He rolled up in bed and buried his hands in his hair. Damnit, he was going to have to go to Stillwater. That's all there is to it. Tomorrow on the morning train.

In the jail the next morning he heard Bull's familiar tread and spoke before he turned around. "I'm going out of town for a few days, Bull . . ." The silence or something made him turn around.

The sheriff had been standing with his back to them when

the deputy escorted her into the jail. He said something and then turned. He didn't speak again, just looked at her. Outside she stayed calm. Inside she was shaking like a leaf on a tree. She'd thought of little else but the time when she would see him again. Would he draw her into his arms and say that he too had thought of little else but her?

No chance of that now. Oh, to have to see him like this! She was so ashamed. She had killed a man and would probably lose her life over it. Just when she'd started to hope that in spite of everything she might one day have a life after all.

"I found her north of town, Jim. I was coming back from number six logging camp when I heard two shots. Found her standing over Junior Buel with a smokin' gun. There was a rope slung over a tree limb. Looked to me like she was plannin' to hang him off the same tree limb that her brother died from."

Deputy Durham saw how Jim was staring at the girl. Then he looked at the girl and saw how she giving Jim a stare right back. A long time went by. "Uh, should I put her in one of the cells?"

"Yeah."

"An' then should I go tell Curly to get the body and bring it in? Or do you want to go look it over first?"

"I'll go look it over first."

But then nobody moved. Bull shuffled in place. Then he scratched his chest. Then he noticed a scuff on the toe of one of his new Hyers hand-stitched boots. Cocking his leg, he licked his thumb and ran it across the mar. Ruint! Damn! The second pair this year!

It was only when he almost lost his balance and the girl put out her hand that he remembered her. He lowered his leg and pointed at the cell door. "Miss, if you would walk right this way please?" She first looked at him as if she'd only just seen him there and then she moved silently through the door.

Two days later Thora Gunnlauger—also known as Thora Gunn—was charged with murder in the first degree.

Chapter 16

In the last year Joe Willie had successfully litigated several interesting cases: a trapper who killed his partner in a knife fight; a woman who shot her husband to stop him from whipping their son; and a fella who celebrated a winning card hand by tossing his hat in the air and shooting a mule that was tied to a nearby hitching rail.

That last one had been especially interesting because he did not represent the celebrant but rather the mad-as-a-hornet owner of the dead mule who had attacked the poor shot with a sickle.

Which he had just had sharpened and which almost took off the man's leg at the knee.

Joe Willie had gotten the charge reduced from attempted murder to attempted dismemberment and entered a plea of temporary insanity. Due to an exceptionally sympathetic jury, (How could anybody be that poor a shot?) he got his client off with a fine, payment of all medical bills and probation.

Admittedly he had handled some controversial clients, but his bread-and-butter cases were more like the one he had just settled the week previous. That case had started out as a simple misunderstanding between two neighbors, then escalated to harsh words, then progressed to open warfare.

Jack Merrit, Joe Willie's client, had purchased a breaking

plough from his neighbor, George Gregory. To cinch the deal Gregory threw in the use of a blooded bull for one month. Merrit used the plough once and it busted. The bull, which Merrit had personally observed covering Gregory's cows practically one every hour, would not cover any of Merrit's cows. Merrit went to Gregory and asked him for his money back. Gregory said that Merrit had busted the plough himself; that when he had sold it to him it had been working just fine. If he'd used it as Gregory told him to, it would still be working fine. Ditto for the bull. The reason why the bull would not cover Merrit's cows was because he was too tight to feed him the special grain mixture that Gregory had suggested.

An insulted and incensed Jack Merrit drove his pigs into Gregory's cornfield. Gregory reciprocated by attacking Merrit with a grubhoe. With great difficulty they were restrained from killing each other by their wives, Edith and Eunice, who—it so happened—were sisters! To the consternation of their wives, both men swore never to speak to each other again.

They might've gone on that way for years, but Merrit could not leave it be. The next day a sign appeared on a fence that faced the main road into town. Barn-red lettering on kalsomined white, it read: BEWAIR OF JUNK SOLD BY GORGE GREGORE.

That afternoon Gregory took the sign down and stomped it to bits, but by the next morning another had appeared. Which met with the same end as the first. The following Sunday, a block notice with basically the same message appeared in a prominent place in the newspaper. Gregory uncased an old Sharp's Big Fifty buffalo gun and used it to try and shoot the weather vane off Merrit's house. He succeeded and also put eleven head-sized holes in Merrit's roof. On the following night—fortunately moonless—Merrit moved Gregory's privy back three feet and cleverly camouflaged the hole with leaves and branches.

When Gregory climbed out the next morning he had a crap line to his armpits and blood in his eyes.

Early on in the fracas Joe Willie had been hired by Jack Merrit to get his money back, which was fifty dollars. Joe Willie's fee was considerably less; a figure not worth getting caught in a crossfire for—although in his lawman days he had placed himself in one for less.

Without either man suspecting his intentions, Joe Willie got both of them in his office. He'd had to present his solution to their problem with his feet planted and a hand splayed on each man's chest, but once an agreement was reached—no small feat in itself—he escorted them outside where they proceeded to try and beat the hell out of each other.

Joe Willie's suggested settlement was simple: whoever won the fight won the argument and the money too.

Joe Willie kept the ear-ripping and eye-gouging to a minimum and with the exception of one huge bite out of one hairy calf, succeeded in seeing that the fight was a fair one. When it was over, the bloodied and battered men shook hands and agreed to abide by the compromise Joe Willie had worked out.

For his fee, Joe Willie pocketed three dollars and each man stood him a round at the Wind Fall. He could have lived without the beers but he was glad to get the cash. Often enough he had been paid in everything but coin: bull hides, pullets, wild turkeys, sacks of grain, half a cow, furniture. You name it, he'd got it.

Hell, he didn't care. He'd always known he'd never get rich practicing law in Two Sisters, Minnesota. Besides, Leon Cheever had left him so much money he didn't have to work another day in his life if he didn't want to.

No, the truth was that he lawyered because he loved competing in a pitched courtroom battle. Sissy told him that when he became a lawyer he'd simply exchanged his guns and fists for words. "I think you'd take on any case as long as it promises to be a challenge." As usual she was right. At least up until now. He was admittedly a little squirrely about the State of Minnesota versus Thora Gunn because his client had indicated that she would not do jail time. Which meant no reduction of the charge. Which meant if he lost the case, his client could hang.

That's what Joe Willie was thinking about that wintery morning. That and the fact that even if he wanted to bow out as defense attorney, the poor girl's choices were, to say the least, limited. Aside from himself, there were only two other attorneys in town: Mayor Rudy Fagerhaug, who himself admitted to being more suited to politics than lawyering, and Nathaniel Worthington, an attorney whose clients were businesses such as the sawmill or the lumber yard and who generally declined criminal cases of any sort. Out of that huge pool of talent was supposed to come a prosecutor too. In most cases, if Joe Willie was either the prosecutor or defender, then his counterpart usually had to be requested from the Cities.

When Worthington was offered the prosecutor's job and when, as expected, he refused it, a court appointed one was requested from St. Paul.

The way St. Paul arrived at the man they sent was unique and infinitely fair. Every attorney—even bigwigs—threw their names in a hat. Granted, many whose name got picked sent some lowling from their staff instead of trying the case themselves but there were as many who simply did their duty. Which was how a horse thief without a dollar to his name could find himself represented by one of the most expensive attorneys in the state.

Dill had just informed him of a wire he had received confirming the appointment of the prosecutor in Thora Gunn's case. Henry Jerome Tippet, a man who had one of the best reputations in the Midwest.

For a brief time Joe Willie toyed with idea that Tippet would decline to try the case himself, but he knew that was wishful thinking. With his eye on the state legislature, Tippet thrived on cases with a potential for wide notoriety. And this murder trial promised to be such a case. Too bad. This sort of thing was the luck of the draw and it appeared that Thora Gunn had been dealt a "folder's hand."

Soon as he got word that Thora had been arrested and had asked to see him, Joe Willie went over to the jail to talk to her. His first client-lawyer conference had been quite a revelation. He asked her point blank how she'd gotten Buel to Two Sisters. Easy, she said. Apparently Buel had been so drunk he would've believed her if she'd said she was George Armstrong Custer.

Actually she said she didn't even have to tell Buel her name. All she told him was that she had been sent by a certain lady at the Wind Fall to escort him back to Two Sisters for the biggest celebration of his life. Half coaxing, half flirting, she had played to his huge ego and it'd worked. All Buel wanted to know was which one of "them whores can't wait to get a holt of me again."

"I can't tell you that," she'd said and threw him what she hoped was a sultry look through her lashes. "That would spoil the surprise, wouldn't it? You'll just have to come with me to find out." Then he had, she said, leaned close enough for his breath to make her stomach flip and suggested "Hey, why don't me an' you go to that hotel yonder an' . . ."

"Because the train leaves in ten minutes . . ."

"Hell, it don't take me long."

". . . and we want to get a bottle first."

"Yeah, that's right. A bottle."

She found a car to themselves and kept feeding him the whiskey she'd bought from a vendor near the station and he slept most of the way. When he woke and tried to wrestle with her she pulled her gun and stuck it in his side. "Drink!" she gritted, and he did. He thought it was funny. Said he had never known anyone who was so bent on having a party.

She'd looked wrung-out after that so Joe Willie didn't bother asking her to go into the actual shooting. There'd be plenty of time for that. Besides, Bull said she confessed to him that she'd done it. Hell, he said when he came on her she'd been standing over Buel's body with a smoking gun.

Joe Willie explained what might happen if they went for broke and that's when he'd asked her about doing prison time. She just looked at the floor and slowly shook her head.

He left when Meline brought the prisoner her breakfast and headed over to the cafe. A sea of sad faces greeted him when he entered. Buddy, Goody, Ben Corliss, Conor O'Malley, Rudy and Dorothy and last but not least, his very own wife, Sissy.

Since he anticipated having to explain client confidentiality at length, he went for coffee first. Between the coffeepot and the dessert tray was a little tented card that read: "Defence Dolars for Thora G." The can was close to full.

Fifty bucks said that several of those dollars were his wife's. He knew his Sissy. The first time the can was passed she probably would have put in whatever money she had on her because she'd have been worried that no one else would throw in and that, consequently, his feelings would be hurt.

Before Joe Willie turned to face them, he rolled his eyes skyward and whispered, "Now I'm buyin' my own services."

Thora left half her food but drank all her apple juice and coffee. She was just sitting on the cot, thinking about the terrible turn her life had taken when she happened to glance up and saw Jim standing in the door. At once he looked weary but unwavering. Silent and strong, like a mountain of rock. Which is, she thought exactly what he had felt like. Skin-covered rock.

Neither said anything for a long minute, both thinking of what had transpired the last time they were alone together.

"Nice day," he said at last.

She looked away. "It's snowing," she breathed.

"Yeah, it is."

She knelt and pushed the tray through the opening and when he bent to take it, their faces were the width of a cell bar apart. Neither moved until she finally gathered enough strength in her legs to stand. It had been that or touch him, and from somewhere she got the notion that he wouldn't have drawn back if she had. Was that, she wondered, what he had in mind?

No sooner did she have that thought than she knew what he wanted. He was probably thinking that her trial could be a long one and that she would be willing to do *that* again in return for certain favors! Sure. That's exactly what he wanted. *What a fool you are, Thora Gunn!*

She turned her back to him and stood stiffly at the window until she heard him leave. Then she had some pretty harsh things to say to herself. Whether it was fitting or not, contact with Jim Horse made her think of all the things that Junior Buel's death had cost her. Things like family, love, home, happiness. Since it happened when she looked at him, it followed that she had to quit looking at him. And she needed to quit talking to him too! It was the only way she was going to get through this ordeal with any degree of dignity. Otherwise, she had a strong notion she would end up offering herself to him, favors or no favors.

She had better take a hold of herself right now. When he spoke to her after this she would cut him dead. She had to.

Chapter 17

The following Monday Henry Jerome Tippet arrived on the afternoon train from St. Paul with an entourage of three: a clerk, an assistant and an investigator. Instantly he became a subject of speculation and the topic of conversation at the cafe, the bank, the mercantile, the barber shop and all the saloons. In short, anyplace where any locals gathered.

Soon as his shift ended at the North Star the desk clerk hurried over to the Wind Fall to impart certain facts about the strangers. Everyone in the room—about twenty people—gathered around young Henry Stensland to hear what he had to say. Unused to such attention, Henry swigged on a courageous beer before he began.

The secretarial assistant, he said, was a mouse-faced man of maybe fifty who was named Oliver Mayburry. He seemed a quiet and thoughtful sort. Unfortunately he smoked a sweet-smelling pipe about which Henry had felt obligated to caution him. "Flying embers, you know."

"Yer gonna see a flyin' Henry if'n you don't git on with it."

The speaker was a huge hairy man named Selmar Nelson, a man who was not known for his kind, serene nature, but rather for stomping people with his canoe-sized boots.

The clerk or apprentice lawyer, Henry said, was a comely young man named Nelson Bacon. "He's the one who has an Eastern accent and prominent front teeth. He wears an interesting ring on his left hand that . . . that . . . looks just like a beetle."

Another glance at Selmer hurried Henry on to the third man, clearly the one who interested him most. Carl "The Claw" Cleary. Like many men with pencil-wide chests, Henry was an inveterate fan of the "squared circle" and the manly art of self-defense. Carl "The Claw" Cleary—Henry reported for those who did not know—was the only man to go over twenty-five rounds with Jake Kilrain. Regrettably, the consequence was a potato nose, ears that resembled stewed apricots more than cauliflowers and enough dough-looking scar tissue around the mouth and eyes to top a nine-inch pie.

Perhaps of further interest, Henry reported, was the fact that they had taken over the entire third floor of the North Star Hotel—all four rooms.

The locals looked at each other, intrigued. "Huh!"

"I'll be damned!"

Young Henry was presented with several broad backs as the men moved away to resume doing whatever they had been doing before he arrived. Young Henry was terribly let down. It had been such a short day in the sun.

"What in t'sam hill're they needin' that extry room for?"

"Mebbe ol' Claw eats live animals an' that's where they'll keep 'em."

"From what I hear about Tippet, he may have to have one room just for his fancy clothes."

"Probably got underwear with the days of the week 'broidered on the butt."

"Naw! He'd put that right acrost the business part!"

Generally Joe Willie judged a man on his merits but the next morning when Tippet twirled into his office . . . (Literally. He wore a cape with red lining and cream-colored box toed patent leather shoes.) . . . Joe Willie took an instant dislike to him. With every hair in place and every seam pressed, Tippet was the sort who made a normal fella nauseous just looking at him. Ten bucks said his pockets were lint free.

Tippet had no sooner introduced himself—and patently neglected to introduce his three employees—than he said he was sure that Joe Willie's client would want to plea bargain.

"We might be agreeable to, oh let's say forty years. I understand she's not that old. Why she could be out before she's sixty." He laid a handful of papers on Joe Willie's desk and said he had "taken the liberty of drawing up the necessary documents."

"Taken the liberty . . ." Who the hell really talks like that? Joe Willie was soon to discover the answer to his own question: Henry Jerome Tippet.

"I'm sure you'll find everything in order. I did not draft the plea myself but I dictated every word to my legal assistant and then, as always, I went over his work with a fine-tooth comb." Fingering his watch fob, Tippet paced one way and then whirled on his toes and paced the other.

"I normally would not suggest a settlement before proceeding with at least some part of the trial, especially in an interesting case such as this one will no doubt prove to be; however, it so happens that I have a pressing need to be back in the Cities by the first of the month." He held up one kidskin-encased hand. "Please consider carefully, Mr. Everett. Should you decline our offer, rest assured that there will be no other and that I will then turn my full attention and substantial energy to prosecuting this case to the wire. Let there be no doubt. I will conduct a vigorous and imaginative prosecution which I am certain to win in the end. Which means, Mr. Everett, that your client loses. Which means—at least in this case—that she stands a good chance of losing her life."

Joe Willie just looked at him. Truth be told, he was sort of stunned. Tippet was a blond, goat-bearded man with muttonchop whiskers and a sparse swirl of hair laminated to the top of his head with some sort of fixit that looked like meringue. God, was this Henry Jerome Tippet?

Ah, but don't underestimate him, Joe Willie warned himself. That was, he'd heard, precisely how Tippet had racked up his record number of wins.

"True, your client will spend most of her life in prison but as I'm sure you'll agree, life under any condition is preferable to death.''

Which is, Joe Willie thought, precisely the opposite of how his client felt about it.

''I thought I'd present it to the judge this afternoon . . . As soon as I have your approval, of course.'' Tippet selected certain other papers from a fancy case and aligned them just so by tapping them on the desk. ''What's his name again?'' He pointed at his assistant who said, ''Rice. Franklin Rice.''

Joe Willie slung one booted, denim-encased leg over the arm of his chair. This could be fun. Provided a man could keep from throwing up.

''I asked my associate here to find out where Rice studied, but no one in Minneapolis knew. Do you?''

Joe Willie played dumb. It was easy. He didn't know what the hell the fella was talking about. ''Where he studied?''

''Yes.''

''The law?''

Tippet gave him a long look. ''Yes.''

''Can't say as I ever heard him say.''

''And you never asked?'' Tippet looked mildly shocked.

''Nuh-uh. I get the idea you think I should've.''

''Good Lord, man, of course you ask! Makes all the difference in the world.''

From a boxy gold case he extracted a ready-rolled cigar. One of his men—the oldest of the lot—handed him a pair of ladies' scissors with which he removed the tip. With a minimum of motion, his man took the tip off the floor, dropped it in his pocket and offered a match. As Tippet bellowed his cheeks the smell of chocolate peppermints filled the room. With a heaven-bent expression on his face, Tippet made his mouth into a cherry and blew smoke at the ceiling. Joe Willie's nose holes seized shut.

''It's been my experience that there's a subtle difference between how a Harvard man interprets the law and how a Yale man will. A delicate variation, almost a nuance if you will.'' He had been looking at something beyond Joe Willie's left shoulder. Now he looked him in the eye. ''What about yourself?''

''What about me?''

Tippet's expression said: Hayseed! "For example, is there a certain school from which you prefer your opponents to have been educated?"

"Ah! Because then they have those certain nuances you mention?"

"Yes." nodded Tippet as if to a child. "That's it."

Joe Willie steepled his fingers and looked at the beams. "I like 'em to be from the school of hard knocks." Tippet gave a little I-knew-this-was-a-waste-of-time laugh.

" 'Cause then they'll more'n likely be good." Joe Willie threaded his fingers and reversed them which resulted in a crack that was only slightly less loud than a rifle shot. "Seems to me that that's when lawyerin's the closest to a fistfight, and in both situations I always feel the best when I beat the best."

Tippet's eyebrows met then rose. "I won't say I'm the best . . ." He gave a self-deprecating chuckle. "Though some say I am. Certainly I am very good."

"Great." Joe Willie nodded. "It'll feel especially good then."

Tippet looked into eyes that were like flint points threatening to combust and knew he'd been had. Everett was no hayseed.

Showing nothing, he allowed himself a scornful noise. "Verbal fencing outside of the courtroom is a waste of my time and energy, Everett. Sparring of any other sort I leave to my esteemed colleague, Mr. Cleary." Cleary and Joe Willie eyed each other for a minute. Tippet, meanwhile, was all business. "Well, Everett?"

"Well, what?"

"The plea, man. What about the plea?"

"Oh, yeah." Joe Willie picked up the papers and dropped them into the spittoon alongside the desk. "We're gonna have t'decline, counselor."

Tippet went tight-faced. "I believe you'll rue that decision, Mr. Everett. To say nothing of your luckless client." He buckled his leather case and slapped Mayburry's thin chest with it. "See you in court, counselor."

Joe Willie tipped an imaginary hat in reply. "Oh, say, Tippet."

He turned, impatient now. "Yes?"

"Don't take up an axe ag'in me unless you intend to grind it."

"What a clever country adage. I must remember it." He looked at Cleary. "Help me to remember that, Carl."

The fighter looked at Joe Willie and nodded. "I don't forget nothin', boss."

Two Sisters' population was large enough to warrant their own judge but after what happened with the last one, the town council put off sending for a replacement for years. Their first judge was Leon Cheever, a benign, seemingly kindly old man who murdered four young women and who was also the man directly responsible for Thora Gunn's brother being hung since it was he who planted the incriminating evidence in the boy's room. Little wonder the town was hesitant to invite another stranger into their midst! Time, however, had helped them with that and the previous year the council applied for and got another judge. His name was Franklin Rice.

Rice had been appointed to the circuit court in the early '80's and in the interim had twice turned down a permanent post. When he was asked why he had finally accepted the job at Two Sisters he looked at the inquirer as if he were a nitwit. "Good Lord, man! Don't you know about the fishing?"

"Fishing? Oh, but I don't fish."

Rice then touched the man's arm as if he had said he had been a cripple since birth. "I *am* sorry!"

Since his appointment he had earned the highest respect of those who stood before him, including Joe Willie Everett. He was strong and stubborn in his opinions and a stickler about courtroom etiquette but he was unfailingly fair and dedicated to the law. Out of the courtroom he had become "one of the boys." He liked to have an occasional drink and regularly met with Ben Corliss to argue politics.

Along with Joe Willie, Jim Horse, Doc O'Malley, Goody Tangen and Rudy Fagerhaug, Rice was a member of the regular poker group that met the third Thursday of every month in the back room at the Mercantile. (Arne Stinson and Curly Frye were alternates who were rarely called upon to fill in as the monthly poker game was a much anticipated event.)

Rice was married to an energetic woman of fifty-five named Clarisse who was a bird of a feather with Dottie Fagerhaug. Within weeks of her arrival, she was a member of the school board, chairwoman of the Lutheran Ladies League and most recently, Directoress of the Annual Raffle for the Poor. Charitable to all in want and unfailingly pleasant, Clarisse Rice was popular with everyone in town. Except on the Fourth of July.

She had a passion for poetry—her own—and every year some unknown person would encourage her to recite her long *Iliad*-like poems from the grandstand. (The previous year there'd been a half a sawbuck reward offered for the name of that *someone!)* The sight of her approaching with a sheaf of papers in hand had a phenomenal effect on the crowd. Rudy said the only time he had ever seen so many people move so fast was the day a prairie fire swept the field.

The Rices had two boys, one who was a career navy man and another who was, as Clarisse was wont say, "attached to the embassy in Belgium."

That last always raised some grizzled eyebrows. "What t'hell's that supposta mean? Attached to the embassy?"

"Attached by hvat dew yew figure?"

The Rices bought the old Johansen farm, the infamous run-down place that had been leased five years earlier by the Gunnlaugers. No matter. Six months after Clarisse got her hands on it, it looked like a country farm in a Currier and Ives print.

Thora knew none of this. All she knew after she looked square at Judge Rice for the first time was that he was the man who had told her that Joe Willie was a pussycat.

For Jim Horse the days before the trial were filled with procedures performed by rote. He escorted Thora to the courthouse for preliminary hearings. He escorted her back when they were done. Twice a day he took her to the cafe for lunch and dinner, and then he took her back to the jail. He went home when Bull relieved him and his only visitors were the spirits who were almost always with him now.

For the life of him, he hadn't figured out what they were trying to say to him. Did they have a message for her? Or were they using her to send a message to him?

Not surprisingly, he also couldn't decide what to say to her about what had happened between them. For starters he figured he probably should say he was sorry. He had been irresponsible, both by making love to her and by letting her go. It was his fault that she was in the predicament she was in.

But he would get to that point and inside him something would say: Here now! Hold it right there. He had let her go because he'd had no business putting her in jail to begin with and because it was a custom among his people that a relative of a murdered man had the right to avenge his death. In the old days, no one would even think of interfering with her right. Besides, he had not *made* her go to Stillwater and abduct Junior Buel at gunpoint.

He told himself all these things and still he felt like shit. Saying that stuff to her might be the right thing to do but damned if he could do it. Why? Who the hell knows! It sure wasn't for want of opportunity. She was only a few steps away all day and many nights. Finally he conceded that it was the girl herself. He had heard of people being stopped dead with a look, but he'd never heard of anyone being stopped dead without one. Yet that's how it was. By never looking at him and never speaking to him—other than when absolutely necessary—she'd made him into a non-person. A non-person shunned by the Ojibwe was looked at like water. Certainly one would not speak to a glass of water.

Hell, that's all right with me. Jim Horse, he reminded himself, does not speak to female persons under any condition, anyway.

Then there came along a night when he thought he heard her call to him. After he righted his chair and picked up his coffee cup, he went in, relaxed and nonchalant.

She lay boxed by moonlight, her hands fisted and defensive on her chest, her face frowning and her mouth tight. He heard a grinding noise and realized it was her teeth. He spoke her name once and then again louder, but she did not wake.

She was in a deep but evidently not a restful sleep. He slid down the wall and sat on his heels and watched her until the eastern sky started to turn.

The following night Thora prepared for bed without much hope of waking rested. She was wondering why she never got enough sleep anymore when she saw something on the wall that was unfamiliar to her. Hanging from a nail above her bed was a narrow wooden hoop. Yarn resembling a spider's web was threaded within it as were two small blue feathers.

Clearly it was an Ojibwe charm of some sort so she knew exactly where it had come from, but throwing it away would be very bad luck and to give it back meant talking to the man she had sworn to ignore. She would leave it there. Why not? She needed all the help she could get.

Joe Willie had argued for bail and did not get it. Now it was a matter of waiting for the jury to be selected, a lengthy process that was delayed for three days running because of snow. Joe Willie was worried. If the several prospective jurors couldn't get into town, the jury selection might not be finished until after Christmas.

The names of every man eligible for jury duty—excluding the judge, bailiff, attorneys or others associated with the case—had been placed on separate pieces of paper and deposited in a foot-square wooden box with a slot on top. Twenty names were then selected with the hope that twelve would become the jurors. Unfortunately, the weather did not relent and selecting the twenty names was all that was accomplished before court recessed for Christmas break.

"I want to get this over with!" Thora cried when Joe Willie told her that Tippet had requested and received an additional week's recess. Joe Willie said he'd argued against the extra recess but because of the special circumstances—namely the prosecutor being from another town and therefore away from his "loved ones"—the judge had overruled him and approved it.

Thora generally ate breakfast in her cell. For supper and dinner someone would escort her to the cafe. In the beginning it was Bull Durham who walked her over but after those first few times it was always the Sheriff himself. She often said she didn't want to eat and he would say: then come and sit and don't eat. If she didn't move, he would stand there and stare at her until she wanted to scream.

The recess was only two days old and already she was half crazy, but it came to her as she was crossing the street that Jim

Horse was right. If it weren't for the few minutes when she was outside in the air, she might go all the way over the edge.

A light snow was falling as they trudged over to the cafe. Someone in a sleigh called "Merry Christmas" to them and Jim Horse raised his rifle in response.

The cafe was decorated for Christmas with tied pine boughs on the walls and cut-out snowflakes pasted on the windows. As usual, it was so packed she thought they would have to stand against the wall gathering water around their boots and the attention of every person in the room but, fortunately, the Everetts and the Fagerhaugs had saved two seats for them. Jim Horse greeted people around the room and then sat beside her.

Everyone sensed her mood and spoke of lighthearted things. Sissy talked about how this was little Joey's first real Christmas. "I don't think he understood the concept of presents last year."

"He does now," said Joe Willie. "I told him he was going to get a new brother pretty soon and he said he'd just as soon not. He went and got the Montgomery Ward's catalog and pointed at what he'd like to have instead."

Dottie asked, "And what, pray tell, was that?"

"A huntsman's bugle and a conjurer's trick and magic box."

"My stars! I can remember when we were happy to get a piece of horehound candy."

Thora had no knowledge of these subjects—Christmas, candy, presents—so she kept quiet. Buddy came in to say hello. Her face was flushed and she wielded a long flat piece of wood of a sort Thora had never seen before.

"Whew! It is sure hot in the kitchen!"

"Sit for a minute," said Rudy and pulled Dottie closer.

Everyone pushed around until Thora's and Jim's legs were melded like two books on a shelf. His leg felt thick and hard and . . . bothersome. Creasing and re-creasing her napkin, she shot him a suspicious look but he was eating and apparently unaware of the contact.

Sissy asked Buddy what she was cooking.

"Lefse."

"Ah!" said Sissy and then found something extremely interesting about little Joey's ear.

"The oven must be very hot for lefse."

"Lefse?" Something in Dottie's eyes said don't ask but Thora did anyway. "What's that?"

Buddy perked up like a dog about to be thrown a bone. "You have never had lefse!"

"No."

"Would you like a sample?"

Thora saw Dottie roll her eyes and grew wary. "Mm. Maybe. What's it made of?"

"Potato, salt, sugar, little sweet cream, little butter. That's all."

Suspiciously. "That's all?"

"Yah!" She hopped up. "I get you a little taste." She paused at the door. "Anybody else? Dottie?"

"I couldn't eat another thing!"

"Rudy? Joe Willie? Sissy? Jim?"

She got a chorus of replies. "Too full!" "Thanks anyway, but no." "Gosh, I'm stuffed."

Once Buddy was gone, Thora told her tablemates. "It doesn't sound too bad. Potato and sugar and butter." Everybody just looked at each other then Joe Willie said, "Let me put it this way: If I was gonna make a break for it, this would be the moment I'd choose."

Within five minutes she understood what he meant. Buddy stood right over her waiting for her to speak. Which was not easy to do with a wad of clay in her mouth. "Well!" she managed finally. "It's sure . . . different."

"Yah! Is good, heh? Want some more?"

Using her tongue she unstuck a gob from the roof of her mouth, braced her hands on her chair seat, stretched her neck and swallowed. "I think I've got all I can handle right here."

"Well, there's plenty. Ssst!" Sissy looked up and Buddy jerked her head toward the kitchen. "Better not forget about you know what."

"I haven't." Sissy leaned forward and placed a hand on Thora's arm. "We've got a surprise for you!"

"What?" She sorely wanted to run her finger around her teeth.

"Jim's bringing you to the Christmas pageant at the schoolhouse tomorrow night."

She gave Jim the full benefit of her cool expression and he

gave her one right back. Her leg, she decided, was either sweating or bleeding.

"How can you do that?"

Sissy answered. "Jim and Joe Willie have cooked up a way, haven't you?"

"That's right." Joe Willie answered. "Here's the deal. Judge Rice told Jim that if he had any disorderlies he needed to toss in jail he could temporarily put you up over at the hotel. Now, if on your way to the hotel you should happen to pass the schoolhouse . . ."

"But you haven't had any drunks."

"I know," said Jim. "There's been a remarkable fall-off in crime."

"Which is about to surge up tomorrow night and then fall off again. Right, Jim?"

"That's the plan."

"Say no more," exclaimed Rudy with his eyes shut. "The less I know the better."

"Isn't that clever?" beamed Sissy.

Damned if Thora could keep from smiling back. Most of the time Sissy was more like a mischievous kid instead of a schoolmarm.

"You'll love the pageant," said Sissy. "The children have been making decorations since way last summer."

"Last summer!"

"Well, that's when the juneberry and chokeberry bushes bear fruit."

"What do you do with berries?" Thora had never seen a decorated tree up close. Now that she thought about it, not from afar either.

"Make garlands. We collected them by the buckets full." She went on, "We made the candles ahead of time too. Since our colors are blue and white this year we put bluing in half the tallow and finished them last month. Joe Willie cut the tree yesterday. That was fun. The entire class went along to select just the right one. We've strung popcorn and colored paper chains and . . ."

Dottie made a hissing noise. "Sissy, we better do the other now. Rudy and I have to stop at Goody's yet tonight."

Sissy nodded. "Yes. Sorry. Jim, can we talk to Thora in the kitchen for a minute?"

A brief look at him and Thora could tell that he already knew about this, whatever it was. She wanted to cry: stop being so nice to me! I don't deserve it. I can't repay it!

"If you promise not to make a break for it out the back."

"She won't."

At least this gave her the opportunity to stand but when she did her leg turned cold and clammy and dead feeling. Barely containing their excitement, Sissy and Dottie ushered her into the kitchen. Indeed it was warm in the kitchen. Both Buddy and Meline were sheeny-faced and smiling like crocodiles. "So you two are in on this as well," said Thora.

"Yah!" They cried in unison. "Lewk!"

Hanging on a wall behind her was a dress. A very lovely dress. "Oh, look at it!"

"It's for you," said Sissy with a hug. "Merry Christmas from all of us."

"For me?" It was a quail-colored dress with full sleeves and a tapered waist. Narrow fancy braiding came over the shoulders and formed a pointed yoke which was trimmed with two-inch cream lace. "It looks new!" She touched the hem like a supplicant at the feet of the Pope.

"Brand new!" said Meline.

"New!"

"See this back here?" said Sissy. "It's called the Wateau back. The very latest thing!"

"Try it on!" cried Dottie.

"Oh, I couldn't."

"Please."

"Oh, no. I wouldn't dare. Not until I'd washed from tip to toe."

"All right. But will you wear it to the pageant so we can all see it then?"

"Yes, I will."

"Promise?"

"Promise!" She wiped her hand hard on her thigh and then touched the sleeve ever so lightly. "Yes, I promise."

Chapter 18

Having earlier arrested the requisite drunks, Bull Durham was now set to escort her across the street to the hotel. She carried the twine-tied bundle that held her new dress. He carried the rest of her things in a small burlap bag.

"Sure is slick!" Bull exclaimed on the way over.

"I hadn't noticed."

"Dang ice! Sometimes I think I ought t'get me some of 'em skates."

"Do you know how to skate?"

"Naw! We didn't have any ice where I grew up. But I figure I can learn."

She put a steadying hand on the deputy's elbow and thought: Better learn walking first. "You could try some snowshoes."

"I did that onct. I'd sooner wear milk buckets."

Bull asked the young clerk for the key and they went straight upstairs. At the door he said, "I'll be right outside here till Jim comes t'get you. In case you need anything."

In case you're planning to escape. Another first, Thora thought, staying overnight in a hotel.

Through the lobby and up the stairs her head had swiveled like a weathervane in high winds, and now the room . . . well, it was like nothing she'd ever seen before. She touched the floral rug then lifted one corner and looked under it. Polished wood underneath a carpet! Same as around it! She ran a hand down the flocked wall paper and burned her finger on a wall light that looked too pretty to be real. The big fancy furniture was so shiny she could see her face in it and there was a four-poster bed with a gold counterpane and four (four!) pillows. Right then there came a light rap on the door. For a second she thought the sheriff was here for her already—then she heard, "Your bath, miss."

She opened the door and two uniformed girls rolled in a big galvanized tub that was shaped like a huge coal hod. When they lifted the cover, scented steam rose in the air.

"Just pull this cord when you're done, miss."

"All right." She hadn't noticed the tasseled cord before and went to give it a closer look.

"Oh, not yet, miss. That calls someone up from the basement to tend you. Unless there's something I can do for you now."

"No. I was going to give it a trial jerk." Another girl came in then with a bar of store-bought yellow soap cushioned on three towels.

"Don't worry. It works all right." She spoke like sometimes she wished it didn't. Then she knelt by the bed to pray!

Thora bowed her head but snuck a look to see what everyone else was doing. The others were ignoring her.

It still threw her when people did that stuff! One time years ago they had stopped in a small river town to buy some supplies. Somehow she had been left standing by herself on the sidewalk. Waiting for her mother to discover she was missing, she had been idly watching the people pass when a lady threw herself down on the broadwalk and cried, "I am a bride of Christ!"

That sort of thing would turn a person against public praying forever.

"Here's the chamber pot, miss."

She had ahold of a flowered pot with a lid and a handle. "Oh, good," Thora said. Both for the pot and mistake.

After pushing the pot back under the bed, the girl stood. "Will there be anything else right now, miss?"

"No, thank you. I've had . . ." She let her eyes roam the room. ". . . quite enough."

At one minute after seven Jim and Thora were making that

same walk down the schoolhouse lane. With heightened senses, Thora was never so aware of crazy things like the feel of fabric on her skin and the crunching sound her moccasins made on the snow-packed path. And the man walking beside her. Which was, she suspected, the reason for all the rest.

With his own attentions equally focused, Jim was intensely aware of how womanly she smelled and how she moved like a soft breeze. He might've told her that—*if* he felt like speaking—but she might as well have been walking with a scarecrow than a man. The sum of their conversation was:

"We can't stay long, you know."

"I know." She looked at him then. "Thank you for letting me go."

"I'd've never heard the end of it if I hadn't."

Jim took her coat and disappeared. Thora looked around. The schoolhouse was overflowing with people and decorations were everywhere. Candles in all the windows and lanterns hung on pegs on the walls. Tacked around the room were drawings of gilded angels and eight pointed silver stars and slightly skewed Christmas trees. Each kid had done a drawing of Father Christmas and several couples were standing in front of them, exclaiming how particularly well a particular drawing had been done.

Thora was awe-struck by the ceiling-high Christmas tree. Gingerbread men, peppermint sticks and other confections of various shapes shared the boughs with blue and white candles, berry and popcorn garlands and paper chains. A little boy with a bucket of water was positioned beside the tree and standing nearby could only be his proud parents, a father with slicked blond hair above a two-tone forehead, a young mother with a swaddled baby in her arms.

"Isn't it pretty?" said the mother.

"I'll say!" They smiled at her and she smiled back and a lump started to form in her throat. She turned.

"Merry Christmas, miss!"

She looked at the boy. "Merry Christmas to you too. To all of you."

Sissy saw her and came over. "Thora! Good you're here. I've been waiting for you to start the program." They pressed cheeks. "You look beautiful!"

"Funny you should say that. It's exactly how I feel about this dress. Thank you again."

"You must know that you would be beautiful in rags! Have you eaten yet?"

"No. Not yet."

"Look." She took her by the arm and led her to one table that held baked ham, roast pork, fried chicken and several casseroles made with either meat, noodles, or rice. Then to another that held strudels and "krumkake, julebrod and fattigman" molasses cookies and fudge with nuts.

"I don't know where to start."

"I know. I started on the desserts. Well, I guess I better set things in motion."

The new teacher, young Nils, was present but apparently willing to take a back seat to Sissy. After all, she and the children had planned the pageant together.

She gathered the children and led them in the Christmas carol Peace on Earth, the Angels Sing and after the applause died, they sang Silent Night. Next she introduced a big-eyed, pigtailed girl of about fifteen.

"Ladies and gentlemen, this is Clara Enger. In honor of her grandfather who perished during the War between the States, Clara now will recite Henry Wadsworth Longfellow's poem, "Christmas Bells," which was written by the poet when his own son was wounded and not expected to survive. Clara . . ." Clara gave a discreet cough and fixed her eyes skyward and began.

I heard the bells on Christmas Day
Their old, familiar carols play,
    And wild and sweet
    The words repeat
Of peace on earth, good-will to men!

And thought how, as the day had come,
The belfries of all Christendom
    Had rolled along

The unbroken song
Of peace on earth, good-will to men!

Till, ringing, swinging on its way,
The world revolved from night to day
A voice, a chime
A chant sublime
Of peace on earth, good-will to men!

Then from each black, accursed mouth
The cannon thundered in the South
And with the sound
The carols drowned
Of peace on earth, good-will to men!

It was as if an earthquake rent
The hearth-stones of a continent,
And made forlorn
The households born
Of peace on earth, good-will to men!

And in despair I bowed my head;
"There is no peace on earth," I said;
"For hate is strong
And mocks the song
Of peace on earth, good-will to men!"

Then pealed the bells more loud and deep,
"God is not dead; nor doth He sleep!
The Wrong shall fail,
The Right prevail,
Of peace on earth, good-will to men!"

Like all good things, the poem and the pageant ended too soon. Yawning toddlers were cocooned in blankets while fathers readied sleighs and wagons. Boys raced outside to get to their caches of stacked snowballs. With shrill shrieks, girls played their part by ducking and dodging, and screaming to be saved.

Thora and the sheriff walked back into town with the Beckstroms, Emily Jones and Conor O'Malley. It was a night for stars. In the sky. On the snow. Glinting off ice-sheathed branches. After everyone paused at the hotel to say good night, Thora noticed that instead of turning off at his lodgings, the doctor continued on with the rest. It looked like he was going to walk Emily home. As if they were sweethearts!

In a flash of self-perception, she identified the unfamiliar feeling she was experiencing. Envy. Earlier she'd envied that young family and now she envied Emily Jones. What an awful person she was! Nonetheless, there it was.

At the front desk Jim asked for the key to her room. It was probably just jitters but she was especially mindful of the three strange men who were sitting across the room, staring at her as if she had horns.

"Here you go, Sheriff. The key to 103."

"Thanks. Have you got a chair?"

"A chair." He looked around and then pointed. "Yes, several."

"You care which one I take?"

"Take? I guess we'd prefer you didn't take any of them, Sheriff." He smiled at his own cleverness.

"I mean to sit on it. Out in the hall."

"Oh, yes! Of course. Say no more. I'll send George Gunderson up with one right away."

The clang of a hand bell made Thora jump. At once the boy she'd seen from her jail window appeared.

"George, take a one of those chairs up to the hall outside of 103. No, not that one. One of those padded ones. Yes, that one'll do."

Jim and Thora moved toward the stairs aware that all eyes were on them. They followed the carpet that went up only the center of the stairs then across the landing then down the corridor. There were spindly-legged tables sitting beneath gilt-framed mirrors and beside padded stiff-backed chairs. In case, she supposed, anyone had a need to look at themselves or rest a minute. Her knees felt like she should make use of one.

She went ahead then stood outside the door and waited. She had no choice. He had the key.

"Thora."

"Don't." She touched a place on the door with her finger and bent her head. "Don't say anything."

With his hands on her shoulders, he turned her toward him but she was looking all around him, not letting him catch her eye.

Jim was hurt. She used to look at him like she hated him, now she wouldn't look at him at all. "Thora, I have some things to say to you."

He was actually going to put the proposition to her! She couldn't bear to hear him say it. "There won't be a repeat of what happened that night. Just . . . just forget about it."

"And if I cannot?"

"Try harder."

Clumping boots preceded George Gunderson who carried the chair up on his head and narrowly cleared the ceiling. Quickly she took the key from Jim's fingers and opened the door.

Surprisingly she didn't sleep as well in the hotel as she had in the jail the last couple of nights. Maybe she was getting used to that little pancake mattress or maybe that charm was working.

Or maybe she couldn't forget that Jim Horse was right outside her door all night. It was the strangest thing. She didn't want him ever to touch her again but she didn't mind that he wanted to. Was she secretly a little crazy?

Thora spent Christmas Day back in her jail cell, but she did not want for visitors. The Fagerhaugs came, Buddy Tangen, Sissy and Joe Willie Everett. Even Emily Jones.

They were becoming friends, she and Emily. Probably because they were both young, lonely and alone but Thora was flattered to know that the other girl desired her friendship. No one had ever tried to be her friend before.

Within limits, they had even exchanged confidences. Emily told Thora she was having a baby but not by who. Thora told Emily her version of what happened the night Junior Buel died. But she did not tell her about Jim Horse.

On the day after Christmas, Emily had finished cleaning and

as she often did, took a seat on her overturned bucket to visit for a while.

"I brought you these," she said and passed some mittens through to Thora.

"For me? She was taken aback. She never expected anything.

"They're not new. I found them thrown away and mended them. Goody had almost the same color yarn."

"I can't tell where they were patched."

"Well, they were."

"Emily, I have nothing for you."

"Funny you should say that. It was only this morning that I was thinking about all the things I have. A job. A nice place to live. I don't need anything else except . . ." She leaned forward and pressed a hand to her back. ". . . maybe a new back!"

"Maybe you shouldn't be doing this sort of work, considering." Thora said that but she was thinking of her mother who worked all the time she was pregnant and had never had a hurt back.

"I'll be fine. Thora . . . ?" Her face was striped by moonlight through the bars.

"Yes?" Emily looked at her then looked at her hands. "What?"

"Well, I was wondering . . ."

"Yes?"

"If maybe you would like to live with me when you get out."

"What makes you think I'll get out?"

"I know you will. First off," She counted her fingers. "Joe Willie Everett is defending you and second because you're innocent. No matter what your intentions were when you brought that man to Two Sisters, he tried to force himself on you. A woman, every woman, has a right to fight back then."

Her voice rose there at the end and she'd waved a reddened fist in the air. Thora didn't know what to say and so said nothing. Neither did Emily and Thora got the impression she felt like she'd already said too much. Save for a rumble of masculine conversation coming from the other room the silence continued until Emily stood.

"Well, I have some cookies to drop off for Doctor O'Malley

before I go home. He refuses to take my money so I told him he'll have to take my cookies." She didn't sound like stopping was much of a chore. "Thora, you don't have to decide about living with me right this minute. I just wanted to mention it now so you could be thinking about it. I'd love the company but there is one thing . . ." She looked at her.

"Yes?"

"I'm worried about the baby."

"Why? Doesn't everything feel all right?"

"Oh, yes. It's not that. I'm worried that you might not care to live where there's a baby fussing in the middle of the night."

Thora snorted. "I can hardly sleep without one fussing." They shared a laugh then Thora asked, "You sure you're all right?"

"I think I am. The doctor says I am. I wouldn't mind if I had more money to see me through the time when I can't work, but at least I'm feeling better. I used to get awful sick in the morning and my . . ." Her voice dropped to a whisper. ". . . my breasts ached so I could hardly bear to have my clothes touch them."

Thora's head jerked up at that but Emily didn't notice.

"Well . . ." Emily stood. "Day after tomorrow will be the beginning of the end."

"I'm not sure I like the sound of that."

"You know what I mean. The sooner the trial starts the sooner you'll be free."

"Think so?"

"Absolutely. See you tomorrow."

"Bye."

For a long while Thora sat as dazed as if she had been hit on the head. All those babies her mother had had and she never mentioned anything about getting sick in the morning and having her breasts hurt. She crossed her arms and touched her breasts.

Oh God! Until Emily said those things she hadn't realized what was happening to her. She was going to have a baby. And its father was her jailor!

Chapter 19

The courthouse was a one-story building with the business end in the front of the building, and a few small offices and the judge's chambers in the back. The courtroom itself was large, windowed on two sides and furnished with benches up to a wood railing that ran the width of the room and separated the audience from the trial participants. The audience sat on rows of benches spaced so they made an aisle on each end of the room as well as down the middle. Judiciously placed around the room were tall hourglass-like cuspidors.

The lawyers sat at two long tables in front of the judge, whose desk was on a raised platform six inches or so above the rest of the room. To his left was a noisy grandfather clock—a gift from the son who was "attached" by something "to an embassy." Beside it was the blue and gold fringed Minnesota state flag and Old Glory. To the judge's right was a straight-backed witness chair. Closest to the small table where the court reporter would sit—but still separated by a good six feet—was the ladder-backed defendant's chair. Opposite that, under a bank of west-facing windows were twelve empty chairs for the jury.

The prosecution waived a formal arraignment of the defendant so the jury selection process could begin immediately. *The*

Daily Clarion carried a front-page account of the action up to and including their selection, and even published a short biography of each.

A female on trial for murder was big news in Two Sisters. Hell, it was big news state-wide.

A few of the venire (men called for jury duty) were excused because of personal hardship or due to the importance of their jobs. Dill Wyatt, for example, because he was the only man who knew how to run the telegraph. Ketil Beckstrom, Meline's husband, because he was the only one who knew how to run the new planing saw at the mill.

Big rawboned Ketil stood in front of the Judge working over his cloth cap in his rough, hamlike hands. "I vant tew dew my dewty, Yudge, but I yust don trust no one on dat ting yet."

The mill had experienced a resurgence of business since adding a tie-manufacturing section that provided the railroad with sawed ties rather than hewn ones. Business was so good it now employed almost a quarter of the town's male population.

"You are excused for cause, Ketil, er . . . Mr. Beckstrom. Next."

Despite those excused they had their twelve jurors in record time. Joe Willie looked them over, left to right.

Erland Nilsson was as bald as a billiard ball but a person would never know it because of a stocking cap worn down to his brows. A big barrel-chested man of about fifty, he and his team of thick-backed oxen scraped the winter-scarred roads in the spring then filled in any holes with sand. For this he was guaranteed two dollars a day but as an incentive he was paid an additional ten cents a rod. It was all that was necessary for a Scandinavian. Nilsson many times earned more than the minimum, and the roads around Two Sisters were the best in a hundred miles.

To survive the rest of the year, he fished and sold his catch to the Northern Lights Hotel or to Buddy's place. One day a man from the Cities offered him five dollars to take him along fishing! Boy, that caused talk! But after that day every once in a while someone else would come up from the Cities, looking for Erland Nilsson and wanting to do the same! It continued to cause talk every time it happened.

Next was a farmer named Gunder Gundersen who had nine children all with names starting with "G." Sissy had taught most of them, but the only names Joe Willie could remember at the moment were Grunde, Gust and George who worked at the hotel and was "a little slow."

Though no more than forty, a scarcity of teeth made Gundersen look old beyond his years. Nine kids might have had something to do with it as well.

Long-time resident Jean Baptiste-Gervais worked during the season as a "river pig," one of the men who rode the logs down river to prevent any logjams. Out of season he was worked as a jack of all trades at the sawmill.

Funny thing about Baptiste-Gervais, he always wore his caulk-soled logger boots. Those who liked him said it was because he had no other shoes. Those who didn't said it was because he liked the manly sound they made on a wood floor. That's how people were about Baptiste-Gervaise. They either liked him or they did not. He had the chancy temperament of a small man and had done his share of brawling.

Next came Arne Stinson who had taken over the leather shop previously owned by Buddy's husband. Stinson had done so well with the business that he had soon had to move into larger quarters. Which was when Joe Willie arranged to sublet the shop for his office.

The white pine was pretty well gone from the woods around Two Sisters but Arne, recognizing an opportunity, had hooked up with a German man with the lofty-sounding name of Ludwig van Brandt and gone into the furniture business. In less than three years the business had become a resounding success and beautiful oak, maple, ash and walnut pieces were now being shipped all the way to Des Moines and clear over to Omaha!

A taciturn, hardworking man who was well liked and highly respected, Arne was—in Joe Willie's opinion—a shoo-in for foreman.

Alf Harper was a teamster who owned four ox carts with which he transported goods from several trading outposts to Duluth or International Falls. Harper was rarely in town but since his permanent residence was Two Sisters he was eligible for jury duty and did not beg off as he could have easily done. It was a hard time of year to be on the road and Joe Willie figured a couple of weeks indoors might be a welcome respite to him.

At twenty-eight the youngest member was Terrance Byers. As the school janitor, Byers was paid thirty cents a week to clean and do minor repairs at the school, and he performed other odd carpentry jobs to get by.

And so it went. Ole Johanssen, tanner; Loren Mitchell, blacksmith; Elmer Homme, gunsmith; Curly Frye, full-time barber and part-time undertaker; Fred Putney and Jack Dawson, pig farmer and dairy farmer respectively. Ordinary working men with, Joe Willie hoped, ordinary horse sense and no highfalutin ideas about justice.

Like her husband, Sissy Everett was also studying the jury and as she looked them over a recurring thought came to mind: why wasn't a woman who was on trial for murder being judged by any women? A person regardless of gender is supposed to be judged by his or her peers—a peer being defined as an equal before the law. How then could these men be Thora Gunn's peers? Her only equals were other women, yet none sat on the jury because jurors are selected among voters and women were not allowed to vote.

To Sissy it seemed another example of the awful injustices that stemmed directly from refusing to grant women full citizenship rights.

Her next column began to take shape in her mind. Headline: *Inequality Before the Law!* Sub-head: *Women in America and The Prejudice of the Justice System.*

''Hear ye, hear ye. The Circuit Court for the County of Crow Wing, Minnesota is now in session. All please be seated.''

On the opening day of Thora's trial ''closed'' signs appeared at the newspaper and the mercantile and Buddy's Cafe. Some signs, like Buddy's read: ''Closed 'Til Dinnertime.'' Some, like the one at Pastor Nels Oulie's house and at the rectory where Father James McWhirter lived, suggested that those souls in want: ''Come to the Courthouse!'' Many proprietors figured everyone knew where they were and so didn't bother with signs at all.

It seemed that the entire town planned to attend the trial. Sissy told Meline that the only thing she could liken it to was when the ice was first off the lake and the walleye were biting.

When all were settled, the judge rapped his gavel once and said, "The matter before the court today is the people versus Thora Gunnlauger. The charge: Murder in the first degree. Miss Gunnlauger, if you please." Thora stood. Joe Willie joined her and stood at her right so that they both faced the judge.

Sissy watched her husband and—as always—she liked what she saw, his square hard hands, his blunt face and sharp eyes. He looked capable and determined and formidable. But she was still nervous as a cat. Buddy, who sat beside her, must have sensed something because she squeezed her hand and said, "It will be all right."

Sissy squeezed back. "I sure hope so."

"Thora Gunnlauger, how do you plead?"

Thora opened her mouth and Joe Willie answered. "My client stands mute, Your Honor."

"Very well. A plea of not guilty will be entered into the record."

It was then that Tippet challenged the venire as a whole.

"Your Honor?" He had a melodious voice, not loud but commanding in tone.

"Yes, Mr. Tippet?" Rice sounded annoyed. He guessed what was coming. They had already discussed the voir dire (questioning of the jurors to see if they can be impartial) at length in chambers!

"If it please the court, Your Honor, I really must go on record about the jury."

The onlookers would soon find that Tippet always posed when he stood to address the bench. If one thumb was hooked in a suspender or in a vest armhole (Today exposing a blindingly white boiled shirt!) then the other hand would be steepled on the table or flitting butterfly-like in the air.

Sighing, "All right, Mr. Tippet."

"Your Honor, I respectfully submit that this jury cannot help but be prejudiced. Simply by virtue of their being longtime residents of this town they have to have been exposed to some degree of bias."

With one eye on Franklin Rice and one eye on the jury, Joe Willie saw Curly Frye lean close to Alf Harper who was sitting in front of him. As one, Curly, Alf and Loren Mitchell stood up.

"What t'hell's that supposed t'mean? Exposed to, uh, whatever that was?"

The judge held up his hand. "One minute, gentlemen. Now, Mr. Tippet, all of these men have been through voir dire . . ."

Like a big bug antenna, Mrs. Willman was working her ear horn this way and that. "What? What'd he say?" Dorothy Fagerhaug, who had the misfortune of being seated next to Two Sister's oldest citizen, tried to holler in a whisper. "Mr. Tippet doesn't like the jury."

"Tell him to quit an' go home then."

The jurors were all talking at once. Rice held up a hand to stay Tippet. "Allow me deal with the jury first." He turned to address them. "The prosecution charges that you gentlemen are . . ."

Curly Frye leapt up again. "We heard exactly what he said! Hell, Judge, you know yourself that most of us is married!"

Judge Rice rapped the gavel to quell the twittering from the audience but Sissy thought that the hand he rubbed across his mouth concealed a smile. "Curly, what the prosecution . . . Mr. Tippet . . . means is that you cannot render a fair judgment because you already favor one side or the other. Not because you were deceitful when questioned earlier, but because you lived through the occurrence and know all the people involved."

"Aw hell . . ."

"No cursing in court, Curly."

Curly chewed his next word first then said, "Bless us but we ain't gonna be unfair! We meant that when we said it at the da . . . durn beginnin' of everything."

"I believe you, Mr. Frye. Well, Mr. Tippet?"

"I'm sorry, Your Honor, but that is merely the tip of the iceberg."

"I feared that might be the case."

"For example, I understand the defense intends to call wit-

NEW YORK TIMES BESTSELLING AUTHOR
JANELLE TAYLOR
DESTINY MINE
SHANNON DRAKE
BLUE HEAVEN BLACK NIGHT
BESTSELLING AWARD-WINNING AUTHOR
GEORGINA GENTRY
SONG OF THE WARRIOR
BETINA KRAHN
MIDNIGHT MAGIC

nesses who can testify to the incident that he feels precipitated Mr. Buel's murder . . . the death of one . . ." He consulted his notes. "Halldor Gunnlauger. That being the case, Your Honor, I wonder how the defense intends to question himself as the sheriff at the time of the murder?"

Joe Willie stood and addressed the judge. "I intend to read the deposition I made at the time and allow Mr. Tippet to question me as he would any defense witness."

"That'll be fine."

"I must protest, Your Honor! That would be highly irregular . . ."

Mrs. Willman again. "What? What'd he say?"

Tippet again. "I am afraid I must make yet another formal . . ."

The gavel met wood with a resounding smack and everyone shut up. The judge wanted to hold his head. Between Tippet and that old crone sitting in the front row he felt a fierce headache descending.

"Mr. Tippet, as you know, a trial must be held where the crime is committed unless you can prove prejudice and you have not, in my opinion, done so. Now. Let's not get into a paper fight, gentlemen. I can poll the panel verbally or have them swear out affidavits that they have no preconceived notions of guilt or innocence. I will do which ever you prefer, but I personally would rather that we poll the panel now, verbally, and get it over with once and for all. Would that be acceptable with you, Mr. Everett?"

"Yes, Your Honor."

"And you, Mr. Tippet?"

The way he said it meant it would have to be. Tippet nodded his assent but he wasn't happy about it.

Each juror was polled again and asked to swear that he was unbiased. All answered in a subdued manner except Curly Frye. "Hell, yes and . . ." He pointed at Tippet. ". . . you tell that fella to watch his mouth."

There was some snickering but Rice rapped hard on the table with his gavel. "There'll be no further outbreaks of any kind including profane ones or this case in which you all show such inordinate interest, will be closed to everyone but the participants." He turned. "And you, Curly, will be replaced."

A hush fell, one so complete everyone in the court—except Mrs. Willman—could hear the pendulum clock on the dais. She leaned close to her beleaguered neighbor again. "What'd he say?"

"That does it!" Angrily Rice motioned to a man sitting at a small desk stacked high with papers. "Bailiff?"

"Yes, Judge?"

The bailiff was Woodrow James, a small scholarly-looking man who had moved to Two Sisters from Rochester some years back. He lived quietly and kept to himself but word was that he had five cats and kept them all indoors, a habit that made him strange by anyone's yardstick.

The judge leaned close. "Woody, who *is* that old bag?"

"Mrs. Willman, sir. She lives . . ."

"Never mind. I place her now."

"Oldest person in town, Judge."

"I know. I know!"

While allowing his nerves to settle, the judge considered the hefty-set woman who had a shock of dandelionlike hair and a face like a dried apple. He'd seen her around town and he recalled thinking to himself that she was shaped just like the shepherd's-staff cane she always carried.

"I wonder how old she is?" Overhearing the judge's musing question was Bull Durham who stood off to one side, supposedly guarding the prisoner. "Older'n God, Yer 'Oner."

"I believe that, too. Well, we can't have her constantly disrupting the proceedings and I have a feeling she'd fight like a wildcat before she'd be expelled." He thought a minute. "Woody, I want you to take a chair and place it right there." He pointed to a spot that was the tip of a triangle between himself and the witness chair, and the jury. "Good! Now, Bull, will you be so kind as to escort Mrs. Willman to her new seat?"

When his instructions had been followed he addressed the old woman who now sat by herself, in the eye of the storm, so to speak. "Now, madam. Tell me . . . Can you hear me?"

"Yes, I can."

"Good. Listen very carefully when anyone speaks and try not to interrupt."

"Well, speak up then!"

"Thank you." The judge turned his attention to the defendant. ''Miss Gunnlauger, the constitution of the United States guarantees you a speedy and public trial before an impartial jury. You are also entitled to know what you are charged with and to confront any witnesses against you and to have the advice of counsel. Do you understand your rights, Miss Gunnlauger?'' She nodded. ''Please be so kind as to answer yes or no.'' He pointed to Woodrow and smiled. ''For the record.''

''Yes, I understand.''

''Good. Now . . .'' To the prosecutor, ''Do you wish to make a formal objection, Mr. Tippet?''

''Yes, Your Honor. For the record.''

Rice nodded. ''I thought you might. Fine. Leave it with Woodrow and I will look it over tonight. Now . . .'' He glanced up. ''Something else, Mr. Everett?''

''My client prefers to be addressed as Gunn. Thora Gunn.''

''All right. Please make a note of that, Bailiff. Mr. Tippet. All right then.'' He rapped the desk with his gavel. ''Bailiff, are you ready?''

''I am.''

''You may begin your opening statement, Mr. Tippet.'' The judge sat back with his arms folded, and Tippet had no choice but to comply.

Until the judge addressed her it had seemed to Thora that everyone had forgotten her. Or that they would like to. She sat directly across from the jury but on the few occasions when she glanced that way everyone on the panel quickly averted their eyes.

It seemed that the people in the gallery were avoiding her too. Except for Sissy Everett or Dottie Fagerhaug or Buddy Tangen. When either caught her eye they all made a point of smiling encouragingly or fluttering their fingers at her.

Since she had now spent several days in court, she had noticed a definite pattern in the way things happened. When they first came in, Bull Durham would seat her and then go back to check guns as people came in the door. When finished, he would carry the armload of weapons up front and drop them with a loud clatter on the small table beside the bailiff. Apparently oblivious to the bailiff's glare, Bull would then go take up his position against the wall at her right.

Jim Horse always stood in front of the double doors that led to the street. His stance was a familiar one. Legs slightly apart, rifle in the crook of his arm. With his hat pulled low it was not possible to see his face but she suspected that he was watching everything with that all seeing eye of his. She often imagined that she felt his gaze touch on her, but since she never looked directly at him she couldn't possibly know one way or the other.

Just like she couldn't possibly know that today he was wearing a dark wool plaid shirt out over buckskin pants which were tucked into knee high moccasins.

Tippet made an imposing opening statement.

"Gentlemen, I intend to prove both motive and premeditation by the defendant. I will show that she harbored a misguided notion of revenge against the deceased which—in her twisted thinking—justified the willful planning of his execution." Tippet moved to the center of the room and deliberately placed his back to her.

"First a word about the victim, gentlemen. Yes. The victim. A person who, according to the dictionary, has been killed, destroyed or injured. A person who is so often forgotten by goal conscious trial lawyers.

"In this case, gentlemen of the jury, the murdered man was Maxwell Buel the Second, also known by his nickname, Junior. He was an unpretentious man who I understand preferred to be called Junior. I will accord him his wish and I do so from here on out.

"Buel's family moved to Two Sisters in the late '70s from New York City and Maxwell Buel, Sr. built the North Star Hotel and started the sawmill operation. Both are still profitable enterprises though their ownership has passed into other hands.

"Understandably, as owners of those establishments, the family used to have considerable standing in this community. Junior, as his father's only son—indeed his only child—contributed to his family ventures on a day-to-day basis, either as manager of the hotel or as his father's right hand man. As a consequence he was someone people were used to seeing here and there around town. No doubt some of you were proud to have called him 'neighbor.' "

That comment caused some people to look at the person next to them and curl their upper lips.

Tippet talked a bit longer about how much the Buel family had influenced events in Two Sisters over the last decade and Thora for one thought that one event he missed mentioning was Junior's part in the death of her brother. The closest he came to it was saying that Buel was not "perfect" and had "erred, but then . . ." He shook his head ruefully. ". . . who among us can say that he is perfect?" Then he jumped ahead to Junior's release from prison.

"Junior Buel served four years for a mistake of judgment about which, by the way, he always professed extreme remorse. Then, finally, the bright day came when his sentence was behind him. Imagine how he felt on that fateful day! At twenty-nine he was looking forward to the rest of his life. His debt to society was paid, and he was free! He survived, gentlemen, for one slim day because . . ." Tippet turned to point at Thora then and Dottie told Sissy she looked like she was trying to become one with her chair.

". . . because the defendant executed him in cold blood. Indeed, she forced him to accompany her here to Two Sisters solely in order to make some sort of ritual of the act!"

He made his voice more reasonable. "Now, my colleague will try to tell you that his client killed in self-defense but you will hear evidence which will prove that claim false. Why, by the defendant's own admission, Junior Buel was not armed when he was shot! And how would she know that, gentlemen of the jury? Because she disarmed him! My dear friends . . ." Some more lips rolled there. "Let me make something perfectly clear. Killing an unarmed man is murder in the first degree. Harbor no misconception about that. It is murder in the first degree."

Joe Willie sat straight and motionless at his desk but to those who knew him well, his restless eyes showed how impatient he was to get started. He was destined to cool his heels a bit longer.

Tippet went on to state that he had all the ammunition he needed to convince the jury "beyond a shadow of a doubt" that they had no choice but to send Thora Gunn to the gallows. Then, finally he appeared to be winding down.

"Once you have heard the oral testimony of the various witnesses and once you have the facts and hard evidence before you, you will have no choice. Not only will you have to convict her of murder in the first degree, but you will have to recommend that she hang as well.

"Did I detect a few flinches? Yes! It is an unpleasant duty! But it is one that you swore you could do. One that you must do! One that by the end of this trial I guarantee that you will have no qualms about performing." He turned to stare at the defendant who sat with a bowed head. "Gentlemen of the jury, do not let her innocent appearance deceive you. This girl . . ." He pointed at her again, straight-armed and with his body as rigid as a matador. ". . . is a cold-blooded, calculating murderess who . . ."

Sissy Everett shot out of her chair like the time in the outhouse when she had felt little legs on her bare buns. "Stop it! Stop badgering that poor girl this instant!" She sat back down, flushed but momentarily quite pleased with herself.

Before his wife's untimely interruption, Joe Willie had been watching the jurors' faces and was gratified to see several frowns. Which was why he was not objecting. The more Tippet badgered his client, the more sympathy the jury had for her. The jury? The whole place!

Despite the pounding of the gavel a rumble rose around the room. From the back someone cried, "Gavekk, darlig mann!" Someone else yelled, "Fand Slyta!" and from another came "Heste Lort!"

Five minutes into the trial, thought Rice, and I am about to lose control of my courtroom. He looked specifically at Sissy and pointed his gavel. She bit her lip and stared at her hands. *My stars! What got into me?*

"Believe me, I'm only going to say this once more. The next time someone speaks out like that, this room will be cleared of all but the participants. I'm not kidding now. Am I understood?" There was dead silence. "Go ahead, Mr. Tippet."

"I was about finished, Your Honor." A little bow. "I will yield to my learned colleague."

In Joe Willie's opening argument he spoke about the real victim in this case, Thora's brother, Halldor Gunnlauger. "My counterpart says we can call Maxwell Buel the second 'Junior.' Good. To cut confusion I'm gonna call the defendant's brother Thor because that's the name this town knew him by. Thor.

Let me tell you how and why he died. First off he was lynched after a trial by fury. The judge was Junior Buel. The jury was four other men who took the law in their own hands only to find out after the deed was done that the real murderer was someone else. Because of them, a poor, simple-minded boy was hung in error."

Thora wondered if she could listen to all of the things that would be said in this courtroom. Earlier she had thought she could, but now she wasn't sure.

"Many of you present can recall the day that Thor was discovered in that old farmhouse. What was to be done with this boy/man? That was the question. Some people said he would have to be sent to the poorhouse in St. Paul. Others suggested the state insane asylum. But there were others—and many are sitting in this room right now—who insisted that there was room for him here in Two Sisters. Those kindhearted souls won out, and in the end, this town collectively adopted him.

"Now, think about that for a minute. If we . . . this town . . . accepted responsibility for him then, in a way, we . . . this town . . . must now account to his sister for his death, because isn't it true that if we had allowed him to be sent to the poorhouse, he'd very likely still be alive today?"

That was a sobering thought and one that made many people exchange looks with their neighbors.

Shattering that significant silence was an angry cry. Over the top of his glasses Judge Rice searched the crowd until he found a squalling baby being bounced around by a red-faced young woman sitting in the back row.

Joe Willie continued speaking but few could hear him, including Woodrow who was trying to record his words. He threw the judge an imploring look.

"Mr. Everett, one moment. Madam, I'm sorry but could you please?"

"I'm stayin'," said the young woman and promptly handed the child off to the young man on her right. Obviously an unwilling recipient of the gift, he tried to hand the baby back but he was pointedly ignored. After an angry whispered exchange, the father got up and stomped outside. With the child.

Jim Horse pulled the door closed behind him and for a brief second Thora saw a smile on his lips. She couldn't've have been more surprised if she saw a snake crawl out of his shirt!

"Please continue, Mr. Everett."

Basically Joe Willie said that he intended to prove that Junior Buel was killed by Thora Gunn in self-defense. He said a lot of other things as well, but that was it in a nutshell.

It was quite late when he finished his statement and resumed his seat. Shortly thereafter, Judge Rice pronounced the court adjourned for the weekend.

That night Sissy waited in the outer room of the jail while Joe Willie talked to Thora. It was not a very long conversation. He was attempting to bolster his client's confidence, but she was very depressed about how the day had gone. Obviously Tippet's opening statement had impressed her more than his had! Riding home, he discovered that Thora wasn't the only one.

Sissy fussed with Joey's blanket for a while and then she asked, "Joe Willie, not that I think it will happen but what will you do if she gets convicted?"

"Then we'll file an application for a pardon."

"Oh." She thought a minute. "What are our chances of getting it?"

He grinned at her. "Hell, I got one, didn't I?"

"Yes, you did!" She smiled back at him and squeezed his arm. "Good. An application for a pardon. Good."

Joe Willie put his arm around her and clucked to the horse. Actually he was less sure than he sounded. John Pillsbury had been governor of Minnesota when he was pardoned whereas the present governor was Lucius Hubbard, a man who publicly and with clocklike regularity advocated a tougher stance on criminals. Rumor had it that he was a woman-hater as well. None of which was very encouraging.

To himself Joe Willie admitted that he was worried. If he lost this case, would Thora hang? It was not an academic question but a real one. And the answer was: mebbe so, mebbe no. As far as sentencing went, it could go either way. Franklin Rice was bound by law to take the recommendation of the jury into account but Joe Willie knew that he'd had no compunction about hanging people in the past. Knowing that during the next week Tippet intended to call witnesses who could and no doubt would attest to Thora's clear intentions to commit murder encouraged him even less.

Sissy had her head on his shoulder. Maybe asleep. She tired easily now, what with the baby and all. He dropped a kiss on her head and got a "Mmm" in reply. Asleep all right. He smiled and snugged her in closer.

Joe Willie had no misconceptions about himself. His face, shaped by work, war, weather and contact with various hard objects, had never been the sort to make girls swoon. But Sissy Heck had swooned. For some crazy reason, she thought he was the most handsome man she had ever laid eyes on! She also thought he was the best attorney in the entire United States!

Hell, he wasn't about to tell her she was suffering from delusions. He urged the horse to go a little faster. He wouldn't disappoint her for the world. He had to win. That's all there was to it.

Chapter 20

Tippet was thorough—Joe Willie gave him that—calling in a parade of unknowns who were asked to testify to Buel's previous good standing in society and then more witnesses who were asked to attest to the fact that he had been a model prisoner. The last witness presented prison records to prove it.

During his cross examination, Joe Willie produced depositions from three fellow prisoners who had witnessed acts of violence by Buel and then he called as a defense witness the clerk from Stillwater Prison, a man named Samuel Swearengen. He was a well-built man in his late forties with heavy jowls that squared his face.

"You knew the deceased pretty well, didn't you?"

"Not pretty well but well enough."

"Is this your handwriting here on this prison record?"

"Yes, it is."

"Then you knew him well enough to make these notes about his progress once a week, right?"

"Yes."

"It was your job to interview the prisoners and note the results of that interview, right?"

"Yes."

"Did you also make note concerning any trouble reported to you?"

"Yes, I did."

"Mr. Swearengen, will you take a look at this prison record for the months of November 1883 and March 1884 and tell me if those notations are in your handwriting."

He took some rimless glasses from his breast pocket, hooked them around his ears and examined the papers. "No, they are not." He handed them back to Joe Willie.

"Whose notes are these?"

"I have no idea. I don't recognize the hand."

"Can you think of any reason why someone would have substituted another's notations for yours?"

"Yes. Because there were notes during those months that would have reflected unfavorably on Buel's review before the parole committee."

"What would it take to get these records changed?"

Swearengen gave a little laugh. "That's easily answered. Money." He went on to say that almost any blemish could be removed from a prisoner's record for a price.

Of course, the implication was that Buel had paid to have his record changed so that when he appeared before the parole committee for the first time, it—and he—appeared lily white.

"Thank you, Mr. Swearengen. Your Honor, I submit these documents as a defense exhibit."

"Will you cross examine, Mr. Tippet?"

"No, Your Honor." Fearing Swearengen might remember the actual notes he made, Tippet declined.

But Joe Willie had plans to return to that issue, at least with respect to an incident that occurred in November 1883. Later that week he called to the stand two former prisoners who had a different angle on the same story. One man had come on a young prisoner lying in a seldom-used hall. He was near death from several knife wounds, but before he passed on he managed to say that his attacker was Buel. The other former prisoner said he'd overheard a conversation Buel'd had with another man a day previous to the attack. Buel did not mention a name but was pretty riled and said that if he "couldn't have him, no one else would either."

The men in the court room exchanged sickened looks; the women exchanged puzzled ones.

Joe Willie left it at that, but that night he spent a long time fending off questions from his naïve young wife.

With few exceptions, business and commerce had virtually ceased, except for the saloons which continued to do a land-office business. (Good somebody was doing it; the land office was closed.) Buddy started making washtub-sized batches of stew—the night before, of course; not when court was in session—which she could easily sell during lunch the following day. Meline Beckstrom doubled her baking output by getting up at four in the morning and whatever she produced in those extra hours in the kitchen she could sell in front of the courthouse between eight and nine. Buddy approved of industriousness. "A person must make straw while the sun shines," she exclaimed.

Occasionally someone in need would enter the packed courtroom and peer through the haze of smoke for Doc O'Malley or Goody Tangen or whoever. If they spotted the person they sought they would hiss and wave until someone would apply their elbow to the requisite person's ribs. Turning with a scowl and then a sigh, the desired person would rise to squeeze past locked knees and raised toes in order to reach the aisle. Those in need soon learned that it'd better be more than a spool of thread or a boil in the nether regions!

Word of the trial had also spread out of state. By the end of the second week, big-city newspaper reporters were arriving from all over. *The Herald, The Mail, The Word, The Evening Post,* and of course, *The Twin Cities' Tribune* were carrying coverage about the "beautiful accused murderess" right below articles about Jay Gould and Jim Fisk.

"We are overrun with small-town newspaper men!" Ben Corliss exclaimed with disgust. The editor of *The Daily Clarion* was having breakfast with Joe Willie and Jim Horse in Buddy's. The cafe had not one vacant chair.

Ben glared at a table of men across the room. "Look at them! All hot shots from some glamour spot like Yankton or Madison. First thing they want is for somebody to supply them with a place to write! Professional courtesy, they call it. Next thing you know they'll be asking me for a place to sleep!" He gave an indigent snort. "Professional courtesy, indeed! Freeloading's what I call it!"

Joe Willie winked at Jim. "Nothin' pushier'n newspaper fellas!"

Ben looked at him and then at Jim and started chuckling. "All right. All right."

"Excuse me, gentlemen."

Everyone looked up—but Jim, who kept cutting up his ham. Ben's face took on a Speak-of-the-devil look! "Let's see, don't tell me. You're . . ."

"Ronald Kellogg. *Bismark Tribune.*"

"Ah, yes. Mr. Kellogg. I'm sure you know that this is Joe Willie Everett and that this is Sheriff Jim Horse."

Jim barely nodded to the newcomer than returned to the ham. Joe Willie hard-eyed him. "You any relation to Kid Kellogg?"

"No. At least I don't think so. But I am kin to Mark Kellogg."

"Mark Kellogg?"

"Yes, he was my cousin."

"Anybody ever call him Kid?"

"No. Just Mark. Well, his mother called him Markey."

Joe Willie shook his head. "Never heard of him." Then, "I wouldn't mind runnin' into the Kid again."

"My cousin uh Mark . . . was the correspondent who accompanied Custer's 7th on their last ride. I'll bet you knew him, Sheriff."

"I wasn't in on that one," replied Jim dryly.

"But you've heard of him . . ."

"Custer or Kellogg?"

Ben and Joe Willie chuckled.

"Kellogg, of course." He was getting nowhere fast.

Jim said, "Can't say I have." He looked at Joe Willie. "You?" Joe Willie shook his head. People in Two Sisters were willing to be agreeable to strangers. With exceptions.

"Well, I suppose that's understandable." The man's tone had turned condescending. "You folks probably don't get much national news around here."

Ben Corliss opened his mouth to speak but something under the table make him hold his peace.

"You *have* heard of the Battle of Little Big Horn?"

"Yeah, we have," replied Joe Willie. "We heard of Wounded Knee too."

Kellogg and Joe Willie had a stare down and Kellogg blinked first. He turned to Jim Horse who was still eating. "Wonder if you'd mind clarifying something for me, Sheriff."

Jim set down his fork and using his thumb pushed his half-full plate away. "I guess."

Kellogg pulled out a small note pad. "For the record, Sheriff, could you tell our readers how the defendant escaped? I understand she was being held for some reason—the rumor is protective custody—and suddenly she's on a train to Stillwater."

"Yeah?"

"Well, some might say that if your office hadn't been lax in your duty, Junior Buel would be alive today."

"I guess you could say that he would."

Kellogg looked from one man to another, incredulous at their lack of concern. "Would you mind clearing the matter up?"

"What matter?"

Was he speaking the same language? "How she managed to escape?"

Joe Willie rolled a toothpick around in his mouth. "She overpowered you, right Jim?"

Kellogg didn't have to hear snickers from the surrounding tables to know he was being made a fool of. "Can I quote you on that, Sheriff?"

"On what?"

"That she overpowered you?"

"Sure."

He closed his book. This was a farce. Well, he'd interviewed difficult people before. Sometimes it worked to get them riled up a bit. Sometimes they'd blurt something out in anger that they wouldn't have said if they'd had time to think about it. It was worth a shot. "On a more personal note, is it true that you are the only Indian sheriff in the United States?"

"I don't know. I never made a study of it."

"Is it possible that right there may have been the problem?"

"What do you mean?"

"Well, doesn't Indian culture condone . . . even encourage . . . vengeance."

"You think the reason I let her go was because I'm an Indian?" That there was some truth to what Kellogg said was what really riled him.

Kellogg winked. "Well, maybe that's only part of it." His tone said man-to-man-you-can-confide-in-me.

From Joe Willie came, "Why don't you quit dancin', Kellogg."

"All right. The sheriff's got a reputation of being a high-blooded man with a big penchant for white women." Several breaths were indrawn. Joe Willie and Ben both started to say something but Jim stopped them with a look. He slowly rose until he towered over Kellogg. "That's a damn lie." Kellogg stopped his furious writing and looked up. Jim Horse leaned close enough for him to see the flecks of yellow in his eye. "I've got a big 'penchant' all right. But it's for all women."

That night Jim was thinking about that conversation as he escorted the prisoner over to the cafe for dinner. He looked over at her and thought: Penchant? Is that what the whites call this slow burn inside?

Thora's spirits were dragging. She couldn't hide her disappointment in the way the trial was going and she didn't feel well besides. She'd stopped throwing up but food still made her queasy and she was having trouble sleeping again. She knew she'd been losing weight. Even the sheriff had started looking at her with concern in his eye. Matter of fact, she imagined that's how he was looking at her now as he held the door open.

Well, she told herself, at least it was better than his usual look. Which was how she imagined a caged fox might watch a pullet.

"Hello, Thora!" Sissy said. A line appeared between her brows. "Are you all right."

"Yes. Why?" *God, she didn't think it showed!*

"You look a little peaked."

"No, I'm fine." Feeling someone's gaze Thora glanced at the next table and met the intense scrutiny of a stranger. She looked away and tried to ignore the man but he stared at her until they finished eating and left.

The next day an article appeared in the *Bismark Tribune* under Ron Kellogg's by-line. Dill Wyatt was the one who warned Ben Corliss as to its contents because he was the one who sent the wire to Bismark. Painting the girl as a *femme fatale,* it hinted quite strongly that Jim Horse had let Thora go to Stillwater in return for certain favors.

Joe Willie was more angry than Jim and Jim swore that if he ever laid eyes on Kellogg again he would roast him head down over a slow fire. Since the vow was made in the presence of several witnesses no one was surprised to learn that Kellogg had left town on the next train.

Unfortunately his was not the only negative article. The *Twin Cities' Tribune* ran an outraged report about an "accused murderess staying in the most luxurious hotel in town" and how she was "brazenly eating her dinner in a public cafe without leg irons, indeed without any restraints at all," and how she "exhibited a haughty mien and festive manner."

Considering how she'd been feeling, Thora would have gotten a chuckle out of any article (if she'd known about it) that intimated that she was having a high old time.

Goody looked up from his paper. "M-i-e-n! Hvat is dat?"

Ben Corliss spoke without looking up from his copy. "Means facial expression."

"Yee-sumchrist! Vhy don' dey yust vrite dat den?"

Of course, Ben editorialized strongly in her favor. Sissy pointed that out to Joe Willie that morning as they shared their paper but he responded, "Fine for public opinion, Sissy, but it's the jury I've got to sway."

Tippet's questioning of the next several witnesses was obviously designed to imply that Thora had not been attacked by Junior Buel—as Joe Willie had insisted in his opening argument—but that she routinely tried to seduce people to get what she wanted.

The tactic backfired with Dill Wyatt, the Western Union agent. "Only thing she ever offered me was a little beaded purse."

That morning Tippet wore a fawn-colored suit, a white shirt trimmed with a tiny strip of ivory lace and a vest with pearl buttons. "You're quite sure she wasn't offering something more . . . personal."

"Hell, I know the difference between a beaded purse an' the other. Don't you?"

"You're excused, Mr. Wyatt," Tippet said and returned to his chair.

Under the cover of some twittering, Joe Willie leaned close to Tippet. "Shame on you, Tippet. One of the first rules of interrogation is never ask a question you don't know the answer to."

Sissy turned to Buddy and nodded sagely. Her Joe Willie knew exactly what he was doing. Oh, yes! Buddy leaned close. "That Tippet always looks like his under clothes are too tight!"

Buddy was right. Sissy contrasted her husband's pleasantly blurred features and easy, persuasive voice to Mr. Tippet who seemed stiffly posed and perpetually frowning. She nodded. "I think Joe Willie's trouncing him so far."

"Me tew!"

"Hey! Do you mind?"

Together they displayed their pinked cheeks to the angry man in front of them and whispered, "Sorry!"

Eventually Tippet got down to brass tacks and called the coroner, Conor O'Malley.

"Dr. O'Malley," Tippet said. "Will you please describe to us the exact location of the slugs in the body."

"Two .44-caliber bullets were fired. One struck the victim in the left lower inner quadrant of the abdomen, about an inch below the belly button. The second . . ." He consulted his notes and Joe Willie saw his jaw muscle working. The same thing happened when he tried to bluff at poker. He seemed to gather himself before he began again.

"The second bullet entered through his right eye and exited his skull eight centimeters above the left ear . . ."

"Excuse me, Doctor."

Tippet held up one hand and paused for effect which earned him a look of disgust from Joe Willie. Today he wore a brocade vest with silvery threads in it. Around his neck and down his shirt was an elaborate arrangement of sea green silk. Goodgawd-amighty!

"Tell us exactly how that bullet was fired."

"Out of a gun."

Snickers from the jury got them a glare from Tippet.

"Let me rephrase that: How did she . . ."

Joe Willie half rose. "Objection to that 'she,' Your Honor."

"Sustained."

Tippet nodded. He didn't really think he would get away with that. "How did the murderer fire the gun? Standing? Or from the ground?"

"Standing, I'd say."

"And the victim? Where was the victim when the murderer fired the second time? Standing or on the ground?"

"The second shot was fired while the victim was in a supine position."

"Whut's supine?" said half the room in unison.

The judge explained. "Face up. On his back."

"Was there any evidence of powder burns?"

"Yes. The material of his shirt was burned from the first bullet"

"All right. Now About the second bullet. Is it safe to say then that the murderer . . . or murderess . . . was standing over the victim with the gun very close to his head?"

Joe Willie stood. "Your Honor, I think I'll object to the word 'victim' and to leading the witness."

"Sustained. Please use 'deceased' and rephrase your question, Mr. Tippet."

He did, but then Conor O'Malley had to admit that it happened pretty much like Tippet said it did the first time around. Not good, thought everyone in the gallery who was rooting for Thora Gunn.

"Thank you, Dr. O'Malley. I have no further questions."

On cross examination Joe Willie asked Conor to give him a summary of his examination of the defendant.

"When did you examine Miss Gunn?"

"The afternoon of the day following the incident."

"What, if any, evidence of a struggle did you see?"

"She had bruises on both arms."

''What sort of bruises.''

''Finger marks.''

''Anything else?''

''A bruise on her chin and contusions on two places on her neck.''

''Do you believe that any of these injuries were self-inflicted?''

''No.''

Joe Willie paced off a square, then asked, ''Was there anything else that struck you unusual?''

''One other thing?''

''Yes?''

''That neither party had a holster.''

''That's not that unusual, is it? A lot of people wear a gun in their belt.''

''But I didn't think a belt gun fit Junior Buel.''

''Your Honor, pure conjecture on the witness's part.''

''I agree. Rephrase your question, counselor.''

''All right. Doctor, did you find evidence of a gun sheath or a casing that would be suitable for a pistol on the deceased?''

''Yes. He had had a special pocket sewn into his jacket.''

''Where?''

''Under the left sleeve.''

''Was there a gun in it?''

''No.''

Joe Willie picked up the boot gun Thora had taken with her to Stillwater. ''Was the pocket made for a gun this size?''

''No.''

''What size was it then?''

''It might fit many guns. For example, the murder weapon slipped into it like a hand in a glove.''

''Thank you.''

Looking at Dottie, Sissy made her eyes thin and nodded gravely.

''What?'' whispered Dottie. ''I don't get the importance of that.''

''Junior was killed with his own gun. That means they must have fought over it.''

''Really?'' said Dottie and leaned back. She still didn't get that out of it.

* * *

When called to the stand, Deputy Sheriff Bull Durham confirmed much of what Conor O'Malley said on cross examination by attesting to the fact that he too thought there were signs of a struggle. Then he recounted when he had heard the shots and how much time he thought had elapsed between the second, final shot and his arrival at the scene. He crossed his long legs and added, "Her face was the color of a wrung out rag."

Dryly. "Thank you, deputy. Now, when you first confronted her did she say anything to you?"

"Yeah." There was a long wait.

"Please tell the court exactly what she said."

Bull worked his butt on the chair first. "She said, 'Oh, God, I've killed him!' "

At that moment a freckled-faced reporter from *The Tribune* took Thora's photo. He had been standing in a little alcove and so had not been observed preparing for the shot.

Coming as a complete surprise, the flash and loud noise caused several men to reach for their weapons and then to look at each other with chagrin when they remembered that their weapons were a snarled mess on a table up front. Jim Horse was on one knee with his gun pointed at the previously ruddy complected photographer. Thora had her face turned away and appeared about to cry.

Judge Reed stood. He was fuming. "Remove that man from this court. He is not to be allowed back under any circumstances."

He could've saved his breath. Jim already had a hold of the man by the seat of his pants and the scruff of his neck and was toe dancing him outside. Several men thought about where his pants were binding and grimaced.

"If any one else attempts such a thing in my court I will fine them one hundred dollars and take their equipment for a year."

"I doubt that fella's equipment'll be usable for a year."

The judge wisely decided to recess the court for lunch. As he gathered his things, he heard the usual rustling of paper and the sound of lids being unscrewed from jars. He looked up and his hands faltered. Mrs. Willman had extracted a piece of chicken from her pocket and was already gumming it into pulp. Several people were half turned in their seats in order to talk to their neighbors as they ate.

They were afraid to leave their seats for lunch because they might not get another one when court reconvened in the afternoon! Rice looked at Woodrow and mouthed: "Amazing!"

And it was. Just look at the number of people who had dropped everything to attend! From listening to conversations and comments here and there, Rice had learned that most all of them were drawn for the same reason. Morbid curiosity. About Junior Buel. About Thora Gunn. How had she done it?

The ones who had known Junior Buel were amazed that a mere girl would've attempted such a thing. Maybe if she was snaggle-toothed and sprouted hairy warts it might've been easier for them to swallow, but an innocent-looking, lovely young thing! Who was she anyway? How had she grown up? What was the story of her life? Some spoke about her in hushed tones, almost as if she possessed some magic power or something.

The bailiff drew the judge's attention from the galley. "Are you going to the hotel for lunch, Judge, or over to Buddy's?"

"Buddy's, I think. Is today Tuesday, Woodrow?"

"Yes."

"Then Buddy's for sure." The Tuesday special was liver and onions topped with thick smoke bacon, all of which the judge liked to smear with a nose-tingling mustard. Clarisse hated liver, so if he wanted it, he lunched at the cafe on Tuesdays.

Just then Meline Beckstrom came in with her young daughter trailing along behind her. Meline carried a tray with apple fritters and donuts for five cents apiece. The little girl carried a tight woven basket with a handle for the coins. Sales, he noted, were brisk.

"Say, Woodrow?" Franklin Rice had a brontosaurus-sized sweet tooth.

"Yes, Judge?"

"Will you purchase one of those apple fritters for my afternoon break?" He extracted a coin from a small vest pocket. "Here. Get one for yourself too."

"Why, thank you, Judge."

"Oh and Woody?"

"Yes, Judge?"

"Crack one of those windows, will you?"

"All right." Woodrow looked at the window then back at him. "Uh, Judge?"

"Yes?"

"It's pretty cold out today."

"I'm aware of that, Woodrow." The judge pointed at the audience. "But I wonder if you're aware of what most of those people have brought for lunch?"

Woodrow paled. "Oh, no!"

"Yes."

"Not again!"

"Uh huh. Hard-boiled eggs."

"I'll crack two."

"Good."

Franklin Rice closed the door that separated his chambers from the now noisy courtroom and immediately loosened his black foulard cravat. He should've passed up that apple fritter. He had been putting on so much weight lately that even his collars were getting tight.

He opened the door to his office and Great Scott! There was the cleaning girl. Passed out on the floor. Her bucket had overturned and soaked her skirt. Or was the stain too dark for water? Great Scott!

Robe flapping, he raced down the narrow corridor, opened the door to the courtroom and spied Woody dropping a coin in Marne's basket. His hissed "Woody!" went unheard over the hum of fifty conversations so he spread two fingers in his mouth and let loose with an ear splitting whistle. All noise ceased and every face turned in his direction. He straightened and drew his dignity about him and motioned to the bailiff.

Woodrow hurried over. "Yes, Judge?"

"Woodrow, please find Conor O'Malley and bring him here right away."

"Is it an emergency?"

"Yes!"

"Yes, sir!" He rushed off. "Conor O'Malley. Find Dr. O'Malley! Emergency!" The room became a bedlam.

When all hell broke lose Thora was following Jim out of the courtroom, headed for Buddy's for lunch, and in that moment of confusion when everyone was either looking at the judge or looking for Conor O'Malley, Davey Cox passed her a double-bladed bone-handled pocket knife with a three-inch blade.

Sissy caught Joe Willie before he went back in the court house. ''Oh, Joe Willie! Emily Jones has lost her baby!''

They were standing out in front, him with his arm around her shoulders, her with her head on his chest. (The Everetts were oblivious to the social stigma attached to a public show of affection. Always had been. Always would be.)

''Hell, I didn't even know she was having one.'' It struck him that others maybe didn't know either and he glanced around but he needn't've worried. Everyone else was already inside. ''Was that what all the hubbub was about?''

''Yes. Franklin Rice found her passed out on his office floor.''

''Damn! That's a shame.''

She tugged on his collar until he lowered his lips for a kiss. ''I hate to miss even one of your wonderful words, Joe Willie, but I'm going to go over to the doc's and sit with her. Conor's there, of course, but she might like to have another woman to talk to.''

His face softened. She was quite a girl, his Sissy. ''Hey, did I ever tell you that you're an acre of sunshine in my life?''

''Not today yet. I'm going now. Kiss me like you mean it.''

''I always mean it.''

''Tell me how much tonight.''

''Deal.''

He watched her trudge toward the doctor's and grinned. From the back she had a shape just like a top. God, he loved her! Suddenly she turned back and pointed at him.

''Don't take anything from that ol' Tippet!''

''Have I yet?''

She grinned. ''Never!''

Chapter 21

When the mantel clock struck three in the morning Emily Jones was still awake thinking about how much she wished she was at home. Home! Home sweet home! Never had that saying meant more! Funny how fast it had happened, but home to her was now—and maybe would always be—that little cabin in the woods.

Though the outside of her tiny cabin was now uglier than ever with its new fresh-peeled logs standing out like raw scars, the inside had been made quite . . . homey. There were two rooms, one a small sleeping alcove, the other a living, eating and cooking area with a clawfoot stove and a muscle-making hand pump.

All the furniture and utensils she had acquired through the charity of the Lutheran Ladies League were supposed to be castoffs but she suspected the iron skillet, pots and a rocking chair with floral patterned cushions might have been purchased outright! There were also no signs of wear on the log cabin quilt or the hand-tied rag rugs or the towels.

Used or new, she owed a lot to those ladies and intended to volunteer her services just as soon as she got on her feet again. If she were ever allowed to get on her feet again. She moved impatiently. She sure hoped Meline had remembered to stoke up the stove this morning and that Marne had left enough milk out for Blossom.

Blossom! Illogically Emily was worried about a cat that, until it decided to adopt her a few weeks back, had probably spent her entire life out of doors.

The small female feline had been standing outside one morning when she went to use the privy. Giving it an ear scratch had been a mistake because it followed her to the privy and cried at the closed door. When she went to push open the door just enough for the cat to come inside, the wind caught it and banged it back flat against the wall and there she sat, staring bug-eyed at the road. The cat, meanwhile, had pranced inside and was doing figure-eights around her exposed ankles.

Fortunately her cabin was the last one along the road.

For no other reason than she liked the name, she called her Blossom. She was not young and not a bit pretty, with a mottled orange coat and only half an ear, but she had integrity and bearing. And she very much liked Emily's nice warm cabin. Sitting on some rags in an egg crate set in front of the stove, she purred so Emily could hear her from the bedroom!

She checked the clock again and sighed quietly. Oh, how she wished she were out of this embarrassing situation where she could grieve her loss in privacy. Unfortunately Dr. O'Malley had insisted that she spend the night in his examining room "under observation." She rolled her head on the pillow. There he sat "observing" to beat the band.

He had his faded denim shirt open at the throat and its sleeves rolled elbow-high to bare frayed cuffs and thick hairy forearms. His head rested on his hands with his face, care-worn and slack in sleep, turned toward her. Such a strong face, not especially handsome but one that had become very dear to her. Which was yet another reason why she wished herself home. Feeling unsettled and weak-willed, she was worried that her defenses would slip and she would break her oath.

Almost from the beginning she'd resigned herself to falling in love with Conor O'Malley. Also from the beginning she had resigned herself to the consequences of unrequited love: a lack of fulfillment and awful unhappiness.

Of course she had also sworn herself to secrecy. Really, how could she have done otherwise? She was a fallen woman soon to give birth to another man's child.

Quite unselfishly—but not without tears—she had been praying that he would find a wonderful woman to love, a life-long partner who would love him back and take good care of him. Someone kind and cheerful who would make sure he ate and slept enough and had all the mahogany-haired children he desired.

Speaking of hair, he also needed someone to remind him when to get his cut! Why, just look at that head! Unruly as a farm kid's! Suddenly his eyes opened and he sat bolt upright.

"I must've dropped off. Are you all right?"

"I'm fine. But look at you."

"Me? Why? I'm all right."

"You're eyes are red as a boil. What good will you be tomorrow?"

"Never mind my eyes." From force of habit he ignored the mantel clock and checked his stemwinder. "Good grief, it's after three! What are you doing awake?"

"I can't sleep here. I want to go home."

"Tomorrow maybe. And you must sleep."

"I can't. I'm not a bit tired."

"All right then." He stood. "I'll brew some tea for us both."

She shook her head. "I don't want tea. I want to go home."

She folded her arms and rolled her head on the pillow. Stubborn as they come, he thought. "I'll brew some tea and after I go to all that trouble, you'll feel bad if you don't drink it."

She sighed. "Oh, all right." Then, "Wait! Doctor . . . please wait a minute."

"Yes?" He turned back but such a painful pause followed that he sat down and put his hand on her arm. He so wanted to see her happy! This moment and always. "What is it?" She chewed her lips and plucked at the coverlet. "Oh, I know. You want sing 'Oh Susannah again'!"

"Good gracious no!" She looked at him horrified, saw he was joking and smiled a little. "You!"

"What then?" The mantel clock ticked once twice and yet again before she finally turned those big pleading eyes on him.

"I was wondering if I . . . will I be able to have other children?"

He expelled a breath he hadn't realized he was holding. "Of course you will. Many women lose their first child and then go on to have a dozen more, all hale and hearty."

"But why didn't my baby . . . wait to be born?"

"It had nothing to do with a fault in your makeup or . . . or in the child's. It just happens."

"But not always."

"Certainly not! Look at all the healthy babies in the world. To which I'm sure you will add your share."

She smiled up at him. "You're . . . you're quite sure?"

"Positive." She searched his eyes and apparently believed what she saw.

"All right then." A big sigh. "I guess I will have some tea."

"Good! If you like we can pass the time with a game of checkers."

"Heavens! I haven't played checkers in years." A pause. "However, I must warn you. I was the champion checker player of my neighborhood."

"And I must warn you that I used to be the champion of mine."

"Was that in Dublin?"

"Yes." She had her lip rolled. "What?"

"European style!"

"I . . . guess so. I wasn't aware there was a difference . . ." He caught her lip twitching then and said, "Just you wait, miss!"

"Hah!"

"Hah yourself!"

He found a tray and placed a fringed napkin on it and started a fire under the kettle and tried to ignore his conscience.

He hadn't been completely honest. Oh, he'd told the truth about her physical condition and her excellent chance for healthy children in the future. But he had lied about her baby, something he simply never did to a patient. No doctor should. What he should have said was something like: "God in His infinite wisdom has removed from your womb a child who would never have survived." Because that was the truth. Her child's multiple malformations had undoubtedly had a great deal to do with her spontaneous abortion.

However he did not because he could not. Lord, what if he had, and she'd asked to see the child? He shuddered, picturing again the misshapen foetus that was awaiting the spring thaw in Curly Frye's back room. Who knew how superstitious she was? Even an objective person such as himself (a person who would supposedly never believe anything inconsistent with the known laws of science) had been shocked by the sight of that tiny face, dented almost as if by a hoof!

He'd decided there and then that he'd not take a chance on spoiling her normally optimistic outlook. She was such a plucky little thing, always smiling, always saucy and he very much wanted things to work out for her.

Now, right there's another lie. The truth was that he wanted to have a hand in working things out for her himself! With sudden clarity he realized that he would marry her in a minute if she would have him. Unfortunately she had never given him any indication that she would.

On a positive note, however, neither had she encouraged any other men in town. At least not to his knowledge. Maybe she had been so emotionally scarred by her experience that she wanted no man!

Ah, but she did want children and so did he. He nodded several times. Thing for him to do was bide his time and watch for the first sign that she might welcome his suit.

He leaned close to the kettle and peered at his reflection. Damn! He ran his fingers through his hair and buttoned his shirt. He stuck his finger in his mouth then into the baking soda jar then back in his mouth and vigorously scrubbed his teeth.

The shrill whistle of the kettle jarred him back to his task. He removed it from the fire and inspected two cups for cleanliness. He blew into one and then augured it out with a dish cloth.

Like his ol' mam used t'say: "When ye wan' somethin' ye mus' blacken yer boots an' be first in line." As he looked for the checkers, he hummed "The Soldier's Song."

* * *

Thora was in a bind. She had done well in keeping her vow to say as little as possible to Jim Horse, but she was worried about Emily Jones and Bull Durham wasn't on duty that night. She would just have to ask.

The door was cracked, the plane of light occasionally broken by his body as he moved around the room. "Sheriff?" He pushed the door open.

"Yeah?" As if the bars weren't enough she had stepped back a bit and clasped her hands at her waist. It wasn't lost on Jim. Nothing was. Not how she looked or what she wore. Nothing.

Her cell had undergone a transformation. There was a three-legged table and extra lantern from Dottie. A blue and gold wedding ring quilt and a spool-backed rocking chair from Buddy. A stack of books from Sissy. A basket of dried fruit and sweets from Meline.

She stood centered in this homey setting. Big-eyed and beautiful as a woodland doe . . . but not as tame. She stopped him from removing the key from his pocket. "No . . . I don't need to make a trip."

In spite of himself, his heart jumped. "What then?" To steady a trembling hand he put it high on a bar but she noticed only how well he filled out his buckskin jacket.

"I was wondering how Emily Jones is. It's been almost a week since she got sick."

"She's home but the doctor won't let her work yet."

"Is she that sick?"

"Not the way I hear it, but the doc's being extra careful. So careful there's been talk."

"What sort?"

"Some're saying his interest must be more than medical."

"Really?" She smiled, then he smiled and suddenly in her mind she was flat on her back again, beneath the slick heat of his body. She felt a stab of response the likes of which she had never felt before. Luckily he nodded and left. Just in the nick of time! She slumped onto the cot. Heaven help her! If he only knew the effect he had on her she'd be flat on her back all the time!

When court reconvened, the animosity between the two attorneys was as obvious as a rat on the kitchen table. Spectators said they found themselves watching the two men so much they often missed key testimony. Some days even simple dialogue between them erupted into a near shouting match.

"Your Honor, this sort of blatant conduct is outrageous."

"Your Honor, I'd like to go on record as . . ."

"That's it!" The judge threw his hands up in the air. "Both counselors up to the bench, please." As the two men reached the bench, Judge Rice leaned down in order to look them both in the eye. "Gentlemen, I cannot take any more. Further, I won't. I'm sick and tired of this bickering."

"But Judge, I have a legitimate objection to Everett's line of questioning."

Joe Willie and Tippet and the judge had their heads close together.

"Then present it to me and not to the room as a whole."

"Judge, you'd already ruled on that objection. If you recall . . ."

Joe Willie felt certain he was making his point until he noticed that the judge's attention was on something beyond his right shoulder. Half turning he found he was looking down the business end of Mrs. Willman's goat horn ear trumpet. She had her eyes closed in concentration, listening for all she was worth.

The three men looked at each other and the only one who didn't see the humor of it was Tippet, who drew back in order to glare down his nose at her. As if it sensed the shift in conversation, her horn whipped around and stopped under his chin.

"Your Honor." He boomed at the top of his voice. "This . . . is . . . ridiculous!" He stomped back to his seat and lit a soothing cigar. Mrs. Willman augured her ear and resumed position. Summoning as straight a face as possible, the judge picked up a pencil and rapped on her horn until she looked at him.

"What?"

"Mrs. Willman."

"Yeah?"

"What are you doing?"

"What's it look like I'm doin'?"

"It looks like you are eavesdropping."

"That's exactly kerrect! Half the time you fellas are whisperin' clear up here where the rest of us can't hear."

"Some of what we say must be privileged er . . . private."

"Why?"

"Why?" He looked at Joe Willie. "The reason escapes me at the moment."

"There ya go. There ain't no good reason."

The judge sighed. "Perhaps you'd be happier if you joined me up here on the bench."

She craned her neck to look at the judge's barrel-backed chair. "What bench?"

"It's just a saying that means 'sit back here with me.'

"Looks t'me like I'd have to sit on yer lap." She gave him a hard look. Up. Down. "If I was gonna sit on some man's lap, it sure wouldn't be yers."

The spectators went wild. Laughing. Talking. Several jury members stood and called out to their friends.

Franklin Rice had little choice. He had to do something. He could not close the courtroom to spectators—Two Sisters was his home. On the other hand, he couldn't overlook pandemonium.

And then on the third hand, there was the substance of his conversation with Erland Nilsson that very morning. Erland had a small shack out on the lake into which he claimed the walleye had been leaping through a hole in the ice.

He slammed the gavel down. "Counselors, this court is recessed until tomorrow."

"What?"

"They scarcely got started!"

"But I rode eight miles!"

"Preposterous! What next?"

It was a disappointed crowd of spectators that shuffled out of the courthouse that morning.

* * *

The following day dawned on subdued participants and chastened spectators. Apparently someone had even had a word with Mrs. Willman. Though sullen-looking, she was thankfully silent, stationary, and seemed content with narrow-eyed looks that traveled up and down the length of each passing witness and an occasional loud noise that sounded like "Titch!"

She was busy. Joe Willie would call several witnesses that day all of whom said they knew the deceased well. Their testimony differed about many things but not about his character. A man who had worked for Junior's father described him best: "A playground bully who never grew up."

Tippet complained. Of course. "Your Honor, I don't see where the defense is headed in proving that the deceased was a violent man. The deceased is not on trial here."

Sissy thought Joe Willie defended his tactics admirably. "Yet it was all right for you to try to prove he was 'Mary Had a Little Lamb.' Your Honor, I am trying to show that Buel was the sort who would readily force himself on a woman in order to then prove that my client had to defend herself from him."

"Overruled. Continue, Mr. Everett."

"Thank you, Your Honor. I only have one other witness along this line."

In what he hoped was a shrewd maneuver—and not the most ignorant thing he had ever done—Joe Willie called his next witness: Hattie Mueller, the owner of the Wind Fall Saloon. As if on cue, Jim Horse opened the double doors wide and there she stood, the owner of the most successful whorehouse in northern Minnesota.

Two Sisters was too small a town for its womenfolk not to have seen its hurdy-gurdy girls, but this was their first opportunity to look their fill. And did they ever!

She had dressed—or overdressed—for the occasion. Though it was only two in the afternoon she had on a pink evening get-up with a gored skirt, black mesh gloves that covered almost all of her arms and a large black hat firmly anchored to one side of her head. Unfortunately it covered half her face which prompted disappointed murmuring from the north side of the room.

The gavel banged and brought a silence so complete everyone (except Mrs. Willman) could hear Hattie Mueller's garters rub against her skin as she swayed to a stop before the bench. Woodrow tugged on his collar before he rose to swear her in.

Sissy's eyes traveled from Hattie Mueller to her husband and then to the plank floor between her feet. It was no secret that Hattie Mueller and Joe Willie had once been lovers. Of course, that had been before she moved to town. Joe Willie had ended the . . . association when he and Sissy came to an understanding. Or she assumed that was the case. Actually she didn't know exactly when the liaison ended because they had never talked about it. It simply wasn't the sort of thing a wife in her right mind would do. She certainly didn't want to talk about it. Not now. Not ever. Simply thinking about Joe Willie doing to Hattie Mueller what he now did to her . . . oh, God, it was worse than a knife in her heart!

Hattie made a production of getting herself settled just so but she was actually observing Joe Willie as he approached. He looked pretty good to her. But then, he always had.

"Miss Hattie, do you know the defendant?"

"No, but I know most everyone else in this room."

It wasn't what she said but the way she said it. "Hussy!" whispered one voice. "Well, I never!" said another. Hattie hid a smile and thought: sling all the slurs you want, ladies. My place'll be jumpin' tonight.

Hattie Mueller was a good businesswoman who had been led to Two Sisters by a fine nose for opportunity. But she had stayed because of another part of her anatomy.

Oh, she knew she'd been a fool. Falling for one of her customers had broken a cardinal rule for women in her line of work. Yet even after Joe Willie married, she'd stayed. She'd figured that a born hellraiser like Joe Willie'd get bored with marriage within a matter of weeks. Apparently she'd figured wrong. Oh, hell, he'd been back in her saloon once in a while—for a beer, a game of cards, a little conversation with a client—but he never once gave her that look and jerk of his jaw that used to make her knees weak and her mouth dry, the one that meant: Upstairs. Now.

She licked her lips and smoothed her skirt. All this time and just the thought of their lovemaking could rattle her. She knew it'd been good for him too. So why hadn't he returned? Obviously it couldn't be Little Miss Bo Peep. My God, just look at her! Oh, she was attractive enough if you liked that scrubbed, wide-eyed look but not now. At the moment she just looked wide. Period. No, what was holding him there was either a political career or his boy. After due observation, she decided it was probably the latter. She and one of the girls had seen them on the street just the other day. Joe Willie'd had the boy up on his shoulders. "She must make him take the kid with him," she told her companion. "I heard the kid's often in his office, crawling around on the floor an' slobbering on the customers' boots."

"Yeah, sure," replied Jewel. "He probably enjoys gettin' his eyebrows ripped out. Sugar, he can't see anythin' but that boy an' his woman. Sooner you come to grips with that, the happier you'll be."

That had made her mad enough to try and think of some little thing that would get his goat and not for the first time she considered taking up with Jim Horse. Her gaze traveled to the big shouldered silhouette in the back of the room. Truth be told, the idea was stimulated by more than spite. From what she'd heard it would not be an unpleasant chore. One of the girls said that an hour with him was like trying to outrun a bull. Exciting, dangerous and not necessarily something a person will outlive. She had been giving it some thought.

Joe Willie's voice brought her out of her musings.

"Miss Hattie, tell us what you know about Junior Buel."

She arched one plucked eyebrow. "Surely not everything?"

"Let me be specific."

"Please."

"He frequented your establishment."

"Yes, he did."

"Did he ever cause you any trouble?"

"Trouble?" The unladylike nose-noise she made caused several women to exchange see-see glances. "Trouble was Junior's middle name. He was a vicious man. Before he would drink himself into a stupor he would either wreck something or hurt someone. Often both. He particularly liked seeing someone helpless."

Hattie went on from there, recounting actual acts of violence committed by Buel. Even toned down for polite society, it was pretty gruesome fare but not one pale-faced person left while she was speaking.

By the time she finished it was almost five, and Junior Buel's reputation was in shreds. The judge declared court concluded for the day.

Joe Willie talked to Thora for about an hour and then drove Sissy home. Her eyes were red and she was silent. Her heart went out to women in such dire straits that they had to let themselves be used by men like Junior Buel.

Joe Willie looked at her then back at the road. ''Darlin', every time I looked at you this afternoon, you were cryin'. Are you sure you want to keep comin'?''

''Oh, yes. I wouldn't miss this for the world.''

''Thora's gonna testify tomorrow.''

''Well, that will clear things up once and for all!''

''Not necessarily. I think she's gonna say she intended to kill Junior Buel and isn't one bit sorry.''

''Oh.'' Sissy looked up at him and for the first time she thought he might actually be worried.

Chapter 22

Joe Willie called his last witness, Thora Gunn. She rose immediately and went to the stand. Having watched all the others, she knew which hand to raise, before the bailiff said, "Please raise your right hand and swear after me." As she did as he asked, she held her other arm across her waist as if to contain a leaping stomach.

As usual she wore her hair in one big braid, but for luck or for courage—she wasn't sure which—she had put on her new dress. Fortunately the weight she had lost elsewhere made up for the weight she had gained in front.

Joe Willie smiled at her. "Miss Gunn, I'd like to begin when your family left Two Sisters—and your brother—behind."

She looked down. She hadn't expected that. Actually she didn't know what to expect. Joe Willie had told her they weren't going to go over his questions or her answers because he didn't want her to sound rehearsed. He'd said she should just answer his questions as truthfully as she could.

Her chin was working and her cheeks were pink. "Anything the matter, Miss Gunn?"

"No, only I'm . . . I'm ashamed to tell about it."

"Why? Tell the jury why." His voice was gentle.

"I'm ashamed that I'm related to someone who did something like that."

"Why did he? Help us understand."

She looked at him and then stared at a spot on the wall. "Because of his dream."

"What dream is that?"

"Ever since I can remember, my father has wanted to go to Alaska. I think it was something he got in his mind when he was little and never forgot. He honestly thought that Alaska was the only place on this earth where he could have a decent life. He never gave any other place a chance. Everywhere we ever went we knew we'd be staying only long enough to get enough money to move along. Sometimes we didn't even take our stuff out of the wagon."

Joe Willie leaned against the wall beside her. "You arrived in Two Sisters when?"

"It was summertime 1879. We left in spring of '80."

"Less than a year."

"Yes."

"Not all of you moved on when you left."

"No."

"Who stayed behind?"

"My brother."

"Because he wanted to?"

She shook her head. "Because he was tied to a post."

Jim watched her put on the same flat blank face that she showed him every day and realized that this practiced look of sober self-control was how she protected her feelings! Now, having reached that conclusion, the next logical question was: what emotion was she hiding from him? He'd have to give that some serious thought. Yeah. Some real serious thought.

"Why was your brother left behind?"

When Tippet started to rise Jim jacked a shell into his rifle. The others were so engrossed in what the witness was saying they didn't even look around, but Tippet did, and then slowly eased back into his chair.

"Because he ate more than he earned."

"Was he lazy?"

"No. He was very willing but somebody else had to stay with him all the time to tell him what to do next." She looked at Joe Willie. "See, he just couldn't understand like the rest of us?"

"Can you give us an example?"

She only had to think a minute. "One time my father hired him out to a farmer who wanted some help cutting his wheat. My father showed him what to do but when we went back to pick him up, he'd cut one strip across the field and never moved over. He just kept going up and down the same path. He ran to my father and pointed with pride. He thought he'd done so well. He didn't understand why my father and the farmer were so mad. Not why he got a lickin' either."

Tippet threw a quick look over his shoulder before he stood. "Your Honor, please!"

Jim allowed him to interrupt then only because she was struggling to maintain control and he knew she'd sooner sleep with a snake than cry in front of all these people.

Rice nodded. "Mr. Everett, please keep to the subject."

"Yes, Your Honor." Joe Willie didn't consider the judge's comment a setback. He'd gotten his point across. "So the rest of the family traveled to the West Coast."

"Yes."

"What happened when you got there?"

"We ran out of money and didn't have fare for the ship. My father started looking around for what he could sell and came upon my sister."

A rumble went through the crowd. "Your sister?"

"Yes. He sold her to a man for fifty bucks and a rifle which he later sold for eight more dollars."

"How old was your sister?"

"Fifteen."

"That was how many years ago?"

"Almost four."

"And how old were you?"

"Thirteen."

"Fifteen and thirteen," Joe Willie repeated and looked back at the crowd. "Did your sister want to marry the man?"

"No. She cried herself sick."

"Why?"

"Because he was old and had no teeth and smelled like a fish pot."

"But she married him?"

"Yes."

"Why?"

"Because she was afraid of what my father would do if she didn't."

"How did you feel about it?"

She paused a second. "How did I feel?"

"Yes."

"Not as bad as Hekla did."

Some twittering here but it quickly died. The girl was perfectly serious. "I felt sorry for Hekla. Scared for me."

"How old was the sister born after you?"

"Eight."

"Mm. I imagine you must've felt like the only shoat left at hog-killing time."

She nodded. "Exactly. I knew I'd be next. And it wouldn't be two years either."

"Why?"

"My father'd always looked forward to getting rid of me. He called me 'that stubborn one' and complained that I was the worst of all his children to raise."

"Why?"

She shrugged. "Just didn't like me I guess."

A lot of women looked close to tears. Even Curly Frye was jerking his chin. "Is that when you decided to escape?" She was shaking her head. "When then?"

"I'd decided to escape way before that. Clear back on the day we left Two Sisters. Only thing that changed was that I knew I had to hurry. The money he got for Hekla wouldn't last long and I'd be next."

On that distressing note the judge suggested that they adjourn for the day. It was a subdued crowd of spectators that shuffled out of the courthouse that night.

Generally someone would call a cheery greeting to either her or Jim when they entered the cafe but not that night. Their entrance was greeted by kindly hellos and sympathetic glances and, from those she didn't know, skittering glances and muffled whispering. Joe Willie and Sissy joined them but they were pretty subdued too.

She felt like an empty pot. Drained, used up and strangely sleepy. She wasn't sure she'd be able to stay awake long enough to eat! Sissy spoke to her twice before her words penetrated her muzzy state. She sat staring at nothing until a family got up and broke her trance. A boy of four or five, a young mother and a father. When they went by, headed toward where the selections were laid out, Joe Willie stood to shake hands with the man. When he resumed his seat he told them that the family was new to the area.

"They just got here last week."

"Where are they from?" Sissy asked.

"A place called Bavaria."

"Never heard of it."

"Me neither."

"It's in Germany," Sissy said, smiling at the boy who had his hands buried in his mother's skirts and his eyes fixed on little Joey. When Joey was prompted by his mother to wave, the boy buried his face too.

"What a fine-looking boy! What's their name, Joe Willie?"

"Kohl. Albert, the father, is the only one who speaks English." He nodded. "He'll do fine. Says he plans to save his money for three or four years and buy a farm. Wants a dairy place so he can sell cheese and milk. Meanwhile he's got a job working for Ketil at the mill. He's planning to better their lot in life; he's already asked Nils Duuos how old the boy has to be before he can enroll him in school."

Having loaded their plates with food, the family was weaving their way between tables when Joe Willie stood again. "Albert, Mrs. Kohl. I'd like to introduce you to my family. This is my wife, Sissy and my son, Joey." Jim Horse stood as well. "This is our sheriff, Jim Horse and this is Miss Thora Gunn."

Jailbird, Thora added to herself.

"Good to meet you all," Albert said and looked at each person in turn. There was no speculation in his eyes when he got to her so Thora figured he was the only person in America who hadn't heard about her yet.

"Well," Albert said.

"We look forward to seeing you often, but now you best eat while it's hot," said Sissy.

"The boy's anxious. It is his turn to say the prayer."

They settled themselves then both parents nodded at the boy. He pinked and then began in a high sing-song voice.

Komm Herr Jesus
Sei unser gast
und segne . . .

A glass rocked as Thora stood.

"Thora, what is it?"

To Jim, she said, "Can we go now?"

"But Thora," Sissy cried. "You've hardly touched your food!"

"I don't feel well."

"Should we get the doctor?"

"No. Please. I just want out of here."

Walking back to the jail she sensed that Jim wanted to say something but not unexpectedly he was silent. He escorted her to the privy and then inside.

As she brushed by him, he drew her into his arms and held her tightly for a heartbeat. Their gazes locked and something passed between them. An understanding. A commitment. Something. Then his hand cupped her head and his lips touched hers with downy softness. She should have pushed him away right then! Instead she leaned into him, as much as telling him he could do as he wished . . . which was to cover her lips with his and kiss her until her knees buckled.

When he released her, he gently pushed her into the cell and pulled the door closed and left. Stunned, she sat on the cot like a burl on a log. If it wasn't for his taste in her mouth and the heat in her blood, she could almost believe it hadn't happened!

Some time later a rustling sound became Emily Jones. With difficulty, Thora pulled herself together. Had Emily been there long or had she just arrived?

"Hello, Thora."

She went to her. "Emily! It seems like I haven't seen you in ages! How are you?"

"I'm fine. Back to work today. I could have started long

ago but Conor . . . Dr. O'Malley . . . refused to let me.'' She pulled over a stool. ''I can only stay a minute. I've been gone all day and I'm worried that my heater's low on wood.'' She smiled. ''Oh, Thora! My cat's had kittens!''

''Really?''

''Yes. Three! I had no idea she was even expecting. Oh, you should see them! The three of them are all different colors.''

''Huh! They don't look anything alike?''

''Not a bit. One's white with orange, one's brown with tortoise stripes and one's black except for its paws and a place on its chin!''

''Huh!''

''I know. If I hadn't watched them be born, I wouldn't have believed they were from the same litter.'' Ruefully. ''I'm trying to get up the nerve to ask Conor if that means they had three different fathers. It's probably true. Blossom struck me as a cat with a past.'' She looked at Thora quite seriously. ''What do you think?''

''I don't know a thing about cats.''

''Me neither. I've never had one before.''

Thora snapped her fingers. ''I know! That bailiff Woodrow told me he loves cats. He told me that one of his cats keeps having kittens and he can't bear to part with them. I'll bet he knows all about them.''

''Good idea! I'll talk to him tomorrow.''

''I'd love to see one when they're bigger.''

''I'll bring one in! Soon as their eyes are open.''

''They were born with their eyes closed?''

''Yes.''

''I'll be. I sure didn't know that.''

There was a little silence. Emily clasped her hands and looked at Thora then looked away. ''You had a hard day today.''

''Yes, I did. I think it might get worse tomorrow.''

''Thora,'' Emily stared at the floor. ''I listened to everything you said.''

''You did? I didn't see you.''

''I cracked the door that leads to the judge's chambers. That's why I'm so late getting home. I stood there and listened instead of doing my work.'' She looked up. ''Thora, I heard what you said about your father and I only want to say that I . . . I understand.''

''You mean you had a father like mine?''

She shook her head and took a shuddering breath. ''On the surface my father . . . my family is nothing like yours. He's a banker and we've lived in the same town all our lives. We all . . . my two brothers and I . . . have always had plenty to eat and nice clothes but things were not really fine.'' She sighed. ''My father drinks. Not for long stretches at a time but when he did he would turn mean and beat us.''

''Us?''

''My mother, us kids, whoever he could get a hold of. There's no reasoning with him when he drinks. He becomes another person. A very crazy person.

''Afterward he was always sorry, provided he remembered what happened. A lot of times he didn't. One night he pushed my mother down the cellar stairs and broke her arm and the next morning he said, 'What on earth happened to you?'

''It was impossible not to feel sorry for him. He always apologized up one side and down the other and we always forgave him because . . . because he was our father and we didn't want him to do it again and because he always promised that he wouldn't. Of course he always did.

''We thought: if only we knew someone who could help him! But then, little by little that changed. I don't know how but pretty soon he had us thinking that his drinking was our fault. If we kids just wouldn't rile him so! Or if Mother would just remember to serve what he liked for dinner.'' Here Thora silently waited through a long pause before she began again. ''One night my mother went to my aunt's house. She'd been ailing and mother was worried about her. Late afternoon she sent a message saying that she was staying over night and for me to make supper for father and my brothers. I did and fed my brothers and got them in bed. I kept everything warm on the stove but my father didn't come home and didn't come home.'' Her voice had fallen to a whisper. ''I never thought . . . I mean he hadn't gotten drunk for over a year.

''I turned the lantern low and waited for him. I fell asleep in a chair and woke when I heard him come crashing in. It was after three o'clock. He was yelling and knocking things over.

I closed the boys' door so he wouldn't wake them. I should have locked myself in there with them. I should have run. But I didn't."

"He beat you." Thora wasn't surprised or shocked. She couldn't count the number of times she'd taken a licking from her father.

"Yes," she whispered. "But in his mind he wasn't beating *me.* He thought I was my mother! Oh, he yelled terrible hateful things. That he was sick and tired of my sick headaches. That he was sick and tired of living with a stone woman. That I would never say no to him again! He went on and on like that, saying real personal things . . . things I never wanted to know about. I tried to get out of the house then but I couldn't get away from him. He choked me and I must've fainted, and then . . . he hurt me." She looked at Thora with swimming eyes.

"Oh, God!" Thora breathed.

"Almost worse than anything was what happened the next day. He remembered nothing. Not a thing! Oh, I hated him then. I believe I would have shot him dead if I'd had a gun!

"I told myself it probably would never happen again but I couldn't stay. I tried but I couldn't even bear to look at him. There was also my mother to consider. Staying would have meant lying to her and oh, it would have been such a mess! Finally, I decided the best thing I could do was leave. To get train fare I sold my clothes and the few pieces of jewelry I had to a secondhand store. I got this far and you know the rest."

"Oh, Emily, I had no idea!"

"I know. I almost didn't tell you but I wanted you to know that other people have survived bad things that happen to them. At least that's what I tell myself. After their misfortune ends, they simply brush their souls off and go on." She put her fingers through the bars and Thora grasped them hard.

"That's what you must do when this is over, Thora. Brush yourself off, hold your head high and go on. That's what I did. No reason to spend the rest of my life stewing about what happened to me. It was not my doing."

Thora stood when she did and offered both hands through the bars. "Emily, what a wise old owl you are!"

"Phooey. If I had half your determination, I'd be in Canada by now."

''Do you still want to go?''

''No. This is probably where I'll live out the rest of my life.'' She smiled a little. ''I guess you could say that I am a little like a bird in one respect. I've only now discovered what a nester I am. Well . . .'' She released Thora's hands. ''I have to go back and look after my little kittens and I have to stop at Buddy's first and pick up some cream for their mother.''

''Thanks for coming by, Emily.''

She paused in the door. ''I didn't have any choice. I wouldn't have slept a wink if I hadn't.''

Chapter 23

The next day Joe Willie came in with a scroll-like thing under his arm. After unrolling it, he tacked it up using nails he took from his pocket and the butt of someone's gun selected from the confiscated weapons table.

Tippet again. "Your Honor, what is that?"

"Looks like a map, Mr. Tippet."

Joe Willie responded. "It is, Your Honor, one on which I intend to demonstrate the path Miss Gunn took on her return to Two Sisters."

"Good God!" moaned Tippet and the judge stopped Joe Willie from going any further. "Did you have an objection, Mr. Tippet?"

He stood and treated those who had not been present when he made his appearance to the full glory of his periwinkle blue suit jacket with black checked pants. A deerstalker's hat dyed a matching blue sat on the table.

"I wondered—again—at the relevance of this testimony."

"Your Honor," Joe Willie said. "Prior to today I asked Miss Gunn to write down the names of the places she remembered along her route in an attempt to prove her whereabouts prior to the incident. As you know, Your Honor, we have a murder with no witnesses. Motive, opportunity and intent are very relevant to the case. Further, my client is claiming self-defense. This information will help reveal the sort of person we're dealing with.''

Rice folded his hands. ''Overruled, Mr. Tippet. Continue, Mr. Everett.''

''Thank you. Now, Miss Gunn, I direct your attention to this map on which Mr. Corliss and myself have marked the rivers and mountain ranges as well as what Indian tribes are known to inhabit each area.'' He pointed to Puget Sound. ''Miss Gunn, earlier you said that you think you started out right about here.''

She nodded. ''Yes, I think that's the place.

''Puget Sound?''

''Yes. The ship stopped unexpectedly one night. The captain called everyone up on deck and told us that they needed to anchor in fresh water for a few days in order to kill the barnacles on the ship's hull. He said that we were going upriver somewhere and as soon as the sailors had scraped them off, we'd all be on our way again.

''Did you know where you were?''

''Not until the captain said Puget Sound that night. All I knew was that there was something out there. I could see lights from the deck. Since I didn't know if there'd be people where we were going, I figured that right there might be my best—and maybe my last—chance to escape before Alaska. My father would be off guard . . .''

''Why?''

''Why? Well, because he'd never expect me to jump into the water.''

''It would be pretty daring but why not?

''Because I couldn't swim.''

Joe Willie was incredulous. ''You couldn't swim?''

''No.''

''You're kidding?''

''No, but I've learned some since then. You know.'' She moved her arms and legs. ''Enough so I can stay afloat.''

Joe Willie gave the jury a look that asked: Do you believe this? and one or two of them actually shook their heads.

''Go on.''

''I unscrewed the cover off a hatch and went down a rope hanging off the back of the ship. I used the hatch cover to keep me afloat and struck out for shore. I thought I was going toward the settlement but it was so foggy I lost sight of the lights. I don't know how long I drifted but one time I got caught in a whirling pool of water and was thrown around in a circle for so long I got sick to my stomach! After that I was very tired. I kept pinching myself to stay awake but it must not have worked 'cause I came to among some rocks and that little town was nowhere in sight." She swallowed hard. "What was in sight was about a hundred Indians! I was scared to death. They were mostly naked and had bones hanging around their necks and from their ears and except for one woman, all their heads were flat in front. It turned out that the woman was a captive who had married into the tribe but I didn't find that out until much later.

"They stood all around me, ankle-deep in the water. One man kept shaking a spiked tomahawk in my face and hollering at the top of his lungs and then about ten of them hoisted me up and carried me off."

She said they took her to their chief and threw her down in front of him. She curled in a ball, freezing and scared silly. He got up and walked around her and then he went around again. He said something and everyone backed off.

"I thought they didn't want to get splattered with blood. I closed my eyes and started babbling every prayer I knew when that half-breed woman leaned close and said, 'Shutup!' I was so shocked to hear someone speak English, I did.

"She took me to a low fire and gave me a blanket and a shell with some mush on it. She told me to eat it and I did. It tasted like rotted fish but I was so hungry I would've eaten worms if she told me to. Two days went by like that and nobody else came anywhere near me. The Indians would watch me from behind the trees and if I stood up, they'd run off. I tell you, if it hadn't been for that woman I would've thought that whole tribe was crazy."

"Why were they afraid of you?"

"They thought I was a spirit. See they were Klikitat Indians and the woman said they believe in this sort of, uh, sea thing called Tamanohus."

She explained that a Tamanohus was very powerful and very

mean and the tyee, or chief, was recommending that they treat her with extreme caution.

"The one with the tomahawk did not believe I was a spirit. I didn't need a translator to know that. Luckily for me, the chief won out."

She said she stayed there a week, gathering her strength and gathering materials she would need for her long trek. The Indians gave her a bow and an otterskin quiver full of fire-hardened arrows, a pair of flints, some snares for hunting, bone hooks for fishing, pemmican and smoked red fish, dried chips from some animal for starting a fire.

"I would've never made it without their help. Why, they even drew me a deerhide map showing the best way out of the area." She smiled a little. "I think they really wanted to get rid of me."

Before she left she wished they had given her a horse but once she started off she realized she couldn't have ridden a horse off the trail anyway. And staying on the trail was too dangerous.

"So you were on your way." Joe Willie pointed at the map. "As near as you can tell, from that Indian camp you moved south through Palouse country to the Columbia River . . ."

"I didn't know the name of the . . ."

"But you said you floated your things across a large river using a hide tacked onto some logs."

"Yes."

"About three weeks from the coast?

"Yes."

"And it was the biggest river you'd come across up to then?"

"Yes."

He tapped the map. "Probably this river."

"I guess. Yes."

"By the time you crossed the Bitterroot Range, the Flathead territory and Blackfoot Country, you'd crossed a lot of water, right?"

She told how she did it. She gathered sticks and tied them together with strips of rawhide. Then she wrapped her belongings in the otter skin the Klikitats had given her and set the bundle on the little wooden raft. She said that was how she taught herself to swim, by paddling along after it. Most of the women thought: My, she's clever! Most of the men thought: Damn, she's pretty!

"After a year or so I started coming down out of the mountains and there weren't so many fast rivers. The grasslands were easier to travel through, but much more dangerous because there was no place to hide."

"Did you see many others?"

She nodded. "I once had two white men on horseback try to run me down and many times I saw Indians. Luckily I saw them before they saw me."

"Weren't you afraid?"

Another nod. "But I had to keep going."

Joe Willie folded his arms. "Must've been pretty tough. How'd you do it?"

She blushed and shrugged. "A little trick I played on myself."

"What?"

"People'll think I'm crazy . . ."

"No. Please."

"I used to pretend I was, ah, something else . . ." Jim Horse did not move or anything but she had felt that eye of pitch on her person as if it were his hand and it was just enough to interrupt her train of thought. She looked at her hands. "A shadow beneath the trees or a ripple in the grass and I'd ask myself: how could a ripple have a blister or a shadow be . . . hungry . . ." Her voice trailed off. Tippet had stood up.

"Your Honor, I protest to this rambling testimony . . ."

He was overruled by Judge Rice again. "The defendant is on trial for her life. We'll give her a bit of latitude." Besides, he wanted to hear the rest of her incredible story!

"Miss Gunn, you said you stopped at Fort Becker. Are you certain it was Fort Becker?"

She looked back at Joe Willie. "Yes, I am. I remember trading some rabbit skins for twenty sulphur matches."

"And some weeks later you made Fort Peck?"

"Yes."

"And then Fort Berthold?" Each time he spoke he was jabbing another place on the map.

"Yes."

"Smack in the middle of Siouxland?"

"I guess so."

"Now, Miss Gunn, near Williston you turned north."

"Yes."

"Why?"

"Because of what you just said: I was smack in the middle of Siouxland."

"Ah." Joe Willie tucked his pointer under his arm and waited for her to continue.

"They were everywhere. One day I came upon a burned out cabin. The Indians had already been gone a couple of days, but another time I saw them attacking four wagons. They . . . they killed everyone on the train, even the kids. It was awful." She looked up. "I didn't know what tribes lived south, but I'd heard that they were even worse than the Sioux so I turned north thinking that I could get around them that way."

"Continuing to walk north . . ." He had his pointer out again. ". . . brought you into the Dakotas, the land of the Cheyenne, Sansarc or Burnt Thigh, Arapaho, Gros Ventres."

"I made pretty good time through that land. Mostly by water. One day I stole a canoe and went a long way even though I only traveled by the light of the moon."

Before she approached the canoe she watched it all night and half of a day. Indians, she had heard, sometimes liked to roll themselves in their blankets and sleep beneath their overturned canoes. By midday, when she was pretty sure the canoe didn't shelter some unbelievably lazy Indian, she scampered down, overturned it and leapt into it and paddled like crazy. Its owner could return any minute and she wanted to be beyond an arrow or bullet's reach when he did.

"How long did you use the canoe?"

"A few days, maybe a week. Until I hit a snag and poked a hole in its side. I didn't have anything to repair it with."

"So you were back on foot?"

"Most of the time."

"Most of the time?"

"One night I saw some Indians camped by a stream." She looked at Joe Willie then looked at her hands. "I waited until night and stole one of their horses."

Jim listened to her tell about how she crept close to the camp and watched them without detection. He heard her describe how some of the warriors wore their hair almost to their heels and how different their clothes were. His face was expressionless but his heart swelled with a strange pride. Crow! he thought. She stole a horse from a band of Crow warriors!

"A confessed thief, Your Honor!" said Tippet and the judge rapped on his desk. "Let her finish, Mr. Tippet."

"Thank you, Your Honor." Joe Willie said, "Just go on and tell us what you remember about that night. You stole a horse . . ."

She remembered all of that night. How could she forget?

The Indians hadn't tied their horses together but used rawhide hobbles so they could graze freely. She crawled to the furthest horse and cut its hobble and led it away. Any minute she expected to hear angry yelling, but she made it across the stream where she threw herself on the horse and rode like there was a brushfire at her back. In a little town called Parkersville she traded the horse for a compass, a rifle and some shot. She traveled many miles on that horse. (And on another one as well, but she sure wasn't going to tell Tippet about bashing that woodsman's head in with a rock! That's all he needed to hear!)

"Roughly two thousand miles." Joe Willie tapped the map and let his eyes rake the room. Look at that girl, his expression insisted. And then look at this damn map! Two thousand miles and most of them on foot! Who knew what it did toward proving her guilt or innocence but there wasn't a man in the room who wasn't saying to himself: "Holy Shit!"

"Your Honor!" Tippet's voice was both sullen and disgusted. "I can't believe we are listening to this deluge of inconsequential hooey!

"An eloquent and logical plea, Mr. Tippet, but one that I will have to overrule."

Jim Horse was so angry he almost shook his head. He would never understand white men. To an Indian it was very rude to interrupt someone who was speaking. If Tippet kept jumping up like that at an Ojibwe gathering someone was likely to introduce the back of his head to the flat side of a tomahawk!

Mm. There was an idea with merit!

"Mr. Everett, if you are at a good stopping place, may I recommend that we continue tomorrow?"

"All right with us, Judge." He bowed to his opponent. "Tomorrow my first question will be: In your own words, Miss Gunn, please tell us what happened the night Junior Buel was shot!"

An anticipatory buzz accompanied the spectators as they filed out. Finally there were only a few people left. Tippet appeared intent on gathering his papers. Actually his mind was racing, selecting possible strategies and discarding them that fast. He couldn't figure Everett out. He appeared to be leading the defendant right up to a witness-stand confession!

Distracted by his thoughts, Tippet didn't notice his entourage of Mayburry, Bacon and Cleary was preceding him out of the courtroom. Suddenly the Sheriff stepped between Tippet and Cleary who went on, unaware the gaggle had halted. Tippet found himself looking into a flint-hard eye.

"Let her talk."

"What?"

"Tomorrow when she's trying to talk, let her."

"Are you threatening me?"

Drawing himself up Tippet prepared to let loose with a scathing set down but then he found he was doing his sputtering at a shadow. Jim Horse was already halfway across the street to the jail. Impotently he searched for Cleary and saw he was just about at the front door of the hotel. Some bodyguard!

"Damn you, Cleary!" he screeched. "Get your fat ass back here!"

Feeling eyes, he glanced around and saw two stout shocked matrons staring at him. "Ladies," he said in his most melodious voice but they huffed off toward that little eatery the locals frequented. "Fat cows!"

Chapter 24

The next day Thora began her story in Stillwater. She told about taking Junior Buel's gun from him on the train when he was passed out and that it was with his own weapon that she forced him to the hanging tree outside Two Sisters. Once there, she said she made a big to-do about throwing a rope over a limb and telling him he was about to die if he didn't tell her who his companions were.

"I admit I was mad enough to kill him then."

"Why?"

"Because he was so drunk! I don't think he even knew where he was and I know that he didn't know who I was. It sort of made it worthless if he didn't know who I was."

Every day the sheriff would take up his position in front of the double doors and stand there for hours on end and never move a muscle, yet now he shifted slightly and drew her eye. She quickly looked away.

"Go on, Miss Gunn."

"Buel really believed that someone was going to have a party for him and got mad when I told him it was a lie. That's when he knocked the gun away. We fought but he kicked my legs out from under me and got me down on the ground. He said the two of us were going to have the party anyway. He held me by the throat while he tried to ah . . . you know.''

The judge spoke here. ''I'm sorry, miss but we don't know. Bite down and tell us what he tried to do.''

''Free himself.''

''Thank you.''

She said she kneed him but he deflected it and was only slightly hurt. The gun lay nearby. When she grabbed it by the butt, he grabbed it by the barrel and she heard a sound like somebody had snapped a rug.

''He looked at me funny. 'Bitch!' he said and sprawled onto his back but he still had a hold of the gun and it went off again. His hold loosened then and I looked at him and said, 'Oh, God, I've killed him!' and then I got sick.''

''Go on,'' urged Joe Willie.

''It was so dead quiet I could hear the crunch of someone's footsteps coming up the hill. It was Deputy Durham.''

He approached with his gun drawn and his other hand outstretched as if it were flat on a door. He said, 'Let the gun slide from your fingers now . . . Easy. Easy. Good.' She dropped the gun. ''Then the deputy . . . knelt beside Buel and said, 'Well, ain't nothin' can be done for him now.' He stood and looked at me. 'You walk ahead of me ma'am, an' please please don't do nothin' foolish.' '' She looked at the sheriff again and then looked away. ''That's it.''

Joe Willie asked her. ''What would you have done if Deputy Bull Durham had not just happened to be in the area that night?''

''I would have given myself up.''

In a surprise move, Tippet requested some additional time for deliberation and received the afternoon. Court was recessed for the day.

Jim stood at the door and waited while people passed things to Thora. A sandwich. Dried fruit. Some just patted her arm. She smiled a little and spoke to a few people but she looked worried. In his opinion she had good reason to be. So was he.

That his friend, Joe Willie, would not get Thora Gunn off had never entered his mind until today. Up to now he had felt certain that Joe Willie had some startling case-winning revelation that would simultaneously set the town on its ear and set the girl free.

Well, if he had one, Jim sure wished he would roll it out. It seemed to him that this thing could go either way, which was not good. A guilty verdict did not fit in with Jim's plans at all.

Yeah, that's right. He, Jim Horse, was making plans.

Normally he did as much thinking as a rock and he never questioned anything. Hell, he had lots better things to do! Who gives a rip why the moon rises where it does or why the earth is round? It was enough for him that things existed. Period. Far as he was concerned, the moon and the earth existed to be appreciated by man. Just as deer, buffalo and fish were created to feed him. Just as woman was made to please him. These things had been decreed by the creator of the first earth. You just don't try to change stuff like that.

Yeah, you do. Apparently you do. And you do a lot of thinking first.

For the first time in his life he was so busy thinking that the sun lifting above the snow no longer drew his eye nor did the plaintive howl of a wolf make him pause. Women who once pleased him now talked too much. Or not enough.

No need to ask himself why. Hell, he knew why. It had everything to do with the girl. So now he had reached a conclusion, the result of all this damn thinking. His fate and hers were meant to mesh. Which was what he intended to tell her when the trial was over . . . once they could meet as man and woman instead of jailor and prisoner. He would tell her about the changes she had brought in him and by some magic—this part was still murky—words would roll off his tongue like water down a fall. She would be impressed. Better yet, she would be won.

But now came the serious obstacle to all his planning. What if she never got out of jail? What if she were found guilty?

Naw, it'd never happen. Hell, he'd seen Joe Willie pull people's fat from the fire plenty of times. Joe Willie had something up his sleeve. Sure as hell!

Then why the hell doesn't he get a move on it? The damn trial is almost over!

Jim caught up with Joe Willie as he was closing the door to

his office. He turned and saw him coming and waited. A soft snow was falling. "Hey, Jim." He pointed skyward. "More snow."

"Yeah," Jim said and then just stood there.

"Worried about how things are going?"

"Yeah. A bit."

"Me too. Well, it's her word against a dead man's, a man whose word was shit when he was alive. That's the case in a nutshell."

"That's it?"

Joe Willie nodded. "That's it." He climbed into the waiting sleigh and turned his horse.

"That gonna do it, you think?"

"If it doesn't we'll figure out something else." He looked at Jim. "She won't hang. Even if I have to spring her myself." He clucked to the horse and Jim watched the sleigh disappear.

Tippet approached the witness on cross examination. "Miss Gunnlauger, were you born in this country."

That question surprised her. "Yes, sir. At a way station in the Ohio Valley."

"Who procured the pistol for you?"

She opened her mouth and shut it again. Coming out of nowhere like it had, that question threw her even more than the first one. She kept her eyes on Tippet's face but out of the corner of one she saw Davey Cox stand up. "I got it for her."

Tippet swirled. Today's outfit: Striped pants. Black broken-tailed coat. Brocade vest with pinkish hues.

"Your Honor, I demand that this boy be arrested as an accomplice." Tippet pointed at Jim Horse. "Sheriff! Arrest that boy! Quickly!" Nobody moved and the room was dead quiet. Fuming, Tippet indicated Jim and asked Joe Willie, "Doesn't that man speak English?"

"About as good as me."

"That's not saying much," he spat. "Your Honor?"

"Davey, you better step back into my chambers."

Dottie Fagerhaug stood. Her face was livid. "What? And have the handcuffs and leg irons slapped on him? Honest to

Pete, Frank!'' Joe Willie leaned over the railing and said something and Dottie slowly sat down.

Court was recessed to handle the problem of young Davey Cox's complicity in the crime, and Thora received a welcome reprieve from Tippet. But naturally she was worried about Davey. If he suffered because he'd helped her, she'd never forgive herself.

The next day came and Davey was not called to the stand. And it was not, as she had feared, because he had been hauled off to prison. He had been placed on probation and sentenced to do ''good works'' in the community.

She didn't know how Joe Willie did it. Either he had lied very convincingly or Davey Cox had, but her relief was short-lived. As she had expected, Tippet was right back at her.

''Now, then Miss Gunnlauger.'' Solely because she'd asked to be called ''Gunn,'' he stressed ''Gunnlauger'' every time he said it.

''Did you intend to kill Junior Buel when you forced him to accompany you to Two Sisters?''

''I thought about it . . .''

He held up one hand. ''Please repeat that for the jury. You thought about killing him when you forced him to accompany you to Two Sisters?''

''Yes, but I shied off . . .''

He held up his hand again. ''Just answer the questions put to you please. Now then, you testified earlier that you fought.''

''Yes.''

''Was he fighting for his life? Or were you fighting for your virtue? Which we already know something about.''

''Objection, Your Honor.''

''Sustained.''

''I'll rephrase. Why did the fight start?''

''Because he was trying to get the gun away from me.''

''So he could keep you from murdering him?''

''So he could do the things he said he wanted to do.''

Joe Willie stood again but Tippet waved him down and switched tactics. ''You have already testified you have been a thief and have killed a man. It makes one wonder what else?'' Tippet strolled away, strolled back.

''What?''

"It makes one wonder what other methods you've employed to get what you want?"

"I don't understand the question."

"I understand you are being represented by your attorney pro bono."

"What's that mean?"

"Without fee. It means that you are not paying your attorney." He shot a look at Joe Willie and smirked. "At least not in coin."

Joe Willie didn't seem to move that fast, but somehow he was across the room and had a hold of Tippet by his collar. With his other hand he hit him in the jaw hard enough to lift him off his feet. His head snapped back and his eyes went white. Joe Willie was cocked, ready to give him another one, but Jim Horse stopped his arm with his hand. None but a few saw that Jim Horse held his pistol by the barrel in his other hand, ready to cold-cock Joe Willie if necessary.

One-handed, Joe Willie shook Tippet like a dog and then threw him to the ground. He tore his arm out of Jim's grasp and turned and they stared at each other. There was a moment when everyone held their breath, then Joe Willie stomped off. It was obvious he was mad as hell and controlling himself with great difficulty. Jim Horse knelt and lifted one of Tippet's eyelids. Bull knelt on the other side.

"I knew Joe Willie was fixin' t'pop 'im. I seen him lay back his ears and I knew. Damn! Got 'im good, he did. He ain't moved yet."

Jim Horse looked up at Bull. "Bull?"

"Yeah?"

"Find Doc O'Malley."

"Here!" Conor worked his way through the crowd and knelt beside the downed man. Nobody said anything for a full minute.

The judge's voice was shaking in anger. "I will see both of you in my chambers."

"Want me to carry him in, Judge?" Bull pointed at Tippet.

"When he comes to will be soon enough."

In chambers, both men knew they were within a hair of getting themselves thrown in jail for contempt of court. "You have carried your adversarial roles too far! Mr. Tippet, I found your comment highly offensive. I can certainly understand how Mr. Everett did."

"I was trying to provoke the witness. Not her attorney."

"Provoke!" Joe Willie half rose. "I oughta . . ."

"Joe Willie! Sit down!"

The judge said he would throw them both off the case if it weren't for the fact that the case was almost ready to go to jury and that there were no other lawyers in town. Both men were fined. Joe Willie one hundred dollars, Tippet fifty. Both left the judge's chambers feeling soundly rebuked. Tippet also felt like he was growing another jaw under his left ear.

Thora spent another uneasy night. The trial was almost over and she realized that she could actually be sentenced to death! For the sake of her child, she had to do something.

From beneath the mattress she removed the knife Davey Cox had given her. Was she capable of luring the sheriff into the cell and plunging a knife into his heart? That was easily answered. She replaced it and started pacing, but about all that got her was sore feet. And one idea: Maybe she should tell the judge about the baby and throw herself on the mercy of the court. What would happen then? After she had the child, would they put her in jail and put the child in a foster home or an orphanage? An ache knotted in her stomach at the thought, but she didn't see that she had a choice. Though she worried on it all night, she was no closer to a solution in the morning.

Summation speeches and closing arguments came next. First the prosecution and then the defense. Tippet, sporting a plum-like growth on one side of his jaw, spoke to the jury in a sermonizing voice about a willful, unlawful murder committed with malice aforethought. He gave a very credible review of the people's case and covered all the salient facts at great length. Joe Willie played with his pencil and watched the jury, most of whom looked bored; they'd heard all this before.

At the end, Tippet said, "The defendant has admitted to killing the deceased but she claims it was done in self-defense.

We know that is a bunch of claptrap. I have proven that the murder was a deliberate act done in a fit of homicidal revenge." He pointed at the jury. "Gentlemen, if you allow this defendant to go free, you are as much as saying that anyone in this town can go out and do the same. Not, I am sure, the sort of message you want to send. For the sake of your town, for the future of your community, you must find her guilty. For your attention during this long process, I thank you."

The room was dead quiet until the judge softly said, "Now we will hear from the defense."

Joe Willie's closing statement wasn't a tenth as long as Tippet's but he started out talking about justice too, saying "It will not be a sign of softness to let her go free, it will be legal murder to convict her!"

Then he talked about killing. Not so much about Thora's killing of Junior Buel but about Junior's killing of Thora's brother, and reminded the jury what a mindless death it had been. "As casual and cruel a killing as I have ever known."

And toward the end, this: "Look at her, gentlemen." Twelve heads turned toward her. She would not meet their eyes but stared at her hands in her lap. Joe Willie hoped the jurors were looking at that alabaster neck and were imagining it with a hemp necklace. He waited until several worked their rears on their chairs or tugged at their collars before he continued. "Justice is your responsibility, gentlemen. Daniel Boone once said, 'Make sure you're right, then go on ahead.' Gentlemen, that's all I'm asking you to do. What's right. If you believe the defendant was assaulted and fought for her life, then she was justified in defending herself, no matter what her earlier intention was."

When both the defense and the prosecution rested, Judge Rice instructed the jury in their duty and in the law as it applied to the case. "It is your responsibility to ponder the testimony you have heard. Talk among yourselves now and give us your opinion."

At this most solemn moment, Mrs. Willman stood up and cried, "Not guilty!"

Having discharged her duty, she tucked her ear trumpet under her arm, retrieved her knotted oak cane and stumped out. The judge gave a longsuffering sigh, waited for the twittering to die and rapped the desk. Hopefully for the last time.

Thora looked up and saw Jim Horse standing in front of her. His face was as impassive as usual, but he nodded once—only a slight movement but in it she imagined she saw pride, approval, encouragement and faith.

It was what gathered her feet under her and allowed her to stand on her own.

Along with many others Sissy congratulated Joe Willie on his fine speech but secretly she was worried sick. Not that she didn't have confidence in her husband's ability. Certainly she did! But . . . but what if the jury came back with a guilty verdict? She put the question to Joe Willie with the hope that in the intervening weeks he'd developed a better plan than asking for a pardon.

"Don't worry, sugar. They're going to find her not guilty."

"I hope you're right, but how can you be so optimistic?"

"I didn't want to say anything during the trial because I was afraid word would get back to the judge and he might've given more credence to Tippet's plea of bias."

"What do you mean?"

"Hell, if any jury was predisposed to a not-guilty verdict it was that one."

"Predisposed? What do you mean? I thought you said they were unbiased."

"Honey, how could they be? They knew Junior Buel and they knew Thor. They've gotta favor a verdict of not guilty."

"But the jury all said . . ."

Joe Willie snorted. "Sissy, if I practice law for a hundred years I don't think I'll ever see a jury more biased than that one."

"But . . ."

"Don't worry, sweetie! It's in the bag!"

There were times she didn't know what to make of her husband and this was one of them.

* * *

Thora paced her cell. Joe Willie had said the jury wouldn't come back until at least tomorrow. He'd also winked at her and told her not to worry. That everything would be just fine. No matter what he'd said she was nervous as a cat.

She stopped. Her lantern had flickered from the wind which meant someone had opened the front door. She waited. Was it word from the jury? No, she heard Emily's voice and the inside door opened.

"... looked like an awful fight, Deputy. One man's head was bleeding a lot."

Bull responded. "Guess I better go see about it. Jim'll be back any minute to take Miss Gunn to dinner."

"Good," said Emily. "I won't be here long. I was almost finished when I ran out of soap."

The outside door slammed and Emily came in but instead of starting to work she flung her bucket down and inserted a key in the lock. "Hurry! Hurry!"

"What . . . ?"

"I saw the key on Bull's desk this morning. Thank goodness he hasn't noticed it's gone. Quick!" She hiked up her skirt. A heavy sweater was tied under it."Put this on. Your coat's in the other room. Here's your gloves and here . . ." She handed her a couple of coins. "It's all I have!"

"Emily, I don't know what to say!"

"Lordy, you don't have time to say anything." She looked at her and smiled. "Thora, you go now. Run as fast as you can."

"I will. Thank you." They came together for a quick embrace and Emily turned off the lantern and opened the door and stuck her head out "It's all clear," she said. "Go!" She gently pushed Thora outside.

"Thanks!"

"Good luck!" Emily stood there and watched until she was out of sight. It didn't take long.

* * *

The next day the jury notified the bailiff that they were ready to render their judgment. Everyone remarked at the speed of it and piled into the courthouse.

Woodrow called the court to order and everyone stood as the judge entered. The jury filed in last and took their usual seats. Arne Stinson stood but the Judge stopped him from speaking.

''We'll wait until the defendant is present,'' he said. That's when a red-cheeked Bull Durham approached the bench. Several noticed that he was working over his hat pretty good. A rumble of whispers spread across the room.

''What is it, Deputy?''

''It's about Miss Gunn.''

''Yes? Where is she?''

''I don't know. Your Honor, the defendant escaped last night. Early last night right before dinner.'' The rumble rose to a roar!

''How?'' asked the judge, incredulous.

''Somebody came in and saw my key on the desk and unlocked the door.''

''You normally leave your key on your desk?''

''Yes, sir, I do.''

''I see,'' the judge said although he did not.

Jim Horse was there. ''Your Honor, in the end the responsibility for prisoners is mine. I'll take the blame.''

''Do you have any idea who did it?''

''No, I don't.''

Bull had told Jim about Emily Jones's late visit and the fight that didn't exist but between them they had agreed not to implicate her. Sure as hell, she was the guilty party, but unless she confessed there was no way anyone could prove it.

''Well . . .'' Clearly befuddled, the judge addressed the jury. ''I guess we need to know if we are looking for a convicted murderess or not. Mr. Foreman. Have you reached a verdict?''

Arne Stinson stood. ''We have, Your Honor.''

''In the absence of the defendant, will you face me please and read it now.''

''We are not looking for a convicted murderess. We found her not guilty.''

''Court adjourned!

The room went wild with big "Whoopees!" and several cries of "Yesss!" and "Oh, thank goodness!" Sissy was in Joe Willie's arms crying in joy and that was his last sight of Tippet, over his wife's shoulder. He packed up his papers in record time and was out the door.

"Good riddance," said Joe Willie.

Sissy pulled back and looked up at him. "What?"

"Tippet just left."

"Good riddance!" she echoed.

Run is exactly what Thora did. Until her side felt like somebody was turning a hot knife in it. They'd expect her to go due north so she went west instead. The night was clear and cold and windless and her feet took her to the cemetery first. Briefly she paused at her brother's grave and then hurried on and didn't stop again until she had reached the crest of the mountain. There she turned and looked at the town. Individual buildings couldn't be made out at this height, only tiny winking lights.

She regretted not saying good-bye to those who had been so kind to her. Buddy and Goody and the Fagerhaugs. Joe Willie and Sissy. She had the sudden painful thought that if she succeeded in getting away she would likely never see any of those people again. Almost made her regret her freedom! Her traitorous mind turned to the sheriff and she wondered what he was doing. Probably saddling up, getting ready to track her down. Maybe others as well, carrying flares, restraining their dogs.

For an instant his image loomed, as if he would stamp his face and form in her mind forever. Tears gathered and the image shimmered. Inside she cried, Run! Go! but her feet were rooted and her eyes fixed. Then he seemed to reach out and fear broke over her. With a jerk, she turned and trotted down the mountain. The sooner she got away from him, the better. Once she put distance between them, she could get him out of her mind. She made a vow right then and there: She'd break herself of thinking of him and that's that. For the sake of her own sanity, that vow was one she had to keep.

And she meant it, too . . . every single time she made it.

She retrieved her rucksack which included her oilskin-wrapped carbine and Wolf Woman's snowshoes, not the sort with the turned-up tips but the old fashioned sort called bear-paws. They were made for short distances and she was forced to stop frequently to knock the snow out of the webs.

She traveled light. Leather whangs held her rucksack and blanket tied across her back so she could carry her carbine at the ready. By the end of the first day it had started to snow lightly. It was hard to see, but she was not complaining since it also covered her tracks.

The first night she made a lean-to of pine limbs, without any canvas or stretched hide. It didn't stop either the wind or snow from entering but by using her body as a shield she was able to build a small fire.

She slept poorly and the next night she found better shelter beneath an overhanging rock. It took a long time to build a warm fire. Dry wood was not easy to find and neither was it easy to get a fire going using only a flint and piece of punk. She ate some pemmican and promptly got sick.

Chapter 25

Newspaper headline: CONFESSED MURDERESS FOUND NOT GUILTY.

"Sheriff!" The voice came from somewhere behind him. A crowd of about ten people were following Jim to the jail. He kept going until he reached the front door of the jail and there he turned and faced them. Everybody started talking first, but the loudest was the same reporter who had snuck a picture of Thora in the courtroom that day.

"Paul Manion, Sheriff, from the *Twin Cities Tribune* . . . Ah, Sheriff, this is the second time this prisoner has escaped your jail."

"Yeah?"

"Well, at least you didn't try to tell us she'd overpowered you again." He snickered to let the lawman know he was just being humorous but then a long and rather uncomfortable silence ensued, filled only with the distant sound of a barking dog. Jim folded his arms and planted his feet, well aware of the man's discomfort.

Manion mulishly continued. "Are you really asking our readers to believe that your deputy routinely leaves the keys to the cells laying about where anyone could get their hands on them?''

''I don't care what your readers believe.''

The reporter's face turned sly and mean. ''So you are sticking to your story that some person still *unknown* . . .'' He came down hard on that last word. ''. . . let the prisoner go?''

''You got it.'' Jim turned then and went into the jail and slammed the door.

The reporter was furiously making some notes in his book. What he had said, what the sheriff had said. Ha! What a joke!

When he finally looked up, the street was empty save for a fellow who had one boot propped back against the jailhouse wall. His hat shaded his face. Manion had been tossed out of court early in the trial and had a poor memory for faces anyway, but it looked like . . . Yeah, it was him all right. Deputy what's his name. The reporter consulted his notes then approached. ''Deputy Durham, right?''

''Yeah?''

''Mind if I ask you a few questions too?'' The man shrugged, which Manion took for assent. He did not, however, act very accommodating.

His publisher, a surly, cantankerous but very crafty old hack—had told him a good reporter will ''suck up to a sucker an' then suck 'im dry.'' He had translated that to mean: establish rapport before you begin asking questions. His attitude turned chummy. ''Say, I don't suppose you've got a match?''

''Yeah, I do.'' The deputy nodded across the street. ''How about that horse's hind end yonder an' your face.''

By the time the reporter had figured out that he had been irrevocably insulted, the deputy had pushed off and was ambling down the street. He was whistling ''Red River Valley'' softly through his teeth.

It was early the next morning. Joe Willie and Jim Horse stood outside the jail. Jim's horse was saddled and ready to ride.

''You don't think she'll come back of her own accord?''

Jim shook his head. ''She'll be on the run for the rest of her life unless somebody tells her the verdict.''

"That why you're goin' after her?"

"Somebody's got to."

Bullshit! said Joe Willie to himself. He cupped a match to his smoke then asked, "Where d'you figure she headed?"

"North."

"Well, that leaves only Canada and Alaska."

"English River country maybe.

"Hell, that's two hundred miles from here."

"Thereabouts." Jim slid his rifle into the boot and went inside. He came back with a rolled blanket which he tied behind his cantle.

"Rudy said to tell you they'll hold your job."

"They better not do that. I might be gone a year."

"Well, I told them I'd fill in for you if it's needed."

Jim paused and looked at him. "How does Sissy feel about that?"

"Fine . . ."

"That's a lie."

Joe Willie laughed. Jim Horse was about the only man alive who could say that to him. "You're right. But, what t'hell, the job's a cakewalk now."

Jim snorted and mounted up. "Watch yourself."

"I will. I ain't used up yet, you know. You watch yourself! I hear it's real chancy country up there." He looked at Jim Horse, looked away. "Guess I don't have to tell you that."

Without added leavetaking, Jim Horse turned his horse north and rode off.

Within a week Jim had crossed into a wild, heavily timbered country that was not really a mountain range but ridges and valleys gouged by glaciers and huge prehistoric rivers. The snow was deep and the trail almost nonexistent. If it got much worse he knew he'd have to find someplace to leave his horse.

A couple of days beyond International Falls he met a lone horseman headed the other way, a gamey-looking mountain man poorly mounted on a hairy-eared, high-withered mare and leading a pack mule that was stacked with skins. Once he drew closer, Jim took note of the bones that were sewed onto his hatband and the hawk feathers stuck in it.

He also took note of the two fresh scalps that hung from a thong on his pommel. They were Indian.

Jim stopped his horse and at a distance of ten yards they eyed each other warily. The old man had sharp bleached-out eyes and skin like a brittle leaf. He nodded and Jim said, "I'm Jim Horse, the sheriff of Two Sisters."

"That li'l town north of Duluth?"

"Yeah."

The old man spat then rubbed his sleeve across his mouth. "Long way from home, ain't ya?"

"Lookin' for somebody." Jim nodded toward the scalps. "Had some trouble?"

"Nothin' I couldn't handle."

"Crow."

"Yeah. Figurin' to steal my stuff t'buy some whiskey, I imagine."

Jim crossed his wrists on his pommel. "Bet you're plenty familiar with this country."

"Your people used t'be too."

Jim shook his head. "I've been away a long time." *Too long.* "Know someplace where I can leave my horse?"

"Yeah. There's a place about forty mile thata way." He pointed. "Used t'be a loggin' camp. They call the ol' man that lives there Indian Ed but he ain't."

"He ain't Ed or he ain't Indian?"

"Both!" said the old man and laughed. "He'll probably keep your horse though."

"Hu'ah!" He looked up at the sky. "The sun is setting."

The old man looked up too. "It shore is. It's apt t'do that every night about this time."

"I have coffee and would share my fire."

The old man nodded. "Sounds good to me."

They ate and warmed themselves and then sat by the fire. The old man offered to share the contents of a clay jug with a cob stopper and did not look disappointed when Jim declined.

There followed a long stretch when the only sounds were of snow falling from a bough or the pop and hiss of a pine cone on the fire. The old man started to talk about an hour into the jug.

"I seen you lookin' at those scalps." Jim nodded but was

silent. ''Those jaspers'd been trailin' me for two days so I laid a trap for 'em.'' He gave a gap-toothed grin. ''Caught me two Crows in it.'' He took a long pull on the jug. ''That's why they call me Crowbait Cates, you know. 'Cause I'd sooner catch Crows'n breathe. I ain't agin' all Indins, understand. My woman was a La-Cotah.'' A wolf greeted the moon and from high in the trees came the flapping of a large night-hunting bird. ''It was Crows that killed her. An' everyone else I ever cared about.'' He looked into the fire for a long time before he went on.

''Ten years we trapped together, my partner and me. Married women from the same tribe, built our cabins half a mile apart. I was gone huntin' one day when they attacked. A score or more I figure. My partner and his woman made it to my place and made their fight there. I found both women and my two kids shot. My partner tortured to death.'' The old man held a burning ember to his pipe and drew noisily on it. ''They earned themselves a lifelong enemy 'cause I have spent most all my time ever since huntin' Crow. Used t'crawl out and meet 'em.'' He made a snake movement with his hand. ''Till I got too played out, but if they come t'me, like those two . . .'' He winked. ''Well, that's another thin' entirely.''

The old man's tongue was growing fur and the more he drank the hairier it got.

''Life would hold no flavor for me after my family was kilt, but I was too caught up with my hate t'know that. Weren't till jus' recently that I realized it. That's when t'hurtin' come.'' A wolf howled. Another joined in and then another. ''You know, it's a terrible thing t'be alone, but it's worse t'be alone an' old to boot.''

He tipped the jug up and a pine-knob-sized Adam's apple bobbed through his beard. Jim was respectfully silent during the old man's long silences. After all, it was not his story.

''Weren't too long ago that I thought careful on it an' decided I was jus' about ready t'leave this life. Not rub myself out, understand, but jus' go on an' go, next time t'opportunity come along.

''Well, when I found out those two Crows were after me, I was gettin' ready fer 'em—outa habit I guess—when I thought: now wait a minute! Hold it right there! Why, this here's perfect.'' He looked at Jim across the fire. ''So I sat there like a big ol' duck an' waited fer 'em. I did! Sat there an' waited to die. Then I'll be damned if some sap or somethin' didn't rise up in me. Annoyed t'hell outa me, but there it was. I couldn't do it.'' As if in a toast to himself, he lifted the bottle then drank again. ''I didn't realize it 'til jus' t'other day, but the same damn thin' that happened t'me was what musta come on ol' Jubal there at the end!''

''Jubal?''

''My partner. My guess is that when Jubal saw it weren't no use, he killed my two young uns first and then shot the two women. Then the only thing I can figure is that when it come down to killin' hisself, he couldn't. He jus' couldn't die like a coward! You follow me, fella?''

Jim nodded. They sat for quite a while. The old man upturned the jug a final time and then kicked it away from him. ''Empty. Well, I'm turnin' in.''

''Your story was well told.''

''Thankee!''

And without further ado, the old man rolled himself into his blanket and instantly went to sleep leaving Jim to stare sightlessly into the embers.

One event changes a man's life forever. A sad story and one that Jim had heard before. The man who put both feet in a bear trap. The man shot because his drunken brother mistook him for a buffalo. The man who'd been struck by a thunderbolt.

Old Crowbait had probably known someone who'd been caught in a trap or shot by accident, but Jim would wager he hadn't known any one thunderstruck before. If he hadn't gone to sleep he might have told Cates that story. It was at least as good as Cates's story had been.

The man was a Choctaw farmer who traded horses with Rope Thrower's father. A middle-aged man, maybe forty or so, he'd been working alone, trying to remove a stump that stood in the middle of his field. Apparently he had gotten a chain around it and was about to start the team of mules moving when he was struck. His son found him hours later. The thunderbolt had blown the stump out of the hole and threw it and the man some fifty feet away. (Nobody ever saw the mules again.)

The son carried his father home and any healer—Indian or

white—who might've helped him was called in by the frantic family. No one knew what the hell to do! He acted dead except for irregular, very shallow breathing. The man stayed very sick for a very long time. Days went by then weeks then months. Almost two years later he came back to life. (And almost sent his daughter out of it. She had been asleep in a bedside chair when he reached out and grabbed her knee.)

He had come back like a bolt ''out of the blue'' his wife said and according to him that's exactly where he had been!

People came from all over. When he could speak he said that he had been living with the thunderbolts. Eaten with them, slept with them. That he had even seen the earth from the back of one. He claimed he had flown higher than the eagle, even beyond the place where the spirits soar. He said he'd had a fine time and didn't know if he was happy to be back or not!

From that moment on, the man thought only of the sun. When the sun was present in the sky he stared at it and wanted to touch it. When it was out of sight, he brooded about it. Many times his family found him standing in that same field, staring up at the sky. If he could get hold of himself, he would do some work but pretty soon there he'd be, back staring up at the sun. A healer was called and another and another. None did the man any good. One said nothing would, that he would never be healed. Obviously on one of those trips around the earth the thunderbolt had flown him too close to the sun, so close that the sun's spirit had gone into his eyes and possessed his head.

Jim rolled a smoke and lit it. It had taken the old man's story to make him see the similarities between his situation and that of the Choctaw man, but now that he considered everything, it was as obvious as a glass eye. When Thora Gunn was out of his sight, he brooded about her and when she was present he stared at her and wanted to touch her.

Clearly he too had flown too close to the sun but he hadn't even known it!

He shook his head in disbelief! Hard to believe but there it was, plain as could be. There he had been, doing his job, minding his business and blam. Everything was changed forever.

Only there'd been no crash of thunder and no jagged streaks

across the sky. No, she'd done it very smoothly, very silently. While he was occupied with her slender shoulders, teacup breasts and silken skin, that damned Thora Gunn had flown into his eye and stolen his soul!

It made him mad for a time and then he became resigned. There was nothing a person could do in a case like that. Just learn to enjoy the rest of his life. He leaned back and grinned. Tough job but he would try.

The old man was packed up before the eastern sky showed any hint of dawn. "Well," he said as he mounted up. "It's been real nice talkin' to you."

Now it was Jim's turn to speak. "Hu'ah!"

Thora had put a lot of miles behind her. One night she quit sooner than she would have liked but she was starved and had come up on a small lake that might yield something to eat. At a spot where a clump of marsh hay came up through the ice she made a hole and stuck a bit of jerky on a bone hook she always carried. Within ten minutes she had two skillet-sized crappies. She gutted them, removed their heads and stuck them on green sticks over a smokeless fire. While they cooked she cut wood and made a branch shelter against a little hill. By the time she had finished the sky was spitting icy snow at her.

That night she sat staring into a veil of white. As usual, she spent her spare time worrying. First off she worried about what had happened to Emily Jones. (God forgive her, but she hadn't even thought about her until that very day!) They had to have figured out who let her out, but even if they hadn't, all they had to do was ask. Knowing Emily, she wouldn't deny it. God, she hoped she hadn't been put in jail! There was nothing she could do about poor Emily, but she stewed about it anyway.

Then she worried that she had probably cost Jim Horse his job. He liked his job and he was good at it, but being the prideful man he was, he might've taken responsibility for her escape and resigned! She could see him doing that. Actually she could see him doing a lot of things. Sitting at his desk and chewing his pencil. Flipping through wanted dodgers. Striding across the street. Blowing on the surface of his coffee. Running his hand through his hair. Talking to Bull Durham. Glaring at Tippet.

And sometimes she could see him standing in the moonlight, wearing only a bear claw necklace.

To her dismay, she started to cry. She gave in to it and let the tears flow. Sometimes she would think of him and a frighteningly powerful longing would come over her. Apparently, this was going to be one of those times.

She didn't know what time she slept but it was close to dawn. She woke shivering and found snow mounded on her coat. A wind switch from the south to the north had almost buried her alive. She quickly packed up and set off. Half froze like she was, it took three miles of fast walking to warm up.

The next day, still heading north, she bought coffee and some soda crackers in a small town called Jones Ferry and that was all she had to eat until she came on a deer standing beneath a solitary jack pine. It turned and looked at her and she expected it to bound off but it didn't. Coming closer she could see why: It must've found a gopher hole through the snow because its hind leg was broken.

She knelt and looked at it and it occurred to her that the poor thing was a lot like her. It had few options and all were bad. It could freeze to death or starve to death or it could be eaten by wolves. Or it could be eaten by her.

She decided the latter was the best all around. She should have cut its throat but she hadn't the stomach for it. She would have to risk a shot or go hungry. Sadly she raised her rifle.

Carrying as much meat as she could pack, she made sure she got far away from that area before she cooked it. She found a place she thought was safe: a ledge that was at the base of an overhang fifty feet above the ground. If it wasn't snowing or pitch night, she could see anyone or anything's approach. There she stayed two days, eating and gathering her strength.

The next days saw her deep into the heavy woodlands, a land of clear running streams and dense towering timber. Her heart was glad. It would not be long now.

Two days later she came on a cabin beside a frozen stream. The door stood open and clothing and utensils were strewn all about the yard. No smoke rose from the chimney but she took her time approaching, moving silent as a whisper and taking great care not to be seen. She needn't've bothered. Both the people inside the cabin had been murdered, the man shot and the woman's throat cut. That was the least that had been done to the woman.

She sawed through the bindings that tied the woman's hands and feet to stakes in the floor and covered her body. Since she could not bury them in the frozen ground, she poured coal oil on everything and set the building on fire.

She hated to destroy the cabin because now no one would see what she had seen: that the footsteps in the bloody dirt had been made by moccasins with something hung off the back.

After that, she avoided open country and did most of her walking in the early morning or before the moon rose in the late evening. Starved and stumbling from exhaustion, she had lost track of the days and nights and so she was actually surprised when she saw Wolf Woman's cabin below her.

Surprised and happy! She was never so glad to see anything in her life! She had lived there for eight months, unwilling to leave the old woman alone while she died. It was the most home she had ever known.

The cabin was in a protected valley now filled with wind-lined snow that seemed to go on forever. She hid in the trees and watched for signs of life but nothing moved on land or in the sky and had not, it appeared, for several days.

That there were no tracks was both good and bad. It meant that no squatter had taken over the cabin, but it also meant that Coco-man had not been there. At least not since the last snowfall. She prayed that he hadn't been shot by some nervous farmer on his way north or worse, been caught in a trap.

There was much to do those first days. Cut more wood. Find food. Cut more wood. Hunt. Re-chink holes in the walls. Cut more wood. She did all of this and more in spite of the fact that what she really wanted to do was put on her snowshoes and go hunt for Coco-man.

The third day she stepped outside. The sun was bright on the frozen land and the air was still and crystal clear. Having eaten and rested, she now felt good. Leaning back inside she took the snowshoes off the peg and tossed them by the door. Then she gathered her rifle, added bullets to the ammunition pouch and stuck her axe in her belt.

She would look for Coco-man and chop some more wood at the same time.

Chapter 26

The morning air was crisp and clean and Jim welcomed the cold wind that tugged at his hat because it also carried the faint scent of wood smoke.

Crouching low he crested a hill and there below was an abandoned logging camp, exactly where old Crowbait had said it would be. The settlement consisted of several run-down cabins and shabby, weathered outbuildings, but the only sign of habitation was one pencil-thin column of smoke.

A dog started barking as he rode in. In clear view he dismounted and fired a shot into the air. When a stranger "shot his wad" in the days before the repeaters it meant that he approached in peace. Jim figured an oldtimer like this "Indian Ed" fella would recognize the signal.

Jim stood in the open yard and tried to ignore the stiff-legged dog that stood about ten feet away. Its ears were laid back and every hair on end. How do dogs bark without ever stopping to draw a breath?

A long time passed so he leaned his gun against the wheel of an ancient wagon and sat down on the dropped tongue. A minute then another slipped by and still no movement from the cabin. He sure hoped somebody showed soon; a stinging snow had come along with the rising wind. Eventually the door opened and a raisin-eyed face appeared.

"What do you want?"

"To talk."

"What about?"

"I'm looking for someone."

"Is it me?"

"No."

"Then you're outa luck—ain't nobody here but me." The door started to close.

"Maybe you've seen the person."

"Ain't seen nobody for four years. Shut up, dog!"

"An old friend of yours says different."

"Ain't got no friends old or new."

"What about a mountain man named Cates?" Nothing. "He told me that even if you had not seen the one I seek you might be interested in taking care of my horse for me. For money."

"American?"

"American."

Like a suspicious turtle, he stuck his head out far enough to eyeball Jim's gelding. The dish-faced bay was probably the finest piece of horse flesh the old man had ever seen.

"Well?" He came outside then.

"Mebbe I will an' then again, mebbe I won't."

He was small and worn-looking and bald as a board but he carried a double-barreled shotgun like he knew which end worked.

"You got good reason to be so suspicious of strangers?"

"I thought mebbe you was gonna steal my dog."

Jim considered the mouse-colored mange-ridden hound. "Another time maybe. I don't feel like eating dog today."

Indian Ed showed Jim some gums that he could've mistaken for his gun bore. "Not today! Ha! Ha!" The laughter ended abruptly. He nodded at the horse. "How much and how long?"

"Twenty bucks and three months."

"Headed north?"

"Yeah."

"What happens if you get et by a bear?"

"Then you got yourself a McClelland saddle worth thirty bucks and horse worth two hundred."

"Two hunnerd!" He tried whistling through teeth which were no longer there. It was not a pretty sight. "Guess that's all right by me."

"Where do you want him?"

He ran his sleeve across his mouth and pointed to a building that had a rail corral off one end. "In there's all right."

Following close behind, he said that the people who'd moved on had left in a hurry and left a lot behind. Did he know that Cates's first name was Crowbait? Did he know that they were fixin' to get a storm?

Jim picked out a stall where the roof appeared pretty good. He led the bay into it and removed the saddle. The old man watched. The horse acted faunchy until Jim settled him with some calm conversation and an oat-filled feedbag. And the old man watched. Jim rubbed the horse down in silence and then he turned and hard-eyed the old man . . . who was belatedly remembering that he had left his rifle propped against the cabin.

"What? I say somethin' wrong?"

Jim stalked the old man until he'd backed him into a corner. "Close your mouth and listen to me."

Indian Ed laid his head between his shoulder blades and swallowed hard—which wasn't easy to do with his Adam's apple pointing at the rafters. "I'm listenin'!"

"You trade off or sell this horse before three months is out and I will eat you. And your dog!" There was no truth to the story that Ojibwe ate their enemies—not dogs either—but he knew some whites who believed that they did.

That's exactly what Indian Ed was thinking. Most people thought Ojibwe meant "puckered" after the unusual seam that they sewed on their moccasins. But he'd once heard that "puckered" was the condition they liked their enemies' skin before they commenced carving!

"How about thirty dollars and I hold the horse six months?"

"Deal."

Indian Ed turned quite a bit friendlier then. He said he had just made breakfast and offered Jim a meal which he gladly accepted. While they were in the barn the snowfall had increased to a blanket of flakes, feather-soft but icy-cold.

Indian Ed's cabin was unkempt and fusty smelling, but it was dry and warm. Jim hung his hat on a deer antler rack and his coat on the back of a chair pulled close to the fire. He sat on an upturned keg next to a plank table. While Indian Ed dished up hot venison stew, Jim asked him about Thora Gunn. It was the same question he'd asked twenty others during the last four months.

"A lone female? Ha! I ain't seen a female alone since '38 down in Mason City. She was a l'il ol' gal who like to, ah, . . ."

Something in the sheriff's face drew him up and he did not expound further. *This is sure a serious fella. Even for a lawman.* "Why would a female travel around these parts alone?"

Not without pride Jim answered, "Because she is Thora Gunn." *And will travel where ever she damn well pleases.*

He described her and in case she had endeared herself to the old man, he explained that he wished the girl no harm, that he was actually the bearer of good tidings. He went on then and told him about the trial—Indian Ed was apparently the only person within a thousand miles who hadn't heard about it—and said that he was trying to find her to tell her she didn't have to hide out for the rest of her life.

Indian Ed just looked at him with those small shrewd eyes, as if he knew there was more to it than that and Jim felt his dander rise. "Well, damnit! You seen her or not?"

"I'm thinkin'." He made his mouth into a cat's butthole and looked at the roof. Finally he said, "No. No. No. Jus' like I tole you in t'beginnin'. No."

Jim set off with the old coot's harebrained cackle grating on his ears.

Chapter 27

A few days after she'd arrived she got a terrible craving for some fish, so she sharpened her spear, repaired a lure made out of a piece of fur and beads and went fishing.

A sandy finger of land ran thirty feet out into the lake. In the summer it was a wild and lovely home to crying gulls, yodeling loons and playful beaver, a spectacular site for watching vivid sunsets or listening to lapping waves. At the moment it looked like such a barren place it could not possibly sustain any life, plant or animal.

One side of the point was a sheer drop-off to a rock-strewn depth of ten feet. The other side gradually declined into a weedy habitat that was a favorite haunt of northern pike. She used her hatchet to break through the ice and then widened it to a foot square. It was bitterly cold. She had a rag across half her face and still the wind sucked the air out of her lungs.

She was bent over, working the lure with her left hand and holding the spear in her right when she felt her neck hairs prickle. She was being observed by someone.

Without lifting or moving her head she scanned as much of the shore as she could and saw nothing. She was, however, surer than ever that someone was present.

As if disgusted with her luck, she pulled up the lure and

stabbed the spear into snow. Then in one move, she dropped to her knee and scooped up the rifle and sighted on shore. A huge wolf was hunkered under the pines. "Coco-man!" He bounded toward her as she raced back along the point laughing. They fell together and tumbled around like pups. "God, am I glad to see you! Let me look at you. Here! Hold still. Quit licking a minute!"

He looked fine to her. Wider through the chest and leaner in the haunches, but he bore no new scars. They fished together and she caught two pike about ten pounds each. That night she made fish cakes, a personal favorite of them both.

"I can't tell you how much I missed you!" Coco stopped eating and twitched his ears at her. She leaned over and scratched between his eyes. He loved that! Suddenly she was sad. "You know, I swear you can understand me." She sighed. "Maybe you are the only living thing that will ever understand me."

She tried to cheer up. At least she had Coco back. "Well, wait till you hear what happened after you left!" She talked to him half the night. At least for that time she was content.

Weeks went by and her life's routine was one totally geared to survival. Heat and food. That's all that mattered in the wilderness. From dawn to dusk she had to work hard for both. The child within her grew, but her body elsewhere got leaner and stronger.

Her friend Coco was gone for long stretches of time, but such behavior was normal. He was no longer a pup. He may have joined a pack or he could have selected his life's mate and formed one of his own! She was happy for him if either were true but still, without him her life was very lonely.

Like it or not, she had formed a bond with those people in Two Sisters and now she who had always been most comfortable alone was never more lonely! She thought of them often. Sissy and Joe Willie, Buddy and the Fagerhaugs. Emily and Jim Horse. Yes, him too.

Him too? Liar! Him first. Him longest. Him most often.

During hard snow days, she spent a lot of time sitting cross-legged before the fire, staring blindly into space, and any fool could figure out why. She was pining. And for a man who had never given her any indication that he wanted anything from her but what he'd already gotten!

If Jim had left any tracks over the last months they would have looked like a huge jagged saw as he zigged and zagged his way over three hundred miles of northern wilderness. But in spite of this all-out effort, he found no sign of her. Some weeks back he decided he had gone far enough to the north and headed west. Then frustrated with his lack of success, he'd recently started south again. Damnit, the girl had either crawled into a foxhole and pulled it in after her or she was dead.

He was still on foot but at a brisk trot he could easily do five miles an hour, hour after hour, even in heavily wooded terrain.

To the north and east lay the huge waterway the whites called the English River System. To the west lay Cygnet Lake, a place where his clan used to camp every spring in order to tap the sugar maples for syrup. Not too many miles to the south was a place where his grandmother went to gather spices like wild ginger and bear berry and mountain mint. He was at home. This land of snow-covered pines and icy streams had been his peoples' since man had memory.

A light snow was falling as he topped a pine-studded ridge to study the mottled landscape below. Though spring was nigh, the land was still stark and winter barren with leafless trees that appeared stunted-looking against the sky.

In the distance were the lights of the town of Menaki. It looked like it had grown since he had been here last. He counted over thirty stove-pipe chimneys doing their part to add to an already murky dusk. Perched at the base of a dark-timbered slope about a mile this side of town was a building easily recognized as a trade outpost.

Such places were often the unwilling recipients of gossip, mail and messages, but if this place turned out to be an exception he could at least buy some coffee. Before he started down he slipped the quilled buckskin cover off his .45–70 Winchester repeater and worked the lever to send a cartridge into the chamber. Menaki had always been a town with little or no law.

The post was built in the manner of the American Fur and

Hudson Bay stations and so was typical of many strung out along that part of Canada. Made entirely of unpeeled logs, the main building was about fifty feet square excluding a long narrow porch that ran across the front. Its deeply slanted roof was made of split cedar and it had one chimney at its peak and one on either end. Its outbuildings were built with sawed lodgepoles.

Moving silent as a cat he ascended the stairs then paused beneath an impressive moose rack that was nailed above the door. When he heard no sounds of mayhem from within, he lifted the leather latch and slipped inside.

The interior had been halved with the store in front and the proprietor's living quarters in back, probably behind a piece of bunched fabric that hung on a pole in a doorway.

The usual stuff cluttered the rafters: traps, snowshoes, galvanized buckets, cast-iron pots. Stacked on the shelves were tins of coffee, tobacco, canned fruit and rodent poison. On one wall was a birch canoe and several pair of crossed skiis. On another was a padlocked slat cabinet that contained several firearms. A Winchester '73 had a bargain price of twelve bucks.

On a counter made from planks laid across hogshead barrels was a stack of prime pelts. Beaver and fox mostly. For a brief moment a head appeared to be growing out of them. "No whiskey. We sell no whiskey!"

Jim stood there, frowning at the spot where the face had disappeared. Damned if there hadn't been something familiar about that man. He moved to a better spot and asked, "What about coffee?" The face reappeared and coal black eyes looked him over top to bottom. "I'll be damned! That you, Fong?"

"Jim Horse!"

"Yeah."

"Jim Horse!" The man stepped from behind the counter and in the worst Ojibwe Jim had ever heard called, "Bring coffee, Betty!" He clasped Jim's hand and primed it like a pump. "Jim Horse! What are you doing in Menaki?"

"I was gonna ask you the same thing. Last time I saw you, you were headed for San Francisco." It was true. Fong had left Two Sisters some four years ago. Matter of fact, it was his job that Sissy Heck had taken at Buddy's when she first came to town.

Fong nodded. "I was going to San Francisco. On train I met a Dutchman who was going to California too. He told me about this place. Said he got into knife fight with man and killed him. Had to leave town very quick."

Velly quik! His English was as bad as his Ojibwe.

"I make offer to buy. Man accept. Gave me a paper with his um . . . " He pressed his thumb on the counter.

"His mark?" Jim supplied.

"Yes. Two people on train witness mark-making and then I come here."

Jim looked around. "Well, it's damn nice, Fong."

"Not nice when I come!" cried Fong with a grimace. "No floor there. Fireplace falling. Mice all over. Dirty! Augh! I have to fix everything." He examined Jim a minute then pointed at the black patch. "Eye sore?"

"Eye gone."

"Gone! What happen?"

Jim replied, "Hurt bad in fight." Damn, it was catching! "I was in a bad fight."

"Huh! I finish here. We sit and talk."

While Fong tossed the furs in a pile on the floor (and tried to imagine the sort of man who could best Jim Horse in a fight!) Jim idly picked up a bottle off the counter. *Sozodont. Guaranteed to cure impure breath, catarrh and seizures of the lower system.*

The curtains parted and a woman appeared carrying a coffee-pot and two mugs. Tag-tailing along behind her were three small, very handsome children. Jim didn't know the woman but she was Ojibwe. He gave her a suitable greeting for a single man to a married woman, respectful but not too friendly.

"These yours, Fong?"

"Yes." Dolefully. "Worthless children named . . . " He pointed at them in turn, stepping down in size with each. "Rain. Sun. Cloud. Worthless woman is my wife, Betty Wildbird."

"Hu'ah!" Jim said. The woman smiled modestly and Fong nodded and grinned, pleased as Punch. "Next one maybe named Snow."

With her shapeless outfit Jim didn't know if Fong was predicting or speculating but he looked at the Chinaman and nodded solemnly. "Snow is a fine name."

They sat and smoked and drank coffee—or at least Jim did. Fong's cup smelled like anibic, an Ojibwe drink that Jim had never acquired a taste for. After a suitably courteous period of time—both by Ojibwe and Chinese standards—Fong asked, "Why are you here now? Not deputy any more?"

Jim explained about Joe Willie's retirement and that he was the sheriff now. Fong raised his eyebrows but didn't comment. Jim told what had happened to the man/child that Fong had known as Thor.

"Big here . . . " He held his hands wide then tapped his head. ". . . but little here?"

"That's him."

Fong shook his head and looked greatly saddened. "Buddy cooked for him."

"Yes."

"Junior Buel!" He grimaced. "Never liked him."

The door opened then and a white man entered, shaggy in tattered skins but carrying a new Remington rifle. A sixteen-inch scabbard hung from his belt and a coon tail hung off the back of each moccasin. He looked like an ape, with a sloping forehead and a big-holed nose. Above a matted beard his face was pox-pitted and his eyes were like ice.

He interested Jim from a professional point of view. Not many years ago a man who fit this one's description had aligned himself with some renegade Indians and robbed, raped and murdered several immigrants who had settled in remote areas. Nobody ever proved who did it and when the killings stopped people thought the renegades had left the area. Seeing him now, Jim wasn't sure about that. There weren't many men as ugly as this one.

The man spared Fong only a glance but he gave Jim a thorough once over. Jim gave him a look right back and smiled a not particularly friendly smile. The man paid for a six-ounce plug of tobacco and left.

"You know that fella, Fong?"

"Only by . . . uh can't remember how to say."

"Reputation?"

"Mm. He is whiskey runner sometimes. Trapper sometimes. Trouble all times. They say he killed a Menomenee man in Kenora and when the dead boy's younger brother—foolish kid of only twelve—hit him, he killed the kid as well. Not because he had to but because he could.'' Fong shook his head. ''Their mother had only two sons and now she has none.''

Betty Wildbird brought more coffee and Jim told Fong that it was a girl named Thora Gunn who had killed Buel.

''A girl!''

''Yeah. The hung man's sister.'' Then he told about the trial and about her escape only a day before the jury found her not guilty. ''That's how come I've been looking for her.''

''How long now?''

''Four months.''

''Four months!''

''Yeah.'' He told Fong that he'd been as far north as Caribo Falls, as far east as Wabigoon River and as far west as Manitoba. Looking off somewhere he finished with a completely unnecessary statement. ''I sure would like to find her.''

Fong studied the other man with a shrewd eye. He sensed that Jim wanted to find her for more than just to tell her she was not guilty and this surprised him. Jim Horse was not the same man he had been when Fong lived in Two Sisters.

The three big-eyed kids and Betty Wildbird had been listening to everything. The woman signaled to Fong and he nodded. ''Betty has something to say.''

Fong's wife told Jim that now that the white man had forced the Ojibwe to stop killing their ancient enemies, there were a lot of Cree, Santee and Teton living in the area. Even many Nadoliessans—snakes in the grass—had crept back. She said that her cousin Mary Loon had taken up with a Nadoliessan. Mary Loon, she added, had never had much personal pride.

Fong gently urged her along. ''And your idea is?''

That since the Nadoliessans traded with those with whom the Ojibwe would not trade she could go ask Mary Loon to talk to her husband's people about Jim Horse's woman. With her honorable husband's permission, of course.

Jim was going to correct her about that ''Jim Horse's woman'' but he decided not to. He sorta liked the sound of it. ''I could not ask you to do that,'' he replied politely. ''It would be a lot of trouble.''

''She wants to go,'' said Fong. ''Mary Loon is her closest friend.''

Betty spoke again. As a clincher she said she would also tell all the "Ojibwe" that she saw along the way. "I am only a worthless woman but maybe . . . " She shrugged and left it at that.

Jim considered what she said and decided it was probably a good idea; all Indians in this part of the country were suspicious of outsiders, even another Ojibwe like himself. Fong sighed dramatically and took the decision out of Jim's hands. "Better go, Betty."

That fast, Betty disappeared and it seemed only seconds later that she reappeared with a blanket drawn over her head and a parfleche bag dangling from her arm. The door quietly closed. "She goes," Fong said. "She goes and leaves me with these worthless children." He turned to his brood but his eyes belied his mournful tone. "Come now and say good-night to Jim Horse!"

As the children dutifully approached, a foul odor came with them. Jim's nose twitched. "God, Fong! Something's crawled in one of their pockets and died."

"No." Fong pointed at his middle boy. "That one has a bad cough."

That same instant Jim placed the smell. A noxious concoction of goose lard mixed with turpentine. He'd had his share of it spread on his own chest when he was their age. It made him think of his grandmother and he missed her.

By the time Fong returned from seeing the children off to bed, Jim Horse had laid out his bedroll in front of the fire. Without looking around, he said, "I assume it'll be all right to stay here tonight?" When he turned he saw Fong had a rabbit-skin blanket over his arm. With a formal little bow he handed it to him. "Jim Horse is honored guest in this poor house."

Betty Wildbird returned in only three sleeps but it took almost a week to get results. A runner came in, a young Cree named Bear Paw. The Cree and Ojibwe had never liked each other. Apparently the Cree did not like Chinese either. After a mean-eyed look at Jim Horse and Fong, he spoke directly to Betty

Wildbird and rudely ignored both men. Jim, however, understood every word he said.

The girl who was sought might live one or two sleeps south of Rat Portage, on the north side of Lake of the Woods. A young woman once brought ducks and fish into an outpost there to trade for flour and coffee, and the trader had remembered her well. Why? Jim asked and was ignored, but when Betty asked the same question the Cree replied that it was because all the ducks the girl brought in to trade had no feet. The trader remarked on this strange thing and the girl said that a sudden storm had blown in and froze the ducks' feet in the ice.

The Cree said it was rumored that the girl was living in the cabin of an old Ojibwe woman who had been ostracized and banished many years ago. The trader thought maybe the old woman was dead. She had been called Wolf Woman.

After the Cree left, Jim thought about how Thora had said she'd found her wolf pup and it all made sense. Rat Portage was so called by the Indians because it was where the muskrats portaged back and forth between the Winnipeg River and Lake of the Woods. The whites called it Kenora. There were many wolves in that area.

Jim bought some .45-caliber bullets for his Winchester and a bag of coffee and left immediately. At the top of the hill he turned and waved and Fong's entire family waved back.

Chapter 28

Jim found the cabin in an area he had always thought was uninhabited . . . other than by bears, wolves and deer, and he only saw it because he knew it was there.

The small structure had been built at the confluence of two streams and was well hidden in a pine, fir and cedar forest. Living trees had been pulled down to form its four corners and Saskatoon bushes filled in the blanks. A canted rock chimney stuck out of one corner yet he saw no evidence of a fire within. Moving closer showed him why. Tied to the chimney were branches that both screened it from curious eyes and scattered the rising smoke.

Careful that he could not be seen himself, he lay down flat and removed some field glasses from a battered leather case. From his bird's-eye view he saw that the valley extended nearly a mile east to west and that the two streams fed into a small snow-covered lake that sat like a bowl of flour to the south. He turned the glasses back on the dwelling.

It was made completely of unpeeled logs chinked with clay and dried moss. Its roof was dome-shaped and covered with rolls of birch bark. He knew the inside would be dark as a cave; wood slats that could be pried off in the spring covered two square openings in front.

He had not seen the wolf, but moving cautiously from tree to tree and staying high, he circled until he was downwind. From this new angle he noted the birch-bark canoe that hung on an elkhorn rack on one side of the building. It was a well-made one, wide in the center and narrow and high on each end. Of the girl he saw no sign yet he knew she was there. He could sense her presence like that wolf of hers could sniff out blood.

Oh, yeah, she was in there all right.

The moon rose and shaded the trees in light and dark and still he laid up there on the ridge. No light came from the cabin but he continued to watch the spot where he knew it was and along about midnight he saw the door open. The wolf came out and the door closed.

Jim rolled onto his back and grinned up at the stars. He had found her!

First thing in the morning he saw her stumble outside, go around the cabin and hurry along a narrow goat-trail path that led deeper into the woods. She returned fiddling with the rope that held up her pants. Not long after that she came out again wearing an elkskin jacket with an axe stuck in the belt. He watched her harness the wolf to a toboggan and disappear into a stand of red oaks. In less than two hours she returned. The toboggan was piled high with stove wood and dangling from a rope around her neck was a good-sized hen turkey. Jim smacked his lips. He was especially fond of roasted hen turkey!

To pluck it she sat in the doorway with the bird on the ground between her legs. The wolf sat patiently and was soon rewarded with the entrails, the head and one turkey leg. She disappeared inside and though she had obviously spitted it over an inside fire, Jim spent the afternoon imagining that the air was filled with the smell of roasting turkey.

She kept busy all day. With a bucket she replaced some chinking around one of the windows, then she hauled water and stacked wood and oiled the runners on the toboggan. By dusk she was inside for the night.

He wrapped himself in his buffalo robe and sat propped against a tree. The moon rose and gleamed dully on the cabin and surrounding trees and soon the sky was full of shining stars of icy brilliance. He heard no human sounds, only the rustling of small animals and the sound of a soft wind through the trees. Twice he heard the honking of northbound geese. Still smiling, he soon drifted into a contented sleep.

Two days and nights went by and still he watched. Each night at sundown when he was sure she was inside for the night, he would explore the surrounding country.

For three miles in all directions he saw no sign of habitation except by the creatures of the wild. Game was plentiful. He spotted tracks of all sizes; from the little muskrat dragging the tip of its tail between its hind feet to the posthole-deep tracks of the mighty moose.

On the third morning he observed her returning with a prairie chicken tied to her sled and decided enough was enough. He tossed aside the jerky he had been chewing on and went to gather his things. It was time to take a look at the lioness' lair. He waited until she left to collect more wood and then he went down.

He closed the door behind him and the first thing he saw was her bed of woven balsam branches. When he touched the flour-sack pillowcase was the first he realized that he had crossed the room and it was a minute before he continued his examination of the cabin.

It was crowded but orderly. Bulrush mats were spread over a dirt floor and buffalo hides had been stretched on the walls for warmth. The windows, nailed shut as he had suspected, had potato-sack curtains bunched to one side and tied with twine.

Suspended from the ceiling were parfleches containing smoked meat and bunches of dried yarrow. A woman's work bag, the base of which was four deer hooves, contained some dark blue broadcloth of the sort traded at places like Fong's. Two deerskins were folded in a corner, ready to work on. Beneath a woven basket of dried squash he found slats that probably covered a root cellar dug deep enough to prevent freezing. On a shelf sat jars of seasonings; wild ginger, bear berry and mountain mint and a sack of wild rice and a jug of maple sugar. The fowl she had caught was on a spit above the banked fire. He twisted off a leg and juggled it until it cooled. God, he was hungry!

He had his hands on his hips and a greasy half smile on his face, when on the smoke-stained oak ledge above the fire he saw a can of Blackwell's Bull Durham! Anger rocked him as it never had before! She had taken a man! Damn her! She had already found someone and invited him to share her lodge! Then racing through his mind was the thought that maybe the man was someone she had cared about before she offered herself to him. That made him even madder. Bah! She had the soul of a slut!

He was so stunned that he did not hear her enter, and he turned the same moment she fired. It probably saved his life.

The bullet knocked him to one knee but he knew he wasn't badly hurt—not like the time he had been shot in the back. Besides pain was the last thing on his mind. What was on his mind was the sure knowledge that he was a damn fool! While he had been mooning around like an idiot, she had taken another!

He roared like an injured bear and charged, batting the gun from her hands and kicking the door closed. Dragging her by the neck he threw her on the bed and threw himself on top of her. For a long minute he just stared at her. Then he kissed her hard, angrily, as if he would remove the other man from his mind with a kiss. It worked. The heat of her mouth spread through him and rational thought went elsewhere. Eventually he lifted his head. "What is that lump?"

"It's your lump."

"Not that! Yours! The one on your stomach."

"Nothin . . . Stop that! Quit it!"

He tore at her clothes until she was bared to his gaze. And gaze he did. So long and so hard her skin felt like it had seen too much sun. Then he put his hand on her rounded stomach. She groaned and drew up her legs. "Don't," she whispered.

"Are you in pain?"

"No!" she spat, angry with herself for her reaction to his touch.

"What then?"

"You're bleeding on my bed!"

He allowed himself to feel the pain and realized that she was right, but a little puddle of blood did not concern him now.

"Whose tobacco is that?"

"What?" It wasn't that she hadn't heard him. He was shouting loud enough to be heard in Kenora.

"Whose tobacco is that over there on the mantel?"

"Wolf Woman's." He saw that she was honestly puzzled. "Why?"

The last thing he remembered saying was, "I may feel like smoking . . . later."

Getting out from under him removed at least a half an inch of skin but she finally stood looking down at him. She didn't care how he got here or why he'd come, but after that kiss she had a feeling it wasn't to take her back to hang. A half smile came to her lips. She cupped her stomach and said, "Look, little one! This is your father. His name is Jim Horse."

Chapter 29

When he came to, she was kneeling on the hearth sharpening a curved skinning knife on a whetstone. She stuck the blade into the fire, held it there and then rose and came toward him.

The bullet had entered a few inches above his waist. She imagined she could see it tenting the skin in front. At least she hoped that was what she was seeing because that's where she intended to make the incision. She had to hurry; he'd already lost a lot of blood. His face was inches from hers. She wanted to stroke it, to draw her fingers across his lips and press her open mouth to his chest. She tore her eyes away and willed the knife to quit quivering.

"I didn't come to take you back."

"Good. Because I'm not going."

He made no sound when she cut the bullet out but she could tell from the way he was holding his jaw that he was in pain.

When she finished, she dropped the bullet on his chest and then slapped a foul-smelling poultice on the incision. He lifted his head. "What's that?"

"A bullet."

"No, that glop."

"I don't know."

"What do you mean, you don't know?"

"Wolf Woman made up the powder. It's got a lot of stuff in it but I think it's mostly puffballs."

"Puffballs!" He knew that "puffballs" had medicinal qualities, but she wasn't having any of his teasing.

"Yes." Indignant. "Dried, ground puffballs."

"With rat tails and frog hairs?"

"And snake eyes, squirrel eggs." She shrugged. "The usual."

"Hu'ah," he croaked. "Feels good!"

His eye rolled like a marble in a plate. He said, "I think maybe I'll rest a minute." And then passed out for two days.

Smells came to him first, those of sage and roast pheasant and baking bread. His mouth watered and his stomach clenched. Lord, he was hungry! He opened his eye. A pheasant was indeed impaled over the fire! How had she known that it was his favorite meal? Steam and a spicy smell rose from a black kettle that was suspended over the fire. Wild rice with onions! Mm. And there on the hearth! A frying pan contained legolet bread—a flat round bread made only with flour, salt and water. He loved legolet bread. She stood and eyed him with her hands on her hips.

"You're awake. Finally."

"Yeah, well, it was a pretty long walk up here."

"What about the wound?"

"The wound? He waved his hand. "It's nothing."

"You lost a lot of blood."

"I always do."

She brought him some green tea and tried to feed it to him with a wooden spoon but he pushed her hand away. "I want the bread and pheasant."

"Not yet. You'll spit it up."

"No, I won't." He folded his arms and set his mouth in a petulant line. "I want the pheasant."

"You haven't had anything on your stomach for two days. You need to start with something that won't make you sick."

"I want the pheasant."

"All right. I wash my hands."

"I hope you did that before you stuffed the bird."

"Listen. I didn't have to patch you up, you know."

He made a conciliatory move which she ignored. Though righteously annoyed, she took a peeled bark plate from the shelf and put a pheasant leg on it, then a spoonful of wild rice with a dollop of maple syrup and a wedge of legolet bread. She handed it all to him and then pointed to the birch bark bucket that sat beside the bed.

"There's the bucket."

When his head stopped spinning and he could speak without spitting up, he said, "Did you know it was me?" She threaded one arm through a rawhide strap and positioned her rifle on her back.

"When?" She stuck a small axe in her belt and pulled on a flop-brimmed hat.

"When? When you fired."

"Yes," she said.

"Most people would've lied about that."

He had spoken to a slammed door. His head met the pillow and selecting the best words in both Ojibwe and English, he cursed soundly.

Suddenly the door opened and she stood there, looking at him and then looking at her feet. "I didn't know it was you." The door closed again. Jim grinned and nodded sagely. "Hu'ah!"

Without thinking about his wound he went to put his hands behind his head and had to choke back a very unmanly—not to mention un-Indian—scream.

She rose at dawn to stroke the fire and knew he was awake, waiting for her to change his dressing. Yesterday she noticed that he liked it. Soon as she put her hands on him, his stomach sank and another part of him rose. She pretended she didn't notice the lump under the thin blanket she'd spread over him, but she didn't think she carried it off. Well, good Lord! She would have to be blind as a bat!

As for himself, he had become quite a different patient from that first day when he pretended no pain. She liked him better when he pretended.

"I think I have a fever," he said. She laid a concerned cheek on his forehead, but his head was cool.

"I don't think you do."

"I think so."

"I don't. Really."

"Better check again."

She did and eventually realized that her chest was practically in his face and the object of a very intense, one-eyed scrutiny.

Next day he started groaning and scissoring his legs and thrashing his head but she was wise to him now and went on about her chores as if he were not there.

Only he was. Oh, yes. And he watched her like a hawk.

She decided that two could play this game and it started to take a lot of time for her to get ready in the morning. Braiding her hair, smoothing her pants, tieing on her moccasins. A lot more time. Had he noticed that her breasts were bigger? She turned a certain way in case he was looking. Then she lifted both hands and smoothed her hair. Then she bent to pick up her hat and glanced at him. Oh, yeah, he was looking all right.

The first warm day, she helped him to a chair and set about cleaning. She rolled up the bulrush mats and swept the floor with a broom made of pine boughs. Then she hauled the bedding outside and aired it by spreading it on some bushes. He watched through the open door, sitting as if he were slumped against a stabbing ache in his side. Of course, he could not walk because if he could walk, he could leave. No, no. He was far from well.

God, he felt good! Spring tinged the hills with green and yellow and soaked the earth with its smells. In the woods he knew he would see wild grass shoots showing through the decayed leaves of autumn, and fiddlehead ferns uncoiling toward the sun, and swarms of tadpoles swimming between reeds still encrusted with ice. Animals were selecting their mates. Birds were looking over prospective nesters, checking for firm breasts and a narrow waist and rounded hips.

Who would have thought the sight of a robin could drive a man crazy with need?

When she came back inside she carried a pot she had scrubbed in the stream and set to air dry. He noticed that she pushed aside his eye patch in order to set the pot on the table. Funny that he hadn't thought of it before but now he wondered if she had recoiled when she saw his face. "Bet you were shocked when you first saw my eye."

She glanced at him on her way to stir up the fire. "You mean where your eye used to be?"

"Yeah." She picked up the sack of wild rice and put some in the pot and added water and covered it with a lid. "Bet you never saw anything like it before."

"Nuh-uh, I never have" She went closer. The scar was the only imperfection in an otherwise splendid face. No need, however, to get him gloating. With her finger on his chin she turned his head into the light. "Does it ever ache?"

"No."

"That's good." She carried the pot containing the wild rice outside and set it in the sun to soak and started off somewhere.

"Hey!" He called after her.

"What?"

"Where you going?"

"To find the hammer. I left it out here somewhere." She was looking around.

He grinned to himself. "Hammer! Hell, I'm starvin' in here."

"You are always starving," she muttered. Louder, she said, "I want to take the wood off the windows first then I'll fix you something."

"I'll be glad when I can feed myself!" He had been playing possum for two days.

She stuck her head inside and almost caught him grinning. "I will be, too!"

When he could no longer claim to be an invalid he got up and started doing his share. But not very fast and not so much that she would start to wonder if he was well enough to leave.

One night she sat on the floor stitching a tear on her moccasin and he sat crosslegged beside her, cleaning his rifle. They were working by firelight. She had washed her hair earlier and it hung in tangled curls to her waist. He longed to touch it. To bury his nose in it. To feel it fanned across his chest.

She fascinated him, sometimes acting like a hopeful little girl, other times like a shrewd old woman. He anticipated spending his life finding out about her. It would take at least that long because he would not want to hurry. Like a kid hoarding a treat to make it last, he would wait until she revealed herself to him. Bit by bit.

"Tell me about your wife."

He looked at her, surprised by the question but she was picking at a seam. "Little Rain?"

"Yes."

"What about her?"

"Well . . . when did you meet?"

"The first spring after I returned from Oklahoma. At the sugar bush."

"What's that?"

"A sugar bush is the place where our clan went every spring to gather maple syrup. We would nail tin pails to the trees to catch the syrup and camp there for a week or two." He smiled sadly. "My grandmother wanted me to go with her. I had forgotten how much I used to enjoy going when I was a kid. The sap kettles were kept burning all night and the people from all the clans would gather around the fires and talk and tell stories."

"It sounds fun."

"It was. And if you had ever sat around a sap fire on a warm spring night, you would understand how easy it is to fall in love. Or to think you've fallen in love. Many children have been started by the light of a sap fire."

He smiled at her but she was still worrying that seam. She was also either blushing or sitting too close to the fire.

"Little Rain's clan was camped nearby and that's when we met. She was very young and so was I and . . . "

He shrugged and intended to leave it at that but she added, "And the sap was running."

"Hu'ah."

"How long were you married?"

"Six months. She complained of a sharp pain in her side, so bad she couldn't walk. I tried to get her to a doctor in time but she died on the way. I once asked Conor what he thought it was that killed her. He said probably a burst appendix and then peritonitis.'' She was looking at him with such sadness in her eyes that he touched her arm softly. ''I think of her with tenderness, but there is only one face in my mind.'' She met his gaze then looked away. Neither said anything for a minute, then she set aside her moccasin. ''I am tired. I think I'll go to bed.'' She made as if to stand and gave a little groan. Instantly he was on his feet to help her. ''What is it?''

''I am just so fat I can hardly get up any more. I'm surprised I haven't tipped over and busted my nose.''

He held her arms until she looked up at him. ''You look too thin to me.''

''Hah!'' She moved but he held her still and there was a deadly silence broken only by the sound of her own heart pounding in her ears. ''The jury acquitted you, you know.''

''Not guilty?'' she said softly.

''That's right. Not guilty.''

''I knew you hadn't come to arrest me.''

He nodded. ''Now you need never fear the law again.''

Instinctively, her voice became flirtatious. ''You came all this way just to tell me that?''

''No, not just for that.''

''For what else then?''

''I think you know.''

Their eyes locked and she looked away first. She moved to the window, and stood staring outside. Her thoughts were jumbled, her wants strange and disturbing. She quailed when she felt him come up behind her. He was going to touch her. She couldn't stand it if he did.

He did and she couldn't.

He kissed her temple and then the corner of her eye. Her lids fluttered closed. ''Please kiss me like you did when . . . No! No, don't . . . ''

''Don't what.''

''Don't touch me . . . there.''

''What about here?''

She heard the smile in his voice. ''Not there either . . . Well, all right. Oh, God! Just don't . . . oh, don't . . . Well, there on my neck's all right. Oooh!''

She sagged against him so he picked her up. "No . . . don't. Put me down." He did. On the bed. "Stop!" She had one hand on his chest but he mashed it between them and buried his face in her hair. Ah, that sweet smell. He remembered that and more. What her nipples tasted like and how it had felt when her body enclosed him like a fist.

"What are you doing?"

"Smelling your neck," he muttered.

Several seconds lapsed. "What does it smell like?"

"You don't know?"

"How could I . . . "

"Like a spring morning."

"Oh." She smiled. She frowned. "Quit it. Stop. Right now." She slapped at his hands but to no avail, one already covered her breast. He looked at her a long minute. "You aren't very big."

"I'm a lot bigger than I used to be!"

"I meant your stomach."

"Oh." Her frown deepened. "You know I was thinking that maybe the baby isn't big enough. You think?"

"I think it is a fine boy who will wait to do his growing until he is outside."

"Good! Yes. That's good."

She smiled up at him. He lowered his head then lifted it then he rolled over onto his back. To the ceiling he said, "Shit!"

She looked at him but he didn't look at all unhappy. Actually he was smiling. She smoothed her hair and pulled her shirt down. "What?"

"Nothing. Just a general comment." He sat up and got his hand under her shirt again. "Don't!" He parted it. "Hey! Quit it!" He pulled off her britches.

"Just let me look at you."

She might've said no but he was already flipping her this way and that.

"You know, of all the naked women I've ever seen I've never seen one pregnant. Here you've changed but from the back . . . nothing." A big hand covered her breast again. "Only here. And here . . . Mm. And here."

"Oh." she said and her eyes drifted closed. The fire brightened the room enough for him to see all that he wanted. Starting with her face, he kissed her cheeks, her temples, her lips and then moved on to all other places he wished and she did not care that her stomach was big and her legs were splayed. She didn't care about anything except how his slow hands and warm lips made her feel.

Later, when she could think clearly again she would be embarrassed by what she had said and the way she had acted, like how she'd snarled her hands in his hair and held him where she wanted him. Thank goodness it was a long time before she could think clearly again. They lay entangled, his arms tight around her, her head on his shoulder.

"What happened?"

"You flew too close to the sun."

"Mmm. Good!"

He woke her in the middle of the night. "One more thing," he said, as if they had just been speaking. "You don't have to run any more, right?"

"Mm."

He pushed her away so he could see her. She was lovely. Flushed. Mussed. Contented-looking. Just as he wished her to look always. She slitted one eye. "What?"

"But if something happens . . . "

"Yes?"

"And you think you need to run . . . " He tapped his chest. "You run here. Got it?"

She nodded. "Got it. Now can I get some sleep?"

Chapter 30

This planning thing may have come on late in life but it was, like dreaming, proving just as hard to shake. Now he was working on a plan for the rest of his life! And hers!

She had told him earlier that she thought the baby wasn't due for some time yet. Had she ever seen one born, he asked. No, she replied, but women did it all the time.

He'd acted unconcerned, but secretly he was worried. Very. Ojibwe women often died in childbirth. Yet when he'd casually suggested returning to Two Sisters, she'd said she didn't want to go back. Not ever? he'd asked and gotten a shrug in reply.

Which is where the planning came in. He'd decided that if she didn't want to go back, they wouldn't. The girl and the child were the most important things to him now. He would do whatever she wanted. Besides, would it be so bad to live like this forever?

He was propped on one elbow, watching her doze. She was a picture of languor, stretched out on the grass with one arm back behind her head, one hand splayed on her rounded stomach. Without opening her eyes, she asked, "Why are you staring at me?"

"I was wondering what you're thinking."

She rolled her head on her arm. "I was thinking that you speak English very well."

He had wished for something more personal. "Do I?"

"I think so."

"I didn't used to. I didn't used to care. But the last couple of years I started paying attention to how I sounded."

"Why?"

"Same reason I took the feathers off my rifle, I guess."

"To fit in?"

"To fit in."

"Was that all it took?"

"I went to the male seminary in Tahlequah for eight years."

"Where's that?"

"Down in the Nations."

"The Nations?"

"South of here."

"Didn't they have schools up here?"

"Yeah, government schools. One on Madeline Island and one at Eagle River but grandmother did not like either of them. Rough boys went there, she said. Fierce Indians who did not live in the now." He laughed. "What she didn't know was that I was the number one rough boy."

"How long did you live down there?"

"Nine years. When I came back I found that grandmother was very ill. I stayed with her until she died and then I went to Two Sisters. I didn't like it very much in the beginning."

"Why did you stay then?"

"Because grandmother made me promise I would. 'Humor me,' she said. 'I am old and it is a dying wish.' "

"Why do you think she felt so strongly about it?"

"She believed that all the Indians who survived with pride would have to adapt to the white man's world."

"But the coyote cannot cry like the loon."

He looked at her. "Who told you that?"

"Wolf Woman."

"Hu'ah! I said those same words to grandmother once."

"And what did she say?"

"Go anyway."

"And you stayed."

"Yeah, I stayed."

"Because you grew to like it?"

"Yeah, I guess."

And now if she should ask: do you want to go back? Would he tell her the truth? Would he say that if not for meeting her he probably would've been sheriff for as long as the town council would let him?

And then what if she asked why?

It was strange, but in a way he felt shame that he as an Indian man should covet the white man's success. That he should desire prosperity, pride and happiness for his children and their children's children made him feel like a traitor to his people, but why? Deep inside, did he believe that it was better to live like a hermit or to wrap his pride and a bottle in a blanket and freeze to death?

It would be easier if she didn't ask. "How come you talk like you do?"

"How do I talk?"

"Good. Educated."

She rolled her head back. "My mother had some schooling when she was growing up and Pa made her teach us kids what little she knew."

"That surprises me."

"Don't be fooled into thinking that he did it out of the goodness of his heart. He did it so that we could get better-paying work."

Something entered the water with a splash, and the taptap of a woodpecker echoed through the woods.

"Tell me what you learned in school."

"As little as possible! I was very poor at Greek, Latin, trigonometry and surveying and very good at history studies—particularly war and the use of weapons."

They both listened to the cry of the first loon of the evening. Its yodel was soon taken up by another and then another. She smiled. He smiled and he opened his mouth to say that she meant everything to him. What came out was: "Were you ever afraid, staying out here all alone?"

"Sometimes in the night when the ice would crack. Sounds just like a rifle." She looked at him. "Hungry?"

"I could eat."

"You didn't have to tell me that." He helped her up and dusted off her behind. He took great care. Patpat. Brush. Pat.

"Any grass on front?"

"No. I was not laying on my front." She might've added: *because it isn't possible.*

"What about flying grass?" He'd turned her and was eyeing her front hard.

"There's no such thing."

"Sure there is. It is carried by grassflyers."

"Grasshoppers?"

"Their cousins. One hops over grass, the other one carries it with him. There goes one right now."

Soon as she looked skyward, he dropped a handful of grass on her front. She looked back, laughing, but his face was serious. Holding her gaze, he slowly and very carefully began to remove the grass and then his hand was under her shirt and his lips were on hers.

That night she was repairing her snowshoes by the light of the fire while he sharpened his knife with a whetstone—he had shot a deer that day and dulled the blade cleaning the meat.

The silence seemed to weigh the air. She looked up and smiled. He smiled back but inside he sighed. Having never been celibate for any length of time, he had not known how difficult it was. It was. Very difficult. He now had a great deal of respect for those holy men who had chosen that state—supposedly so they were not distracted by carnal thoughts. Seemed to him that it made a man think of little else!

"Tell me about the old woman who used to live here."

"Wolf Woman? Her real name was Anna Sure Hunter." She used her teeth to bite some sinew. Strong sure teeth. "She never told me what happened that caused her to be banished, but I guessed it was a man."

"Was she made unhappy by her banishment?"

"Not that I could see."

"You think some men might be worth risking banishment?"

She shrugged and then forgot that she wasn't supposed to look at him. As usual he wore his buckskins and an elkskin vest but no shirt and no shoes. And as usual the display of bare feet, chest and arms did strange things to her insides. To herself she posed the question: Would banishment be worth it for a man like you? Yeah. Oh, yeah!

Spring came in full force, and with it came the rest of the migratory birds of the wilderness. Long-legged blue herons, yellow-rumped warblers, broad-winged hawks and ruby-throated hummingbirds. Atop a tamarack that leaned perilously far out over the water, two eagles refurbished a stick nest that was already six feet across. These latecomers had to get busy; the early birds like the wood duck and loon and Canada goose already had eggs in their nests.

Every day dark clouds scudded in from the lake and dropped a little rain and the land grew greener. Wildflowers bloomed in the lowlands and meadows, and wild asparagus grew tall enough to cut—provided they could get there before the rabbits and deer! Trees sprouted bumps that became leaves overnight.

They spent most all of their days together now because Jim was afraid to leave her alone for long. It was a good thing that's how he felt, because she insisted in going everywhere with him anyway. They shared most duties, even the hunting, but after two meals which were prepared by Jim, she did all the cooking. They tapped the maples that grew on the other side of the lake and gathered syrup. They fished and smoked big bass and pike and as always they spent a lot of time replenishing their supply of stove wood.

They both loved the woods and often paused to watch the wildlife around them. A cow moose and her calf. A lumbering black bear and a bristling porcupine. River otters, muskrats and beavers. A swimming turtle with only its head above water.

Once they stopped to watch a family of loons. The two chicks rode sedately on their mother's back but the father loon was making a spectacle of himself swimming, diving and dancing on top of the water.

She turned to him with a look that said "Look at that show-off!" He gave her a look back that said, "Hey! It is a man's right! Those are very fine chicks."

At that moment neither one could imagine that they would ever feel this close to another human being.

As time went on Jim had to go increasingly slower to compensate for her ungainly pace. Then one day she said she felt fine but not well enough to go trekking through the woods all day. After that he did the hunting alone but he never ranged far and never failed to bring back something.

It did his heart good to return and see the smoke curling from the chimney and the small light in the window. He would shift whatever game he carried on his shoulder and smile. This was his home. Unless she was someplace else.

He prepared for the child's coming by attempting to do the things that were normally done by the woman's family. He tried to make a tiny pair of moccasins which could be fastened around the baby's ankles but when finished they looked more like tobacco pouches than moccasins. Which brought a sudden thought: Why not use a tobacco pouch for a moccasin? What a fine idea! He couldn't believe that he was the first person to think of this time-saving idea and he decided that the extra hours entailed in fashioning moccasins must be part of the birthing ritual. Otherwise why would women make extra work for themselves? He found two pouches that were being used for storing herbs, and aired them and presented them to Thora. She praised him highly for his fine work.

He had less trouble making a cradleboard. All it really required was cutting a straight piece of oak and then lining it with rabbit skins. To hang above the baby's head he fashioned a charm out of reeds, feathers and buckskin.

Thora watched his strong square hands make these things for his child and she knew that no matter what happened between them, he would love their baby. As for more than that, who knew? She supposed everything would be settled after the baby was born and that much anticipated event was foremost in her mind. Her thoughts often turned to the task before her. She wished she knew exactly what having a baby entailed.

She would find out sooner than expected, one dusk when a light rain made a soft patter on the roof and a soothing stillness had settled over the woods.

Jim was whittling a new soup ladle when he heard a sigh and glanced up. She was standing at the window using a brush made of porcupine bristles tied on a stick. She looked beautiful, her face tinged pink from the sunset, her hair like a silver cascade. Another sigh and she lowered her arms.

"I will brush your hair for you if you like."

"It's all right."

Later he twice said something that she didn't hear. Strange. He watched her for awhile then finally he set down the knife and went to her.

She covered the hand he put on her shoulder but her eyes were dreamy and far-looking. He looked in the same direction and saw a robin bathing itself in a newly formed puddle. In the stream beyond, a hen duck was teaching her little ones how to forage, a lesson that apparently required a lot of quacking and upturned rears. Eventually the ducks had rounded the bend and disappeared but still she stared at their wake. He turned her toward him. "What is it?"

"It's coming."

He looked at her, mildly curious. "What's coming?"

"The child."

"The child!" He stuck his face in hers. "THE CHILD?"

"Yes."

His naturally brown cheeks turned pale as paste. "But it's too soon!"

"I don't know what I can to do about that."

"We better find a doctor . . . "

Looking at him like he was crazy she pushed his hand away. "That's one thing I know for sure. I'm not going anywhere."

"Maybe you better try to stop it!"

"How?"

"I don't know. God, isn't this sort of thing instinctive?"

"Not for me it isn't."

Having grown up as an only child—a *male* only child—the birth process was foreign to him. "How long will it take?"

"It took three days for my mother once."

"Three days!"

"She said her first one took even longer. I guess I could be at it for quite a while."

She was wrong. It seemed to her that the child was born in an embarrassingly short time.

It seemed to Jim that the child did not come for years.

Decades. It went on and on until the universe had become a blur before his eyes.

After an interminable night of pacing, moaning, pacing, by dawn she was kneeling on the bed. She would come up on her knees and press her hands on her stomach and pant like a run-out dog. Then, when the pain passed, she would sit back, a slumped and lifeless rag. Her hair clung damply to her head. Her body was shiny with sweat. His too, like he'd just come from swimming. He would dab her forehead and then his own. He'd never felt so helpless. None of the pain from any wounds he'd ever experienced had been as difficult on him as this was on her! Did all children come this hard?

"Oh, God, it . . . hurts!"

"Don't let it. Remember when you were a shadow beneath the trees or a ripple in the grass? Do that now."

"Don't you think I already tried that. God!"

"All right. All right. Let's see . . . "

"You . . . go!" She slapped at his hands. "Just go away from me!"

Half annoyed, he stood there a minute and then he inched back. "Did I ever tell you about the time I killed two turkeys with one shot?"

She frowned up at him. "What?" Pant Pant.

"It happened about three miles from Tahlaquah . . . "

"Oooh, Go! Go! . . . never . . . speak to me . . . " Groan. Pant ". . . again."

"A perfect boy!" He held the boy at arm's length and smiled at her but she'd gone from a writhing harridan to a dead person with a particularly loud snore.

His smile drifted into a frown. What a mess. Thora. The boy. The bed. A big slimy mess.

Using warm water and very soft hands, he washed his son first. On the outside he was a splendid-looking boy but Jim worried that something was wrong with his limbs, which were rubbery and took off every which way. He decided to say nothing and hope that either she didn't notice or that his limbs hardened in a hurry.

After he slid the boy into the cradleboard he tackled the bed.

By gently rolling the new—and still snoring—mother first one way and then another, he was able to get the buckskin cover out from under her without waking her. He folded it up and carried it outside and buried it. Then he washed her and made a napkin from the downy insides of several cattails.

He stood a minute and watched her sleep. Then he looked at the boy in the cradleboard. Then back at her.

A sudden unpleasant thought had him leaping across the room and extracting the boy a mere instant before he unleashed a foul torrent that would've made a terrible mess of the rabbit skins . . . And which made a mess of his father's feet instead.

He cleaned the baby again then put a down pad between two soft rags and tied it around his waist with a leather whang. Then he laid the boy beside his mother and covered them both with the blanket.

After he'd cleaned between his toes, he cleaned the cabin, which looked like it had been visited by a moose. With an abused sigh, he sat and then immediately stood again. He had done the things ordinarily done by the women relatives of the mother but had forgotten the proud father's part entirely.

He went outside and fired a gun into the air then he built a huge fire, around which he slowly and ceremoniously carried the baby four times. Unfortunately holding the baby at nose elevation announced that the boy had already soiled the napkin he had made so he replaced that yet again. He made a mental note that in the near future they would need many more cattails and, for right now, a lot more water. Using a rag *the second time* he removed from the fire the very hot empty pot which had once held water, he carried it to the stream and refilled it.

Finally finished and feeling quite put upon, he slumped in the chair. Almost immediately, the rag fell from his hand. He slept.

The next morning dawned clear and beautiful and Thora woke feeling wonderful . . . until she tried to sit up. Gingerly she lay back and looked around. Jim was sleeping half reclined in the chair with his legs wide spread and his feet forked like a duck. The baby was a swaddled lump on his chest.

She lay back and smiled. She couldn't imagine ever being happier! Her son and her man. My family. These two people will be my family forever!

* * *

She recuperated so rapidly he had to practically tie her down. Within a week she was running around healthy as a . . . well, as a horse.

She had told him that having the baby wasn't instinctual but rearing and caring for it obviously was, because she was a natural mother. Loving. Attentive. Kind. Under her care the boy grew longer and firmer every day.

They argued about his nature, which he thought was most like hers because he was so robust and vocal, and which she thought was most like him because of how much he loved to eat. Undeniably the latter was true. He was so vigorous he could burp and slurp and even pass wind while he suckled! He was quite strong for his size. He once latched onto his father's finger and held it such in a viselike grip Jim had to sit there for an hour until the baby's fingers relaxed in sleep.

"You know, I just remembered what he reminds me of." The boy, who had just finished eating his fill, lay sleeping between them.

"What?" She had been almost asleep herself.

"It's a thing I saw once."

"What sort of thing?"

"They called it a coconut." He touched the boy's head with its tuft of deep red hair. "He looks just like one."

"A coconut. I've never seen one."

"It's a big nut with hair. From some island." She looked up at him and the moon on her face showed it was frowning. He quickly added, "But a very handsome nut! With very beautiful hair!"

Later she woke to find him pacing. "Now what?" she asked, not lifting her head but following him with her eyes.

"I've been trying to think of a name we can call him until he is old enough to take a name of his own." He stopped. "What do you think of Charley?"

She chewed her lip. "I was thinking of Halldor after my brother. But you're right. He is an American and Charley is an American name."

"Good! That's settled then."

She nodded and smiled down at the baby. ''Hello, little Charley.'' She frowned. ''Charley . . . Horse.''

''A fine name.'' He nodded solemnly. ''Almost as fine as the name I have given you.''

She lost her train of thought. ''You've given me an Ojibwe name?''

''Yes.'' He crawled back into bed.

''What is it?''

''None-So-Pretty.''

''Oh, Jim!'' she said and sighed happily. ''That's a lovely name!''

He kissed her forehead and then nuzzled her neck. Her womanly smell drove him crazy. ''It is a mountain flower, pretty but very strong. If picked in the fall, the yellow and white flowers will last all winter long.''

She blushed prettily. ''Thank you.''

''It is also sometimes called Indian tobacco or cotton weed.''

A vertical line appeared between her eyes. ''Cotton weed?''

''Mm. My people use it as a tobacco substitute. Some claim it can cure ulcers, but I've never known anyone . . . ''

Was it she who had once complained about Jim Horse being too silent? ''That's all right!''

He removed his lips from her neck in order to look into her eyes. ''What?''

''I don't need to know all that other stuff. Just the flower part.''

''Hu'ah!'' Strange, he thought. She was usually so inquisitive about things.

Chapter 31

Coco had disappeared a few days before Charley was born and still hadn't returned two weeks later. It was the longest he had ever been away and Thora was worried about him. As soon as she felt up to it, they put the child in the cradleboard and strapped it on Jim's back and went in search of him.

Taking the same direction the wolf did when he left led them to a rocky footpath not obvious to any but an experienced tracker like Jim. Higher up, where the path was less rocky they found wolf scat and some tracks that she recognized as being Coco's. Then, some hours later they found him. To her delight (and a twinge of sorrow), he had a family as well, a young female lighter in both weight and color than himself and two pups so fat and square-bodied that they could've have been mistaken for shoats!

Sitting on a hill above the den they shared the draw-tube telescope Jim'd had the foresight to bring along. The den was in a fish-shaped hole at the base of a sandstone cliff. A toppled spruce tree partially camouflaged the opening, which Jim said looked like an old fox hole. ''Wolves'll often take over the abandoned dens of other animals.''

Thora was proud of Coco. He was a very indulgent father, roughhousing with the two pups for quite a while and, even after he lay down, remaining compliant when they walked on his face and bit his tail. But understandably he eventually reached the end of his tether. Lifting his head he barked what must've been quite detailed instructions because the two pups tore off and began to mark every rock, tree and bush in the area. Left alone at last, Coco lay down and appeared to sleep.

"Poor guy!" Thora said.

"Why?"

"Now his wife's creeping up on him . . . Oh, look at her!"

"I can't. You have the telescope."

"She's waited until he's asleep to . . . Oh! Oh! She just bit him on the butt!"

Apparently it had not been a playful nibble because Coco yelped and got up and they rose up like dancers and batted their paws at each other in mock battle.

"God, she's demanding!"

"That's enough! Give me that scope." He stretched across her but she withheld it. "What do you mean, 'that's enough'?"

"You! You are jealous of a bitch dog!"

"I am not!"

"Why, you are!"

"You can have the scope back. But I am not jealous."

They watched the wolf pack for hours, as pups and adults joined in digging, playing, marking and chasing each other all around the den.

By dusk when they headed back to the cabin, Thora was tired but reassured about her friend. What a wonderful life he had, but more to the point, what a wonderful life he had . . . without her!

Sadly she knew that this was how Coco-man was supposed to live. Not penned or cabin-bound but free as the wind. Wild things should be able to choose to stay wild or to become civilized. Coco had obviously chosen the wild.

She ignored the inner voice that reminded her that Jim Horse had chosen too and his choice was quite different from the way he was living now. They hadn't discussed it but he acted like he was going to stay with her. Because of Charley or because he wanted to be with her. Could be either. Could be both. Maybe someday she would find out. Then again, maybe not. Things could just go on as they were now. One thing she had learned long ago: don't question good fortune. Just say: Thank you, Lord!

When they stopped so she could rest and feed Charley, she told Jim that she wouldn't worry about Coco's well-being if it weren't for the trappers. Coco could hold his own against other wolves or predators but no wolf could survive a well-laid trap and what was in most instances a slow and painful death.

"Let's you and I split up and look for traps. That way we can cover as many miles as possible."

"No."

She looked up. "No?"

"Such a trip would be too hard on you and Charley. A hunting wolf will range as much as fifty miles from its den."

"You're right. We'll wait another week or two and go then."

"No."

"No?"

"I'll go tomorrow."

"Alone it would take you weeks to cover that much territory. Wouldn't it be better to wait until I can go with you?"

"No."

"No? Why not?" He said nothing. "Why wouldn't you want me with you?"

He stood and offered his hand. "You know why." Their eyes met then and she knew why. She could see it on his face and hear it in his voice. Oh, yes. She knew exactly why.

She used the time he was gone for healing and thinking. And missing him! Whatever questions she'd had about Jim had gone with Charley's birth. She wanted to spend the rest of her life with him. Preferably in one spot.

Charley kept her busy during the day but he slept most of the night. If he woke her at all it was about an hour before dawn. She placed a chair by the window and fed him there while she watched the sunrise. It was no coincidence that it was also the direction from which Jim should return.

Jim came back smelling of the woods and of smoke and looking very tired. While he ate deer stew and legolet bread, he told her that in all the ground he had covered he had only found three traps. They'd been laid by the same man but they were over thirty miles distant, to the west. "I think most trappers have given up on this area."

"Good. Wolf Woman is smiling to hear that."

After dinner he washed and swam for a time and came back with a light blanket wrapped around his waist. He sat on the bed, propped against the wall and played with Charley for a while. He talked about how much the boy had grown and mentioned the unusual color of his eyes. She kept herself busy and answered him with soft murmurs and no talk. When Charley fell asleep, he lay propped on one elbow and remarked on the strength of the boy's legs, at how smart his expression was . . . and then he fell asleep himself. Like the child, he lay on his face with both arms and legs flung out.

She eased the baby off the bed and fed him and cleaned him and put him in the cradleboard. Then she quietly undressed. She had washed and braided her hair that morning. Now she untied the leather thong that held it back and brushed it loose.

Earlier she'd stood on a rock above the water and imagined that she was seeing herself through his eye. She hoped that he would find her appealing. Her body was different, softer and more rounded but only in a few places.

Very quietly and very carefully she lifted the blanket and nipped him smartly on the rear end. She got a pillow-muffled response. "The damn mosquitos are terrible this year!"

"One bit you?"

"Right on the butt."

"Huh!"

He sat up and raked his hands through his hair and saw her standing in the firelight. His eye flickered and narrowed.

"There's no room for me in the bed." Her voice was shaking. She was almost afraid of the way he was looking at her.

"Come then," he said gruffly and held out his hand. Their fingers met and their gazes locked and she had one knee on the bed when he flipped her under him. He gave a grunt of satisfaction and stared down at her. Then he touched her lips with his and whispered her name. Using his hands, he pressed her up into him. "Now?" A soft sound escaped first then she nodded and whispered, "Now."

The demon gleam in his eye contradicted an overloud sigh. "God, you're demanding!"

"The one time I want to talk you don't want to talk."

"People don't talk about things like that."

"My people do. If they are married. I'll bet white people do too."

"I don't think so."

"They must. Otherwise how would they know what pleases their partner?" Nothing. She had her eyes shut tight, pretending to sleep.

"Suppose I was to do this . . ." He dipped his head.

"Argh!"

"And then suppose I did this . . ."

"Mmft!"

"From those two words I am to understand which you prefer?" Nothing. He shrugged. "Guess I'll have to try again and listen harder."

"Both! Oh, both. Bothbothboth!"

"Good. Then the wolf call must've meant that this time was better than the last?" Nothing. He nudged her.

"What wolf call?"

"The one you gave earlier."

"You!" she said and punched him playfully.

He turned onto his back and sighed happily and closed his eye. God, he felt good! She punched him again only not so playfully this time.

"Oh, no you don't!"

He opened his eye. "What?" He lifted his head the better to see her, but she dropped her gaze shyly. "God! You really *are* demanding!" He moved his hands over the curves of her back then down around her buttocks. He lifted her and pulled her onto him.

"What's this?"

"I need to rest my knee wound."

"What were you resting before that?"

"My back wound."

"Ah."

"We have a lot of wounds to cover! Mm. Many wounds. Ah! Yes, many many wounds."

Later—in a moment of quiet repose—he shattered the silence with a very good imitation of a wolf, and scared her witless.

Thora felt loved. For the first time in her life, she felt truly loved. He had not said it, but with his gentle hands, and heated lovemaking, she knew that he loved her. She was never happier than she was during those days and it seemed to her that their idyll would never end.

Chapter 32

They were at the bottom of the rough, stump-studded path that led to the water. Charlie was asleep on a deerhide mattress, Jim and Thora lay facing each other on the grass. It was dusk. The light from the cabin glistened on the water and their nightly serenade of tree frogs had begun. An eagle circled high above the pewter water looking for perch and sunfish. A mayfly dipped its transparent wings too close to a clump of lilies and disappeared with a splash.

She had just fed Charley and there was that faint milky smell about her that Jim found so provocative. His hand played in her loosened hair. "How did you like your swimming lesson today?"

"Swimming lesson, my butt. We never get beyond floating . . ."

She saw a hard black shadow and then they were upon them. Jim pushed her roughly aside the instant a shot was fired then he fell backward, into the water. Spirals of red rose as he sank beneath the surface. "No!" she screamed. She grabbed for the baby only to have it snatched from her and thrown by its heels into the tall grass near the water's edge.

She turned to face her attackers. One was a Hunkpapa Sioux. He had a big nose, snake eyes and no chin. The other was a white man wearing grimy buckskins. His moccasins each had a coon tail hanging off the back.

"Well, if it ain't little miss mophead. 'Member me?" he asked and pushed up his matted hair on one side to show her a scar.

Briefly it registered that he was the crazy woodsman who had attacked her, but her thoughts were on Jim and the baby. She had heard no more from either! She ran away from the water, hoping to decoy them in the direction of the cabin but they caught her easily and wrestled her to the ground.

"Lookee here, Black Fox. Buck naked and all ready for us. Grab 'er arms good."

The dry-dead smell of them filled her senses. She made no sound but she fought fiercely, for her life and for the life of her child—and prayed that it wasn't too late. She bit and scratched and clawed but the white man kicked her in the head, a stunning blow that knocked her senseless and rolled her to the water's edge.

"Now, damnit, you hold still!"

Through blurred eyes she saw him stand over her and undo the rope around his waist. She turned her head away. Suddenly there was Jim Horse rising out of the water. For a second she was frozen at the sight of him, pagan naked and half covered in blood, but his panther-like scream loosed her. She kicked and somehow pulled free of the Sioux. Jim scooped up the ugly one's belt and slung the scabbard off the knife as he dodged the tomahawk the Sioux threw. Drawing his knife, the Sioux gave his battle cry "Hoka hey!" and charged, but Jim threw the white man's knife into his chest. Clasping it, the Sioux sunk slowly to his knees and was dead before he met the ground. The white man had his carbine raised but Jim knocked it aside and they came together like the clash of horned sheep.

She ran to find Charley, fearing that he'd landed in the water but he lay in the grass, stunned and red-faced. When she scooped him up he found his breath and started wailing lustily. His anger increased when she laid him right back down again.

Jim and the renegade were having a terrific fight, rolling in the grass and grunting like animals. Both were blood-smeared. They tore apart and circled each other, arms loose, fingers twitching. The renegade saw a chance and charged but Jim hit him in the head with laced hands. He was staggered and clearly surprised that Jim would use his fists like a white man.

In the instant when his foe was stunned Jim bent over the dead Sioux to retrieve the knife. He whirled and was only just able to check his throw.

Thora had straddled the renegade's back and was trying to scratch his eyes but he easily slung her off. With amazing quickness, Jim was on him with a killing slice to the throat. Chest covered with blood, the renegade fell onto his back and died. Instantly Jim was on him and had his hand tangled in the dead man's hair. As the knife descended, he gave a primitive victory yell.

She grabbed his arm with both of hers and only just stopped him. "Jim! Jim!" His teeth were bared and his eye glazed like a black marble. He looked at her but it was a long minute until she knew that he actually saw her. Something stirred in that inky depth then he blinked. "Charley's crying," he said calmly.

"He's just mad." She stood and stepped back and watched him bury the knife hilt-deep in the dirt.

She returned with the baby, whom she'd comforted by giving him her breast. "Quick! Go up to the cabin." She picked up her shirt. "Your head's bleeding a lot."

"WOMAN!"

"What?" Her voice was muffled, as she was pulling on her buckskin shirt. Her head popped through the opening and there was his bloodied face, stuck in hers.

He looked furious! A muscle popped in and out on his jaw and sparks danced in his eye. "What?"

"When we get back to the cabin, I will beat you blue!"

And with that he stalked off.

She looked at the two dead men, sprawled beside the water like broken dolls and then scooped up Charley and hurried after him. "Why? What did I do?"

He slammed into the cabin practically tearing the leather hinges off the door. She stood in the doorway and peered owlishly inside. After hearing several loud noises, she started getting mad herself. "Don't you dare make a mess in there!"

He was back, still naked as a scalded hog. He grabbed her wrist hard and jerked her inside. "Listen to me, woman!"

"I am listening. How could I not?"

"Pay good attention then! I fight . . ." Here he pounded his chest with his fist. "You . . ." Here he poked a hard finger at her. ". . . do not fight! You . . . patch me up." He threw her wrist aside. "Now. Get at it!" He sat and pulled the buffalo robe over his shoulder and shut his eye.

God, he was serious! She put Charley in the cradleboard and hurried to get the bag of medicines.

"What would have happened if I'd been killed?"

She'd been almost asleep. "What?"

"I said, what if I'd been killed. You and Charley would have been left here all alone. Provided you survived what those men had in mind."

He was staring outside. She reached up and turned his face toward her. "Jim, I can take care of myself and a baby. It would be awful to have to do so, but I can do it." He jerked his jaw away. "What?" she asked. "Something else is bothering you. What is it?"

He was silent for a time, then, "What about Charley in the years to come? Growing up all alone. He'll end up wild as a bear. And what about you? No friends. No real life except the struggle to stay alive and keep from being taken." She rested her head on his shoulder and thought about it. "Didn't you like Two Sisters?"

"I did. Very much."

"Then why don't you want to live there?"

She shrugged. "I'm sort of embarrassed about things."

"About killing Junior Buel?"

"That and you know . . ."

"No, I don't know. What?"

She pointed. "The baby."

He thought a minute and then turned her toward him. "We are married here . . ." He touched his chest and then hers. "And here . . ." He touched his temple then hers.

"But not in the books."

"But that's an easy thing to solve!"

She looked up at him. "Would you marry me in the books?"

"Yes, I would."

She chewed her lip. ''I know how much you liked your job and you're right about Charley. He needs to go to school.''

''What about you? Couldn't you be happy there too?''

''Yes, I think so.'' She took hold of his hand hard and looked intently up at him. ''There's one thing.''

''Yes?''

''Wherever we go I want to stay. No bouncing around from town to town for Charley or any others we have. Deal?''

''Deal.''

She turned and leaned back against him. ''Well, that's settled then.''

''There's one other thing to consider.''

When he first said that, she thought he might have read her mind because she had just been thinking that if she lived in Two Sisters she would at least have a chance to get a lead on the those three men. But then, suddenly she knew what he meant. She sat up. ''Coco!''

''Yes.''

''We can't take him with us!''

''No. Sooner or later he would be shot by somebody. Not because he was doing anything wrong. Just because he's a wolf. Besides, he has a family now.''

''I know.'' She was crying a little. ''But when we go there'll be no one to protect him from trappers.''

''Coco's pretty sharp. That spot he picked for a den is way to hell and gone. He'll teach the rest of them what he knows and they'll be all right.'' He waited and finally, she said, ''Can we wait until he comes back so I can say good-bye to him?''

''Anything you say, Ogema.''

It was an Ojibwe word she'd never heard before. ''What's that mean?''

''Boss.''

''Oh, right! I sure felt like the boss this afternoon when I got my eyelashes burned off.''

''I was angry.''

''No foolin'!''

''What do you think? Jumping on that man's back! Crazy woman! Well, it is over now.'' He looked at her. ''Unless you intend to bring it up every three or four days for the rest of my life.''

She sniffed. "I don't want you to holler at me like that."

He knew it. She was going to bring it up for the rest of his life.

There's no denying that the cabin had special meaning for her. In leaving it and Coco, she was giving up what had been her only home and her only friend. But she knew Jim was right. She belonged with Jim and Charley. Jim's work was in Two Sisters. Coco belonged with his pack.

When the time came to say good-bye, she walked with Coco to the end of the clearing and explained everything to him. She cautioned him at length about traps and hunters. Then she told him that Jim had said that they'd come back for regular visits. It was a tearful and whiny parting, but it was bearable for both.

They waited out a week of rain and left on the first clear day. Jim had told her about the "crazy old coot" called Indian Ed and she wasn't disappointed when she saw him. Why the old man would want to live way up here by himself . . .

She was thinking that when she realized she'd been willing . . . no, she'd been happy . . . to do the same.

It was fortunate for Indian Ed that Jim's horse appeared so well tended and fed. Jim offered the old man his money, but he was so taken with Thora, it was a moment before he noticed his outstretched hand.

"You a rich man, Sheriff?"

"No."

"Well, it must be love 'cause you sure ain't much to look at."

"You got a looking glass, old man?"

"Looking glass? No. Why?"

"Never mind."

They left old Indian Ed scratching the skin on his head.

Jim walked and Thora rode with Charley in the cradleboard on her back. She had something to say but a barking dog followed them until they'd gone over a mile. When they'd finally cleared what the dog considered his territory, she said, "This is a beautiful horse, Jim."

"Hu'ah!"

"What's his name?"

"Horse."

"Huh!" she said. A minute later she started to chuckle.

"What's so funny?"

"I was just thinking that it's a good thing you never signed up for one of those Wild West shows!"

He answered sort of huffily. "You don't think I could hold my own?"

"No, it's not that. I was thinking of the barker." He looked at her. "You know, the person who announces the acts." She cupped her hands around her mouth. "Ladies an' gentlemen. Hold onto your hats! Tonight we have the thrilling and exciting riding team of Indian Jim Horse and his horse, Horse."

"Very funny."

"I thought so."

Chapter 33

The reason why Sissy saw them first was that she couldn't bear to witness the awful thing that was happening behind her back. Her baby Joey was sitting on a board laid across the arms of Curly Frye's barber chair and he was about to get sheared like a sheep.

"A boy's supposed t'look like a boy!"

Joe Willie was right, of course, but that didn't mean she had to like it. So she'd deliberately turned her back and looked out the window. Idly fanning herself and baby James Richard, she was soon distracted by the activities on Superior Street. Two boys sauntered by, shouldering fishing poles and carrying a can of worms. A family was loading supplies onto a buckboard. Voices shrill with excitement brought a smile, and she watched a group of girls who were scratching a hopscotch form in the dirt. Summertime in Two Sisters! she thought. Soft, sleepy summertime.

Regrettably, summer also meant hot sultry days, muggy airless nights and bugs! Lots of bugs. The window stood open in the hopes of catching the meager breeze off the lake. Unfortunately it also caught the attention thousands of flies and mosquitos. Smudge pots were burning on all the street corners but about all they did was leave a film of black on the windowsills.

Goody Tangen came out with a bushel basket and started replenishing his vegetable table and she was wondering if he had any beets . . . and there they were, Jim leading a horse on which sat Thora Gunn and a baby!

"Oh, my stars! Joe Willie!"

Joe Willie jerked the newspaper he held, afraid that he'd been caught not supervising the hair cutting and the kid's head had been shaved. But his wife was leaning out the window, waving one arm and crying, "Yoo-hoo! Hello! Over here!" Muttering that he hoped she wasn't going into a new line of business, he went to the window to take a look himself and there stood Jim Horse, grinning and waving back at him. "Well, I'll be damned!"

(What a stroke of luck! Both of his parents had charged out of the barber shop and left him all alone. Now the barber was leaning out the window and paying him no mind at all. Little Joey Everett cast around for something to get into.)

They all went to the cafe and, of course, word travels fast in a small town. Soon several people were crowded in the little eatery and it was a party.

Thora showed the baby to Buddy. "Well, Buddy, here's your . . . Goodness, Jim." She looked back at him. "What would Charley be to Buddy?"

Buddy took the child and said, "How about I call him grandson?" She held the baby out from her, and her eyes teared. "Oh, Gudmund! Lewk vhat a beutifewl baby!"

As soon as she brought him close enough, Charley smiled and raised his arms Christ-like and got a snapper-like hold on each of her coiled braids.

As a large contributor to the church, Buddy was able to prevail on Pastor Oulie to perform the ceremony on very short notice and they were married the next day in as nice a ceremony as anyone could wish. It was held in a little side chapel which was soon jam-packed with well-wishers.

Except for clean brushed buckskins Jim didn't get all gussied up, but Thora wore Sissy's wedding dress. It was a little too short, but she looked so beautiful nobody noticed. And oh, my, was she lovely! Sissy had worked her hair into a pouf on back of her head and encircled it with wild columbine and Queen Anne's lace.

"Dearly beloved!" The pastor had a commanding voice for a such a small man. "We are gathered here in the sight of God and in the presence of this gathering to join this man and woman in holy matrimony."

It was obvious to anyone present how much in love they were. Why, Jim could scarcely take his eyes off her, and Thora was the same. Both, however, wore solemn expressions. Neither was taking this lightly. Oh, no.

". . . is not to be entered into by any unadvisedly, but reverently and discreetly, and in fear of God.

"James . . ."

"Jim." he said softly, not taking his eye from Thora.

"Jim, wilt thou have this woman to be thy wedded wife, to live together after God's ordinance in the holy estate of matrimony? Wilt thou love her, comfort her, honor and keep her, in sickness and health, forsaking all others, keep thee only unto her, so long as ye both shall live?"

"I will."

Pastor Oulie had Thora repeat her vows and then said, "With this ring I thee wed . . ."

That part got Jim's attention and he cast furtive glances around the room. Buddy saw what was wrong and stopped mopping her eyes long enough to say: "I have the ring." With that she stepped forward and removed the ring that had been on her finger since the day she was wed. There was a hushed argument with the bride and groom, but then Buddy resumed her place. Minus her wedding ring. Though crying worse than ever, she wore a beatific expression of happiness.

Pastor Oulie began again. "With this ring I thee wed, with my body I thee worship, and with all my worldly goods I thee endow . . ." Jim placed the ring on Thora's finger and then lifted her hand and lightly brushed it with his lips.

"Those whom God hath joined together, let no man put asunder . . ."

A proper, restrained kiss and it was done. They were married in the books! The room broke into loud laughter and whoopees. Bull Durham pulled his gun and pointed it at the ceiling and almost didn't remember where he was.

Sissy was deeply moved and cried through the whole thing. For days afterward she could start up again just thinking about it. She told Joe Willie that she'd been overcome by the sight of little Charley who had been strapped on Jim's back the whole time they were being married. "Those big eyes went right through me . . . Oh, dear!"

"Eyes? Huh!" replied Joe Willie. "It was the drooling that got me."

The day after the wedding, Joe Willie was in court and didn't get to his office until midafternoon. Buddy Tangen came in practically before he had a chance to get the windows open. "Hey, Buddy! What can I do for you?"

She sat down and waited for him to take his seat. "Something very important, Joe Willie."

He knew that right off; she wore her Sunday hat with the blue paper flowers and a white ribbon that tied under the chin.

"I want to make a testament."

"You mean a will?"

"Yah. A will?"

He hard-eyed her. "Anything wrong, Buddy?"

"Nothing is wrong. I just want a will." She pointed. "Get paper and write."

"I've got a paper, Buddy."

"Good. Write."

Sighing. "All right. Shoot!"

"Shoot?"

"Begin."

A few seconds of fidgeting, then, "How do you begin?"

He laid down his pen. "Buddy, the first thing you need to do is make a list of all the things of value that you own."

"Ah. Well, there is the cafe and my house. And some land along the old sawmill road . . ."

By the time Joe Willie laid down his pen again, he had quite a list. "Buddy, you are a well-propertied woman. If I wasn't already married, I'd marry you myself."

She blushed. "Al and me worked hard all our lives."

He covered her work-roughened hand with his. "I know it

and you deserve every damn thing you have. Now, what do you want to do with it all when you're gone.''

''Well, we had no little ones, Al and me, so I guess I can leave it to whoever I want.''

''That's right. Generally people leave their stuff to their kin. Isn't Goody your closest living relation?''

''Yah, but Goody has plenty of his own. No, I want to leave something to Jim and Thora.''

''All right. What?''

''The land along the old sawmill road and some money.'' She leaned forward. ''Joe Willie, could I give it to them right now?''

''You can give it to them any time you like.''

''Good. Write that down then.'' She leaned over to watch him write. ''Sawmill land and money. Good. They can start building themselves a nice cabin right away.''

''Buddy, that's about one of the kindest things . . .''

She brushed him off. ''Now then, the cafe I want to leave to the Beckstroms. But not now . . .'' (Buddy was from the generation that died in the traces.) ''After I go.'' By way of explanation, she added, ''Marne and Lars are my godchildren, you know, and that Meline's a hard worker. If something should ever happen to Ketil she could make a good living from the cafe . . .''

By the time she was finished, there were bequests to the church, and her dishes and some antiques to Sissy, some mementos for Dottie and Rudy. And finally, money enough to see Davey Cox through the University. Provided he wanted to go. Davey's mother was dead and his father a no-count who had run off some years back. Like with Thora's brother, some in the town had taken Davey under their wing, and Buddy had been one of them.

Buddy said, ''Sissy tells me he's smart enough to go to school, provided he keeps himself on the up and up.''

''If he turns out to be an outlaw, do you want me not to give him the money?''

''Well . . .''

''Speak of the devil!'' Davey Cox had just come in.

Buddy turned in her chair and looked at him and she thought: Yah, give it to him even if he's an outlaw.

"Help you with somethin', Davey?"

"That's okay. I can come back."

Joe Willie looked at him and was reminded of the night that he and Jim Horse had taught the kid how to fight, or more aptly how to fight and win. He knew their instructions had helped because a few days later he'd seen Floyd Dobber with a battered face and a changed attitude.

"Wait outside a minute, Davey. I'll be finished pretty quick."

He told Buddy it would take him a week to get the papers drawn up and to let him know if she'd changed her mind about anything in the meantime. (It wouldn't really take him a week but he always gave people some time to modify their wills. Nine times out of ten, they'd come in with some little something. Fifty bucks said Buddy Tangen did not.)

"I feel much better," she said as she left.

"Good!"

When he motioned Davey inside and when the hemming and hawing was done, Joe Willie got his second surprise of the day. The boy wanted to know how to obtain the services of . . .

"A whore?" Davey nodded, red as a beet. "How old are you now?"

"Sixteen. Well, almost."

Joe Willie played with his pencil. "Sixteen's old enough for most I reckon." He couldn't miss Davey's gleam of anticipation. "Now just hold on a minute. I didn't say it was old enough for you."

Joe Willie built a twirly and lit it and studied Davey through the smoke. The boy was at that stage where he was growing a couple of inches a night. His clothes looked too big and his skin too small, and the most prominent things on him were his hands, his feet and an Adam's apple that was the size of some men's heads. In spite of that, he would be a manly-looking man when he filled out. Wide through the shoulders. Long-jawed.

"Well, all right. I'll go along and smooth things out for you. One word of advice first." Joe Willie said. "Always treat a whore as kind as you would treat any other woman. First off, because it doesn't cost you anything and second off, when a man treats a whore good, she's liable to treat him good back."

"Why? I mean not that I wouldn't but . . . why?"

"You'll understand that better later."

When Joe Willie stood to get his hat, Davey found that he couldn't stand the first time he tried.

"Well? You coming or not?"

Joe Willie wasn't surprised to see Marne Beckstrom sitting on the step outside his office. That little girl followed Davey like stink on a hog. Sure enough, the instant she saw him she latched onto his leg and cried, "Dav-eee!"

"Crimany, Marne! Look at your face!"

The little girl crossed her eyes then giggled. "But I can't see my face, Davey."

Joe Willie shook his head. "She's a mess, all right. What've you been eatin', Marne. Mud?"

"Probably." While he spoke, Davey reached in his back pocket and pulled out a none-too-clean handkerchief. "Just a minute, Joe Willie. With his hand on her shoulder he escorted her to a nearby trough.

Joe Willie watched him brush aside a horsefly and wet his handkerchief and mop the kid's face. He shook his head. That kid needed more than a good swabbing.

Once Davey had divested himself of Marne, he and Joe Willie proceeded to the Wind Fall. Davey entered first—not because he wanted to but because Joe Willie's big flat hand was plastered between his shoulder blades.

Precisely at the moment her husband entered the saloon, Sissy came out of Goody's directly across the street. She lifted her hand to call out to him then slowly lowered it.

It was too early for Joe Willie to be finished for the day. Actually he'd said he expected to be so busy he'd probably be home late that night. She stood there and puzzled on it for a minute and then the image of Hattie Mueller's sly face came to her like a thunderclap. Try as she might, she could think of no earthly reason for Joe Willie to be going into that place but one.

She and Joe Willie had resumed their enthusiastic love life after the baby was born and she'd thought it was better than ever. She'd thought he thought so too.

Maybe she'd thought wrong! Maybe during the time before the baby was born he'd felt it necessary to go elsewhere. Elsewhere being Miss Hattie Mueller. Then, maybe he had been so happy with the resumption of his affair, he'd decided to maintain it. It happened, she'd heard, even in the best of families. But not in mine! she cried inside.

Try as she might, she could not stop herself from crossing the street for a closer look.

Joe Willie strolled over to a table in back where it sounded like a good natured argument going on. Davey followed uncertainly, nervous as an old soldier at a fireworks display. He was getting a whiplash from trying to look everywhere at once.

"What seems to be the trouble, boys?" Curly Frye, Conor O'Malley, Ben Corliss and Goody Tangen were playing five-card stud. One card down. Four up.

"We were discussing," explained the doctor, "a medical phenomenon known as intermittent alligator arms."

"Oh?"

"This hand's enough to make a grown man cry," said Curly loudly.

Goody bet and Conor raised by tossing a coin into the center pile. "When Curly here wins a pot these long gorilla-like arms come out to rake in the dough. But when the bill comes for a round of drinks, those same arms shrink up into alligator arms."

"I raise," said red-cheeked Curly louder still.

"Anything you can do to cure it, Doc?"

"Anybody gonna see me, or not?"

"We thought maybe shunning."

"That ought to work."

"Or maybe tar and feathering," said Ben.

"Always persuasive. Provided you get the tar good 'n' hot."

Lucy, the bargirl came along with four beers on her tray and Curly lunged to his feet. "I'll get this one."

Conor winked around the table. "Well, what do you know? A spontaneous remission. Very interesting."

Davey saw the proprietress enter and his throat closed like a cellar door in high wind.

"Hello, Joe Willie."

Hattie Mueller was wearing a black shiny dress that hung

down to her elbows and made her chest look like it had two big light globes growing on it.

"Well, well. What can I do for *you?*"

Joe Willie indicated Davey, who was trying not to look at her chest and ruining his hat. *Those can't be real. Can they?*

"Brought you a new customer, Hattie."

"Oh?" She leaned back on the bar and smiled up into Davey's face. "Hello."

"This here's Davey Cox."

"I've seen you around town. What's your pleasure today . . . Dave?"

Davey looked at Joe Willie who nodded and said, "Go on."

"Yes," Hattie urged. "Please do."

Davey'd been repeating to himself what Joe Willie had said he should say: *Ma'am, I would be pleased to entertain a lady for a spell.* Leaning close, he whispered . . . nothing. His mind had run and hid on him.

I'd like to entertain . . .

If one of your ladies is entertaining . . .

Is there any entertainment?

Finally, in a hoarse whisper he blurted, "I came for a woman!"

"Well, I didn't think you came to get your corns pared," said Hattie. Turning professional, she stood back and ran her eyes over him. He'd be tall. Hell, he was already tall. Scrawny though. She tilted her head and looked at his feet. Big, ungainly and wide as a butter paddle. Mm!

"I think I'll take this one myself. Unless . . ." She walked over to Joe Willie and stood an inch away from touching him. "Unless there's something I can do for you?"

"No, Hattie darlin'. I have become something I'd always thought was rare as snake eggs."

"What."

"A happily married man."

She laughed to cover her disappointment and replied, "So are ninety percent of my customers, sugar. Well, no matter." One finger played with his vest buttonhole while she smiled up at him. "You could at least give me a kiss for old times' sake."

Rooted to the boardwalk outside the window, Sissy's shocked

brown eyes widened and then became so brimful she could scarcely see. Marne tugged at her skirts and cried, "Can I see too?"

"No, Marne." Choked. "As a matter of fact, I believe I've seen all I need to see myself." She scooped up Marne and staggered off.

When their lips parted, Joe Willie looked at Hattie with true affection. "Girl, you must've had at least twenty chances to get out of this life. Why don't you marry one of these ol' boys hangin' around here an' have yourself half a dozen kids?"

"Joe Willie! You know how much I love my work!" Her glossy eyes belied her laugh but then she motioned to Davey. "C'mon, sugar," She winked at Joe Willie over her shoulder. "Guess I've got a point to prove."

When she started ascending the stairs, Davey looked at Joe Willie with eyes that were as wild as an unrode mustang. He scuttled closer and put his lips next to the older man's ear. "Joe Willie, what if I can't do it?"

"What if you can't do what?"

"You know! I'm . . . I'm not sure I can . . ."

Joe Willie looked at Hattie's rear pendulating like a grandfather clock and had to hide a smile. He clapped the boy on the back. "Well, Davey, I guess you'll just have t'do the best you can. That's all anybody's got a right to ask of a man."

There was a long minute when Joe Willie figured it could go either way. Davey's Adam's apple bobbed like a cork and his eye twitched and it looked like one leg had become shorter than the other. But then, glory hallelujah, he squared his shoulders and marched off to battle.

Chuckling, Joe Willie turned back to the bar and hooked one heel on the railing. Well, his words may not have helped any other part of Davey's body, but Joe Willie hoped they'd stiffened his backbone . . . he'd trust Hattie to do the rest. "I might as well have a beer, Asa."

"You bet, Joe Willie."

Drinking his beer made him a bit sentimental and he found himself remembering another gangly kid and his first woman. He caught the eye of another man at the bar and nodded.

Out of force of habit, Joe Willie looked the man over. He had a sort of lean hungry look that Joe Willie recognized and it made him curious. Men of the stranger's sort were not that common in Two Sisters any more. He nodded at the man. "Buy you a beer, stranger?"

"Why, that's mighty white of you."

Turned out he wasn't as professional as he looked. It only took two drinks to get the man talking. He was from St. Louis and had come north after "a speckled nigger named Lester Greene. Supposed to be headed in this direction."

"What's his price tag?"

The man's eyes met Joe Willie's with a look of recognition. "Three thousand."

Joe Willie blew air through his teeth. "The money's improved considerably since I was in the business."

"Well, ol' Greene's sort of a special situation."

"Killer?"

"Rapist. On top t'regular reward, a lot of the rich townsfolk tossed in the pot too. He forced some hoity-toity white woman, down in Little Rock, and they don't take that sort of thing lightly down there. Nossir! Not a black man messin' with a white woman."

While the man talked, his eyes moved on something over Joe Willie's shoulder. Without making much of it, Joe Willie turned and followed the stranger's line of sight . . . outside the window and over to where Emily Jones stood on the landing leading to Doc's office. She was shaking a rug out and looked real fetching with her hair loose and her cheeks like cherries. He turned back and looked the newcomer square in the eye. "We aren't too keen on rape up here either. Last winter we tied an ol' boy out on the ice and let the wolves have him." He tossed down the last of his beer. "Well, good huntin', hear?"

"Yeah. Thanks."

To the bartender, Lyle breathed, "Jesus! I thought they had all the savages rounded up down in the Nations!" but apparently the bartender was no talker.

Lyle Jenkins carried his beer outside and watched the big guy go into a lawyer's office across the street. Funny, he had figured him for a kindred soul. Certainly not one of 'em damned lawyers!

Something caught his eye. That little cleaning gal again.

Now she was sweeping off the landing, turning this way and that, twitching that cute little butt at him. He smiled a little. Couple of weeks up here might not be so bad after all.

Down in Little Rock, Lyle had greased the palm of a fella who had been in jail with Greene before he made his break, and he'd found out that Greene had an old buddy who worked on one of those flat-bottom barges sitting beyond the harbor. Lyle figured Greene intended to hitch a ride to Canada. Lyle planned to nab Greene before he got on board but he could have as long as a two-week wait. He had grabbed a fast train north while Greene was probably staying out of sight during the day and traveling at night.

Lyle tapped tobacco into a paper trough then licked it into shape. He ordinarily did not like to go two days without a woman, but he also did not like to go without whiskey. Finding Northern whores more expensive than their Southern sisters meant that Lyle'd had to choose between one or the other. Then he'd remembered the little cleaning gal. He first saw her pussyfootin' it across the tracks the day he stepped off the train. Subsequent careful observation had told him where she lived and that she lived alone. All that way from town too. He picked at a sore on his neck and grinned. Perfect.

Chapter 34

When Buddy and Goody called them downstairs to talk one night, they found a setting that had ''official'' written all over it. Goody was in a freshly boiled shirt, buttoned all the way and Buddy was without her apron. Pie and coffee had been laid out using Buddy's special dishes. ''Sit,'' she said. ''Eat.'' Dutifully Jim and Thora sat and ate while Buddy and Goody passed the baby back and forth.

When they'd finished, Goody and Buddy exchanged a look and Goody produced a document from his back pocket. Buddy spoke. ''Jim, you and your family are our only living relation.''

''That's what you tell me.''

''We neither one of us have kids. Anha died so young and I never could keep a baby long enough to birth them. Anyway, because of that, you will get everything when we die.'' She held up a hand. ''Wait please. We aren't going yet but we want you to get some of what we have now because you need it now. Living upstairs is no good.''

''It was plenty good for me.''

Goody shook his head. ''Now is different. You have a wife and baby.''

Jim was silent. What could he say?

"Come go for a walk with us. We want to show you something."

The property they showed them was two miles outside of town along the old sawmill road. It was heavily wooded and bisected by a deep unnamed stream that was eight feet wide and crooked as lightning across a summer sky. Since the stream emptied into Lake Superior, it was a natural spawning ground for walleye and northern pike, black bass and countless smaller species like crappie and bluegill and perch. A little clearing—perfect for a cabin—backed up to a line of aspens that bordered the water.

Jim had some money set aside and he had been thinking about buying some land. Maybe, he thought, this is just far enough off the beaten track to appeal to Thora.

Goody and Buddy left them to talk it over. Buddy took Charley with her in case the night air should bother him. The baby had the constitution of an ox but they didn't argue with her.

Thora and Jim stood hand-in-hand and listened as the water whispered and the leaves quaked. Smoke blue clouds floated overhead. In the west the sun dropped below the horizon and as if in homage, a loon yodeled and tree frogs commenced to sing.

"I can live here," she said.

He grinned. "Good," he said as he pulled her down with him onto the ground.

"What are you doing?"

"We better consecrate the land. An ancient Indian rite."

Joe Willie had no idea that the reason why Sissy was acting so strange was due to his visit to Hattie Mueller's place the previous evening. All he knew was that something was definitely wrong. He might as well have kissed the doorknob goodbye that morning.

To say her behavior preoccupied him was putting it mildly. While crossing the street, a wagonload of wood narrowly missed maiming him for life and he didn't even hear the driver's frenzied cursing. It preyed on his mind through lunch and most of the afternoon.

''Damnit!'' he said.

''Hvat?''

Joe Willie looked at the client who sat beside his desk. ''Nothing. Go on, Goody.''

Goody had come in to see if Joe Willie could do anything about a bad debt he had. ''I ferget now vhere I vas.''

''You were about to tell me how much Carlson owes you.''

Goody dug in his bib pocket. ''I yust lewk-ed dat up tew-day.'' He handed the slip to Joe Willie.

''Mm. How long's he owed you the money?''

''Tree yearss.''

''Three years!''

''Vel, I don't like tew push.''

''Obviously. Have you ever asked for your money?''

''Yah-shure but Yon Carlson says dat all da stuff vas no gew-ed.''

''What was no good?''

Goody handed him a ledger book and pointed. ''All dis stuff right here.'' He read: Rat Poissun. Han Saw. Six plugs Snoose. Udder Cream. Two gallons Beers.

Joe Willie flicked the paper. ''Carlson had the balls to tell you that all this stuff was no good?''

''Yah! All yunk he says!''

Joe Willie stood and started pacing. Goody watched him with a vertical line between his eyes and wondered why was he was so upset.

Joe Willie was looking at the ledger but he was seeing his wife.

There must be someone else! His Sissy! God, it was like taking a knife in the groin! He would've never believed it of her. Never in a million years. Still, better men'n him had been fooled by a woman. He rammed his fist into the wall and Goody about lost his shoes. ''I'll kill 'im,'' he gritted.

''Hvat?!''

Joe Willie took his gunbelt from a peg on the wall, slung it on and tied it down. Goody's eyes acted like he was watching a ping pong match. And when Joe Willie yanked a desk drawer out to its limit, Goody's heart became intimately acquainted with his tonsils.

Staring at nothing, Joe Willie pulled out his gloves and

threaded them on slowly . . . slowly. Then he flexed his hands and narrowed his eyes. Goody's mouth dropped open then abruptly shut. "You wait here, Goody. I'll be back 'fore you know it." And with that he was gone!

For a full minute Goody was so stunned he was stuck to his chair. "Yee-sumchrist!" he cried. He leapt up and ran out and sped across the street as fast as his old legs allowed, and flew into Buddy's. When the door banged back, Buddy looked up, all set to tie into whoever had rattled her dishes on the wall. "Gudmon! Hvat iss it?"

"Stopp den mannen!"

"Hvem?"

"Hent hjelp oyeblikkelig!"

"Hvem?!"

"Yoe Villie hass gone gauken!"

"Cuckoo?"

"Yah! Cuckoo!"

When Joe Willie got home Sissy was gone and so were the two kids. He stomped around, missing the pot of stew on the stove and the smell of fresh-baked bread that filled the air. "I'll kill 'im and then I swear I'll tar the livin' daylights outa her!"

He was throwing together a bedroll when the sound of her voice came in through the open window. He stood motionless for a heartbeat and then he raced outside and there she was, kneeling by one of the flower beds. Digger thumped his tail when he saw Joe Willie but didn't bother to rise. The two boys were asleep on a blanket nearby not, as he had imagined, on a train with their new daddy.

Sissy had a rag tied around her hair and was stabbing at the dirt—acting exactly like a woman who's been curried the wrong way—and with long overdue insight, he realized that she was madder'n hell. At him! Why?

It had rained early that morning and though the sun had come out hot and strong, it was still a bit muddy. Which would never stop Sissy. She'd work in her garden under almost any weather condition with the exception of snow. She said it relaxed her when she was too tired. He never had made sense of that but figured whatever made her happy.

And that's exactly how he wanted her. Happy. With him!

He stepped off the stairs. She looked up and her hands stilled. She forgot herself and talked to him. "Joe Willie! What are you doing home?"

He lifted her up by the elbows. "I came home to find out why you're mad at me." She turned her face away. "Sissy!"

"I'm not saying."

"You are!"

"I'm not."

"You are! Sissy, you will tell me what's wrong or we'll stand here till kingdom come!"

She made her lips flat and set her chin but he finally got it out of her. She was stunned when she heard his explanation. "Davey Cox wanted to . . . to . . . but he's only a child!"

"Who claims he's losing his sight an' growing warts on his palm."

Her brows drew together. "What does that mean?"

"Never mind Davey Cox now. We're talkin' about us." He paced off a ways then back. "Exactly what did you think, Sissy? That I was going in there to have a woman for myself?"

"Yes!" she spat and started to cry. Sissy Heck Everett did not go *boo-hoo.* She wailed like a fire siren. "I followed you and looked in the window and I . . . I saw you kissing that . . . woman!"

"Oh, God!" Joe Willie sat heavily. "You were never meant to see that."

"I'm sure not!" she huffed.

He grabbed her hand and pulled her onto his lap. She struggled but he wrapped his arms around her and held her captive. "Now, you listen, Sissy Heck . . ."

"Everett! And don't you ever forget it!"

"Girl, how could I? Why would I want to? Now hush an' listen. Do you know how far out of line you are? About as far as I was, thinking that you'd run off with another man."

That got her attention. "You thought I'd run off with another man?"

He told her about how his imagination had gotten the best of him, how he'd raced home expecting to see her in the clutches of some soon-to-be-dead stranger. "Now that I'm clear-headed

I realize that no man would have the cojones to go after my woman! As long as I have breath . . .''

She interrupted; he was getting himself all worked up again. ''Oh, Joe Willie!'' She clasped his face between her hands. ''As long as you have breath in your body, I'll be your woman. Only yours. And you'll always be my man.''

''I will.''

''Only mine.''

''Only yours.''

The two boys were put to bed quite early that night. So was their mother.

Chapter 35

August settled over Two Sisters like a blanket, and its citizens started to reap the fruits of their labor. Tomatoes, peppers and cucumbers sweetened on the vine and the sweet corn filled with flavor. Potatoes were dug and squash admired. Weeds and kids seemed to grow a foot overnight.

It was hot! Women who sat on their front porches to shell peas or shuck corn made sure they kept their bare feet tucked under their skirts but men threw caution to the wind and worked without their shirts, chopping wood, sweating and fighting flies, hard pressed to remember foot-long icicles on the eaves and snow drifts that were eye high. It was a peaceful, endless time.

It was also a time of serious trouble for Thora and Jim Horse.

The problem had been there right along, festering like a skin deep piece of glass but it was not brought out into the open until a series of events that began with a visit to Mrs. Willman . . . who was still the oldest person in town.

That day was so hot the sun hurt your eyes and no breeze moved the air. Thora was pulling Charley behind her in a wooden wagon with broad side-boards and wide wheel-rims.

Much larger wagons rattled by them headed for the grain mill, scattering bits of wheat and rye in their wake.

When she reached her destination she saw Mrs. Willman bent double in a rock-enclosed garden. A steady stream of old lady curses were coming from her mouth. "Sassafras! Jumpin' Jehoshaphat's jewels!" Mrs. Willman did not hear her call, so Thora pushed open the wooden gate, pulled the wagon in and went closer. "Need help, Mrs. Willman?"

"Arh!" The old lady grabbed her heart and turned furious eyes on her. "Lands sakes alive! You like t'scare the pee outa me!"

"I'm sorry. I thought you heard me."

"What?"

Thora raised her voice several decibels. "I said I thought you heard me. Can I help you?"

"Oh, my durn trap's in these berry bushes an' I was jus' tryin' t'get it out without gettin' scratched t'bits." She looked over Thora's shoulder and broke into a toothless grin. "Oh Lordy mercy! There's little Charley!"

"Hal."

"What?"

"Hal. I was going to start calling him Hal."

"Sal's a terrible name for a boy. I'm gonna call him Charley."

Thora sighed and shrugged. "You might as well. Everybody else does."

While Mrs. Willman clucked Charley under the chin, Thora dislodged the trap without "gettin' scratched to bits" and found a live squirrel in it. "Mrs. Willman! You've caught a squirrel in your trap. I'll skin him for you if you like."

"Oh, lands, girl! I am not gonna eat him."

"No?"

"No, I'm gonna drop him into that barrel there." She indicated a rain barrel sitting where the eaves came together. "Trap and all."

"Why?"

"Because the little beggar has been diggin' up my bulbs."

"Oh, gosh." Thora had killed plenty of squirrels herself but only when she was hungry.

Mrs. Willman gave her a calculating eye. "What? You got a funny stomach?"

"No." She shrugged. "It just seems a little . . . harsh I guess."

"Harsh? Hah! Not half so harsh as dashing their brains out against the house."

"Mrs. Willman!"

"That's what I used t'do. Put them in a burlap sack an' . . ."

Thora was shocked. And from such a nice grandmotherly sort. "They are just doing what comes naturally."

"They can do it at somebody else's place." She'd picked up the chain and slung the trap by it. "I'm sure glad I didn't catch a skunk again. One let me have it full blast last year."

"Oh, no!"

"Yeah, same thing'd happened. The critter had walked the trap into the bushes jus' like this little fella, but instead of goin' inside an' getting my spectacles, I reached in an' pulled the trap out. I got my nose about an inch from its tail afore I seen that stripe. Then I seen that it was lifted."

The squirrel was racing around the trap, trying to maintain its balance. "You know, Mrs. Willman, I was just thinking of fixing Jim some squirrel stew."

"Well, here then. You take him. But you'll need more'n one."

"Yes, I know but he'll be a start."

"You want t'skin him right now?"

"No, I've got several stops to make. Think I could borrow your trap for a day or so?"

"Well, sure, but not too long. I've got to keep at these critters every minute."

"I imagine." Looking around. "My, your garden sure is nice."

"It is. We've had nice rain this summer. Say, want a few tomatoes? I got way too many t'eat."

"Well . . ."

"How's that new place comin'?"

"We're living in it, but it doesn't have any stairs and the floors aren't finished . . ."

"How about some carrots?"

"Well . . ."

"Sure you do. You've been too busy buildin' your new place t'garden. Say, could you use some pole beans?"

"Well . . ."

When she left Mrs. Willman's place she was carrying Charley and pulling the wagon which was filled with a squirrel cage—complete with squirrel—a sack of tomatoes, a bag of potatoes, a basket of beans and a bunch of carrots. All of which was overlaid with a huge cutting of delphiniums and lilies and roses and daisies.

She pulled the wagon almost home before she released the squirrel. He was a nondescript gray squirrel, like hundreds of others. Nonetheless she lectured him on the advantages of some neighborhoods over others.

She told Jim about it that night, just in case Mrs. Willman should ask him how he liked the squirrel stew. He laughed and then asked what she was doing clear over there.

"Well, I happened to think . . . the tree was on her property." She was changing the baby's napkin and so didn't notice how Jim was looking at her.

"What tree?" he asked though he already knew.

"The tree they hung Halldor from. I thought maybe there might have been something she would remember that she had never remembered before." She handed the baby to Jim. "There! All cleaned up for Daddy."

"Did she remember anything?"

"Mrs. Willman?" She shook her head. "She's so dotty I doubt she'll soon be able to remember her name."

"Since we've been back you've talked to about every one in town."

"Well, if I have then I guess I'll have to start all over again."

She walked to the window and stood looking out. "Somebody has to know something. I'll just keep asking until someday someone makes a mistake." She turned but the room was empty. "Jim?"

She went out on the porch and saw him walking down the path that led to the water. The baby was looking at her over his shoulder. Going swimming she supposed. "Well, you might've asked me if I'd like to go along!"

She thought no more about it but Jim did.

Chapter 36

Word had come of a yellow fever breakout in Duluth. Over two dozen people had succumbed to the dreaded disease already. Medical men and willing nurses were out on their feet from administering round the clock care to the ill. Conor O'Malley was leaving to lend his help. He told Emily Jones to contact him if anyone in Two Sisters came down with the awful symptoms.

"It begins with pain, fever and trembling. It's not until right before the end that the victim gets a yellow skin and starts vomiting blood." He settled his hat. "Now where is my . . ." She pointed at a bag made of grainy black leather. "Thank you. All right then, I'm off."

"I'll be terribly worried about you."

He looked at her. "Will you?" Impulsively he took her hand. Unfortunately it held a wet rag.

"Oh, Doctor! I'm sorry."

She used her apron to dry his hand. Took her time about it too. Though he was perilously close to missing the train, Conor was rooted by the tender feel of her hands on his.

"There!" she said and looked up into those intent brown eyes.

"Emily, I . . ."

"Yes?"

He chewed on his next word so long she was quite disappointed when it finally emerged. "Emily . . ."

"Yes?"

"We really must have a talk when I return."

"About my work?"

"No. Yes! About a new occupation I have in mind for you."

She smiled. "Will I like it?"

"God, I hope so."

Emily was thinking about Conor later that week. She was pacing around the cabin, circling the table and then the chair. (While it was true that she was concerned about Conor O'Malley, her concern did not manifest itself in pacing. She had a long piece of string tied to her belt and a following of gamboling kittens.)

No one in Two Sisters, thank heavens, had shown any signs of illness and although word came from Duluth that the disease was on the wane, Conor O'Malley still had not returned. Gosh, she missed him! The longer he was gone the more lost and vulnerable she felt. Especially since that man had started following her around.

He'd said his name was Lyle. Not if that was his last name or his first name. Just, Lyle. She'd scarcely acknowledged his impromptu introduction—certainly she had not reciprocated with her name—but since that first day she'd seen him almost every time she went into town. Too often to be coincidental. She had a bad feeling about him. Very bad.

Something—or someone—must've been trying to forewarn her that night. It wasn't an hour later that he showed up at her cabin, calling to her like a neighbor lady over a picket fence. "Yoo-hoo!" She looked out the window and saw him standing by the gate. His sweat-stained hat was pushed back on his head and he was grinning at the door. She thought he might be a little drunk. He cupped his mouth. "Yoo-hoo!"

"What do you want?"

"I thought maybe you and I could sit out here on the porch and watch the stars come up."

"What?"

"I said I thought maybe . . ."

"Never mind. I heard what you said. You get off my property right now!" It wasn't her property but he didn't need to know that. She hurried to the other window and checked for a light at the Beckstroms'. Nothing! Fear washed over her. She was trapped. She was helpless. Oh, God!

No sooner had she locked the door and put the bar across the window than she heard his footsteps on the porch.

"C'mon out now, girley. Let's have us a little talk."

"If you don't leave right now I will shoot you!"

"Ooowee! Listen to you! Why, I . . ."

"Say, fella. Vhat are yew dewn up dere?"

Ketil Beckstrom! Thank goodness! She peered through a space in the shutter and there indeed was wonderful big, burly Ketil. Unfortunately the entire family was with him. Ketil didn't look so rough with little Lars in his arms. Emily heard only snatches of the conversation.

". . . come acourtin' . . ."

"Vere yew ast tew?"

"I guess I don't see that that's any of your business . . ."

"I guess I made it my business. Emily!" he called. "Dew yew vant dis fella here?"

"No!" Emily sang out. "I do not!"

"Dere yew go, fella. Get yewrself back tew town."

"Now jus' a damn minute . . ."

Ketil said something to Meline and handed Lars to her. Meline said something back that earned her a sharp word from Ketil. Carrying Lars and dragging Marne by the hand, Meline scurried down the path that led to their cabin. Marne, never one to miss a thing, was looking back and forth between her "Da" and the stranger.

"Now den," said Ketil.

Emily had her eye pressed to the shutter so hard she would have a ridge on her cheek for an hour. Height-wise they were about equal. Width-wise Ketil made two of Lyle. But she was afraid Lyle was carrying a pistol!

There followed some low talk between the two men. Finally Lyle leaned and spat and hitched his belt. Then, thank goodness, he turned toward town.

Ketil came up on the porch and Emily opened the door. He

took one look and exclaimed. "Lewk at yew, Emily Yones! Shaking like a tree!"

Ketil wanted her to come and stay with them but she insisted she couldn't start to do that every time some little something came up. Ketil cautioned her to lock her door and bar all her windows. Later Meline came over with a cow bell and demanded that she put it by her bed in case Lyle returned. She had a restless night but no unwanted visitor.

Conor O'Malley returned the next day and, of course, Two Sisters being the size town it was, immediately heard about the "cowboy who had been pestering Emily Jones."

He was waiting for her when she showed up to clean that afternoon. "Oh, Conor! Dr. O'Malley! Thank goodness!" Her eyes went all over him, searching for signs of illness. His eyes were underscored with dark crescents but otherwise he looked hale and hearty and yet somehow . . . different. He had his hands on his hips and that box-jaw stuck out a foot.

"What's this I hear?"

"What have you heard?" Her smile faded.

"I want to know the circumstances of this thing!"

"The circumstances of what thing?"

"About this . . . roughneck who's been hanging around your place."

"I did not encourage his attentions." She set down her pail and faced him. "But I didn't know I had to ask you if I wanted to accept someone's suit."

"Has he been bothering you? Answer me that."

"He came by my place one night and . . ."

"Did he scare you? Ketil said he thought you were scared."

"Well, I was a little . . ."

"That's all I wanted to know." He tore off his tie and removed his suit coat and stormed out.

"Good grief!" she cried and ran after him. She caught up with him in the middle of Superior Street. "What are you going to do?"

"Knock his block off."

"You're going to fight him?"

He looked at her and snorted. "What? You think I can't

fight?'' He was stomping along, rolling up his sleeves as he went. ''I grew up in the streets of Dublin, my dear, and can contend with the best of them.''

Lyle had stepped out of the Wind Fall. Conor looked from Lyle to Emily. ''Is that him?''

''No.''

Lyle called, ''You looking for me?''

''I am!'' boomed Conor.

At that Joe Willie and Jim Horse came out of Joe Willie's office. Across the way Curly Frye stepped out of his shop holding a leather-covered razor. He was soon joined by a half-shorn man wearing a striped apronlike thing around his neck. Goody had been sweeping his walk but he instantly dropped his broom and shifted his glasses from his forehead to his nose.

About to cry, Emily was wringing her hands and doing little hops. ''Stop him!'' she cried to Joe Willie. Hop! ''Sheriff!'' Hophop! ''Stop him, Sheriff!''

Nobody moved. Matter of fact, Joe Willie and Jim Horse spoke then shook hands!

Lyle slouched against the porch post and grinned. Conor spat in one hand then spat in the other. ''Do you come down here or do I come up t'get you?''

Emily kissed Conor's bruised nose first and then his split lip. He opened his eyes and looked up at her. ''Emily?''

''Yes, dear.''

''Am I dead?''

''No.''

His eyes drifted closed. ''I thought you were an angel.''

''Silly! You won!''

''I did?''

She nodded. ''You were wonderful!''

''Emily?''

She leaned back and looked at him. ''Yes?''

''Did you know that you're kissin' me in the middle of the street?''

''Yes, I know. I think I'll do it again.'' And did.

''Emily Jones.''

She leaned back again. ''Yes?''

"Will ye marry me?"

"Yes, of course I will."

Says herself an' then right back at the kissin' an' the lovin' again. Like his ol' mam used t'say: Blacken yer boots an' be first in line. An' remember t'jab with yer left!

Conor folded his hands and ankles and enjoyed.

The door to *The Daily Clarion* had a sign on it that said, "Open! Come In." Thora took it at its word and did. She was greeted with the strong odor of newsprint, ink and paper but nothing that was breathing.

"Hello? Yoo-Hoo?"

She found the editor clear in the back sitting at a rolltop desk from which every nook and cranny sprouted papers like a weed patch. Obviously he was oblivious to the bell that had announced her entry and her calls. She moved closer. He must've seen her then because he jumped a little.

"Oh! You gave me a start! Have you been here long?" Rising, he scooped some papers aside and offered her a chair. "I get so involved. Please be seated."

"Thank you." She looked around and thought, What a mess! but meeting his slightly curious gaze, she smiled and said, "What an interesting place!"

"Thank you. I think so. Although there's so much to do I do tend to get a little . . ." He waved a hand over the litter. ". . . scattered."

"It's the result that counts, Mr. Corliss, and your paper is wonderful." She smiled winningly and hoped he didn't ask her what other papers she had read.

"Such words are music to my ears. It's grown so much! You know, the paper started out with only two pages. Now we're up to six and have increased the page size to five columns each!"

"Imagine that!"

"Yes." He had both hands on his knees and was leaning forward, watching her closely. She wondered if he gave everything his full attention.

"Would you care to look around?"

"Yes, I would."

He showed her around, describing the printing process in such detail that she wished she hadn't evidenced such interest.

"It's difficult to keep the reader's interest day after day."

"You don't have any trouble keeping mine, Mr. Corliss. I especially like 'This Day in History' and of course, Sissy's column."

He nodded. " 'Mr. I. Rate.' That's a very popular column with everyone. Sissy's a natural, you know."

"Where do you get all your other material?"

"I have worked a deal with the *Pioneer* paper out of St. Paul. Talk about a growing paper! Originally it was a little tiny thing set up to cater to settlers from other countries."

"Is that so!"

"Yes. Well, they're kind enough to send me Scandinavian tidbits and I send them news of the area." They returned to the desk and resumed their original seats.

"No wonder the paper's so popular."

He clasped his hand around his raised knee. "Well, I like to think that at least the paper gets read before it lines drawers or wraps apples or insulates attics." She laughed and he laughed. She looked around again.

"There must be something I can do for you."

"Well, actually there is . . ."

"What?"

"Do you save copies of all your old newspapers?"

"Why, yes. I keep at least one copy of all previous editions. Why?" Understanding dawned and his smile faded. "You're still trying to get a lead on your brother's murderers, aren't you?"

"Yes, I am, and I thought it might help if I could read the papers from back then."

"Of course you can, but did you know Joe Willie read them all again at the time of your trial?"

"No, I didn't." She moved close to the edge of her chair. "But I'd still like to read them myself. Here's the thing . . ."

She explained that perhaps there was some little thing that hadn't meant anything to anyone else but that would leap right off the page at her, seeing as how she was putting a fresh eye on it and all.

"All right," he said. "You stay right here." He brought a

lamp over and set it on the table. "And I'll go get them." He went down some narrow stairs. "They should be in chronological order. Just take a minute."

That was when Jim walked in. He stood at the door, smiling quizzically. "Hey! Buddy said you might be over here."

"I left Charley with her for a bit."

"That's what she said. So what's going on?"

"I was just . . . asking Mr. Corliss about some things."

"What things?"

"About some old papers." She brushed her hair back. "I . . ." She looked at Jim. "I wanted to read some of his old papers."

"Here they are!" Ben Corliss came up, his face red from bending over and panting a little. He held a stack of papers in his arms. Jim strolled slowly over and looked at the dates, then at the headlines and then he looked at Thora.

And then he left. Not a word did he say but she knew he was mad. So did Ben Corliss.

She stood. "I guess I'll have to look at them later, Mr. Corliss. I'm sorry to put you to all this trouble, but . . . I think I better go home."

"I understand. I'll just put these right on this table and if you want to come back another day . . ."

"Thank you."

That night Jim told her she had to quit asking people about the men who hung her brother.

"Why?"

"Because people think you suspect them. Or their brother. Or their cousin. Or their father. Thora, people are startin' to avoid you."

He walked away, into the other room. She followed. He turned and folded his arms. Both his tone and his stance were stiff.

"I've told you about the sort of men who used to work for Buel's father. Junior always had a bunch of 'em hanging around with him. The kind of men with shady reputations or none at all. They supposedly worked at the hotel or at the gaming tables, but all of them were hired guns. I'll bet good money that three of those men had a hand in the hanging. Not Rudy or Goody or Curly or any of the others who've made Two Sisters their home.'' He looked at her. She was sitting on the bed, not looking at him now, but at the baby and he could see tears on her lashes. The baby gurgled and blew a spit bubble then, as if sensing something, fell silent. ''Thora, you have to let go of it or we cannot live here.''

She looked at him. To think that he was not happy with her . . . oh, she'd rather take a beating with a stick! She burst into tears. ''I don't know how.'' He knelt and pulled her into his arms. ''I can't seem to quit! Help me!'' He held her for a long time, then, ''I don't know how to help you, but maybe I know someone who can.''

He told her to pack for a three or four day trip and then rode into town to let Bull know he would be gone for a time. When he returned he had a dappled mare that he must've rented from Art Wright at the livery stable.

''Where are we going?''

''To see the nenan'dawi'ined.''

''The who?''

''The man who has the power to call the spirits.''

Chapter 37

They set off at once. It was a warm day but Jim pointed out some of the less obvious signs of fall. Red squirrels that had become more active, mushroom caps that were being eaten by black bear and white-tailed deer and a flock of swallows, the earliest migrating birds, who were gathering for their flight south.

It was mostly a silent trip. They talked, but only about unimportant things. At night all three slept under the same blanket and though he held her with special tenderness, he did not make love to her. Which was just as well. As far as worry went, her mind was in the worst condition it had ever been in. "People are startin' to avoid you." His words and his stiff disapproval of her had cut her to the quick. She imagined awful things. Like their having to leave Two Sisters because no one liked her. Or worse, that Jim would stay and send her away. Outside she made her face calm and clear. Inside she wanted to drum her heels on her horse until she got to the healer.

Oh, God, she hoped he could help her!

With no snow to contend with they made good time and at dusk on the second day Jim turned in the saddle and said, "Almost there."

"Good."

Soon they came upon a small gathering of eight or ten structures, a hodgepodge mix of dome-shaped wigwams, peaked lodges and bark houses. Deerskins were stretched over pole frames but there were no outside fires. It was a settlement of some duration; below the village was a ditch to carry rain water and snow melt away.

Several people came outside as they approached. Women wearing rawhide headbands and buckskin shirts over calico skirts, men wearing high-crowned hats and corduroy trousers beneath long-fringed jackets. Considering the size of the village, there seemed to be an unusually large number of kids. As if he'd read her thoughts, Jim grinned at her and shrugged. "Our favorite winter pastime."

They stopped beside the largest structure, an elm-bark lodge, and a young boy ran over. He wore brushed buckskins and beaded moccasins and looked well fed and healthy. Jim touched his head and spoke softly to him before he turned over his horse. From beneath a line of black bangs he gave Charley and Thora a thorough going-over as Jim helped her dismount.

"I'll do the talking, hear?"

"All right."

"The nenan'dawi'ined will not address you directly. He isn't being impolite. It just isn't done."

"All right."

After entering the lodge, it took a minute for her eyes to adjust enough to see an ancient woman who sat shadowed in a corner. She stood and held out her arms for the baby. When Jim nodded, Thora shrugged out of the cradleboard and handed him to her. Then the old woman indicated that they should be seated around a low fire.

On a reed mat across from them sat an old man with milky eyes set in a leather and bone face. His yellowy gray hair was long and loose. He wore a thrummed buckskin shirt with red porcupine-quill work and elk teeth strung on a thin necklace of braided hair. Jim addressed him as "grandfather" though she knew he was not his kin. "Grandfather, this is my woman, None-So-Pretty."

"Hu'ah! You have brought her to see me."

"Yes."

"What is wrong with her?"

"She has lost half her thoughts."

"Where are they?"

"Stuck on an awful hate."

"Who does she hate?"

"Some men who harmed her kin."

All this had caught Thora off guard. She'd expected a long session of small talk, but apparently the nenan'dawi'ined did not believe in wasting time.

Jim shook his head. "It is not good, Grandfather. Even when our hearts are touching I sense she thinks of revenge. Her need to exact punishment colors all her thoughts and therefore colors all of mine. I think that in a secret place this hate is waiting to destroy us."

"Why doesn't she just kill the men who have hurt her?"

"She has killed one of them."

He gave a satisfied grunt. "Killing of enemies brings comfort and consolation to a person."

"Sometimes."

The old man nodded. "Sometimes. Other times the person stays filled with hate no matter how many are killed."

"That is what has happened. She is not free to go on with her life. I fear that she will only grow more hateful and will teach that hate to our children."

"You may have to throw her away."

When Jim seemed to think Thora looked at him with shocked eyes. Finally he said, "I'd hate to do that."

"You may have to. What about the other important things?"

Jim asked, "Which ones, Grandfather?" And Thora thought he already knew.

"Is she dirty in her personal habits?"

"No."

"Careless in her housekeeping?"

"No, Grandfather."

"Is she always pleasant to be around?"

"Mm. Mostly pleasant. She travels very well and is appreciative of the earth and its animals." Thora allowed herself a little smile. "But she will not bear much criticism." Frown.

"Does she welcome you under her robes at night?"

"Welcome me?" Jim Horse looked at her with an amused glitter in his eye. "She makes my bones go weak . . . I need only to look at her and my throat swells.'' Softly he added, ''And that's not all.''

''Hu'ah! But remember! There are always other women.''

''Not for me, Grandfather. When she first left me, I ached inside. My heart turned to dust and I was without spirit. I doubted the value of my life.''

Was this her Jim speaking? She wanted to rub her eyes and ream out her ear with her finger. Instead she stretched out a tentative hand and touched his arm.

''The first moment I saw her she wrote her face on my mind. I thought of nothing else. When she left, I went after her.'' He gave her a nighttime look and she was glad the lodge was so dim. His words were inflaming her! That he should feel so about her and say it! Oh, God! It was all she could do not to fling herself on him and bear him to the ground!

''Hu'ah. Good!'' The old man said and nodded.

''I found her and I made her mine . . .''

''Good!'' Another pause, then, ''Well, it seems to me that it is only this hate. Deep inside she will never be right until she settles this thing.''

''Yes, Grandfather.''

The old man thought for a minute then he held up his hand. ''Wait. I have thought of something else.''

''Yes?''

''She isn't one of those women who is also a man, is she?''

Jim thought. ''Like that Nadowessioux?''

''Yes. Finds-Them-And-Kills-Them.'' The old man looked very grave. ''You cannot please one of those women-men, my son. I tried one of them once and I don't believe a man can make them happy.''

''Her heart is very brave, as brave as any warrior I have ever known, but unlike Finds-Them-And-Kills-Them, this one is . . .'' He gave her another burning look then. ''. . . all woman!''

Thora swallowed a groan and bit the inside of her cheek and clenched her legs.

''Hu'ah!'' the old man said and did not say more for a long time. ''Well, I will try to work with her.''

''Thank you, Grandfather.''

She thought they would leave then, but they didn't. The old

man sat and smoked a while and then he said. "I'll tell a story now."

"Hu'ah!" Jim said.

And he proceeded to do so. "Once there was a man named Wa-B-Na-Se. (The Falcon) This man was never satisfied with what he had and always coveted his neighbor's belongings. This man's horse or that man's bow. His covetous nature had shown itself when he was very young and it never went away. When he was full grown, it was no surprise when he coveted another man's wife. Unfortunately she was of his same clan and therefore would have been forbidden to him even if she was not already another's woman.

"Her name was Ka-Beck-A-Nung (The End of the Trail) and she was very beautiful, but her name was true: she was destined be the end of the trail for someone. The Falcon stole the woman away for many days of . . ." Here the old man struck his fist in his other hand several times. "What do the white men call it?"

Jim grinned at Thora who was blushing brightly. "It's all right, Grandfather. She's familiar with it."

"Hu'ah. Well anyway, when he brought the woman back she was so ashamed that she threw herself away. Furious and heartbroken, the young husband attacked The Falcon and got rubbed out. The elders captured and held The Falcon. It was up to the husband's father, being the wronged party, to either forgive The Falcon or kill him. They led The Falcon to the old man and The Falcon sunk to his knees. He knew he was in a lot of trouble so he was very persuasive. He said he would spend the rest of his life atoning for his sins. That he would become the old man's son and hunt and care for him forever. He made such a strong plea for his life that the old man forgave him. Then when The Falcon was walking away, the old man ran after him and shot him in the head.

"He had forgiven him but he still could not allow him to live. He said that if he did not kill The Falcon, he would have to kill himself for he could not live and know that The Falcon lived too." Then he said, "Many times, the price of hate is a life all alone."

Everyone sat silent, listening to a barking dog and the noise of the wind in the trees. Thora's thoughts were jumbled by the end of the story, but one thing he had said kept repeating itself in her mind. "Many times, the price of hate is a life all alone."

Jim, meanwhile, was thinking about old Crowbait Cates and he was sad.

Eventually the old man made a motion and Jim stood and held out his hand to assist her up.

"I will try to get her to see her enemies in a dream. If that doesn't work maybe the spirit messengers will give her the solution to her problem." He shook his head. "I don't know what could be worse than getting a message in a dream and not acting on it. I hope she knows that."

"I'm sure she does, Grandfather."

"All right then. I will start tomorrow."

Through the open door the old man watched the two young people walk off. They were indistinct blurs but he could see that the girl was hanging on the man's arm and rubbing against him like a cat. The old woman watched with bird-bright, knowing eyes. "They have forgotten the child," she said.

"They won't be long," he said.

Once they were away from the wigwam, Thora grabbed Jim's arm hard. She wanted him so much she was half crazy! "Take me somewhere!"

"What?" He looked at her then and saw the quickening in her eyes. She was almost breathless with need. "Where?

"I don't care. Somewhere private. Hurry!"

He looked around. "Behind that tree?"

"Yes! Yes! Wherever."

Once behind the old oak they shared the kind of kiss that looked they were trying to eat each other then pulled apart, wild-eyed and panting, and looked at each other.

"God!"

"Yes!"

She reached for his belt and he pulled at her pants, but their need made them clumsy. Groaning with frustration she slapped his hands away and tore at her clothes. He spread his legs and leaned back against the tree and she crawled him like a bear. Their coupling was swift and hard like a tornado had grabbed them and spun them senseless. When it was over, she hung on him like a bib.

He slitted his eye and looked around. Too late to worry about it now but for her sake he hoped no one saw them. She roused and rolled her head back. God, he loved that slack-mouthed, glazed-eyed look of hers.

"Oh, Lord!" she gasped.

"You took the words right from my mouth."

"Don't move!"

"No."

"God!"

"Yes."

Eventually, however, he lost control of that part of him that she wanted him to never move. He lowered her and held her and after a time she roused herself further. "How do I look?"

"Lovely, but you have some bark in your hair." He plucked it out.

"Your eye patch is snagged on your ear."

"Thank you." He retrieved it but he was too caught up in her to put it on. God! If that's what talking got him, he would start putting goose grease on his tongue tonight!

They stood there awhile, Jim leaning against the tree, her melded to him when suddenly she jerked. "I forgot Charley!"

He chuckled. "I know. Calm down. We'll go back now and get him."

"I suppose they know what happened."

"I suppose they do."

"You go in and get him."

He laughed outright.

"Hush!" She removed a twig from her pants leg. "Come on now and don't you dare laugh. We must both look very serious."

As they walked back she pretended to examine a mushroom on a birch and then the sky. She smiled and nodded at two passing women and frowned when they both covered their mouths and giggled. She shot a look at him and stopped walking. "Quick! Your patch! Oh, damn!"

"Where is it? What?" Having just hung it back on his ear he knew exactly where it was. He pretended to look for it on the ground but she already had it in her pocket.

"Damn! I told you . . . oh, here come some more people. Act normal."

"I am normal."

"Talk!"

"About what?"

"What's a Nadowessioux?"

"Our word for an enemy. Like the Lacotah and Dacotah. The white man heard it and adopted it and shortened it to Sioux. It stuck. The Sioux even use it themselves now."

"Who is Finds-Them-And-Kills-Them?"

"A famous Crow warrior who was also a woman."

"Here come some men!"

Taking pity on her, he steered her beside a fast-running stream that soon widened and became a small mountain lake.

"What about Charley?"

"Charley's fine. We'll take a minute to ah . . . compose ourselves."

The village was located high in the mountains where the cooler weather had already started to color the woods. The aspens were turning gold, oaks a deep red and the sumac would soon look like it was ablaze. Interspersed here and there were green fir and cedar and blue spruce.

"I thought there were many Indian women who fought as warriors."

"Not like this one. She was stronger than any man ever matched against her. Too strong to be a woman, yet she was."

Jim drew her to one side so that they cautiously skirted a large hump in the ground. They had stopped at a place that overlooked the lake on one side and a mass of hills on the other. Wind moaned through the trees and windblown waves broke against the rocky shore, yet beneath the sounds of nature it was strangely silent, almost eerie. "What is this place?"

"The burial grounds of the Mound Builders."

"Mound Builders?"

"They were an ancient people who used to live here many hundreds of years ago. They got their name because they buried their dead in pits and built mounds over them. Until I was older and knew better I used to dig around here."

He told her that on various occasions he had found stone weapons and tools here. Pieces of pottery. Shells that had obviously been used for something. One time he said he found a huge tooth, the biggest—he was quite sure—ever found in the world. "I still have it, in a parfleche bag somewhere."

They both fell silent. She looked up at him but he was staring far away, as if he were listening to someone speak. She turned him toward her with a hand on his arm. "Did you mean those things you said?"

"What?" he asked, knowing full well what she meant.

"About how you felt when I left."

"Ah. You mean that part about my heart turning to stone?"

She looked at him, pained. "Dust. You said it turned to dust."

"Oh, yeah. Dust."

Teasingly she lifted her hand as if she would strike him but he easily caught it and pulled her to him and turned her face up to his. "I meant every word I said and more. The words of mere mortal beings cannot express how I feel."

"Oh, God!" She rested her head on his chest. "That is sooo good!"

The next day she reported to the madodo' wasinum—the sweat lodge—and was invited to enter by the old woman.

Centered within the lodge was a heated stone that glowed red-hot in the dark. A birch bark bucket containing water sat on a woven reed mat. The woman dipped a bunch of dried grass in the water and sprinkled it on the stones. Steam rose.

"This will take our message to Mide Manido."

Interestingly enough it was the woman who seemed to be in charge now. The old man was there but in the beginning he only sat silently smoking.

The woman said she would prepare an asin'ipua'gun for Thora which would help clear her mind. She handed Thora the stone pipe and she smoked it although it made her feel fuzzy. In a soft voice, almost a whisper, the woman asked her to recline on a bulrush mat which, she explained, covered sweet grass and pine needles. Sacred stones surrounded a low fire of sage and juniper needles that had been laid in a circle. The old woman marked the palms of Thora's hands with blue paint because, she explained, blue was the symbol of peace. Then while somewhere, someone played a cedarwood flute, she striped her face with red for day and black for night.

When she was finished she explained that because Thora's

o'djitcag—her soul or spirit—was not at rest, she must listen very carefully to the words of the djaskid so that he could clear her mind and allow her spirit to cohabit with her mind.

The warmth of the fire and the flute and the old woman's voice were all very relaxing. The old man unwrapped his medicine bundle of sacred objects, none of which she was allowed to see, and started to chant the ancient sacred songs that asked that Thora have a ina'bandumo'win (vision). That was the last earthly thing she remembered.

Next thing she knew she was standing on the shore of a huge lake. A few yards away she saw her brother in a boat with two young Indian men, sleek, brown-bodied men with indistinct faces like smooth flat eggs.

Her eyes were hungry for her brother and she had never seen his face more clearly. His eyes were bright and his mouth wide with laughter. His cheeks were pinked high on the bone and he looked so happy he seemed lit from within. "Halldor!" she called. He saw her and his smile widened.

"Gosh, your hair is long!"

"I know. I like it. It's warmer in the winter and keeps the bugs off my neck in the summer."

"Oh."

The lake was flat and shiny as a silver plate but very deep. One step into the water and she was wet to the thighs. "Halldor!" she motioned him in, but he waved her off. He was about to catch a fish. His friends cried words of encouragement. He was hanging over the boat but she could see that his eyes were wide with excitement. He held the pole high in the air then his arm dove into the water and came up a monster muskellunge! He turned to show her and then he gently put the fish back into the water.

"Halldor, come here so I can touch you!" But his two friends paddled the boat away. He stood and waved good-bye. He was smiling.

"I think I fell asleep.

"Why? What do you remember?"

"Very little. Mostly what the djaskid said at the end, when I woke up." They were alone in a small bark house they'd been given to use.

"What did he say?"

"He told me that my brother talked to me through him."

"All right, what did he say?"

"Not very much. A lot." She rubbed her head. "I can't remember everything."

"Maybe you aren't supposed to remember everything right now. Maybe you'll remember some of it as you need it."

"Maybe. For sure he said that the end of a person's life is only a step into his next life in the spirit world. But that sometimes the dead person is held back because his kin on earth cannot let him go."

"What do you think? Is that true?"

"I don't know. I have to think about it." Then, "Right before I left he said that there is no reason for tragedy in life. He said that I should stop looking for a meaning because there isn't any. Tragedy just . . . happens. He said some people get so busy looking for meanings in life, they forget to live it."

"What did you say?"

"I said, 'Hu'ah!' "

The same boy brought their horses out when they were ready to leave. Before Jim took the reins he walked around both horses and saw that they had been curried with great care, that their hooves were oiled and that the mare's mane had been braided. Jim knelt before the boy and spoke to him.

"You have a way with horses." The boy looked at his feet but he was pleased. "I would like to tell your father. Where is he?" The boy replied in sign: Dead. "Your mother then?" Gone. "Who cares for you?" When the boy pointed to an old woman sitting outside a wigwam, Thora thought: she takes good care of him in spite of her age. Jim switched to English.

"Do you go to the government school?"

"Hu'ah!"

"Can you speak English?"

The boy shrugged.

"Speak English. Never forget the old ways but speak English every chance you get, then when you are old enough, you can come to Two Sisters and look me up. I will help you find a job."

The boy responded in English. "Can I be a horse tamer like you?"

"Like me? Ha!" He pointed at Thora. "She's the horse tamer!" The boy was staring at her with shock, so Jim smiled to show he was teasing. "You can be anything you want. Provided you learn English. Now, remember, come to Two Sisters if you want a job. All right?" The boy nodded. "All right. Think you will be able to recognize me?" The boy looked at Jim's scar, the place where there was no eye and nodded. Jim removed his bear claw necklace and dropped it over the boy's head. "Now I will be able to recognize you too." Thora thought the boy was going to his knees, he was that awed. Meanwhile Jim went and knelt in front of the old grandmother. Thora hoped he was giving her whatever money he had on him.

They followed the lake southward. On one side of the trail they had the beauty of a tree-lined northland lake; on the other the shadows of the sheltered woods, but because Thora was preoccupied with the things that had happened in the village her mind had withdrawn from the present and she saw neither.

They stopped in an inlet. Some canoes were sluggishly moving through a swampy bog where tall grasses grew above the water. The sight of Indian women pulling the long stalks over their canoes and beating them with sticks brought her out of herself.

"What are they doing?"

"Harvesting wild rice. Haven't you ever seen it done?"

"No. Never."

"It looks like a good crop this year. It was a wet spring."

To think these women's ancestors had done the same thing in the same manner for hundreds and hundreds of years made her feel one with all those who women had gone before her. Forgotten women who loved men and reared their babies, who'd toiled and laughed and cried and then passed on—out of this world. Her heart swelled and she was happy to fall into place behind them. She had much to be thankful for. She said as much to Jim.

"Hu'ah!" he replied and got ready to be the number one thing she was grateful for.

"Thank God we are here now. Together."

"Here . . . ?" He pointed at the ground. "Or in Two Sisters?"

"Here. There. Wherever. Just look around us! It's America! Don't you love America?"

He looked at her but she was staring at the wild rice bog. "Sure."

Inexplicably she was annoyed with him. "That's something I want to talk to you about. If you can talk like you did back in the village, you can talk now."

"I did talk. I said, 'sure.' "

"I mean about unimportant things."

"Why would a person speak about unimportant things?"

She turned her horse and started off. Her words trailed back to him. "Right there's your main problem. You can't make small talk."

"About America?"

"America. Wild rice. Whatever."

"Look, if I said everything I know about wild rice right now, then our talks about it would be finished forever. This way we can talk about wild rice for the rest of our life. Little by little." She shook her head and went on.

He cupped his mouth. "Besides, we are in Canada."

Epilogue

They went back to the cabin in the woods. Thora wanted to return to the place where so much had happened to them, and she wanted to check up on Coco-man. That last thing, she told Jim, she would like to do alone. He said he understood and he did. She needed to think everything over and a person can only think well when he is alone and in the woods.

She rose before dawn, prepared food for Charley and Jim and then packed for an overnight stay. She didn't know if she would be gone that long, but she might. Either way, Charley would be all right without her. Since her milk was going, he had been eating what his father called ''mush'' anyway.

After lengthy instructions concerning which mush when, and after several good-bye kisses, she was ready. She wore buckskins and knee-high moccasins. A rawhide thong held back her hair and an elkskin encased the carbine across her back. Jim watched her stride off into the woods and thought: in some ways she is even wilder than me!

The route was familiar to her but she took her time getting there. Since it might be a while until her return, she wanted to make sure she remembered everything: the fragrance of the pine needles she crunched underfoot; the sun-dappled majesty of the two-hundred-year-old pines that shed them; the sound of

Canada geese honking overhead; the chatter of angry squirrels. Beside a pond she sat and watched two beavers refurbish their lodge and in a secluded copse she searched until she saw the great horned owl who had drawn the attention of a noisy pack of crows.

Stopping as often as she did meant she arrived after dark, so she camped on the lookout spot that night and was on the bluff above Coco's den in time to watch the rising sun throw streaks of gold on the land. That's how she spent the rest of the day, watching the wolf pack.

She was delighted to see Coco looking sleek and well fed, as did his pups. They had grown so much!

Unfortunately Coco's wife seemed the same to her, a beautiful wolf but definitely demanding. Well, she supposed that wasn't her concern. Coco had to live with her . . . the witch, and she apparently made him happy.

It appeared they had adopted an old beat-up wolf into the pack. He was scarred and lame and probably wouldn't have lasted long on his own. She didn't know wolves did that and thought it was particularly charitable of Coco. She congratulated herself. All in all, she had done well with the raising of her first young.

Not surprisingly she thought a lot about what the holy man had told her and in her heart she knew he was right. She had to forgive and forget or become so bitter of spirit that no one would want her company. How, though? She asked that she be given the answer and pretty soon she was. From somewhere came the idea that she must pray for the men who had killed her brother. A man a month, and at the end of five months she should go back and begin at the beginning. She had to do it until the need to know them was lifted or until she forgave them no matter who they were.

When she left this place she had to try and leave it all behind her. Hate for her father. Hate for the men who had murdered her brother. Hate for anyone who had ever harmed her. Or she had to be willing to take the consequences, which might mean the loss of Jim's love.

All of her life she'd wanted love and a family and she'd almost let hate come between the first person who had given her both!

She stood at last and saw Coco stand as well. His tail was moving hesitantly and he seemed to be looking at her. "Bye, Coco, my friend! Have a long and very happy life!"

She walked all night in order to get back as soon as possible and arrived midmorning. She found her family down by the water, where she and Jim used to spend so much time. It looked a lot different from the last time she saw it. For one thing, the grass wasn't tramped down and bloodied. And the two bodies were gone.

Charley slept folded in a blanket. It was warm in the sun but fall was not far away. In the shady places at the water's edge there were ice crystals on the grass. Jim stood and welcomed her into his arms. "I missed you!"

"I missed you too."

He held her close and she felt his lips on her hair. "I'm ready to go home, Jim."

"Good!"

She sighed and looked around. "But you know, I will always think of this as my first home."

"Are you sad?"

"A little."

"We can come back here to live when we're old and broken. It will be a good place to die."

She stepped back and pulled off her shirt. "That's a comforting thought!" She dropped her pants and then dashed for the water.

As she treaded water to keep warm she watched him strip off his clothes. He straightened and smiled at her, a splendid male, framed by the woods and rugged country behind him.

There's some who believe that there's no animal so wild it won't respond to kindness. Looking at him through a stranger's eyes, she would have to say she wasn't so sure about that.

They would not be without their ups and downs, she and Jim—they were two round pegs wedged into square holes—but they had each other and Charley and those to come. And they had the good people of Two Sisters.

She watched him wade in and smiled a little smile. Oh, good! Looks like it's time for another swimming lesson!

ABOUT THE AUTHOR

Wynema McGowan presently lives in North Central Minnesota, the state with ten thousand lakes and a preponderance of people with blond hair and blue ears.